UNLEASHED CHAOS

A Novel of the Breedline Series

by SHANA CONGROVE

Novels of the Breedline Series by Shana Congrove

Sweet Chaos

Total Chaos

Unleashed Chaos

Sins of Chaos

THE IMMORTAL

Available wherever books are sold online

Author's Acknowledgments

Dedicated to all my talented friends on FanStory.com, especially Neal Owens, author of *Mirrors of Life*. Without your helpful advice and continuing support, none of this would exist. Good friends are hard to find. Thank you for being mine.

As always, immense gratitude to God's loving grace. Thank you for giving me guidance and courage with everything I do.

To all the readers, family, and friends: Thank you for stepping into my fantasy world of the Breedline. I appreciate your love and support!

The Legend of the Breedline

Imagine all the myths, legends, and folktales that both captivated and terrified you as a child—*the monsters under your bed, the boogeyman in the closet, werewolves, vampires, witches, demons, ghosts, and so on*—really existed.

The story I'm about to tell you goes beyond unbelievable. This is the legend of the Breedline.

The story goes that a secret species of humans born with an identical twin had the power to shift into wolves. Some say it is an old tall tale, ancient lore derived from Native American legends, known mainly as stories of shapeshifting creatures.

For the Navajo and other tribes of the Southwest, each has their own version of supernatural creatures called skin-walkers, but each boils down to the same thing: a majestic being capable of transforming itself into a wolf, coyote, bear, bird, or any other animal. When the transformation is complete, the human inherits the speed, strength, and cunning of the animal whose shape it has taken.

So the question remains...

Do supernatural beings really exist among our mundane, humdrum existence?

The thing about myths, legends, and folktales is sometimes they're true.

How do I know, you ask? Because... I'm their queen, and this is our story.

Prologue

Berkeley California, thirty-six years ago

Lisa Wellington huddled in the dark and drew the blanket snugly around the tiny infant she had cradled in her arms. The night air was chilly, wiping away the previous warm, sunny afternoon. She said a silent prayer as she hid among the trees in the middle of a wooded field. Tears slid down her cheeks as she stared up at the cloudless and star-filled sky.

Her escape had been a miracle. An explosion had damaged the cell where she'd been kept prisoner. She'd managed to get away before the guards found her. She had given birth to twins only a week ago and was severely weakened by all she'd been forced to endure.

After it had been leaked out about her ability to heal others, an underground group of government military officials, consisting of unethical scientists, kidnapped her. She'd been treated like some magic wand they waved at a wound or an illness, expecting her to make it all disappear. The worst experiment she'd undergone was when a German scientist named Dr. Hans Autenburg forced her to heal a patient with mental illness. For days Lisa had known what it truly was to be insane. Although thoughts of suicide had consumed her, her unborn twins had kept her mind focused. And then a ruthless physician named Dr. Hubert Crane, who served as her pediatrician, wanted to experiment on her babies after they were born. Dr. Crane was without humanity—the kind of monster who would skin an animal alive just to see how much pain it could endure before its death.

She hated them for using others that had similar unique gifts. Not only did they kidnap humans, they took Breedline against their will, forcing them to change into their wolf. They endured painful cellular modifications, mutated into a hybrid species. To them, they were just objects to provide them with knowledge and power. But now Lisa had run out of options. She managed to get out alive with her daughter Tessa, regretting the decision to escape without her son. Someone had taken Steven before she could get to him.

The weight of her responsibility was exhausting. Trying to figure out her next plan of action was proving difficult. How was she going to provide for a baby, alone at seventeen? She couldn't go back home to her family. That would put them in danger. She knew her abductors were probably already searching for her, and she had no choice but to stay on the run. That was no life for a child.

Her mind drifted to the father of her twins. When she was abducted, she severed the telepathic link they shared, to keep him safe. Kenneth was born with the genetics of a Breedline. Her worst fear was that she would never get the chance to see him again.

In a way, she supposed it was for the best. If she tried to go back to her loved ones, they'd never be able to live a normal life, and she was determined to keep them out of harm's way.

The sound of a soft coo brought her back to reality. As Lisa looked down into her daughter's angelic face, more tears fell from her eyes. She reached up and wiped them away, refusing to fall apart. She was stronger than this, and she'd be strong again. She just needed to find a safe place for her daughter.

She froze when she heard a noise in the distance. She snuggled the baby against her chest and gently rocked, trying to keep her soothed. She would never be able to live with herself if they took her daughter away.

As she waited in silence, ghosts invaded her mind. Lisa wondered if her sanity had been sacrificed and worried she'd suffered through one too many experiments. She came back to focus when the sound of footsteps drew near. Then she heard a man call out her name. The voice was quiet in the dark, barely above a whisper. It wasn't until he stood a few feet away that she recognized his face.

It was David, one of the guards who brought meals to her every day. As time had passed during her captivity, they'd secretly become friends. He'd promised he would find a way to get her and her twins to a safe place.

She took a halting breath and whispered, "David... I'm over here."

As he followed her voice and got closer, she noticed he held an automatic rifle, and though he shifted so he was standing next to her, his gaze was still trained on the distance, watching, never once looking down at her.

"Lisa, we need to get out of here." He kept his voice low. "There are guards looking for you, and they're not far away." He peered down at her. "Are you strong enough to walk?"

When she nodded in silence, he held out his hand. With all the strength she could muster, she kept a tight hold on her daughter and grasped his hand. As David helped her stand, her heart dropped when she caught sight of the look of despair on his face.

"I'm sorry, Lisa." He shook his head. "I couldn't get to Steven in time. Dr. Autenburg's men took him."

"Promise me..." She swallowed back tears. "...after we get my daughter to a safe place, you'll bring me back to get my son." There was a fierce edge to her voice that reflected strength her body didn't have. But with determination, she would find it. She would take the risk of getting captured again if that's what it took to reunite with her son. She had to make sure Steven had a chance for a normal life and not one filled with painful experiments.

David nodded. "Then we need to leave now. I've got a vehicle hidden not far from here. Where do you want to go?"

As she looked down at her daughter, a burst of hope warmed her insides. This baby in her arms was a miracle, a precious, living breathing gift from God. Lisa didn't want to let her go, but she knew she had to do what was best for Tessa. If Tessa stayed in her life, it would be one on the run. Both her children deserved a chance to have a normal childhood, away from danger lurking in the shadows.

Lisa lifted her chin and said, "Take me to Midway, Kentucky."

He nodded. "Let's get moving."

David helped her get to the Jeep he had hidden behind an old barn. When he opened the door for her, she noticed two car seats in the back and a bag sitting beside them, apparently full of baby things. Before she climbed inside, she said, "Thank you, David. I couldn't have done this without you."

As they drove away, he was on edge, keeping a constant look out the rearview mirror until his neck ached from all the back and forth. Focusing on the back seat, he was relieved the baby was sound asleep, happily snuggled in the car seat, appearing content. Looking away, he glanced at Lisa and said, "Do you have family in Kentucky?"

Lisa stiffened against the seat belt. When she thought about his question, it brought back memories of her family. "Yes," she finally said. "My older sister lives there with her husband, John. Wanda practically raised me after our parents passed away."

David frowned. "What happened to your parents?"

Lisa looked down and shrugged. "They died in a car accident, but I don't think it was accidental," she said, raising haunted eyes to his, hurt brimming in her liquid gaze. "I think their death had something to do with the people who took me."

David's lips drew thin and guilt swamped his eyes. It went against his grain to ever put a woman or child in danger. He had no idea the people he worked for were involved in illegal activity.

He opened his mouth to speak but then fell silent. His gaze riveted to Lisa as she looked away and stared out the window. Her demeanor told him she was holding back tears. Sensing her pain, he changed the topic. "Did your family know about your abilities to heal?"

Lisa averted her stare from the window at the passing scenery and looked to him. "Yes. My parents knew before I was old enough to walk."

"What about other people?" he asked. "How did you manage to keep it secret?"

"I just didn't use my abilities," she said. "My parents drummed into me from as early as I can remember to keep it a secret. No one outside our family was ever to know."

David's brow arched. "That shows remarkable restraint. What about Tessa and Steven's father. Does he know?"

"No." She shook her head. "I thought it would be best if he didn't know."

"You mean... you never used your gift... ever?"

"Just once. Kenneth's mother became very ill, and there was a chance she wouldn't survive. Her illness completely devastated him, so I secretly healed her."

David smiled. "You're special, Lisa. And I don't mean because of your abilities. I think you're the kindest person I've ever met. You deserve a happy life."

"Thank you, David." She smiled a little. "Thank you for being so kind to me."

She said nothing more, because if she did, she would break down and fall apart. Just for the moment, she didn't want to think of a future—an impossible future—she couldn't have.

After three days on the road, they finally arrived in Midway, Kentucky. Lisa must have dozed off because she awoke when David gently nudged her shoulder.

"We're close, Lisa."

She sat up, wiping her tired eyes, and then studied the roadway in front of them.

"Do you think your sister will be home?"

She released a sigh and mentally said a silent prayer. "I hope so."

A half hour later, Lisa could feel her pulse rising as they drove down a long country road that led to her sister's farmhouse.

David reached across the seat and put his hand on her shoulder. "You're doing the right thing."

She turned to him with tears in her eyes and nodded.

The road leading down to her sister's farm was narrow and dusty. The moon shimmered as she looked at the dark sky. In other circumstances, she'd be happy, but this was not the occasion. She had no other choice but to ask her sister and brother-in-law to raise her daughter.

As they parked in front of a two-story house, Lisa sat in silence and stared out the car window. After a long moment of building up the courage, she turned to meet David's gaze. "Please wait here." Her voice was laced with tears. "I won't be long."

David quickly got out, reached in the back seat for Tessa, and handed her to Lisa. With the diaper bag draped over her shoulder, and Tessa securely tucked in her arms, she walked to the front door. Her heart pounded in her chest. Before she reached up to knock, she looked down at her daughter and said, "I will always love you, Tessa."

Thirty minutes later, David saw Lisa come out of the house alone. She'd been forced to do the unthinkable... give up her own flesh and blood. When Lisa got into the Jeep, she sat staring ahead in silence, completely broken. David understood the sacrifice she'd made. Her children deserved a chance to grow up in a traditional home without the fears of being kept in a cage like an animal.

She wiped her tears and said, "Let's go find my son."

David reached for Lisa's hand and gave it a gentle squeeze. He waited a moment, as though to allow her to gather her emotions, and then turned on the ignition. "I promise I'll do whatever I have to do to keep you—and your son—safe."

She stared up at him in awe, so shocked by his reassuring words that she couldn't even begin to know how to respond. What could she say to that? It comforted her that he was so resolute and that he now included Steven in his vow to protect. But he was just one man, and this was not his fight. And yet she needed him. He was the only person she would allow herself to trust.

As they drove through the night, fog hovered low to the ground, making the visibility nearly impossible on the road ahead. When David and Lisa arrived back to the compound, the trap had already sprung. Dr. Autenburg and Dr. Crane's men had blocked the front entrance with weapons aimed in their direction. When the Jeep came to a screeching halt, dread rose in her throat, tightening until it was hard to breathe.

David kept his hands on the steering wheel, and Lisa flinched when several guards approached her door. At the same time, David's door flew open and more guards surrounded their vehicle, motioning for them to get out. When Lisa looked at David, he whispered, "Don't run, Lisa. Just do what they say."

In surrender, they slowly stepped out of the Jeep. Lisa screamed when a shot fired and David dropped to the ground.

When she tried to run for him, a guard caught her by the arm. Lisa managed to twist free and rushed over to him.

She dropped to her knees beside him. "Please, no..." She shook his shoulders. "David!"

But he wasn't moving. David's glassy eyes stared out with an empty gaze. Lisa could see a thick trickle of blood down the side of his face.

She flinched when someone grabbed her by the arm. When she turned to look, a face of pure evil stared back at her. With all her strength, she tried to pry herself free from Dr. Hubert Crane's tight grip. But it did no good. He was too strong.

Lisa was narcotized and smuggled out of California to a prison laboratory near Munich, Germany, where all the horrific experiments began.

Subjected to endless and painful tests, Lisa suffered years of isolation. Refusing was not an option. Dr. Crane used her son as a threat. If Lisa refused to comply with their physical torture, they systematically tormented her with insinuations of Steven's death. In the end, Lisa was bound to an operating table and mutated into a new specimen they called *Lilith*. Even though her heart froze, never to beat again, and most of her memories erased, she was still alive. They transformed Lisa into something which went against the laws of nature... an abomination created by power and greed.

Blinded by their scientific craving, Dr. Hubert Crane had made a crucial mistake. He'd created his worst nightmare. Already born with the gift to heal, Lisa's abilities developed and grew, changing with each experiment.

She used her new skills of mind manipulation on all of Dr. Crane's men. One by one, as they turned on each other, the facility erupted in chaos. The only two who managed to escape, taking Steven with them, were the two physicians.

In a heated rage of fury, she burned the laboratory to the ground and cursed her revenge. As she watched everything burn, a clear memory of the past suddenly assailed her. She caught a vague remembrance of two babies lying side by side in a crib, each with emerald green eyes. In her subconscious, she could hear someone singing a lullaby. Then the soft melody shifted into a nightmare. The memory of her babies being torn from her arms came to her in a flash. Instantly, she covered her face and fell to her knees.

"Please..." the words painfully broke from her throat. "Don't take my babies!"

Overwhelmed by raw emotions, she slowly lowered her hands and looked up at the sky, ready to surrender the last threads of her sanity. She closed her eyes, unable to bear the memory. It was more than she could withstand. All of it seemed like a dream, moments drawn out of real life as if they belonged to someone else. And then they were gone as though they had been scrubbed from her memory. Her children faded into nothing, leaving behind a blank slate. It was as if the images had never existed at all. She opened her eyes and watched as everything around her turned to ash.

Both physicians went quiet for years, as though they had disappeared from the face of the earth. Years later, Steven escaped, and police discovered Dr. Hans Autenburg's mutilated body back in Berkeley, California.

Dr. Hubert Crane sought new backing from billionaire clients with a hunger for research and hired more men to hunt down Steven.

Chapter One

Death was messy, painful and without rules, especially when you were faced with decisions to risk your life and the lives of the ones you loved.

An hour later, as Tessa opened her eyes, she realized she was back at the Breedline Covenant, safe and sound, lying on top of a padded examination table.

"I think she's awake," Cassie said, looking down at Tessa with a cheerful grin on her face. "Welcome back, Tessa."

She felt like hell, and her entire body was stiff, but she was alive.

Jace suddenly entered her field of vision as he leaned over her with a worried expression in his icy blue eyes.

"Are the babies—"

Jace smiled and took her hand in his. "They're fine, sweetheart."

Tessa exhaled a sigh of relief and closed her eyes. As she drifted off into a peaceful sleep, everything had seemed to have worked out as it was supposed to. That path she had been set upon to help the Breedline fight in battle against the Chiang-shih demon had taken her precisely where she was meant to end up—safe back in Jace's arms.

On the other side of the room, Celina blinked as tears filled her eyes when she heard her Aunt Helen say, "I'm sorry, Celina. The injury to your spine is beyond my expertise. You'll need an orthopedic surgeon."

"I thought I was going to be okay," Celina said. "I mean... I figured it was just a head injury. I wiggled my toes and..." She swallowed back tears. "Will I walk again?"

"I have faith you will." Helen's voice suggested hope.

"We'll find you the damn best," Kyle chimed in. "No matter what it takes."

"I'll find her an excellent surgeon," Helen said. "You have my word."

Kyle's shoulder sagged a bit as if all the air had escaped him at once. When he nodded, Helen checked the IV in Celina's arm. Before she left the room to give them privacy, she looked over her shoulder and said, "Don't stay too long, Kyle. Celina needs rest."

When the door clicked shut, Celina felt Kyle's hand on hers. The connection between them eased her in ways she couldn't explain.

In truth, everyone in the Covenant was now her family. Aside from her Aunt Helen, they were the only real family she had left.

Kyle leaned in close and captured Celina's mouth in a quick, tender kiss. "I'm so glad to have you back safe."

"Me too," she whispered just as her consciousness slipped from her grasp and she drifted asleep. In her heart, she believed she would come back to Kyle whole. One way or the other, she was going to walk again.

* * *

When Tessa awoke, Jace was right by her side, sitting in a chair, holding onto her hand. "How are you feeling, honey?"

As she gazed into his eyes, she saw him for all he was: a fierce fighter, a compassionate lover, a lost soul, the fearsome Beast, and the bonded mate who was now her family.

"Forgive me," she murmured.

He shrugged. "Why would I need to forgive you?"

As she thought about all their ups and downs, he'd always put her first. In that moment, she unleashed all her emotions and fell apart.

He grabbed a box of Kleenex and placed it in her lap. "Please don't cry, honey."

She snatched a tissue out and wiped her eyes. "I'm sorry for being so hardheaded," she finally said. "I shouldn't have risked the lives of our unborn children. Can you forgive me?"

"There's nothing to forgive." He stared at her with compassion. "You did what you had to do to save the lives of others. But part of it's true." He chuckled. "You're definitely hardheaded."

She laughed, and he loved the sound. "I love you." Her teary eyes stared into his. "You've always done the right thing by me... always putting me first before anyone else."

Jace grasped her hand and placed it over his heart. In another attempt to repair his completely botched effort of proposing, he said, "You never gave me an answer. Will you marry me, Tessa?"

Tessa smiled up at him, so much love in her eyes that it took his breath away. God, she loved this man. "Of course, I'll marry you."

Jace smiled. His dimples beamed on each cheek.

"You knew I would say yes, didn't you?"

He leaned over and gently kissed her lips. "I was praying you would."

"Good." She placed her hand against his face. "Then it's settled."

Tenderly, he gathered her close and held her. As he pulled from their embrace, he reached into his pocket. When he brought his hand back out, Tessa gasped in surprise.

"Oh, Jace... it's beautiful."

Jace took the ruby ring that was inside a small, black velvet box and slid it on her finger. "Alexander passed this down to me, to give to you. It was my great grandmother's wedding ring." Then he placed his hand over her rounded belly. "Soon, we're going to be a happy family."

"I love you, Jace Chamberlain."

With his fingertips he traced over her stomach and whispered, "I love you more."

Chapter Two

Two weeks later...

The Breedline Covenant was alive with chatter, laughter, and the warm smiles that only came from being with family. Everyone that resided in the enormous estate was present and accounted for. Even John and Sarah—Jace and Jem's human adoptive parents—were there.

Sarah had cornered Jace as soon as they'd returned after the Breedline finally destroyed the Chiang-shih demon, concerned for Tessa's pregnancy. He had assured her she was fine, but he hadn't shared the fact that he'd proposed to Tessa. He was saving that surprise for when they made the official announcement.

Jace's twin brother Jem, and Alexander—their biological father—knew, but they were keeping it quiet, not wanting to ruin the big surprise.

Thanks to Doc Helen's handiwork and fifty stitches later, Tessa was up and around a week after the battle with the Katako. He'd snapped her shoulder open clear to the bone. She knew she was back to her usual self because she'd been up half the night... making love with Jace.

Early in the morning, Jace and Tessa headed downstairs toward the kitchen to meet everyone for breakfast. As they stood outside the door, Jace was grinning so wide his face was starting to get sore from all the smiling. His eyes glittered with excitement as he took hold of Tessa's hand. "Let's announce our engagement," he said.

Tessa grinned and squeezed his hand. She was as eager as a kid at Christmas. She loved the way Jace was drawing it out for maximum effect. She wanted to savor this moment for as long as possible.

When they stepped through the door, everyone who mattered to them was inside. Jace cleared his throat and then called for attention. "Tessa and I have something we'd like to share with everyone."

The chatter inside hushed, and all eyes directed toward the happy couple.

Jace glanced down at Tessa and gave her a look so filled with love she would never forget it. She felt warmed all the way down to her toes by the contentment that rested so effortlessly on him.

He took a deep breath and lifted his chin, his smile growing so broad that his teeth flashed. With his hand entwined with hers, he blurted, "We're getting married!"

The smiles in the room were instantaneous. Sarah clapped her hand over her mouth as tears filled her eyes. No longer able to contain herself, she dropped her hand as squeals of excitement burst from her lips.

"Oh, my..." Sarah rushed over and pulled Tessa into her arms.

A chorus of cheers and congratulations went up, and everyone gathered into a big group hug.

John pushed his way in and gathered Tessa into a huge hug, but he was careful not to squeeze too tight. He kissed her cheek, and when he spoke, emotion coated his voice. "I couldn't be prouder." Then he put his arm around Mia. "What a blessing to have both my sons lucky in love with two lovely young ladies."

"This calls for a toast," Jem said as he held up a glass. "To Jace and Tessa... congratulations. I love you both."

Everyone was quick to grab their glass and toast to the happy occasion.

Alexander looked between Jace and Jem and said, "I want to congratulate you both." And then he averted his eyes from his sons and looked directly at John and Sarah. He had so much respect for the couple it was hard to put into words. He was grateful that they raised his sons when he couldn't. "I'm so grateful for everyone in this room. I don't know where I'd be without any of you."

Tessa's eyes roamed over the room at every single face and said, "Our sons will be the luckiest children who ever lived to have such a loving family."

Another round of congratulations swept through the room, relieving some of the solemnity.

Jace briefly closed his eyes, merely absorbing the vibrations of so much joy. He was moving into a future filled with the promise of brighter days and happier times.

After the celebration and breakfast, Jem strode down the hall with Jace to hit the gym. The happy announcement about Jace and Tessa getting married had lifted everyone's spirits and brought excitement back into the Covenant, especially since Jem and Mia decided to push their wedding ahead of schedule. They were getting married in eight days.

Tessa met with Mia to help her finish the last-minute wedding details and to show off her engagement ring. When all the arrangements were final, and Mia was satisfied with all the choices, Tessa smiled at her and reached for the door. "You're going to make a beautiful bride, Mia. Jem's going to love the dress."

"Thank you, Tessa." Mia sat on her and Jem's big bed. "I couldn't have done this without all your help."

"You're welcome, and don't be nervous. Everything is going to go just fine."

When Tessa left, Mia nervously rubbed her sweaty palms over her jeans as she thought about walking down the aisle. When it came to marriage, most girls looked forward to being presented to their fiancé by their proud father, and their mother was supposed to be sobbing when she saw her daughter walk down the aisle in her wedding dress.

Mia, on the other hand, was walking down the aisle by herself. There was no one to give her away, and no one would be sitting on the bride's side of the room.

She leaned against the headboard and thought about the only family member she had but didn't even know. She was thinking of her twin sister, Eve. They were separated at birth and grew up without even the knowledge of one another. And now her sister was alone and pregnant... with Sebastian's twins.

As her thoughts shifted toward Tessa's pregnancy, she wished Eve could be like her. Tessa was more like a sister to her than a friend. Eve had done terrible things to her, but Tessa didn't hold a grudge toward Mia, even though she looked identical to Eve.

At least she knew the Covenant and Jem's family had accepted her. But everything else in her life before she met Jem had not been good. Maybe that was also the cause of her jittery nerves. She feared the things she'd done in her past would come back to haunt her. Jem was a miracle, almost too good to be true.

A knock on the door brought her head around. She frowned and sat up on the bed and called out, "I'm coming."

When she opened the door, she was surprised to see Jem's father. He held something small in his hand. "I hope I'm not intruding," he said.

"No... of course not, Alexander. If you're looking for Jem, he's in the gym with Jace."

"I'm actually here to see you," he said with a nervous pitch in his voice. "I was wondering if I could speak with you. I mean... you're going to marry my son, and I thought it would be nice to talk, but if you're busy—"

"No, please..." She moved aside and motioned him in. "Come in. I just finished going over all the wedding plans with Tessa." She gestured toward the table and chairs in the small kitchenette. "Please, have a seat."

Before he sat down, he said, "Are you sure I'm not imposing?"

"Of course not." She smiled, pulling out a chair across from him.

When he sat down, he put a small, velvet box on the table. "I wanted to give you something before the wedding. It belonged to Jem's great-grandmother."

She looked at him, surprised.

"Open it," he said with a smile.

When she opened it, her eyes widened at the beautiful, antique diamond brooch inside. It was the shape of a butterfly. "Oh, Alexander... it's gorgeous."

"Would you wear this at your wedding?"

"I would love to wear it, but are you sure?"

He nodded. "It's a wedding gift. My grandmother would have loved for you to have it, and it would mean a lot to me."

"But what about Tessa?" Mia shook her head. "This should go to her."

"Jace gave her my grandmother's wedding ring," he said. "Please, Mia. I want to pass it down to you, then your children, and then on to their children. I would like to keep it in the family."

"It's breathtaking." Her voice glittered with excitement as she admired the brooch. "Thank you, Alexander."

"You're welcome, Mia." His smile broadened. "And there's one more thing. Since you don't have a father, it would be an honor if you would let me walk you down the aisle."

That's when the tears started. Mia instantly covered her mouth to stifle her sobs. Finally, she nodded and lowered her hand. "I would like that more than anything," she said, blinking more tears.

"So would I," came a voice from behind.

When Mia and Alexander turned to look, they saw Jem with a look of approval stamped all over his face.

"Son..." Alexander said as he rose from his chair.

As Jem came forward with his hand extended, Alexander took hold. It wasn't long before Jem tugged his father into a tight hug.

Mia put her hands over her mouth, clearly overcome with emotion as she watched father and son finally embrace for the first time. *You never know where life is going to take you*, she thought. Sometimes, the journey led you down a road with new surprises. And as it seemed, the ones they were heading toward were not bad... not bad at all.

Chapter Three

As dawn grew near, Sebastian wrapped up his first night back in control of his life after Jace's beast destroyed the Chiang-shih demon. And it was freakin' fantastic not having that *thing* possess his body.

What was *not* so hot was the fact that everything felt different without his beloved Eve. He felt deflated without her, as if all the life had been sucked out of him. Bottom line, without Eve by his side, everything seemed to be just a shadow of what it used to be. His mission was to get her back and then seek revenge against the Breedline.

A quick check of his watch told him he had only two hours left before closing time at the private club where he and Eve used to share a room. With the ability to conjure a portal, he traveled to the parking lot at the speed of lightning. Shit at the club grew seedier as midnight closed in, and the escorts that worked here—who looked like they just stepped out of a porn flick—were bringing in clients like bees to honey.

Suddenly, he caught a whiff of a heady aroma. When he turned to look, he saw a woman entering the bar. He realized without a doubt the long-legged blonde was a Breedline. His appetite instantly flared.

When he started forward, a massive figure stepped into his path. Sebastian halted and stood face-to-face with Corbin Azzo.

"Master... is that you?"

Before Sebastian could muster a response, the sound of heavy footsteps coming from behind caught his attention. As he spun around, he tucked one hand inside his jacket and felt for his pistol. To his surprise, he stood facing Samuel and Fredrick Mercier—both Breedline twins—who had gone traitor against their own kind.

One thought that went through Sebastian's mind as he stared at the two losers was he didn't want to be the ringleader of anything anymore. He didn't want to walk that stretch of hell on earth trying to keep others in line. All he wanted right now was to get Eve back where she belonged. Back in his arms and in his bed.

Sebastian shot them a look of distaste and said, "Sorry... I'm not the person you think I am. The Chiang-shih demon is dead."

Samuel's mouth dropped and Fredrick muttered, "Sebastian... is that you?"

"Yes, you idiot," he replied with a clear smirk in his voice. "You serve no purpose with me." Sebastian waved them away. "So begone."

"What about the Breedline Covenant?" Samuel said. "Don't you want revenge? They killed your father."

Sebastian shrugged and said, "Frankly, I don't give a damn. So, go on with your pathetic lives and stay out of my way."

"We need to talk," Corbin interjected. "It's important."

Sebastian looked at Corbin and rolled his eyes. "I don't care what you have to say."

Although the three of them were most likely strung with weapons, Sebastian turned and walked away. He had better things on his mind before the three stooges had rudely interrupted. And it had a smokin' body and the Breedline blood he craved.

As he made his way inside the club, loud music thumped while women dressed in bits of leather paraded by on client patrol and men glared at one another. He moved through the bar and sat down in the VIP section. When the waitress came up to his table, she tilted her hips and said, "What's your poison, sweetheart?"

"Shot of Patrón."

"You got it, darling."

When she sauntered off, Sebastian's eyes roamed through the crowded bar for the woman he'd spotted earlier.

Moments later, the waitress placed a shot glass on his table. Without hesitation, he tossed it back and said, "Bring me another, and start a tab."

Three shots later, he finally eyed the leggy blonde across the bar. It didn't take long for her to notice him. She gave him a look of approval. Sebastian's features were both gothic and alluring. He'd never had trouble picking up women in his life. They practically fell into his arms and straight into his bed.

His long, jet-black hair and his chiseled face stood out among the other men in the joint. And he had the kind of body that looked ready for all sorts of action.

The blonde across the club smiled at him and picked a cherry out of her pink liquor. She swirled her tongue around the stem like an invitation. A smile emerged from Sebastian's lips as he imagined her tongue in other places.

She watched as Sebastian rose from his chair and headed in her direction. Her eyes practically feasted on his body.

Finally, he stood facing her and extended his hand. "Let's go somewhere quiet."

Damn... she thought. *His voice is like a sex-phone operator, all husky and mad sexed-up.*

"Aren't you going to ask my name?"

He flashed her a smile. "Does it matter?"

She shrugged and took hold of his hand.

As Sebastian guided her back to his old private room upstairs, it wasn't long before he had her bent over a chair.

When he finished, he slapped her on the bare behind and zipped up.

She pushed her skirt down and pouted her bottom lip. "You're not going to leave me hanging, are you?"

"You don't honestly expect me to care whether you get off." He laughed. "Remember, I'm the one paying you."

For a moment, she seemed confused by his smug statement. She tilted her hip to one side and pursed her lips. "Did you *really* just say that?"

"What didn't you understand?"

"Fine..." She groaned. "Then pay me."

Sebastian pulled out his wallet. "What do I owe you?"

"Since you're such a bastard..." She flipped her hair back. "...that will be five hundred."

He grabbed her by the arm. "Don't be a bitch."

"Screw you," she said as she drew back her free arm and slapped him across the face.

Now things were starting to get interesting. First, there was screaming. Then a bit of a struggle came next. But in the long run, it all played out in Sebastian's favor. When he satisfied his hunger, he left the blonde unconscious on the floor. Before he ducked out of the room, he tossed the money beside her and said, "Consider this your lucky day."

* * *

As Eve's lids grew heavy, someone or *something* came to her room. At first, she saw nothing, just a shifting patch of shadow, and then a shimmering figure evolved out of the darkness. Surrounded by a brilliant glow, he had beautiful black wings that unsheathed from his back. She could feel the warmth from his body as he hovered above her bed. His face was a human face with sun-kissed skin and long, wavy, dark hair. His glowing eyes were slit-pupiled like a cat's. Looking into his mesmerizing features, Eve seemed calm in his presence.

She lifted higher on the pillow and said, "Who... are you?"

He leaned in, and when he smiled, two pointed teeth peeked out from under his top lip. "My name is Raphael," he said in a soft voice.

"Are you an angel?"

"Yes. I am the angel of healing."

Eve furrowed her brows. "Why are you here?"

"To heal your unborn children," he said as he glanced down at the place that held two tiny lives. When he placed his hand on the small swell of her belly, she felt a warmth all the way down to her toes.

In a matter of seconds, it was as though a weight had been lifted. Eve felt free of all the demons that had haunted her from the past.

The look the angel gave her made her eyes flood with tears. His expression was of forgiveness and comfort. "Worry not, my child," he said. "The hate in your heart will soon fade and love will take its place." Then he began to sparkle as if his skin was covered with thousands of tiny diamonds. "When you wake, you will have no memory of me."

Moments later, he vanished from her room. Eve closed her eyes drifted into the most beautiful dream. It was filled with a future of a loving family.

Chapter Four

When morning finally came, Eve was shocked when she opened her eyes and saw a black cat next to her in bed. It was sleeping, all nestled in the blanket. She smoothed her hand over its sleek fur and said, "How did you get in here?"

The feline purred in response.

Suddenly, a nauseous feeling came over her. Eve quickly got to her feet and rushed to the bathroom. As she put her face over the toilet bowl, her stomach automatically settled before she got sick. When she went to put her hand on her belly, her eyes rounded in stunned disbelief. "What—"

Her stomach was the size of a basketball. It was as if it had magically grown overnight. Although she was only four months along in her pregnancy, she looked to be ready to give birth at any minute. Then, out of nowhere, she felt a lot of movement inside.

Her first instinct was to reach for the phone to call the Breedline's physician. Instead, she sat on the top of the toilet lid and rested her forehead in the palm of her hand. She knew a succubus's pregnancy went by fast, but this? She wasn't expecting it to be so sudden.

For her past crimes against the Breedline, she'd been placed in a guarded guesthouse that was attached to the Covenant. It had one bed and bath, a small dining area, and a tiny kitchenette. After she gave birth, the Breedline council would decide her fate. She hoped for a lesser punishment since she willingly gave herself over to the Breedline and helped Sarah Chamberlain escape from the Chiang-shih demon.

Eve released a long sigh as thoughts of Sebastian came to mind. Was his soul back after he'd been freed of the demon's possession? If so, was he searching for her?

She forced her thoughts away and went to the closet for something to wear. After going through all her clothes, she realized not a single thing would fit. Finally, she settled on a pair of sweatpants with an elastic waist. As she looked to the bed, she noticed the cat was gone. She looked under the blanket and under the bed, but the cat was nowhere to be found. Tossing the search aside, she headed down a small winding stairwell as her mind went straight to food. The sudden spike of hunger hit her so hard she felt like she hadn't eaten in days.

After deciding on a can of soup, she poured the contents into a pot and heated it up. Minutes later, she poured it into a bowl and dug in. The warm, salty liquid tasted perfect as it ran down the back of her throat and into her stomach.

Without warning, her stomach churned. She barely made it to the trash as it all came back up, reverse as it went down. When it finally came to an end, she sat back down. She wondered if she should call the Breedline physician. It was possible that she was getting close to delivery, or maybe it was blood she needed.

Her first instinct was to try to escape. Although that would get her nowhere, considering she had two guards posted outside her door, plus she had no place to go. Surely if she asked, they would provide her with proper medical treatment.

Deciding to ask for a doctor, she went to the door. When she opened it, both guards turned to greet her. With one hand on her stomach and the other used to prop herself up, she suddenly became dizzy. She lost her balance, and as she tilted back, one of the guards rushed over just in time to catch her fall.

"Hold on, miss," the guard said in a Scottish accent. "I'll get you the doctor."

Eve silently nodded with her head in the crook of his arm.

The guard carried her to the Breedline's examination room while the other guard called for help. When he entered the room, he gently lowered her onto a thinly padded table.

"I'm going to be sick," she mumbled into her hand.

Quickly, the guard rushed toward a trash container and grabbed it. When he brought it over, she dry-heaved into it. After her sickness had passed, she eased back and gestured him to take it away.

"Are you sure you're done?" the guard asked.

"Yes, I think that's all I have left in my stomach."

When he went to sit down, he had to squeeze into the chair. His massive body overflowed the armrests and the back cushion.

"What's your name?" Eve asked.

"Mah name is Bruce." He cleared his throat. "Bruce Carmichael."

"Thanks for helping me, Bruce."

He gave her a slight nod.

"Do you have any children?"

He shook his head.

"Are you married?"

He gave another shake of the head.

"Sorry... I'm just trying to make conversation," she said. "I guess it's my nerves."

Suddenly, the door came open and a young female came in. "I got here as fast as I could." She smiled and placed her hand on Eve's shoulder. "I'm Cassie Chamberlain. Helen's tied up in an emergency at the hospital. I'm a pediatrician at the Bates Hospital. Would it be all right if I examined you?"

For a split second, Eve worried about the physician not knowing anything about her species. There were anatomical differences in the two. What if she couldn't help her?

"Yes, of course," Eve finally said. "But... you do know I'm a half-breed, right?"

Cassie nodded. "Yes, I do. If it eases your mind, I helped Helen deliver Tim and Angel's baby. She's also a half-breed."

Eve nodded as a single tear slipped down her cheek.

"Don't worry, Eve. Everything is going to be okay." Then Cassie turned to the guard who was standing by the door and said, "And you are?"

"Bruce Carmichael." He quickly moved closer and extended his hand. "I'm her guard."

Cassie shook his hand. "Going by your accent, you must be a Scottie?"

He nodded. "Aye."

"I take it you've been ordered not to leave Eve alone?"

"Aye, ma'am."

Cassie looked away, focusing back on Eve. "Okay, so let's start off with a blood sample to speed things along."

A few minutes later, Cassie filled a few small vials with blood. Then she found the chart Helen had for Eve. After she looked over the file, she said, "Have you been taking the prenatal vitamins Helen gave you?"

When Eve nodded, Cassie said, "Your chart says you should only be four months along and... with twins?"

Eve nodded again.

Cassie rolled a chair next to Eve and sat down. "I'd like to do an ultrasound so we can see what's going on."

"Can we do it now?"

"Absolutely," Cassie replied. Then she opened a drawer and retrieved a small tube. "This is ultrasound gel. It will be a little cold, but it will help transmit signals between the ultrasound probe and the skin's surface."

Eve nodded and Cassie pulled back Eve's top, revealing her rounded belly. Eve flinched at the cold sensation when Cassie squirted the gel onto her bare skin.

Cassie moved the probe across Eve's stomach and said, "Let's see if we can hear the heartbeats."

Moments later, the sound of a tiny rhythm came from the monitor. As Cassie continued to move the ultrasound probe, another rhythm could be heard that almost kept up with the first one.

"Yup, we have two heartbeats," Cassie said. "They're healthy and strong too."

Eve was speechless. As she looked at the images displayed on the monitor, tears instantly slid down her cheeks.

Eve wiped her tears away. "Are the babies okay?"

Cassie looked away from the monitor and focused on Eve with a smile. "Yes, they're perfectly healthy. Due to your genetics, the babies will be full-term in about two weeks. You should be ready to deliver by the end of this month."

Eve went completely still as she grappled with what Cassie had just told her. "Two weeks?"

"That's normal for your species," Cassie explained. "Don't worry. I'll make sure Helen and I are here to monitor you until then. Would you like to know what the sexes of the babies are?"

"Please..."

"You're having boys."

Instantly, Eve inhaled a deep breath and slowly exhaled. Then she lost it all over again as tears flowed down her cheeks.

"It's okay, Eve." Cassie's voice was soothing. "You're going to be fine."

Cassie's words filled her with hope, and her caring heart humbled her. It made her *want* to be a better person. Then she felt the babies move. At that moment, a flush of joy flooded through her body, making her feel alive in a way she hadn't been in a very, very long time. Eve fell in love with her sons at that moment. She smiled through her tears, and her sons were the cause of it.

"Thank you, Miss Cassie."

She handed Eve a slip of paper and said, "It's a picture from the ultrasound."

Eve's eyes lit up. "I can't believe it." She held up the picture and said, "Look, Bruce... it's a picture of my babies."

When he moved next to Eve and looked at the images on the small picture, his mouth formed a broad smile.

A knock at the door suddenly caught their attention. Then it cracked open and Angel peeked her head in. "Is it okay if I visit with Eve?"

When Eve nodded at Cassie, she motioned Angel inside and said, "We just finished. Come on in, Angel."

Angel pushed through the door, carrying her daughter, and moved next to Eve. "How are you?"

"I'm much better. Thank you, Angel."

"Eve is getting close to her delivery date," Cassie said. "We just found out she's having boys. Isn't that right, Eve?"

Eve held out the ultrasound picture. "They're growing so fast. I can't believe they'll be born so soon."

When Angel looked at the photo, she smiled. "Congratulations, Eve. I'm glad you and the babies are fine."

Before Eve could respond, Natalie stretched her little arm out and pointed to Eve's belly. "Baa-beez," she mumbled around a light giggle.

"Yes," Eve said. "There are two babies in my belly."

"Please let me know if you need anything," Angel said. "I want to make sure you have everything you need to feel comfortable."

Eve blinked tears. "Thank you."

Angel's kind words made Eve's heart swell with so much raw emotion. It made her feel at ease even though her life was in turmoil. It was hard to explain... even to herself, but suddenly everything felt different, from the way she looked at everyone in the Covenant to how she looked at herself. *Maybe there is hope for me after all,* she thought.

Chapter Five

Kyle leaned against the wall across Celina's bedroom with a cigarette between his lips. His nerves were off the charts. He put a lighter up to his face and flicked the little wheel several times, but it wouldn't ignite. "Dammit," he said in a low voice. Finally, he gave up and put it away.

He thought about Celina on the other side of the wall, lying in bed... paralyzed. He needed a drink, and a whole bottle of whiskey would just barely take the edge off. Now was not the time to get stupid drunk though. Celina needed him sober.

Inside the room, Celina's body felt all wrong, both cumbersome and weightless at the same time. Her only hope was the tiny spasms she felt in the muscles in her legs and feet. *Surely, I won't be like this forever,* she tried to convince herself. *My healing powers should be kicking in by now.*

At the sound of a light knock, she looked up. When the door opened to a crack, Kyle peeked inside. "Hey, babe. You up for a visit?"

"Sure." Her voice sounded weak.

Kyle pushed his way in and took a seat next to the bed. Celina was stretched out from under several blankets, immobilized with a neck brace running from her chin to her collarbone. The IV in her arm linked to a bag that hung on a metal pole, and there was tubing down below that plugged into a catheter.

"How are you feeling?"

"I'd be perfect if I could get out of this bed."

His eyes softened. "I know, babe."

"Have you heard from Helen?"

Kyle gathered her hand in his. "Sorry, babe. I haven't talked to her since yesterday."

"Kyle... you don't have to do this."

"What are you talking about?"

"You don't have to be with me through this if you don't want to."

"Of course I want to be with you." He lightly squeezed her hand. "I couldn't bear the thought of being without you."

She smiled and nodded.

"You have to have faith, Celina." He brought her hand to his lips and pressed a kiss to her soft skin. "I promise I'll do everything I can to help you, but you've got to trust in me."

"I do." Her eyes blinked sleepily. "I have faith in you, Kyle."

* * *

Chester Ewan—a Guardian of the forest—felt helpless knowing Celina couldn't use her powers of a Wicca to heal her broken body. At that moment, he knew he had to help her. His plan he envisioned had to work. He had to convince Jem to use his powers to heal Celina's spinal injuries. Although there was the possibility his powers, if they could not be controlled, would be dangerous. Nevertheless, they had to try. Chester knew once he explained to Jem what he was capable of he wouldn't refuse to help. It simply wasn't in Jem's hardwiring.

With the ability to move past any barrier, Chester didn't bother to knock. He used his powers and drifted inside Jem's room.

"Chester..." Mia bit out, clutching on to the towel that was wrapped around her body. "What the hell are you doing here?"

Chester quickly covered his eyes. "I'm sorry, Mia. But I don't have time to explain. I'm looking for Jem."

"Haven't you heard of knocking first?"

He hesitantly lowered his hands and gave her a puppy-eyes stare. "Sorry... but it's important that I speak to him."

She let out an aggravated sigh. "Jem is not here. What's so important that you couldn't take the time to knock?"

"I may know a way to heal Celina, and I need Jem's help."

Mia rolled her eyes. "Why didn't you say so in the first place? He's in the library."

"Thank you, Mia. By the way, congratulations on your engagement."

"Thanks, Chester." She raised a brow. "But promise me you'll knock next time."

He bowed his head. "You have my word."

When Chester left, Mia quickly got dressed and went down the hall to Tim and Angel's room. Tim would be furious with Chester for not coming to him first. He was the council head of the Breedline, and before any decisions were final, they had to present them before Tim and Tessa.

Mia walked past all the other doors and hung a right that led to Tim and Angel's room. As she reached up to knock, the sounds of a child's laughter filtered through the door.

"It's open," Tim called out.

When Mia opened the door, she saw Natalie sitting on the floor playing with Jace's cat. Natalie looked away from the black feline and focused her bright eyes on Mia with the biggest grin. It wasn't long before the toddler got to her feet. She held out her little arms and squealed, "Mee-uh!"

When Mia scooped Natalie into her arms, she hugged her neck. As she released her, Natalie pointed to the door and said, "Baa-beez!"

Mia looked at Tim, baffled. "Did she say... babies?"

"She's talking about your sister's babies," Tim explained. "Eve's guards rushed her down to the examination room earlier. Helen was at the hospital, so Cassie took her place and cared for Eve."

Mia's eyes rounded. "Is she all right?"

"Yes, she's fine. Apparently, Eve's due date is in two weeks."

"But how can that be? Eve is just four months along."

"Mia... didn't you know?"

When she shook her head, Tim said, "I guess I expected you to."

She shrugged. "Expected me to know what?"

"Due to your genetics of a half-succubus, a pregnancy lasts no more than four months. That's why Angel had Natalie so early." He tilted his head a little. "Hasn't anyone ever told you?"

Mia felt dumbfounded. "I've heard this before, but I guess I thought it was just a myth. Growing up in human foster care wasn't exactly what I call helpful when it came to my species."

"I'm sorry, Mia. If you ever have any questions, I'm sure Angel would be more than willing to talk to you."

"Thanks, Tim." After a long sigh, Mia said, "So, what will happen to Eve when she has the babies? I mean... will she be punished with prison time?"

"Eve's punishment will be up to the council," Tim said. "They will put in consideration that she helped Jace and Jem's mother. That could give her a lesser punishment. The council will also make the decision where her twins go." He hesitated and said, "I hate to say it, but unless a family member steps in to take them, they will go to a foster family."

"The only family member they have is... me."

"I don't expect you to take on that responsibility, Mia."

"But her children are innocent in all this," she said. "They don't deserve to be tossed over to strangers. I know what that's like."

"Mia, you and Jem are about to be married. Have you two talked about having children?"

Natalie pointed to Mia's belly and said, "Baa-beez?"

"No sweetheart." Mia's eyes softened. "There's no babies in there."

"Jem's got a big heart, Mia. Especially when it comes to kids. It wouldn't hurt to ask him."

"You mean... ask him about taking in Eve's children?"

When Tim nodded, Mia considered his idea for a moment. It was a suggestion she couldn't even wrap her mind around.

"If Jem did agree to take in Eve's twins," Mia said, "how do you think everyone else in the Covenant would feel? I'm not sure if Jace could even tolerate having Sebastian's children raised in the same household as his."

"I think you're underestimating everyone," he said. "Go talk to Jem first. If you need help, you've got me and Angel's support."

"Thanks, Tim."

"Angel also told me something about Eve," Tim said. "Since Angel is half-succubus, she sensed that Eve wanted to right her wrongs. Angel thinks being a mother has changed her in some way."

"Do you think I should go speak with her?"

Tim nodded. "Yes, I do."

As Mia lowered Natalie to the floor, she said, "Oh, I almost forgot why I came by. Chester came into my room looking for Jem. He said something about healing Celina, and for some reason, he needed Jem's help."

Chapter Six

As Chester hurried downstairs in search of Jem, his primary concern was for Celina. He was not the kind of man to leave a lady in distress. With his mind focused, he rushed into the library and searched through the shelves stocked with books. Moments later, he saw Jem leaning against a bookshelf.

Jem looked up when he heard someone call out his name.

"Hey, Chester. What are you doing here?"

"I'm looking for you."

Jem came forward and said, "Is something wrong?"

"I need to speak with you about something urgent."

After Chester explained the special abilities Jem wasn't aware of, his response was an exhale that lasted about five minutes past infinity.

"Will you help her?"

"Of course," Jem finally said.

The part where Chester explained about the dangers went unspoken at first. Sometimes the situations placed before you didn't give you options. Without a doubt, family was everything to the Breedline. Your mate, your blood, and the friends you considered family... that was your whole world. And along with that belief, as Celina suffered, so did everyone else in the Covenant.

The sound of a door opening made them turn to look. As Tim moved in their direction, Chester's body began to fade into a shadow.

"Chester, there's no need to be nervous. It's just Tim," Jem said realizing what it was like to trip on the outside world and fall into the Breedline rabbit hole. Having to reveal their secret world to his adoptive parents had proven difficult. When it came to someone of an entirely different species, the mix could raise complications.

When Chester relaxed, Jem told Tim about their plan to help Celina.

"We'll see how Celina feels about this," Tim said. "And of course, we'll need to run this by Tessa. Nothing gets decided without her final word."

* * *

After Mia spoke with Tim, she decided to visit her twin sister. She had a lot of questions to ask Eve. Sure, she hoped to finally be at peace with her, although she wasn't holding her breath for a miracle. *Could it be possible,* she thought, *that motherhood had changed Eve?*

Mia walked down a narrow hallway and stopped in front of a mirror. The image staring back at her was identical to Eve's, down to the length of her long, black hair, the crimson color of her eyes, and her pale skin. With a sigh, she looked away and kept moving until she reached the Covenant's guesthouse.

A guard greeted her as she came to the front entrance. Moments later, he escorted Mia inside.

"Your sister is here to visit you," Bruce said as Eve came downstairs.

Mia looked at Eve and said, "I would like to talk if that's okay with you?"

"Of course," Eve said. "Please..." She gestured Mia to the bar in the small kitchen. "Make yourself comfortable."

When Mia took a seat at the bar, Eve sat in the chair across from her.

"I heard your due date is coming soon."

"In two weeks," Eve said, placing her hand over her rounded belly. "I'm having boys. Would you like to see the ultrasound picture?"

Mia nodded. "Sure."

After Eve placed the photo on the table and Mia saw the images of two tiny lives, her eyes filled with tears.

"Oh, Eve... they're precious."

"Thank you, Mia. I can't believe how fast they've grown. They practically grew overnight."

"Did you know," Mia swallowed in mid-sentence, "that our species carried a baby for only four months?"

"I hadn't a clue."

Mia sighed. "Me neither."

"Yeah." Eve rolled her eyes. "I guess we didn't get that memo."

Mia laughed. "I guess not."

"I never thought you'd come to see me," Eve said. "But I'm glad you did."

"Eve, can I ask you a question and get an honest answer?"

Eve nodded. "I promise to be truthful."

"Is Sebastian the father..." she briefly hesitated, "or is the Chiang-shih demon the father?"

"I'm not sure." Tears gathered in Eve's eyes. "But I will love them no matter who their father is. They didn't ask to be created."

"No, they didn't," Mia said. "They are not at fault no matter the circumstance."

"Thank you for understanding. It means a lot to me."

"There's another reason why I'm here," Mia said. "Depending on what happens after the twins are born, and what the council decides, there is a possibility you will serve time. That means the boys will be placed into foster care."

"I know." Eve's lips trembled. "But what are my choices?"

Mia reached for Eve's hand. "Let me care for them."

"You would do that?"

"Yes, Eve."

Eve squeezed Mia's hand. "Oh, thank you, Mia."

"You're welcome, Eve." Then Mia slightly tilted her head. "Can I ask you a personal question?"

When Eve nodded, Mia said, "How can you bear to love Sebastian? He's done such horrible things."

Eve lowered her head and inhaled a deep breath. As she exhaled, she lifted her chin and said, "He saved me, Mia. When I ran away from my foster parents, I was homeless on the streets. He took me in and gave me a place to stay. When my foster father finally found me, he forced me back. Sebastian found me after I had been beaten and raped... and killed him. After that, I felt safe. He's always cared for me. I know he's ruthless and done terrible things, but he's all I've ever known. I will always love him."

"I'm sorry you went through that. I understand now. I want to help you, Eve. I'll make sure your children never have to suffer the way you did."

"What about the Covenant?" Eve said. "Surely everyone will oppose to having my children raised here."

"Tim and Angel have already given me their blessing. But I haven't talked to Jem yet. I know he will be compassionate and understanding. Tessa has a big heart, and she will help me, but Jace is the one I'll have to convince. His hatred for Sebastian goes deep into his soul, but I think once he's a father himself, he'll come around."

"Can you ever forgive me, Mia?"

"Give me time, Eve. I've already come this far. I'm not proud of my past either. Sometimes it just takes others longer to find the right path. Have faith, Sister. You'll get there too."

Chapter Seven

When Helen returned to the Covenant, she went upstairs to give Celina the good news. She'd stayed up for hours, searching for a surgeon of the Breedline species. At the San Francisco General Hospital, they recognized Dr. Kenneth Craven as one of the best and experienced doctors in the field of orthopedics. After Helen had pleaded Celina's case, he'd agreed to do the surgery.

Standing outside Celina's bedroom door, her hands fidgeted with the lapels of her white coat and then the stethoscope in her pocket. With her own patients during many trauma incidents, she'd always kept her cool. It was her trademark. This was personal though. The person on the other side of the door hit close to home. Although Celina was Helen's niece, she seemed more like a daughter.

After a time, the Covenant's examination room was finally set up with proper equipment, but it didn't have everything. They would have to transport Celina to the hospital's OR, where Helen could assist with the surgery if needed.

Before she stepped inside, she took a deep breath and pulled herself together. When she opened the door, Celina's face brightened. Tim stood next to her bedside with anticipation stamped all over his face.

"Did you find a surgeon, Aunt Helen?"

"Yes, honey," Helen said as she approached Celina. "Dr. Craven is one of the best in his field."

Celina smiled. "That's great news."

Tim glanced down at Celina. The thought of someone so young having to live with the loss of mobility took his breath away. Even if you were a couch potato, life in a wheelchair would seem like a death sentence.

"How soon can I get the surgery?"

"You have an appointment first thing in the morning," Helen said. "Dr. Craven wants to examine you before we schedule the surgery."

"I don't mean to interrupt," Tim said. "There's something else that has been brought to my attention. It has to do with another possible option other than surgery."

Helen shook her head. "What are you talking about?"

Before Tim could explain, someone clearing their throat caught their attention. When they glanced over, Jem and Chester stood in the open doorway, waiting for permission to enter.

"Please," Celina said. "Come in."

As they came forward and moved next to Celina, Helen and Tim stepped back. Before Chester spoke to Celina, he leaned down into her field of vision and smiled. His big eyes were a bright green, but not any shade of green she'd ever seen. His pointed ears reminded her of a Sindarin Elf from *The Lord of the Rings*.

"Jem has the power to heal you, Celina."

Her eyes rounded. "But... how?"

"He is the Chosen Son," Chester said. "The powers he bestows are far greater than any species I have encountered. They are powerful enough to bring back the dead."

"How do you know this to be true?" Helen asked.

"I am a Guardian," Chester said. "We know all."

Helen averted her eyes from Chester and looked to Jem. "Did you know this?"

Jem shook his head. "I had no idea."

"If Jem can truly heal me," Celina chimed in, "I want to see if it will work rather than go through with the surgery."

"Celina, you need to know my gift could also be deadly," Jem said.

"Absolutely not," Helen urged. "I won't allow such a risk."

Celina looked up at Helen and said, "Shouldn't this be my decision? Surgery is risky too. Besides, Chester said Jem had the power to bring back the dead, so..."

"Please, honey," Helen said, her voice pleading. "Let Dr. Craven at least examine you first."

"I agree with Helen," Tim said. "Let's see what the surgeon says before we make any hasty decisions."

"They're right, Celina," Jem said. "I think you should try the surgery first."

Celina didn't look at Jem, but she could feel the weight of his stare. "All right," she said, releasing a sigh. "But if the surgery isn't successful, I'm going to let Jem try to heal me. I can't live with the fact that I didn't try everything possible. I'm not going to spend the rest of my life in this bed."

The sound of someone clearing their throat put an end to the conversation. When they looked to the open door, Kyle was standing there. "What's going on?"

"Helen found a surgeon," Celina said. "I have an appointment first thing in the morning."

Kyle ambled forward and stood beside Jem. "Did I just hear you say you have the power to heal her?"

Jem was quiet for a moment. "Yes, but there is a chance it could kill her. I've never done this before, Kyle. It's a huge risk."

"But it's my risk and my decision," Celina said. "If the surgery isn't successful, I'll do whatever it takes to walk again."

When Kyle moved next to Celina, he grasped her hand. She felt the warm strength of his palm in hers. As he stared at her, his gaze was intense. "I promise you, Celina." He lightly squeezed her hand. "I'm not going anywhere. Even if you can walk or not, I'm always going to be with you."

She smiled. "Well then... I guess it's settled. You're stuck with me."

Kyle winked. "I wouldn't have it any other way."

* * *

Mia left her sister's confined living quarters and went to her and Jem's bedroom to wait for him. She stopped in front of a mirror as soon as she went inside. As she stared at her reflection, she wondered how Jem was going to react when she asked him about taking in Eve's twins. A sudden feeling of dread came over her. What if he refused?

She flinched and turned to look when the door opened. Jem immediately sensed Mia's anxiety. He came forward and said, "What's wrong, honey?"

As he waited for a reply, she found herself speechless. She took a deep breath and said, "Jem... I need to talk to you about something important."

He reached out and drew her in close. "Of course, honey. What's on your mind?"

"Eve is going to have the twins soon. After her trial, she'll most likely be sent away. It would kill me if my nephews go to foster care."

Jem frowned and took a few steps back. "What are you asking, Mia?"

"I want…" She swallowed the knot that had formed in the back of her throat. "…to take in the boys."

The silence and the strained look on Jem's face intensified. The look in his eyes peeled back layer after layer until she felt bare and vulnerable under his scrutiny. Finally, he said, "Do you know what you're asking?"

"I know it's a lot to ask," she said. "But I'm the only family they have. They're also your blood kin. No matter how much you hate Sebastian, he's still your half brother."

"I'm sorry, Mia. I cannot take in Sebastian's children. After what he has done to Tessa, it would destroy Jace if I agreed to do this."

"But, Jem…"

He held up a halting hand. "Please, Mia. Do not ask me this again."

As he turned to leave, she said, "Where are you going?"

"I need to get some air."

"Please, Jem. Don't leave upset."

He moved to the door, and before he opened it, he said, "I just need to be alone for a while. I've got a lot on my mind."

When he stepped out of the room, he leaned his back against the door and hung his head. He was positively numb. Aside from the fact he'd just found out he had the power to heal, not to mention the part about having the ability to bring back the dead, he felt guilty about what he just said to Mia. He loved her with all his heart, and he wanted nothing more than to make her happy, but he could not do what she asked of him. If he chose to take in Eve and Sebastian's children, it would drive a permanent wedge between him and Jace. That was something he could not live with.

As Jem headed downstairs, the training room came to mind. A good hour or so on the treadmill would help clear his mind.

After several minutes of sobs and tears, Mia finally emerged from the bedroom. She saw Tim heading her way the second she stepped out.

"Tim...," she bit back tears. "Have you seen Jem?"

He noticed she'd been crying. "I saw him go downstairs. Is something wrong, Mia?"

"Jem is upset with me."

Tim shrugged. "Why?"

"I asked to take in Eve's twins."

"I take it he disagreed?"

Mia nodded with tears streaming down her cheeks.

Tim came forward and placed his hand on her shoulder. "I'm sorry, Mia. But you can't blame him for his first reaction. This is a tough decision that involves his brother."

"I know," she said. "But I just can't bear the thought of my nephews going to live with strangers. It would break my heart if they were mistreated."

Tim lowered his hand and said, "I'll go talk to him. Maybe I can make him come to reason."

"You would do that?"

His eyes softened. "Of course. I understand how you feel. Your nephews are not to blame for their parents' bad decisions. They deserve to be with family and to grow up in a good home."

She smiled a little. "Thank you, Tim."

"So, do you have a clue to where he might have gone?"

"Maybe the training room," she said. "When he has a lot on his mind, that's the first place he goes."

Tim nodded. "Don't worry, Mia. We'll figure this out."

Moments later, Tim braced himself before he walked into the weight room. When he stepped inside, Jem was on the treadmill in a fast sprint. His brows were clenched tight and he looked miles away, lost in deep thought.

Tim moved closer and said, "Hey, Jem, can we talk for a minute?"

Jem nodded and hit the stop button. Before he hopped off the treadmill, he reached for a towel and wiped his face.

"I take it you spoke with Mia, am I right?"

"I'm not trying to get in your business," Tim said. "But as your friend, I thought you needed a shoulder. Sometimes it's best to talk things out. Believe it or not, you're a lot like your brother when it comes to expressing your feelings. You two tend to bottle things up until you reach a boiling point. It's not the best solution, especially for Jace."

"Yeah, I guess you're right." Jem exhaled a sigh. "It's just a lot to take in. I mean... I love kids and I would accept Eve's twins, but how am I supposed to explain all this to Jace? He would never come to reason. This would tear him to pieces if I agreed to take in Sebastian's children. He would hate me."

"I think you're underestimating your brother. Sure, he'll be pissed at first. But when he has time to think about it, not to mention when he's a father himself, he'll see things in a different way. Besides, what if no one gave you two a chance because of your biological father? I mean, he was possessed by a demon, for crying out loud. John and Sarah adopted you and Jace because they loved you unconditionally. They didn't care about your past or where you came from."

"Damn," Jem said. "I feel like a complete ass."

Tim reached out and clapped a hand on Jem's shoulder. "Go talk to Mia. Do the right thing. Those boys deserve a chance. We'll deal with Jace later." He chuckled a little. "Hell... if we have to, we'll tie his ass up and gag him until he comes around."

Tim's words filled him with determination. Strangely, calm acceptance finally settled over Jem. He extended his hand. "Thanks, Tim."

Tim smiled and took his hand into a firm handshake. "You're welcome, Jem."

Chapter Eight

Sebastian left the leggy blonde in his room and went back to the club. He headed straight for the VIP section and slid behind a table. As he leaned back into the padded booth, he watched the lights flicker down on the crowded dance floor.

When a waitress brought him his usual two shots of Patrón, Sebastian became annoyed with the noisy group behind him. A bunch of middle-aged men with gold watches and silk suits laughed like the blowhard drunks they were—to the point that the loudest of them slammed back in his seat and knocked into Sebastian. That didn't go over to well.

He turned around and let loose a few f-bombs.

One of the guys, who had a goatee and a ponytail, almost identical to the image on the cover of Zig-Zag cigarette papers, cranked his head around and shot Sebastian a dirty look.

Sebastian glared back at the guy and reached for his drink. He quickly tilted his head back and swallowed the vodka in one gulp.

A moment later, as he was about to take another shot, zig-zag guy banged into his seat. Sebastian shot forward and spilled his drink. "Son of a b—"

"Oh, sorry..." the guy chuckled. Then he turned around with his drink in his hand and lifted his pinkie at Sebastian. "Didn't mean for you to spill your drink... fag."

Sebastian growled low in his throat and reached inside his jacket for his pistol. Before he retrieved it, a tall guy came up to Sebastian and put his hand out to stop him.

The stranger turned to the other table and said, "Gentlemen, is there a problem?"

Sebastian looked up at the guy in stunned disbelief. It was as if he was looking into a mirror at his own reflection. The guy could have been his twin. "What the hell..."

Zig-zag guy peered up at Sebastian's doppelganger with a confused look on his face. Then he motioned to his buddies and said, "Look guys... it's dumb and dumber."

When everyone at the table burst into laughter, Sebastian snarled his upper lip.

A waitress came up to the table just as Sebastian started to get up. She smiled at Sebastian's doppelganger and said, "Hello, Mr. Carlyle. Would you care for a drink?"

"Please, Tanya." He dipped his head. "Bring me a bottle of Dom Perignon."

"Yes, sir," she quickly replied and then turned toward the other table. "Would you gentlemen like another round of drinks?"

Before zig-zag guy could reply, Sebastian's doppelganger said, "Tanya, just bring them their bill. They were about to leave." He looked to the men. "Isn't that right, gentlemen?"

The zig-zag guy's eyes bulged. His mouth dropped at the pair of glowing eyes staring back at him. "Uh… yeah," he muttered. "We were just leaving." He reached into his jacket with a trembling hand and took out his wallet. After he fidgeted with the contents inside, he laid down several bills and said, "Keep the change." Seconds later, they rose from their table and hurried through the exit.

Sebastian's doppelganger gestured toward the empty seat across from Sebastian and said, "May I?"

When Sebastian nodded, his look-alike sat down and faced him.

Sebastian glared at him. "Who the hell are you?"

"I'm your twin brother, Thomas Carlyle."

Sebastian damn near swallowed his tongue. "My stepfather said you died at birth."

For a moment, Thomas kept silent and stared at Sebastian with avid curiosity. Finally, he said, "Your stepfather was a bastard and a liar."

"That's why I killed him," Sebastian shot back. "So, where have you been hiding all these years?"

"I've lived in England most of my life with our mother's sister, Cathryn."

Sebastian leaned back and crossed his arms. "How did that go?"

"Although I was raised with money, she made my life a living hell."

Sebastian smirked. "Is she still alive?"

"No. Cathryn passed away a year ago. The good news is, I inherited her fortune."

Sebastian cocked a brow. "So, aren't you a least bit curious about our birth mother?"

"Tell me. What's she like?"

"Dead," Sebastian said. "I killed her too."

Without as much as batting an eye, Thomas reached inside his Valentino sports coat. Before he brought his hand out, Sebastian quickly pulled out his pistol. He leaned across the table and said, "If you even think about trying something—"

"Hold up," Thomas cut him off and held up his hands. "Calm down, Brother. I'm just reaching for a cigar, that's all."

Sebastian tucked his weapon back inside his jacket. "You need to know," he said, squaring his shoulders, "I don't trust anyone, especially when it comes to family."

"I completely understand," Thomas said, retrieving two cigars from the inside of his suit pocket. "I think you'll like this brand." He handed one to Sebastian and leaned back to light up his. "They're dark, but smooth."

Sebastian flicked up a flame from his lighter and leaned forward for the inhale. As he took the smoke in, he could feel his brother focusing on him.

Thomas exhaled a perfect white cloud that momentarily fogged his features. "So, what do you think?"

Sebastian exhaled the expensive stogie. "I like it."

Thomas grinned. "I knew you had good taste."

"How did you know where to find me?"

Thomas rolled his cigar between his forefinger and thumb. "Lilith told me."

"Who the hell is *Lilith*?"

"A goddess," Thomas simply said.

* * *

After the talk with Tim, it wasn't long before Jem left the training room and headed upstairs to apologize to Mia.

As he entered their bedroom, he could hear running water coming from inside the bathroom. He cracked open the door and peeked inside. Mia was taking a shower. Although the room was full of steam, he could see her through the thin glass barrier that separated them. God, she was beautiful. His eyes softened and his heart ached. He could sense her emotions as she stood underneath the water's spray with her head down. Mia was heartbroken.

When he stepped inside and called out to her, Mia's reaction was instantaneous. She opened the shower door and held out her hand, inviting him in.

He instantly hardened.

He quickly slipped out of his clothes and took her hand. As she guided him inside, he stood facing her and said, "I'm so sorry, honey. Can you forgive me?"

She nodded as tears fell from her eyes.

"We'll do the right thing and give Eve's children a loving home," he said. "I promise, somehow, it will all work out."

Her lips trembled. "I love you, Jem."

"I love you, sweetheart."

Instantly, they reached for the other at the same moment. Their mouths finished the journey as their lips crushed together.

* * *

After Celina's first appointment, her surgery date was scheduled, and today was the big day. As Helen arrived at the Covenant, she was anxious to get Celina transported to the hospital.

When she went upstairs, she met Kyle in the hallway outside Celina's room. Just as she was about to say something, Kyle spoke first. "Are you sure she'll be safe in a human hospital?"

Helen's placed her hand on his arm. "I spent years working in that hospital when I first got out of medical school. I'm familiar with all the rooms and all the equipment. There is not one square inch of the facility I don't know like the back of my hand. Dr. Craven and I will work together and make sure she is safe. And Tim will have a guard outside her room until she's released."

"I can't bear to have anything happen to her again."

"Trust me, Kyle. We'll take care of her."

"Can I have a minute with her in private?"

Helen nodded. "Of course."

Kyle went to Celina's room and tapped on the door. "Celina… it's me, Kyle."

"Come in," came a sleepy voice.

When he opened the door, he said, "Helen is here for you. She's got an ambulance waiting outside to transport you to the hospital."

She nodded in silence.

He approached her bed and placed his hand over hers. "I'll be outside in the waiting room until you're done."

Before she could reply, the door opened, and Helen put her head in. "Celina, we have to get going."

"Okay, I'm ready."

Kyle stood right by her side, wishing he could take her place. "I'll be right behind you," he whispered to her. "I'll follow the ambulance."

Before the paramedics loaded Celina into the ambulance, Kyle grabbed one more glance at her. Helen got into the ambulance and when the doors closed, Kyle headed to his car.

Within the next hour, Celina was getting prepped for surgery.

A nurse flipped through Celina's paperwork—which Helen was going to make sure she confiscated after all this was through—and said, "Where are her consent forms?"

"I've got all those," Dr. Kenneth Craven said as he walked into the room.

In his fifties, he was a tall, attractive man who resembled the actor George Clooney. Kenneth's salt-and-pepper hair was thick, and he wore it parted on the side. He had a square masculine face, captivating emerald-green eyes, and looked as if he kept in shape. All the nurses wondered why such a handsome and intelligent man would be single.

Kenneth moved next to Celina and said, "I promise, Celina, you're going to be just fine. We're going to take good care of you."

"Thank you, Dr. Craven."

He stroked her shoulder and nodded at the anes-thesiologist.

Chapter Nine

The first thing Celina saw when she came awake was a blurry image in the chair beside her bed. She must have been in a back brace because she felt confined, like being stuffed into a turtle's shell.

As her head finally cleared, she became aware of the beeping next to her bed and the stiffness in her back. She looked down and saw an IV that was attached to her arm. Her eyes followed along the tube that ran up a metal rod. Attached to it was a bag filled with clear liquid.

Celina looked around the room and realized she was not in the one she'd been in previously. She inhaled through her nose and recognized a familiar scent that reminded her of Kyle's cologne.

"Kyle..."

Suddenly, she heard movement and then felt a warm hand. "Shhh... I'm here, baby." He lightly squeezed her hand. "You're okay."

"How did it go?"

"Your surgery went fine. I'll go get the doctor and tell him you're awake."

After Kyle left, it wasn't five minutes later that he came back with her surgeon.

"Hello, Celina," Kenneth said with a handsome smile. "You did well. I reset the vertebrae, and your spinal cord wasn't compromised entirely."

Celina lifted her shoulders and tried to re-adjust her body, but the contraption she was in kept her from moving. "Will I walk again?"

Kenneth didn't immediately reply. He just kept his stare, and his expression told Celina it was not good news.

"Please tell me. I want to know the truth."

"The surgery was not a failure, but I don't know if you will walk just yet. Time is going to tell us more than anything else."

Celina closed her eyes, and her heart grew heavy. She lifted her lids and blinked several tears. "I see."

The door to the room cracked open, and Helen peered inside. "Oh good, you're awake."

Celina tried to smile as Helen came in, but her lips formed a tight line. The silence that stretched out in the room seemed to last forever.

Immediately, Helen moved next to Celina. "It's going to be okay, honey. You're going to heal from this."

"Am I?"

Helen nodded. "You have to stay positive. Your state of mind will reflect your healing."

"Are you in any pain?" Kenneth asked.

Before Celina could respond, she inhaled sharply when pain instantly shot through her body.

Celina's visible agony splintered Kyle's heart. He grabbed a tissue and wiped away her tears while Kenneth administered something for the pain.

After her tears had been dried, and her pain eased, Celina looked up at Kenneth. "Do you think there's a chance I could walk again?"

"I honestly can't be sure. The rules are obviously different for you since you're a Wicca. So, anything is possible."

She nodded. "Thank you, Dr. Craven."

"When will she be released from the hospital?" Kyle asked.

"In two weeks," Kenneth replied.

Celina's expression melted. "Oh no. I'll miss Mia and Jem's wedding."

"I'm sure they'll understand," Kyle said.

Celina sighed. "What about the back brace? How long do I have to wear it?"

"You'll need to wear that for at least three months," Kenneth explained. "After that, you should be good without it, but I wouldn't do anything strenuous for another six months."

"I'll make sure she has everything she needs at the Covenant during her recovery," Helen said.

Kenneth nodded an approval and focused on Celina. "I'll be back in an hour to check on you. If you need anything, just press the call button by the bed. A nurse will be on duty at all hours to assist you."

"We also have a guard posted outside your room," Helen mentioned. "It's just for a precaution."

When Kenneth stepped out of the room, he saw a petite woman with long, brown hair moving in his direction. He instantly got a strange feeling. She looked oddly familiar. She was holding hands with a tall guy that had long, blond hair. As the couple came up to him, she said, "Excuse me, are you Celina's surgeon?"

Out of nowhere, a splintering pain slammed into Kenneth's head. He braced himself against the wall to keep from dropping to his knees.

Tessa moved closer. "Hey, are you okay?"

He froze and focused on her face. She reminded him of someone from his past. Then he reached out to her and said, "Lisa..."

Tessa tilted her head a little. "I'm sorry. You must have me confused with someone else. My name is Tessa."

As Kenneth swayed, Jace quickly grabbed his arm. "Whoa there, Doc," he said, holding Kenneth steady. "You don't look so well. You want us to get a nurse or something?"

Finally, Kenneth managed to get his mouth to work and gasped. "My head..."

Tessa shot Jace a look. "Honey, go find a nurse."

Jace averted his eyes from Tessa and focused them on Kenneth. "Doc, maybe you should sit down."

Kenneth held up a halting hand and hung his head. "Just let me get my feet under me."

"If I let go of you," Jace said, "you're not going to pass out on me, are you?"

"No." Kenneth slowly shook his head. "I'll be fine."

The second Jace released his arm, Kenneth's knees buckled, and he tipped forward.

"Shit..." Jace muttered as he took hold of Kenneth before he went down.

"Hang tight, Doc," Jace said, helping him to the floor. "I'll be right back."

When Jace hurried to the front desk, Tessa knelt by Kenneth and said, "Hold on. We're getting you some help."

Finally, two nurses came over with Jace close behind. When they knelt in front of Kenneth, one of the nurses said, "What's going on, Dr. Craven?"

"I don't know," he croaked out. "My head. It feels like it's going to split open."

The nurse turned to her coworker and said, "Page Dr. Carrington."

The second she got to her feet, Helen came out of Celina's hospital room. When she saw everyone gathered around Kenneth, she rushed over. "What happened?"

"He's complaining of pain in his head," a nurse said.

"Kenneth..." Helen reached out to him, realizing he was in a great deal of pain by the look on his face. "Can you tell me what happened?"

He instantly covered his face and gasped into his hands.

Helen looked over at Tessa and Jace. "Did you see what happened?"

Jace nodded and Tessa said, "We came over to ask if he was Celina's surgeon and he just fell against the wall, complaining of pain. He looked like he was going to pass out. Jace caught him before he hit the floor."

Helen turned toward a nurse. "Let's get him a gurney and get him down to X-ray."

The nurse nodded. "Yes, Dr. Carrington."

"No gurney," Kenneth gasped out. "A wheelchair will do."

Helen heaved out a deep breath. "Okay, get Dr. Craven a wheelchair."

When the nurse left, Helen reached into the pocket of her white coat and retrieved a small medical instrument that looked like a tiny flashlight. "Kenneth, can you open your eyes for me?"

He lowered his hands and nodded. As he slowly lifted his lids, Helen placed the light to his right eye and examined his pupil. After she looked into both eyes, she said, "Your retinas look normal." Then she reached for the stethoscope around her neck and took hold of the blood pressure cuff the nurse handed her. As soon as she finished, the nurse arrived with a wheelchair.

Jace quickly got to his feet and helped the nurse get Kenneth into the wheelchair.

Before the nurse wheeled him away, with Helen by his side, Kenneth looked up at Jace and said, "Thank you."

"No problem, Doc. Hope you get to feeling better."

Moments later, Helen and the nurse took Kenneth down to the second floor to Radiology and wheeled him inside. They were greeted by the technician, "What's going on with you today, Dr. Craven?"

Kenneth looked up at the technician. "A hell of a splitting headache, that's what."

"I think it's more than a headache," Helen chimed in. "I've ordered for him an MRI."

The imaging technician nodded. "There's also something going around. I've had four nurses and some other staff that have been suffering from nausea and headaches lately."

Helen didn't ask Kenneth any further questions. Then again, he didn't know there needed to be anything to share. Nobody had a clue about his past, or what he did outside the hospital, mostly because he'd never shared his personal life with anyone. He'd kept his private life to himself.

The technician wheeled Kenneth to an examination table. "Do you think you can stand, Dr. Craven?"

Kenneth looked up at him, confused. *What was the question?*

When he didn't instantly reply, the technician said, "You okay, Doc?"

"Yes," Kenneth finally said. "I'm sure I can manage on my own."

Helen rolled her eyes. "I think we should help you. The last thing we need is for you to take a tumble."

Kenneth nodded. "Whatever you say, Dr. Carrington."

After the MRI, Kenneth was feeling better and standing on his own two feet. Looking over his results with Helen close by, the technician clapped his hand over Kenneth's shoulder. "Everything looks normal. Go home and get some rest. Looks like you might have caught that bug that's going around."

Helen shot Kenneth a look. "You're not thinking of driving yourself home, are you?"

Helen's question didn't register. Even though Kenneth's headache had backed off completely, his mind was miles away. He was thinking of the young woman he'd saw earlier and how she looked so much like someone from his past. Someone he dearly loved. *Could it be,* he thought, *that was just a coincidence?* No matter how many years went by, he would never forget Lisa. His life would be easier if only he could.

The technician frowned. "Doc... you okay?"

Kenneth shrugged. "I'm sorry, what was your question?"

Helen groaned. "I'm driving you home, Kenneth."

"Yeah, I think that's a good idea. Thanks, Helen."

On the way to his Condo, Kenneth stared out the window, his mind in a whirlwind. He couldn't stop thinking of Lisa and why she disappeared without a trace. Although he couldn't explain why she left, or where she might have gone, he'd spent his whole life searching for her. It was as if she had vanished from the face of the earth.

Chapter Ten

A week later...

Jem nervously shifted his weight back and forth between his feet. Suited in a black tuxedo, he anxiously waited in the Covenant's foyer below the grand staircase for his bride to appear.

Jace stood by his side, representing as best man. Tessa stood as Mia's maid-of-honor in a strapless chiffon gown. Reverend Mike stood behind Jem, waiting to proceed with the ceremony. Other members of the wedding guests assembled in a half circle across the way.

Among the guests were Jem and Jace's Uncle Jackson. He'd arrived early that morning from East Hampton. Standing beside him were their adoptive parents, John and Sarah Chamberlain, and their little sister, Cassie. Tim stood by Angel, who held on to their daughter Natalie. Casey Barton and Kyle Jones—Jem and Jace's best friends and bandmates— stood proudly while Kyle held on to a camera, ready to catch everything on video for Celina to view later.

Helen Carrington was standing next to Kyle with a tissue in her hand, wiping her tears before they smeared her mascara. Chester Ewan and his wife Amelia stood alongside Helen. The rest of the Guardians were spread among the other guests, all dressed in their finest attire.

Behind a grand piano, Drakon's amazing pipes sailed up and filtered all around the room. Halfway through the melody, Jem felt like he'd just died and gone to heaven. Standing at the top of the staircase, with her arm entwined with Alexander's, was his beautiful bride. Mia was breathtaking. The cream gown she wore rendered him senseless and captivated the whole room. The miles of satin skirting falling about her slender body brought out the sniffles from all the ladies watching from below.

As their eyes met, Jem mouthed the words, "I love you." The smile Mia gave him made his chest swell.

Taking careful steps, Alexander guided her down the staircase.

When the ceremony commenced, Jem and Mia said their life vows. When Reverend Mike gave the cue, Jem leaned in and pressed his lips to Mia's.

As they turned toward the guests, the Reverend said, "I present to you... Mr. and Mrs. Chamberlain."

Cheers and claps from everyone echoed all around the room. After they made their way through the rows of people, Jem reached for Mia and held her close. He kissed her and said, "I love you, Mrs. Chamberlain."

"I love you too, honey."

When Jem released Mia, John pulled her into a soft embrace. "Welcome to the family, Mia. I'm proud to have you as my daughter."

"Oh..." Mia's voice trembled. "Thank you, John."

Sarah stretched up on her tiptoes and wrapped her arms around Jem. "I love you, honey." Then she turned to Mia and held out her arms. "I love you too, sweetheart." When Mia reached out to her, Sarah pulled her into a hug. "You're officially part of the family now."

Cassie darted over with her arms out. "Now I have a sister!" She hugged Mia and turned to Jem and wrapped her arms around him. "I'm so happy for you!"

Jem kissed the top of her head. "Thank you, sis."

With a firm handshake, Jem's Uncle Jackson said, "I'm proud of you, Jem." He faced Mia and hugged her. "You look beautiful, Mia. We're glad to have you as part of our family."

Mia's eyes filled with tears of joy. Her heart raced with excitement. She was part of a family now.

The celebration started rolling with voices, laughter, and a lot of sparkling champagne. There was a feast set out, starting with creative appetizers and then the sit-down dinner.

Afterwards, they presented the traditional bride-and-groom cake cutting.

Jem cut a small piece and gently fed Mia with his hands. And then Mia cut a small square, held it in front of Jem's lips and, to his surprise, she tenderly put it into his mouth. After it was all done, he leaned down and kissed her.

Everyone clapped and cheered at the happy occasion. Jace raised his glass high and said, "Cheers to the happy couple. I wish you many years of love and happiness."

As the guests lifted their glasses of champagne and cheered, Alexander said, "I would like to make a toast." He smiled with tears in his eyes. "To my son. Your giving spirit and your love have earned you a precious gift... your beautiful bride." He looked to Mia and smiled. "Mia, you are indeed a gift from heaven, and we welcome you into our hearts, and we rejoice in Jem's good fortune that he found you, and you him."

"Cheers!" Everyone stood with their glasses raised and drank in honor of the bride and groom.

When everyone at the table took their seats, Jem rose from his chair. "I would like to make a toast to my beautiful bride." His voice was thick with emotion. "Mia, the day I met you, my world stood still. I had always hoped to meet someone like you but wondered if such a woman even existed. But when we met, you exceeded all my expectations. You are my perfect fit. And so today, as we join our lives together, I give you *my* heart." He grasped her hand and lightly squeezed. "I want you to know as we journey through life, we will do so as partners, lovers, and best friends. I love you, Mia."

After his toast, there wasn't a dry eye in the room. As tears slid down Mia's cheeks, she stood up and placed her head against his chest. "Jem Chamberlain..." She looked up into his eyes. "You're my *everything*."

Jace rose from his chair and hollered, "Let's start the party!"

As the music to their favorite song began, Jem said, "Dance with me, sweetheart."

When he guided her to the dance floor, he pulled her close. Their bodies meshed as they swayed to the romantic tempo.

"Together forever," Jem whispered close to her ear.

"Always," Mia whispered back.

* * *

Jace quietly slipped out of bed, trying not to wake Tessa. He was eager to be downstairs when Jem and Mia got back from their honeymoon after a few days at a relaxing B&B near the beach.

While he got a shower, Tessa snuck out and headed to the kitchen. She was eager to try the fresh strawberries Angel had picked up for her at the farmers' market. Everyone in the Covenant was spoiling her after they got the news of her pregnancy.

So far, she and the babies were healthy, well into her sixth month and feeling great. She had plenty of energy, no more morning sickness, and two babies that did laps under her rib cage every time she ate, especially if chocolate was involved.

Tessa's pregnancy was nothing she'd prepared for. She planned on her and Jace getting married before even talking about having children. After the initial shock had worn off when Helen first told her she was pregnant with twins, and already four months along, she'd fallen in love with the idea of having Jace's babies. She pictured two little, blond-haired boys that were the spitting image of their father. Just a smaller version.

She was hoping that, like most women, her labor would be normal. The only thing she wished could be part of her children's lives was her biological parents. Her mother abandoned her when she was born, and she had no idea who her father was. She'd been raised by her aunt and uncle, not having the slightest clue about the Breedline species. Her Aunt Wanda and Uncle John didn't know anything about her real bloodline. Although her aunt and uncle never talked about it much, Tessa had a twin out there somewhere in the world.

"Are the berries any good?"

Tessa turned around and said, "Mia... you're back!"

After they embraced, Tessa said, "Did you have fun on your honeymoon?"

"It was incredible," Mia said as she dipped her hand into Tessa's bowl of strawberries. "How are you feeling?"

Tessa smoothed her hand over her rounded belly. "They're really starting to grow."

Mia took a bite of the strawberry. "So, what does Jace think about becoming a father?"

Tessa chuckled. "He talks to my belly every night, right before we go to bed."

"Are you serious?"

"He's already got names picked out. He wants the first born to be named after Jem. I hope that's okay?"

"Oh..." Mia's eyes softened. "Of course it is. What about baby number two?"

"We're naming him Jax."

"Where did he come up with that name?"

"Jace and Jem's Uncle Jackson."

Mia smiled but Tessa noticed the sadness in her eyes. "Is something bothering you, Mia?"

She nodded with a sigh. "It's Eve."

"Do you want to talk about it?"

Tessa listened quietly as Mia began to explain to Tessa about her and Jem's decision to take in Eve's twins after they were born.

When Mia finished, Tessa was silent for a moment. Then to Mia's surprise, Tessa reached for her hand. "I understand, Mia." She smiled. "The children are innocent. They deserve a chance to have a good life, and I know you and Jem will provide that for them."

"Thank you, Tessa." Mia's voice trembled. "I needed to hear that."

"Now all we have to do is convince Jace," Tessa said. "I'm not sure how he'll take the news."

Mia raised her brows. "I know."

Moments later, after Tessa left, Mia thoughts were consumed with worry. She couldn't stop thinking about how Jace was going to react when he found out about her and Jem's decision to take in Eve's twins.

After she took a seat behind the kitchen bar, she leaned forward and placed her hand over her face.

"Hey, honey," Jem said as he sat down beside her. "Are you okay?"

Mia lowered her hands and sighed. "I told Tessa about us taking in Eve's twins."

"Oh... what did she say?"

"She gave us her blessing."

"That's great, honey." He put his arm around her. "So why do you look so sad?"

"I'm worried how your brother is going to take the news, and so is Tessa."

"We'll get through this, Mia." He pulled her close. "I love you."

Mia leaned her head on his shoulder. "I love you too."

Chapter Eleven

When Celina was brought back to the Covenant, she'd been moved into another room other than the one she'd stayed in. It was larger, and yet everything seemed the same. She was lying in bed in a state of total confinement. The back brace she had to wear was stiff and uncomfortable.

Thoughts of Kyle came to her, and she found herself thinking about the conversation the two of them had before her surgery. He'd told her he would be by her side no matter what the outcome was. Celina would never forget what he looked like, standing over her bed, his eyes full of compassion and love.

In truth, what future could they have if she never walked again? She would be a burden, a useless body, having to let others care for her. Meanwhile, Kyle would still be a young, vibrant, sexual male deserving more than what she could offer.

As the door slowly opened, Helen walked in, and it was a relief to focus on something else.

"Hello, sweetheart."

"Hi, Aunt Helen."

Helen looked down at her niece with concern brimming in her eyes. "Are you feeling any pain?"

"No, I'm fine." Celina forced a smile. "Have you seen Kyle?"

"He's downstairs in the kitchen. Don't tell him I told you, but he's making breakfast for you. It's probably supposed to be a surprise."

Celina smiled for real this time as the image of Kyle preparing food for her came to mind. "I'll make sure I have a surprised reaction when he enters the room."

There was a long pause, and then Celina asked, "How are you and Alexander doing?"

"Let me just say things are moving along slow, but I do adore him. We're both alike in so many ways. He's very independent, and he's sort of old-fashioned when it comes to dating."

Celina reached out and brushed Helen's arm. "I'm so happy for you, Aunt Helen. You deserve to be in love."

"Thank you, honey. You deserve the same too."

"But what if I never walk again?" Celina's voice cracked. "How can I give Kyle what he needs?"

Helen had no easy answer for that one. And before she could respond, Kyle walked in. "Good morning, sunshine," he said with a tray in his hand. "How 'bout breakfast in bed, babe?"

With a surprised expression on her face, Celina said, "That sounds great."

"Stop torturing yourself," Helen whispered close to her ear. "It will all work out."

Celina smiled again, and some of the agony eased, replacing it with hope.

A shadow passed through Celina's eyes, and Helen knew she was thinking of something about the past. It most likely had to do with the death of her parents, or her twin sister, Taliah.

Helen leaned down and pressed a kiss to her forehead. "I've got to get to the hospital. I'll be back later this evening to check on you. Page me if you need anything."

Kyle placed the tray of food on the nightstand. "Thanks, Helen."

When Helen stepped out, she sagged against the door and said a silent prayer. Hopefully, God would see her niece through all this. She was too young to be confined to a wheelchair for the rest of her life.

When her phone buzzed, she snapped back to reality. She dug it out of her purse and looked at the caller ID. She recognized the number.

"Hello, Kenneth."

After a short pause, Kenneth finally said, "Helen, I hope I'm not interrupting anything. I called the hospital, and the receptionist said you hadn't made it in this morning."

"You're fine. I stopped by to check on Celina before I left for the hospital."

"How's she doing?"

"She's not in any pain, but she's still frustrated. Although you can't blame her for feeling that way, considering her condition."

"Of course," he said. "I completely understand."

"Is everything all right, Kenneth? You're not getting another headache, are you?"

"No, no," he said. "I'm fine. But I was wondering if I could speak with you in private. Maybe meet in the hospital's cafeteria over coffee, say in an hour?"

Helen glanced at her watch. "Yes, I've got time. Are you sure you're okay, Kenneth?"

"Don't worry. I just need to ask you some questions about my incident at the hospital the other day. Of course, this is something confidential."

"Okay. I'll see you in an hour."

"Thank you, Helen. I appreciate this."

When the call ended, Helen frowned deep enough to wrinkle her forehead. She wondered what was so confidential that Kenneth wanted to discuss. Was it about Celina's surgery? Putting it in the back of her mind, she stuffed her phone back in her purse and headed to the hospital.

Almost an hour later, Helen pushed inside the hospital's cafeteria. She noticed Kenneth sitting at a table with his head hung low. He was staring at his cup of coffee, seemingly lost in thought.

When she came over to the table, she cleared her throat. "Kenneth..."

He quickly looked up. "Oh, hello, Helen." He rose to his feet and pulled a chair out for her. "Would you like a cup of coffee?"

She sat down. "I'm fine, thank you. So, what did you want to talk about?"

His hands shook as he tried to find the courage to explain to Helen what was going on. Finally, he found the nerve to say, "I need to ask you something important."

Helen nodded.

"Can you tell me about the young woman that helped me the other day?"

* * *

Sebastian reached for the bottle of champagne, and after he corked it, he poured himself a drink. Before he took a sip, he said, "So, what the hell do you want with me... Brother?"

Thomas smiled, flashing his white teeth as well as his fangs. "You know, I was actually looking forward to getting to know you for a minute. But now, with your cocky and condescending attitude, I'm not so sure."

"Cut the shit," Sebastian said sharply. "What do you want?"

"I want you to join us."

"Don't tell me." Sebastian barked a laugh. "You want me to join you and this *Lilith*. Am I right?"

Thomas nodded. "Something like that." He leaned in closer. "Don't you want Eve back?"

"How do you know about her?"

"Lilith knows all, especially when it comes to females who are expecting."

Sebastian's eyes rounded. "What—"

"Didn't you know, Brother?" Thomas shrugged. "Eve is pregnant, and she's having twins."

* * *

The hospital's cafeteria fluorescent ceiling lights illuminated Kenneth from above, hitting his salt-and-pepper hair and his scruffy facial hairs he obviously neglected to shave. Going by the tone of his voice, and the tired expression in his eyes, Helen figured he hadn't slept well.

She looked surprised by his question. "You must be talking about Tessa, the Breedline queen."

His eyes widened, and his mouth opened, but no words came out. Finally, after he blinked a couple of times, he found his voice. "I had no idea she was our queen. Now, I feel like a total idiot." He let out a deep breath. "I feel terrible. I didn't get the chance to thank her. I hope she doesn't think I was disrespectful."

"Of course not," Helen said. "I'm sure she completely understood. You were half conscious, Kenneth. I could take you to the Covenant to meet her if you like. You can thank her personally."

"If you don't mind me asking, what's her last name?"

"Fairchild," Helen replied. "Why?"

A shadow crossed over his face. For a moment he simply stared off into the distance in silence.

"Kenneth?" Helen reached for his hand. "Are you all right?"

With her hand on his, Kenneth's focus came back. He opened his mouth to speak but seemed lost for words once again. Helen warred with herself over whether to press him further. She was curious why he'd asked Tessa's last name.

Finally, he said, "I think Tessa is my daughter."

Helen's jaw dropped. "But... how can that be? Are you sure?"

Kenneth's eyebrows shot up and then came together as he stared at Helen. One thing that he was sure of, Tessa was the spitting image of his *beloved* Lisa. She'd been only seventeen the last he laid eyes on her, but the resemblance between the two was unmistakable. And now, after Helen revealed Tessa's last name, there was no doubt in his mind. Tessa was his flesh and blood.

He relaxed his brows and briefly closed his eyes. "Tessa is identical to a young woman I bonded with when I was just a teenager. Her name was Lisa Wellington. I loved her so much, Helen. I wanted to spend the rest of my life with her." His voice grew raw with emotion. "A year later, she just vanished. The only family she had was her older sister Wanda and her husband, John. They told me Lisa was pregnant and decided to run away. I lost contact with them after that. It's like they all completely vanished from the face of the earth. One minute they lived in this area, the next they'd moved, leaving no trace behind. And now that you mentioned the name Fairchild, she must be my daughter. That was her sister's last name."

Helen's eyes softened. "I'm sorry, Kenneth. It must have been hard for you after all these years not knowing."

"Thank you, Helen."

"Tessa didn't know she was a Breedline until last year," she explained. "She had mentioned she was raised by her aunt and uncle. I remember Tessa saying they lived somewhere out in the country. I think in Midway, Kentucky."

"Tessa has a twin," Kenneth said. "Is she here in Berkeley?"

Helen shook her head. "Tessa has tried to locate her, but so far she's been unsuccessful."

"The young man that was with her at the hospital," he said with a curious expression. "Is he Tessa's husband?"

"No, he's her fiancé," Helen replied with a smile. "His name is Jace Chamberlain, and he loves her very much, Kenneth. You would approve of him. But there's one more thing you should know."

After another moment of silence, Kenneth's throat tightened, and the tension in his jaw grew rigid anticipating what Helen was about to tell him.

"If Tessa is indeed your daughter, you're going to be a grandfather soon."

Kenneth took a deep breath. For years, he'd expected to hear something—either from Lisa herself or her sister. As more years slid by, however, he'd started to give up hope. Kenneth understood firsthand how families of missing persons felt. And God, that dreaded cold stretch of not knowing was the worst. He'd given up all hope after he no longer woke up in the middle of the night wondering. Now, he'd finally found his *daughter*.

Kenneth grinned. "I want to meet her, Helen."

"I'll arrange it," she said. "You're going to be proud of her, Kenneth. She's got the courage of ten men and a heart of gold."

Chapter Twelve

Early the next morning, Sebastian woke with a stinger of a hangover. *A hot shower sounds next to heaven*, he thought as he rubbed his temples. The room was closing in on him as he tried to process everything that had happened in the last few days. He'd met his twin brother and found out Eve was pregnant. Unfortunately, she was kept under lock and key by his archenemy. It all seemed so unreal and yet it was real.

An hour later, after showering and changing into clean clothes, he decided to call his twin brother. Even though Sebastian rarely prayed, he'd thanked God his brother had shared the information about Eve. This evening, they would meet to discuss their next move. Thomas had offered him a deal he couldn't refuse.

"Hello, Brother," Thomas answered on the second ring.

Sebastian breathed out heavily over the phone. "I'm in."

"Good." Thomas's voice expressed instant gratification. "I'll meet you in the club's VIP section at nine."

"I'll be there." At that point, Sebastian hung up. His head pounded. There was nothing further to discuss over the phone. It wasn't like he was going to shoot the shit with his brother—although, even if he had, chitchat wasn't going to get him what he wanted.

* * *

Upon waking, Eve thought she'd lost control of her bladder, but as she moved the blankets aside and scooted over, she saw blood on the sheets. Soon after, she felt an excruciating pain in her lower back.

Everything happened so fast after that. It was like watching someone else as she went through the motions, moving by too quick to comprehend. And suddenly, Eve managed to compose herself enough to call the guards.

Not long after she ended the call, she recognized the voice coming from downstairs. It was Bruce Carmichael.

"Can you hear me, Miss Eve?"

"Please, I need help." Eve closed her eyes, pain contorting her features. "I think I'm in labor."

Eve's voice was so faint Bruce could barely hear her. While the other guard called Helen and waited by the door, Bruce charged up the stairs, taking two steps at a time.

He leaned over Eve and said, "Hang on. Help is on the way."

She didn't remember much about being transferred onto a gurney and rushed downstairs—except for the constant pressure she felt in her lower abdomen. As Eve looked around, she saw blurred images of people with their mouths moving and their eyes meeting urgently across her. She couldn't hear their voices. All she heard was the throbbing pain ringing inside her ears.

Rushing past the Covenant's side entrance, Bruce and Tim carried Eve into the examination room as Helen and Mia held open the doors. Eve felt her body lowered until she was on top of a firm surface. She squinted her eyes when a light above shined down.

"Tim..." Helen urged. "Please go find Cassie. I'm going to need her help."

After Tim left, Bruce was reluctant to leave Eve's side. He stood, arms crossed, his gaze never leaving her as Helen scurried back and forth, preparing to do an examination.

Mia placed her palm on Bruce's shoulder. "I'm going to need you to wait outside. Don't worry. Eve's in good hands."

He nodded in agreement, but his expression stayed grim. Bruce grudgingly left the room so Helen could do her job. But he remained close, right outside the door.

When he stepped out, Helen put her face above Eve's. "Can you hear me, Eve?"

With her lids squeezed tight, she nodded in response.

"Where are you having pain?"

Eve gasped. "My lower back... and my stomach."

Helen wheeled the ultrasound machine next to Eve as Cassie pushed her way into the room. After Cassie hurriedly scrubbed up, she placed a blood pressure cuff on Eve and prepared an IV.

Helen moved the ultrasound probe around Eve's stomach with her eyes on the monitor. Seconds later, she turned to Cassie and said, "One of the babies' heart rates is slowing, and she's still bleeding heavily. We need to deliver the babies. Eve has an abruption."

Mia grasped Eve's hand. "You're going to be okay, Eve."

Helen came back into Eve's view. "We're going to have to put you under. I don't have time to do an epidural, okay?"

Eve nodded as tears slid down the corners of her eyes. Before Cassie placed an oxygen mask on her, Eve's voice cracked, "Wait. I want to tell Mia the babies' names in case—"

Mia leaned closer. "Nothing's going to happen. Everything will be just fine."

"No," Eve's voice was urgent. "Please, just in case."

Mia nodded. "Okay."

"My first born is Tidus." She forced the words. "My second born..." Eve blinked her eyes until they completely closed.

"Eve..." Mia squeezed her hand.

Eve's eyes slowly reopened, and she finally said, "Arius..."

"Okay, she's under," Helen said. "Mia, I need you to step outside. We need to get her ready."

The minutes stretched, seemingly feeling like days. Each minute ticked by with agonizing slowness. Bruce was unable to stay seated as he paced back and forth while Mia, Jem, Tessa, Angel, and Tim sat waiting, their expressions somber.

They didn't try to force Bruce to sit down and relax. They all had a clue he'd developed a fondness for Eve.

No longer able to contain herself, feeling sorry for Bruce, Mia rose and went over to him. To his surprise, she placed her hand on his arm. "Don't worry, Bruce. Eve's strong-willed. She'll be all right."

He managed a half smile. "Thank you, Mia."

When Mia sat down next to Tessa, her shoulders sagged as if all the air had escaped her at once.

Tessa reached for her hand and squeezed lightly. "She'll be just fine, Mia."

Mia turned in her direction, her eyes instantly going warm as she registered Tessa's sincerity. "You've got a big heart, Tessa. I don't know how you do it."

Tessa looked at her confused. "Do what?"

"After all Eve has done, you still forgive her."

"I'm not the only one with a big heart," Tessa said. "You and Jem are the most generous people I've ever met. Taking care of her children is beyond what anyone else would do."

Mia smiled and looked away, staring at the examination door, praying her sister and her nephews would be safe in God's hands.

Inside the examination room, Helen and Cassie traded medical terms along with metal clanging sounds and suction noises. They were both focused and in control.

"Okay, here's baby number one," Helen said, handing the baby over to Cassie.

As Cassie wrapped him up in a warm blanket, he let out an ear-piercing cry. "He's definitely got a healthy set of lungs," she said as she placed him in a neonatal crib and cleaned him before she went back to assist Helen with baby number two.

"I've got him," Helen said. When she handed the baby to Cassie, she quickly bundled him in a blanket and placed him next to his brother. While she wiped him off, the baby opened his eyes. Cassie immediately covered her mouth and gasped.

"His eyes..."

Helen looked at Cassie. "What's wrong with his eyes?"

Cassie became confused when the baby's eye color suddenly shifted back to normal. She lowered her hand and said, "How—"

"Cassie, we've got a problem," Helen said. "Eve's still hemorrhaging. I need your help. We're going to have to do a hysterectomy."

Cassie shifted her focus back to Helen. "I'll take Mia the babies."

"Make it fast," Helen said.

Cassie pushed the crib into the waiting room and said, "The babies are fine, but we're going to have to do an emergency hysterectomy on Eve."

Everyone was excited to see the twins, but worried about Eve.

"Which baby is the first born?" Mia asked.

She pointed to Tidus and said, "This is baby Tidus. As soon as we're finished with Eve's surgery, I'll let you know how she's doing."

Mia blinked tears. "Thank you, Cassie."

When Cassie went back into the examination room, Mia looked down and saw two of the cutest little babies with dark hair, bundled inside blue blankets. She reached into the crib for Tidus and said, "Welcome to the world, sweetheart."

Jem came over and reached for Arius. He cuddled the baby close and whispered, "Hey there, little man."

When Arius opened his eyes and cooed, Jem gasped. "What the—"

Mia averted her eyes from Tidus and looked at Jem. "Is something wrong?"

"His eyes..." Jem croaked out. "They're black."

Mia came over and looked at Arius's eyes. They were a shimmering gold, exactly like his father's. She looked up at Jem and said, "His eyes look just like Sebastian's."

When Jem looked at Arius's eyes a second time, he was stunned. "But... I could have sworn they were—"

Abruptly, the baby in Mia's arms let out a piercing cry taking the focus off Arius. Everyone immediately crowded around Jem and Mia to get a look at the new arrivals.

"Oh, they're beautiful," Tessa said. "Can I hold him?"

"Oh course." Mia handed the fussy baby to her, and in no time, baby Tidus stopped crying when Tessa rocked him in her arms.

Before Jem could collect his scattered thoughts, Mia offered to take Arius. As Jem handed the baby to Mia, he felt completely taken back.

Angel reached out and smoothed her hand over Arius's soft curls. "Look at all that gorgeous hair."

Mia looked at her and smiled. "Would you like to hold him?"

"How can I resist?" Angel said as she reached for Arius. "They're both so precious."

Drakon came into the room with Natalie in his arms and said, "Someone is dying to see the new arrivals."

Tim went over to his daughter and said, "Look, Natalie." He pointed to the babies. "You've got someone to play with."

Drakon chuckled. "She'll definitely keep those boys on their toes soon enough."

Angel focused on Jem and said, "Have you told Jace about taking care of the babies yet?"

Jem shook his head and sighed. "Not yet, but I'll talk to him."

"I'll help in any way I can," Tessa said. "Jace will need time to adjust, but I believe he'll come around."

"Am I the only one…" Jem hesitantly said, "…concerned about Arius and Tidus inheriting the demon's genetics?"

"The thought has crossed my mind," Tim said. "All of us will have to take on the responsibility of monitoring their behavior as they grow up. If we're lucky, they'll turn out to be just fine."

An hour later, Cassie and Helen finally came out of the examination room.

"We've got good news." Helen smiled. "Eve's surgery went well."

Mia blew out a sigh of relief. "When can I see her?"

"You can visit her for a few minutes," Helen said.

"Thank you both. If it weren't for you two, Eve and the babies—"

Helen nodded and Cassie said, "You're welcome, Mia."

As Mia stepped into the examination room to visit with Eve, Helen moved next to Tessa and said, "Can I speak with you in private?"

Tessa nodded. "Of course."

When Tessa handed the baby back to Jem, she followed Helen to a small seating area across the room and sat down.

Helen kept her voice low. "What would you think if I said I may have found your biological father?"

Tessa's eyes rounded. "What…?"

After Helen explained to Tessa about what Kenneth had told her, she said, "How can you be sure he's my father?"

Helen reached into the pocket of her white coat and retrieved a small box. "If you agree, I can do a DNA test with just a cheek swab. I've already done one on Kenneth."

Tessa's eyes lit up. "Let's do it."

Chapter Thirteen

An hour later, Cassie went upstairs to her and Drakon's bedroom. When she went inside, she heard the water from the shower. As soon as she opened the door, her heart leaped. Although steam covered the glass barrier, she could still make out Drakon's image as he stood inside the shower. His chiseled body made her weak in the knees.

When he noticed her, he smiled broadly and motioned her inside. She quickly slipped out of her clothes with her mind focused on him.

Drakon opened the shower door. "Come here, sweetheart." He extended his hand. "Join me."

She took hold of his hand. The second she stepped inside, he instantly pulled her close and pressed his lips to hers. His kiss instantly ignited her arousal.

"Please..." She blinked in desperation. "Make love to me, Drakon."

"Are you sure this is what you want?"

"Yes..."

"You know what this will mean," he whispered, "if we go all the way."

"Please, Drakon. I'm ready."

He nodded. "Let's take this to the bedroom."

Moments later, Drakon swept her off her feet and carried her to the bed. When he eased her down, the mattress dipped as he positioned himself above her. His massive body dwarfed hers as he leaned in and put his lips to hers. She gazed into his half-lidded eyes. "Drakon..." Her breathy tone was ripe with surrender. "I need you." Her body moistened with a heated desire. To his surprise, she shifted on the bed and parted her legs as an invitation for him to ravish her.

He purred his approval and deepened the kiss. As she gasped, his tongue invaded her mouth and skillfully stroked over her own. Goose bumps prickled over her skin when his hand trailed over her bare shoulder and slowly inched down her arm. Cassie closed her eyes, absorbing the feel of his caressing and sensual touch. While his hand worked its way lower, in a matter of seconds, she felt a heat bloom within her that nearly took her over the edge. She arched her back and moaned against his lips.

For a fleeting moment, he released her mouth and then shifted his body so that he was looking down into her eyes without pressing his weight on top of her. His stare was intense and full of desire. "I love you, Cassie." His blue eyes were dark with need. "You're my everything."

Before she could reply, he captured her mouth again. Without as much as a thought, she grabbed onto his shoulders, wanting to feel his warm skin and his weight on top of her. He held back for a moment, but then relaxed, realizing what she needed from him, and finally eased his body onto hers.

He gathered her close, so close, she could hear the rhythm of his heart beating wildly inside his chest.

Cassie's hands smoothed across his muscular back and down to his hips, her flushed body writhing against the warmth of his flesh. "Please," she said in a throaty murmur that nearly undid him.

His mouth came down over hers, kissing her as if he'd die if their lips were parted. "I'll go slow and easy," he murmured against her mouth.

"Please... just take me."

Drakon's breath escaped in a long hiss and every muscle in his body tightened as he slowly glided inside of her.

Cassie gasped and tensed at the instant fullness.

His hips went completely still. "Are you okay?" he whispered, waiting for her response.

"Please don't stop," she groaned.

He leaned down to kiss her at the same time he pushed forward again.

She panted frantically as his hips moved rhythmically, pushing her closer to the edge. With her eyes squeezed tight, she gripped the sheets and arched up as high as she could while his weight pressed down on her.

The pressure that had built up within her finally gave way. It was like nothing she'd ever known. Wave after wave of ecstasy splintered through her.

The sounds Cassie made brought Drakon to his own release. As he shuddered inside of her, tears gathered in his eyes. Cassie was his, and he was *forever* hers.

When he finally pushed himself up, he watched the series of emotions that flickered across her face. The purposeful look in her eyes told him she was close to shifting.

He reached out to her. "It's okay, honey. I'll be right here with you every step of the way."

Every particle in her body was changing... changing in a way she had never experienced in her life. Cassie's entire body began to expand and stretch by the second. Her fingernails and toenails tingled, and her skin itched as soft, dark fur began to burst out of every pore, covering every inch of her bare skin. She could even feel her teeth descending and her mouth lengthening.

As her transformation continued, Drakon watched in amazement. There were no words to express her Breedline wolf. She was simply *beautiful*. God, it made such sense that he'd bonded with her.

In her new form, Cassie felt her throat open with a howl, but she did not give in to it. Instead, she moved toward Drakon on teeter-tottering limbs and let out a light whimper.

"You're beautiful, sweetheart," he said, smoothing his fingers through her soft-coated fur.

Moments later, when Cassie shifted back into her human form, she stared up at him and sighed in utter contentment at the look in his eyes. No words could simply replace the way he looked at her. It was as though there was no one else in the world for him.

Words bubbled up inside her. She was grateful and amazed that a man like him existed. She leaned forward and kissed him warmly, pressing her mouth softly to his. "I don't know what to say," she said. Her voice grew shaky with emotion. "I feel complete now."

Drakon reached for her hand and laced his fingers with hers. "I love you with all my heart. I can't wait to make you my wife."

She glanced down at their entwined fingers, watched as his thumb caressed the top of her hand. Then she looked into his intense blue eyes and said, "Me too."

* * *

When Jace got wind of the news about Eve giving birth, he decided to go down to the training room and blow off some steam. As he headed downstairs, his cell phone went off. He reached into his pocket and looked at the caller ID. It was his brother.

When he swiped to answer, he put the phone up to his ear and said, "What's up?"

"We need to talk."

"About what?"

"About Eve."

"What's there to talk about?" Jace said with a clear smirk in his voice. "I already heard she had that bastard's twins."

"Yeah, about that," Jem hesitantly said. "I need to discuss something with you concerning the twins."

"Oh... what about?"

"I'd rather not discuss this over the phone."

"Okay," Jace said. "Well, I'm headed to the gym. We can talk there."

The kind of conversation he was going to have with Jace would definitely not mix with heavy objects. "On second thought," Jem said, "it can wait. Give me a call when you're done working out."

"You sure?"

"Yeah, I'm sure."

Jace pushed his way into the gym and looked across the room at the sounds of grunting and groaning. Realizing it was Kyle and Casey, he waved in their direction, and then hopped on a treadmill. About a half hour into his workout, he caught a whiff of Tessa's perfume. He instantly slowed down his pace and said, "Hey, sweetheart. Whatcha doin'?"

"Looking for you."

He straddled the treadmill and leaned over with his lips puckered. When Tessa reached up on her tiptoes and kissed him, he said, "Is everything okay?"

"I was wondering if we could talk for a minute."

His brows instantly rose. "Are our babies okay?"

"Our babies are fine, Jace." She smoothed her hand over her rounded belly. "It's about Eve's."

Jace rolled his eyes. "You know how I feel about that, Tessa. I can barely tolerate knowing they're here in this Covenant. I want them out of here as soon as possible."

"Jace, please. Don't talk like that. Those children are innocent. They are not responsible for their parents' behavior."

He hit the stop button and grabbed a towel. "I'm sorry, Tessa." He wiped the sweat from his face. "But I just don't care. When it comes to anything relating to Sebastian, I have no sympathy or patience."

"Well then, you're not going to like what I'm about to say."

He clenched his brows. "What's going on?"

"I've agreed to let Jem and Mia take in the twins."

"What...?" He shot her a look. "Oh, hell no." He raised his voice. "Over my dead body!"

"Those boys are innocent, Jace. Think about it. What if no one cared for you and your brother? John and Sarah adopted you and Jem. They loved you two like their own children. They didn't care where you two came from or who your parents were. They just wanted to give you a happy life. Don't you think Tidus and Arius deserve the same chance?"

He heaved out a deep breath. "I can't believe my own brother betrayed me."

"Please, Jace—"

"No, Tessa," he cut her off. "I don't want to discuss this any further."

"You have no choice," she firmly said. "I've made my decision."

He glared at her in frustration. "Fine."

Before Tessa could say another word, Jace stormed out of the training room.

Overhearing their heated conversation, Kyle and Casey came over.

"Are you okay, Tessa?"

Tessa released an aggravated sigh. "No, not really, Kyle. I guess you heard."

Kyle nodded and Casey said, "Is there anything we can do to help?"

Tessa's lips formed into a partial smile. "Thanks, Casey. But Jace needs to work this out for himself. Although, if I were you, I would stay clear of him for a while."

"You don't think he'll do anything crazy, do you?" Kyle said. "I mean... Eve is staying in the guesthouse, and she has guards and all, but you don't think he would—"

"No," Tessa said. "It's Sebastian he wants to kill. You might want to give everyone you see a heads-up. I'll talk to Tim."

"I think that's probably a good idea," Casey said. "You want us to let Jem know what's going on?"

Tessa nodded. "I would appreciate it, guys."

Meanwhile, outside the weight room, Jace paced up and down the hallway. *Of all the decisions Tessa has made*, he thought, *this was the worst one.*

As he made yet another trip down the hall and back, thoughts of his own brother's betrayal hit hard, and it pissed him off even more. He pushed his hand through his long hair and let out a deep breath. Then he silently cursed over and over. If he had half the sense—and given the way he handled things sometimes, which had been seriously debatable, if not downright wrong—he would march to the guesthouse and strangle Eve.

Instead, here he was, trying to control his anger while he wore a path into the floor. On that note, calming down was his primary focus before his Beast reared its ugly head. And that's when he found himself in front of the weight room again. He had an inkling why he kept stopping there. He tried to stop his hand from turning the door handle, but it did no good. When he opened it, Tessa stood there, facing him.

Before he said a word, he just stared at her with a lopsided grin. He knew he'd overreacted, and he felt like shit. Finally, he said, "I'm sorry, Tessa."

Her eyes instantly softened. "Oh, Jace..."

"I know it's not the boys' fault," he grudgingly said. "They're just like Jem and me. They didn't get to pick their parents. I guess they deserve a chance too."

Tessa lifted on her tiptoes and framed his face in her small hands. "Thank you, honey." As he leaned in, she kissed him. "I love you, Jace."

"I love you too, Tessa."

"There's something else I wanted to tell you."

Jace's forehead wrinkled. "Please don't say we're adopting Eve's twins."

She laughed. "No. This is good news."

"Thank God." He blew out a sigh of relief. "So, what's the good news?"

"Helen found my biological father."

Chapter Fourteen

Upstairs in her room, Celina lay in bed, waiting. She was not good at patience at the best of times, and she felt as though days had passed since Kenneth had done his last evaluation. When she looked down at the foot of the bed, she noticed Jace's cat cuddled by her feet. The sound of his purring seemed oddly comforting to her.

A light tap on the door caught her attention. "Come in," she called out.

As Kenneth came into the room, he brought with him a laptop.

"Sorry, I'm running late," he said. "How are you feeling today?"

"Wishing I could get out of this bed."

"I know you do, Celina." He gave her a look of sympathy and sat down next to her bedside. "Helen and I were firing up this laptop this morning." He set up the computer where she could view the monitor. "I think you'll want to see what's on it."

As Celina looked to the screen, she instantly recognized the image of her room. The frame was frozen until he moved the little white arrow, and then the picture became animated. Her brows furrowed as she focused on the image of herself, lying in bed and glowing. Then the video captured her sitting up by herself.

"How can this be?" Her eyes rounded. "I sat up." Her lips curled up like a bow. "I actually sat up!"

"Yes," Kenneth said. "You sure did."

"But... on the video, I'm glowing. How is that possible?"

"We were hoping you could tell us," Helen said as she stepped into the room. "Have you ever done this before?"

"No." Celina shook her head. "Not that I'm aware of."

"Helen and I talked it over," Kenneth said. "And we came up with a theory. We think you unconsciously healed yourself."

"This is so bizarre." Celina shrugged. "Whatever the case, I'm just grateful it happened."

"Kenneth and I..." Helen briefly glanced at Kenneth, "...well, we think somehow your powers of a Wicca have become stronger. We believe you can stand on your own."

Celina looked between Helen and Kenneth, astonished by her aunt's theory. "You really think so?"

"Let's give it a try," Kenneth chimed in.

She looked down at her legs and concentrated on her toes. Without much effort, they began to wiggle. Her eyes lit up. "Did you see that?"

"Oh, Celina," Helen said. "That's wonderful."

"I think I can do this," Celina said as she swung her feet off the side of the bed and flexed her legs.

"I won't let you fall," Kenneth said. "Now... let's see you stand."

As she placed her bare feet on the wood floor, she felt the coolness on her soles. Exhaling a deep breath, she squared her shoulders and pushed off the bed. Her muscles twitched, and her legs wobbled, but before she lost her balance, Kenneth put his arm around her waist for support.

"I can't believe it," Celina boasted. "I'm actually standing!"

Helen smiled. "You sure are."

Although Celina stood, her lower body was weak.

"I want to try and walk."

"Maybe you should take it slow," Kenneth cautioned. "I don't think it's a good idea to push yourself just yet."

"I just want to try and go to the bathroom on my own."

When Kenneth nodded, Celina tried to step forward, but she couldn't pick up her foot.

"Shift your weight," Kenneth said as he moved in behind her. "Here... I'll help you."

She felt Kenneth grasp the back of her thigh and lift her leg. By instincts, she knew to lean forward and place her weight gently as he put her knee in the correct position. With his guidance, she walked to the bathroom. Before she went inside, Kenneth said, "Call out if you need any help."

Moments later, as Celina came out, she met Kyle's smiling face. Instantly, they reached out for one another.

"I can't believe it," Kyle said, securing his arm around her waist. "It's a miracle."

"Back to bed, Celina," Kenneth urged. "I don't want you to overdo it."

By the time Kyle had helped her back in bed, she was out of breath.

"Don't worry," Kenneth said. "Since you haven't been active in weeks, it's expected that you'll be weak until you get your strength back. Just don't overdo yourself. Your body has been through a lot, and it needs time to adjust."

Celina nodded. "Thank you, Dr. Craven."

Kenneth placed his hand on hers and said, "You did all the work, kiddo. Somehow, you healed yourself. It's the only explanation I can come up with. There's no way the surgery could have worked this fast."

"Get some rest, honey," Helen said as she bent over and kissed Celina's forehead. "I'll stop by later to check on you."

"Thanks, Aunt Helen."

When Kenneth and Helen left the room, Celina looked at Kyle and said, "You're not leaving too, are you?"

"Heck no." He winked. "I'll be right here until you fall asleep."

Celina smiled and thought about how patient he had been through all this mess. Their relationship was still new, growing and deepening each day, but it seemed as though they'd known each other a lifetime. Sure, they still had a long way to go. There was a lot more to discover about one another. And now, things were hopeful after the incredible miracle she'd just experienced.

She scooted over and patted the bed. "There's plenty of room for two."

"You got it, babe."

As Kyle stretched out in bed next to her, he wrapped his arm around her. When she nestled her head on his shoulder with a contented sigh, he realized he had a promising future right here in his arms.

Outside Celina's room, Helen smiled at Kenneth and said, "So... are you ready to meet your daughter?"

"Are you kidding?" He smiled like a kid at Christmas. "I've been waiting for years to meet her."

As Helen led Kenneth downstairs and through a set of double doors, his heart leaped into his throat. Sitting in an oversized chair was the young woman he recognized from the hospital.

Helen patted Kenneth's shoulder and smiled at Tessa. "I'll give you two some privacy."

The second Helen left them alone, Tessa rose from her chair. "Please..." She motioned Kenneth over. "Would you care to have a seat?"

As he came forward and faced Tessa, he said, "I don't know if I should hug you, or bow."

"I'll take the hug," she said, holding back tears.

Kenneth smiled and wrapped his arms around her. "I never thought I'd find you, sweetheart."

Tessa opened her mouth to reply, but all she managed to get out were teary sobs.

"It's okay." He patted her back. "I'm here for you now."

When Tessa pulled from their embrace, she said, "You're going to be a grandfather."

"That's wonderful, Tessa. I'm so happy for you. And Helen said you were having twins."

"Yes, and they're boys."

"This is the best day of my life," he said with tears in his eyes. "I've found my beautiful daughter and now I'm going to have two grandsons."

As they shared each other's stories, Tessa felt as though some of the missing pieces from her childhood were starting to come together.

"I want to introduce you to my fiancé," she said.

"Yes," Kenneth said. "I remember. Tall, handsome young man with long blond hair. And as I recall, he was very helpful when I had that dizzy spell at the hospital the other day."

"Yep." Tessa grinned. "That's my Jace."

"I'm looking forward to meeting him," Kenneth said, grinning. "Officially that is."

Tessa wiped at her eyes. "After all these years... I thought you didn't want me."

"Oh, Tessa..." Kenneth released a sigh. "I'm so sorry. Please, never doubt for one minute. I've never stopped searching for you or your mother. It nearly killed me when she took off. I just can't understand why she left." He shook his head. "It doesn't make any sense. Although we were young, I planned on living the rest of my life with her. Lisa was my beloved."

"Do you think she's still alive?"

"I don't know..." He bit back tears. "...but now that I've found you, I have hope."

"I promise," Tessa said. "I'll do everything I can to help you find her. And maybe we can find my twin."

"That would mean a lot to me." Emotion knotted his throat. "Thank you for accepting me in your life." Then he reached into his pocket. When he brought his hand out, he held a gold-cross necklace in his palm. "I want you to have this, Tessa. It belonged to your mother."

"It's beautiful." Tears slipped down her cheeks. "I would be honored to wear it."

"Thank you, Tessa."

Chapter Fifteen

As Eve rested, she wondered what fate had in store for her next. After the birth of her two beautiful twin boys, she knew her time with them was short. She had to face her punishment for her past crimes against the Breedline, which meant they would be separated soon.

When sleep wouldn't come, she decided to get out of bed. Slowly, she maneuvered her feet to the floor and stood on wobbly legs. Out of nowhere, a familiar scent perforated her senses. She looked to the bedroom door and gasped in stunned disbelief.

"Hello, my darling Eve."

"Sebastian..."

"Yes, my beloved," he said as he came forward and reached out to her.

Her eyes searched his face. "How can this be?"

"Shhh... I'm here now." He wiped at the tears that slipped down her cheeks. "Everything is going to be okay. I'm getting you out of here."

"But, what about our—"

"Sons..."

Eve tilted her head in question. "How did you know?"

As Sebastian smiled, the sharp points of his fangs peeked out from under his top lip. "I'll explain later. We need to hurry before the guards come."

"But... I don't want to leave my babies."

"Where are they?"

"They're with my sister."

He leaned down and captured her mouth, kissing her softly. "I promise, I will come back for them."

* * *

Aside from the Covenant's gym, the game room was Jace's favorite place to hang out. It had a flat-screen the size of Texas, leather couches and recliners soft enough to qualify as beds, a wet bar, two pool tables, and a stage big enough for his band's instruments while they practiced before a gig.

While everyone enjoyed all the benefits the game room had to offer, Tessa was fond of its most recent addition. The snack bar included a soda fountain, an ice cream dispenser, and a popcorn machine. Hot, buttered popcorn and a root-beer float went together well, especially during her pregnancy.

After Tessa officially introduced Kenneth to Jace, he invited him to a game of pool. Although Kenneth hadn't played in years, he loved the game.

"Take it easy on me, Jace. It's been a while since I laid eyes on a billiards table."

"Ah, don't sweat it." Jace clapped his hand over Kenneth's shoulder. "It's like riding a bike. Once you get started, it'll come back to you."

"Yeah, well..." Kenneth chuckled. "I haven't ridden a bike in ages either."

As Tessa watched them pick out their pool sticks, she suddenly gasped when she felt her stomach move. It was if the babies inside were having a wrestling match.

Jace looked over. "Is something wrong, honey?"

"It's just the twins." She had her hands over her rounded belly as if she was cradling the tiny lives inside. "I think they're fighting for room."

Jace sat down beside her and placed his palm on her belly. "Whoa..." His eyes widened. "Feels like they're trying to kick a field goal." He looked over at Kenneth and said, "Come feel this."

Kenneth sat down on the opposite side of Tessa and looked at her as if he was waiting for her approval.

She nodded at him. "It's okay."

When Kenneth placed his hand on her belly, his eyes rounded. "Oh, wow. They are active. That means they're healthy and happy."

Tessa placed her hand over Kenneth's. "So is their mommy."

Jace shot to his feet. "Okay, that's enough baby talk. Time to play some pool."

Kenneth took a square of blue chalk and polished the tip of his cue. Across the green felt, he watched as Jace lined up his angles and said, "Nine in the corner."

There was a smack... a roll... and a clunk.

Kenneth raised a brow. "Nice shot, Jace." Then he positioned himself on the other side of the table. When he lined up, ready to knock one of the striped balls in the side pocket, it unfortunately tapped the eight ball. It rebounded and went in the far-left pocket. "Damn..." Kenneth groaned.

"That's the game," Jace said. "Ready for round two?"

Before Kenneth opened his mouth to reply, Bruce Carmichael rushed inside and said, "Eve's gone."

* * *

Sebastian vanished through a portal, taking Eve with him, and brought her back to the room they used to share at the club.

He guided her to the bed. "You need to rest, my beloved."

When she slipped under the covers, she rested her head against a pillow and said, "I didn't think you would want me back."

Sebastian's eyes softened as he sat down beside her. He gently smoothed his thumb over the side of her face. "Why would you ever think such a thing?"

She instantly broke down into tears.

"Shhh," he soothed, kissing her temple. "I could never stop loving you."

"I thought you wouldn't want me when you found out about the twins."

Between one heartbeat and the next, he just stared at her for the longest time. "You are my beloved. How could I not want you?"

She fought back the tears and searched his face for sincerity.

"I look into the future and see you, Eve," he murmured. "I promise, we're going to be together as a family."

"I want you to promise me," she said. "If something happens to me—"

Sebastian instantly placed his finger up to her lips. "Hey... don't talk like that. I'm not going to let anything happen to you."

She briefly closed her eyes. God, she wanted to believe him. Wanted it with everything she had.

* * *

As soon as Bruce announced Eve's disappearance, Tim and Drakon came inside the game room with Jem following close behind.

"It was Sebastian," Drakon said. "He used a portal to get into the Covenant. I caught it on the video footage in Eve's room."

Jace tossed the pool stick on top of the billiards table. "Son of a bitch."

Kenneth shrugged. "Who's Sebastian?"

"It's a long story," Jace grumbled. "Here's a short version. Sebastian is the father of Eve's twins. And I swear, the bastard has nine lives."

"They didn't take the twins," Jem said. "Tidus and Arius are with Mia."

Tessa breathed a sigh of relief. "Thank goodness."

"So, how long has it been?" Jace asked.

"An hour ago," Drakon replied.

"Dammit!" Jace said. "We're already an hour behind. So why are we standing around? We need to find the bastard."

Tim held up a halting hand. "I want everyone to keep a level head. We need a plan before we go off half-cocked. When it comes to Sebastian, it's likely he's not working alone."

Jace wrapped his arm around Tessa and gathered her close. "What's our plan?"

"We need to make sure everyone in the Covenant is notified. I'll see if Celina can put a spell on the estate to block Sebastian from using the portal to get in. And no one leaves." Tim looked to everyone. "Are we clear?"

When everyone nodded in agreement, Tim shifted his focus toward Bruce. "I still want the guesthouse guarded. I want eyes on this place twenty-four seven."

Bruce nodded. "Aye, sir."

92

Chapter Sixteen

Eve woke to the sound of voices coming from the other room. Listening carefully, she could hear Sebastian talking to another man who had an English accent. He mentioned her name a couple of times. Then he said something about one of the twins having a birthmark. That's when she realized he was talking about Arius. He had a birthmark in the shape of an S on the bottom of his left foot.

She quietly pulled back the blanket and swung her legs off the side of the bed. When she stood, her body felt renewed and fresh. When she opened her robe and removed the gauze that covered the stitches from her surgery, she was amazed. It was as if her skin had never seen a scalpel. Then she remembered Sebastian offering her his vein last night. His blood had already healed her.

After she secured her robe back, tying a belt around her waist, she tiptoed out of the room and down a narrow hall. As she got to the end, she leaned against the wall and eavesdropped on their conversation. That's when she heard Sebastian refer to the other man as Thomas. Her eyes rounded when she heard Thomas call Sebastian his brother.

When she peeked around the corner, she instantly gasped and ducked back into the hallway. *Shit!*

"Come, Eve," Sebastian called out. "I'd like to introduce you to someone."

When Eve stepped around the corner, she couldn't believe what her eyes were telling her. It was as though she had stepped into the *Bizarro World*.

As Sebastian grasped Eve's hand, she moved next to him with her eyes locked on the man that looked identical to Sebastian.

"Eve, this is my twin brother, Thomas."

"But I thought he was... dead."

Thomas slightly bowed his head. "As you can see my dear, I'm very alive." He held out his hand. "It's a pleasure to meet you, Eve."

She released Sebastian's hand and took hold of Thomas's. "How did you find each other?"

"I've lived most of my life in England with our mother's sister," Thomas said. "Not long ago, my Aunt Cathryn passed away. When I found our birth records, I was shocked to find out I was a twin. I had no idea Sebastian existed. That's when I decided to find him." He tilted his head a little and smiled. "And here we are, reunited after all these years."

"Thomas has brought something rather important to my attention and it has to do with our son, Arius."

Eve looked at Sebastian, confused. "What are you talking about? Is something wrong with him?"

"No, sweetheart," Sebastian said, reaching for her hand. "As a matter of fact, Arius bears a powerful mark."

"What does his birthmark have to do with anything?"

In the brief silence that followed, Thomas said, "Tell her, Brother."

"Tell me what?"

"Arius has inherited the Chiang-shih demon's powers," Sebastian replied. "He has unimaginable gifts that can be useful in taking over the Breedline species."

"No..." Eve pulled her hand away from Sebastian. "That's not true. Arius is good. Both my sons are good."

"You should be grateful," Thomas said. "It's a privilege to be his mother."

At that moment, Eve searched into herself and saw something she despised but could not ignore. She had no memory of the woman that had given birth to her, but she knew too well the story of how she had cast her out because she was a half-breed. Eve had desperately wanted to be claimed all her life... to belong to a loving family. Instead, she was tossed in and out of foster homes, tortured and degraded. There was no way she was going to let anything happen to her children. She would raise them to be good, not evil.

"Come now, Eve," Sebastian said, offering her his hand again. "You must accept the inevitable. We will raise our sons to be kings."

"I won't let you brainwash my son," Eve said. "I swear to you..." She turned toward Thomas. "...to the both of you. I will not allow Arius to be raised the way you intend."

Sebastian stared at her, utterly perplexed. "What's happened to you, Eve? Don't tell me you care about the Breedline."

* * *

When Jace and Jem informed everyone in the Covenant of the current situation, they met up with Drakon to view the security cameras.

Drakon rolled back the video. As soon as a bright light appeared in Eve's bedroom, the footage revealed a man as he stepped from what looked to be a portal. As Drakon zoomed in, they recognized Sebastian on the video. The look on Jace's face expressed a murderous rage, especially when Sebastian glanced up at the camera with a smug look on his face. It was as though he was laughing at them all. The last thing on the recorded video was Sebastian and Eve disappearing through the illuminated gateway.

"Well, I guess that proves my theory," Jace said with a snarl marring his face. "That bastard does have nine lives."

"Whatever the case," Jem said, "Sebastian will be back. I'd bet on my life that he's coming for Tidus and Arius."

Drakon nodded. "And we'll be ready. When he does return, I'm going to personally nail his ass to the wall."

"Oh, believe me," Jace said through gritted teeth, "that will just be the beginning of his pain. When I get done with him, he'll wish he'd stayed in hell."

Jem heaved a deep breath. "Until then, we'll need to keep a close watch on the twins. The moment we turn our backs, Sebastian will make a grab for them. He's too arrogant and far too self-assured not to try."

Drakon shut off the security footage and said, "Have you heard if Tim talked to Celina about creating a spell to block Sebastian from using a portal to get into the Covenant?"

"He's with Celina right now," Jem said. "Hopefully she can do it."

"Celina is one helluva powerful Wicca," Jace said. "That should be a cake walk for her."

"Let's hope so," Drakon replied.

95

Over the next half hour, Celina worked on a spell to shield the Covenant. If her powers were successful, Sebastian would not be able to use a portal to get inside the Covenant.

"It's done," Celina said. "I've created a barrier."

"Thank you, Celina," Tim said.

"What about another Wicca?" Kyle chimed in. "Could they break the spell?"

Celina grudgingly nodded. "It's a possibility. If indeed Sebastian knows a Wicca, the barrier can be lifted. But it would have to be a very powerful one to undo my spell."

The expression on Tim's face told Celina without words the turmoil of his thoughts. "If Sebastian finds a way in," he said, "we'll be ready this time. Drakon is taking care of the security cameras, and I expect everyone in the Covenant do their part. We'll have to split up into shifts."

"I'll volunteer a shift," Kyle said.

"Count me in too," Celina chimed in.

"Thanks," Tim said, looking between Kyle and Celina. "We'll need all the help we can get. I'll make sure the Guardians know what's going on. Maybe they can keep watch outside the Covenant."

Moments later, as Tim left Celina's room and made it halfway down the stairs, the doorbell rang. Before he reached for the door, he looked at the security camera. He recognized Helen, but he wasn't sure who the young woman standing beside her was. Although her face looked familiar, he couldn't place her name.

Tim opened the door. "Hello, Helen." He stepped aside and motioned them in. "Please, come in."

When they entered the Covenant, Helen said, "Tim, you've met Lila Demont, haven't you? She's Victor Demont's daughter."

Tim nodded. "Oh, yes. I thought you looked familiar. The last time I saw you, you couldn't have been any older than twelve or thirteen. Now look at you. You're all grown up." He extended his hand. "It's good to see you again, Lila."

As Lila reached for his hand, she took notice of the enormous crystal chandelier above him. "It's nice to see you too. It's been so long since I've been inside the Covenant. I almost forgot how spectacular this place is."

"Well, you'll have to visit more often," Tim said. "We've added some new additions. You'll have to check out our game room. Everyone seems to gather there in the evenings. You're welcome to stop by anytime."

"Thanks." Lila smiled. "I'd love to."

"So, how's your father doing?"

"He's fine," Lila said. "Although he's about to drive my mother nuts since he's retired. I think he's going stir-crazy not knowing what to do with himself."

Tim chuckled. "Tell Victor to give me a call. I'd like to catch up with him."

When she nodded, Helen said, "Lila just started working at the hospital as a medical lab technician. She's helping me with some research I've been working on. I hope it's okay if we use the examination room."

"Sure, Helen," Tim said. "You shouldn't bother with asking. Our home is considered yours. If there's anything you need, please, don't hesitate to ask."

"Thanks, Tim. I appreciate it."

Before they headed to the examination room, Tim looked at Helen and said, "While you're here, could I speak with you in private for a few minutes?" He averted his eyes from Helen and focused on Lila. "You don't mind, do you?"

Lila shook her head. "Of course not."

"Please, Lila," Tim said. "Help yourself in the kitchen. You remember where it is, don't you?"

"I'm not sure. It's been so long since I last visited."

"Go through the dining room," Tim directed, "and take a left. It's through the double set of swinging doors."

"Gotcha." Lila nodded. "Thank you, Tim."

After she made her way to the kitchen and stepped inside, her eyes instantly went to the gorgeous guy sitting at the table. He had beautiful long brown hair and handsome regal features. His bone structure alone was the definition of perfection. And going by what she could see, his body was as stunning as his face.

He looked up when the door closed. His mouth fell open when he saw her standing inside the kitchen. She was breathtaking. Words alone could not express how beautiful she was. Her big brown eyes were enchanting, and her honey-blonde hair was like silk. He suddenly had the urge to run his fingers through the long strands. Out of nowhere, he felt movement in the fly of his pants.

In the silence that followed, their eyes locked for what seemed to be an eternity. Before he rose from his chair, he nonchalantly adjusted his pants and said, "Hello..."

Lila blushed at the alluring tone of his voice. She felt like her knees were going to buckle. In a breathy sigh, she said, "Hi."

He came forward on shaky legs and extended his hand. "My name is Casey Barton, and you are?"

"Lila..." Her voice cracked. "Lila Demont."

"It's nice to meet you, Lila."

He was oddly nervous. He'd never felt nervous with anyone in his life. He was always confident, poised, and self-assured, especially when it came to the opposite sex. Women always flocked to him without so much as batting an eye.

"It's nice to meet you too, Casey," she finally said and took hold of his hand.

When their hands made contact, the sensation almost brought them to their knees. It was as though something had zapped them with a jolt of electricity. But instead of pain, they felt an instant arousal. It was tantalizing and euphoric, almost druglike. Then the word beloved came to mind, whispering into their subconscious in the most soothing and loving voice.

"Whoa..." Casey finally let go of her hand. "Did you feel that?"

Lila could only nod. She felt out of breath and a little lightheaded.

When she didn't reply, Casey said, "Lila, are you okay?"

She looked at him wide-eyed and opened her mouth, but the words would not come. She was too busy trying to decipher what she'd just experienced. Going by the tingling between her thighs, she had a good feeling what this was. *Oh, God,* she thought.

Casey hurriedly grabbed a chair and placed it behind her. "Lila, I think you should sit down."

When she plopped down in the chair, he grabbed one for himself and scooted it in front of her.

She cocked her head to the side and simply said, "What just happened?"

He sat down and pondered an explanation. And then he recalled what he had heard from the other bonded males in the Covenant. *Was this what it felt like to bond with your Breedline mate?* No matter how much he wanted to, he couldn't deny his instincts. There was no doubt in his mind. He had just experienced what it was to bond with his soulmate. Although he would have appreciated a warning of some kind. The life he once knew was about to drastically change. Then again... sometimes shit just happened when you least expected it to.

Casey released a deep breath and came back to focus. Instead of saying what was on his mind, he leaned forward. As though Lila could read his mind, she leaned in too. Their mouths met in the middle. Amid their passionate kiss, Helen and Tim abruptly stepped inside the kitchen.

Chapter Seventeen

Thoughts of her twin sons had soon commanded the majority of Eve's mind. She played and replayed scenes from their too-short time together until her heart ached. They were so tiny and defenseless. The moment she looked into their eyes, she took a vow to protect them. No matter what Sebastian and Thomas had told her, deep down in the very pit of her gut, she knew Tidus and Arius were pure of heart. Then her mind became a whirlwind. Maybe they were better off living in the Covenant. *Is it possible*, she thought, *that Mia and Jem could give them a better life?*

Hours later, when sleep finally took hold, the bed dipped and brought her eyes back open. She instantly sensed Sebastian's presence and flinched away from his touch.

"Please, Eve..." Sebastian scooted closer. "...don't be angry with me."

In the silence that followed, he reached out to her. "Please..." His tone was pleading. "Talk to me."

Moments later, she rolled over and looked at him with tears in her eyes. Before she could open her mouth to speak, she found herself wrapped in Sebastian's arms. His body shook as he held her. "I love you, Eve," he whispered close to her ear.

When Sebastian pulled from their embrace, he reached out and smoothed his thumb over her cheek, wiping the tears away.

"I want my sons back," she said. "And I want us to move away from all this. I want us to be a family."

He nodded. "I promise. Soon, my darling Eve."

* * *

Casey flinched and pulled away from Lila when he heard someone clearing their throat. When he looked up, he saw Tim and Helen standing in the doorway. The look on their faces made Casey feel like a kid with his hand caught in the cookie jar.

Lila turned to look, and Casey croaked out, "Hello, Tim... Helen..."

In the awkward silence that followed, Tim said, "I see you two have made friends."

His statement made Lila's cheeks warm and Casey grin like the Cheshire cat.

Helen placed her hand over her heart. At that moment, she realized the young couple had most likely bonded, which meant they were going to be a part of each other's life forever.

"Oh..." Lila finally said. "Hi, Tim." She nodded at Helen and then rose to her feet. "I guess you're ready to get to work."

"If you'd like to visit with Casey a little longer," Helen said with a smile, "that would be quite all right with me."

Lila averted her eyes from Helen and looked to Casey, her cheeks going warm beneath the heat of her gaze. "It was nice to meet you, Casey."

Casey instantly stood. "You too. Maybe we could go for lunch or dinner sometime."

"Sure." Lila beamed. "That would be great."

Casey reached into his back pocket and retrieved his phone. "How about we trade numbers?"

Lila nodded with a bashful smile. "Okay."

After they exchanged numbers, Lila moved toward the door, and before she left with Helen, she glanced over her shoulder and waved at Casey.

He smiled and waved back with Lila's lovely voice replaying in his mind.

Tim stood inside the kitchen with his eyes on Casey, who hadn't moved from his position.

Finally, Tim waved his hand in front of Casey and said, "Ahem... you all right, buddy?"

Casey came back to focus. "I think Lila and I bonded."

Tim cocked a brow. "You do realize she's Victor Demont's daughter, right?"

"Yeah," Casey muttered. "I'm sure he'll be thrilled when he finds out."

"Listen, Casey. We don't get to pick our mates. Our Breedline natural instincts choose them for us. If you want, I can talk to Victor. We go way back."

"Thanks, Tim." Casey sighed. "I may take you up on that offer."

Tim could see the real concern in Casey's eyes. He reached out and patted him on the shoulder. "Once Victor gets to know you, I'm sure he'll give you his blessing and welcome you into his family."

"Well, I hope you're right."

"Don't worry too much, Casey. Everything will work out." Before Tim stepped out of the kitchen, he glanced over his shoulder and said, "Congratulations, by the way. It would be a relief to see you finally settle down."

As soon as the door closed, Casey collapsed back in his chair. He leaned forward and covered his face with his hands. His thoughts were consumed with Lila and the incredible experience they'd shared but also the secret he kept. Casey thought about Lila, savoring the magical sensation that hope for a real relationship could be a possibility no matter how unlikely it probably was. And he briefly considered that he could be setting himself up for a broken heart. It would kill Lila if she found out what he truly was. And she wouldn't be the only casualty. If the Breedline Covenant found out, the whole house of cards would fall.

* * *

Located in downtown San Francisco...

As Steven Pasquale rode in the back of a packed bus, he noticed a man across the aisle that appeared odd. He was pale and thin-boned, wearing dark-tinted glasses and a long, black trench coat. Every now and then, he noticed the creepy-looking guy staring at him from out of the corner of his eye. It looked as if he was watching his every move. Then it dawned on Steven. Could the man be one of Dr. Autenburg's hired henchmen? With his nerves on pins and needles, he quickly decided to get off at the next stop.

When Steven climbed out, the streets looked deserted. That's when he realized he'd gotten off in a bad part of town. After a half hour of searching for a place that was open, he finally found a hotel. He'd almost walked past it, thinking it was just an old, abandoned building before he noticed the neon sign. The vacancy light flickered on and off, buzzing endlessly as if it was on the verge of burning out. The sign above the run-down entrance was hard to read due to the worn paint.

Steven went on full alert, scanning his surroundings before making the decision to go inside. For some reason, a cold chill washed over him, creating goose bumps on his arms. He stopped at the entrance and looked up. He noticed the windows had been boarded and the stone structure had eroded from the city's pollution. It was obvious the building had been neglected for years. The humid air suddenly stirred, sending trash from the sidewalk into the street. The air smelled of garbage and something else. Something thick and sour that filled his throat and made his stomach lurch. Shifting back to focus, he noticed several streetlights were out, though the one closest to the hotel's front window cast a dim glow over cracked glass.

Where were all the people? Steven wondered. Although it was two in the morning, in San Francisco, the city never looked this deserted. He swallowed back his nerves and reached for the door. When he stepped inside, he looked for someone at the front desk but found it unattended. The place looked haunted... cursed. He spotted a bell on the counter, and as he moved toward it, his pulse quickened with each step. The instant he started to ring it, a growl froze his hand in midair. His heart hammered inside his chest. For a second, he wondered if he'd imagined it.

Finally, he found the courage to look. Slowly, he turned around and called out, "Hello... is anyone there?"

A dark silhouette stepped from the shadows, and as it came closer, Steven instantly recognized the dark figure. It was Dr. Markus Ludwig, a twisted colleague of Dr. Hans Autenburg. He wore a black trench coat and a flat-brimmed hat. Following alongside the mad physician was a deranged-looking man. He had pale skin and tattoos covering his bald head. A snarl marred his unsightly face, revealing the tips of sharp-pointed teeth. The guy looked at Steven with pure hatred.

To his surprise, another dark figure pushed its way through the shadows with the swiftness of a serpent and stood on the opposite side of Dr. Ludwig. Steven recognized him as the same creepy man that sat across from him on the bus, except he wasn't wearing the dark-tinted glasses. He focused on Steven with blood-red eyes and a smug look on his face.

Steven stood in silence with a sudden urge to shove his fist through the creep's chest and wipe that grin off his face for good.

"Hello, Steffen," Dr. Ludwig finally said in a German accent. "Your time has run out. Come with us peacefully, and no harm will be brought to you."

Steven shook his head and took a few steps back. "You're not taking me back," he said through gritted teeth. "I'd rather die than go back to that hellhole. I'm through living like an animal trapped in a cage. I'm no longer your science project."

Dr. Ludwig lifted his chin and let out a seedy, bone-chilling chuckle. Then his humor quickly turned to fury. When the mad physician snapped his fingers, two enormous creatures emerged from the shadows. It was then Steven realized what they were. They were two of Dr. Autenburg's specimens he'd created. A Breedline hybrid of some kind.

With dread curdling in the pit of his stomach, Steven watched as the two unnatural hybrids stalked forward on all fours, snarling and growling.

Seconds later, Dr. Ludwig and his cronies looked at Steven in stunned disbelief. His transformation came instantly. Steven's skin took on a luminous sheen, expanding until his frame grew twice the size. Powerful muscles bulged atop his bare chest and claws jutted from his hands and feet.

He charged head-on and pummeled into one of the hybrids. After he easily snapped its neck, the second hybrid raced toward him with its ears flattened against its enormous head. As it struck Steven, the noise was like nothing Dr. Ludwig had ever heard. The howls of rage changed to a whimpering defeat and ended in dead silence. Without hesitation, Steven severed the hybrid's spinal cord and threw it at Dr. Ludwig's feet.

The mad physician stepped behind his bald henchmen and shouted, "Shoot him!"

Before the man could fire his weapon, Steven lunged at Dr. Ludwig. A bone-cracking sound came next. Then the physician dropped to the floor with his neck twisted in an unnatural angle.

When the red-eyed henchman reacted and lunged forward, he stopped in his tracks as Steven shoved his fist through the guy's chest cavity. As he fell limp to the floor, the unmistakable sound of a gun being cocked suddenly came from behind Steven.

"Don't move," the tatted, bald guy said.

Everything seemed to move in slow motion. Steven whirled around at the speed of a blur, slicing the guy's throat with his razor-sharp claws. The blast of the gun echoed like the crack of lightning. Simultaneously, the bald guy flew back, blood spurting from his throat, and Steven fell to his knees, clutching his chest.

Chapter Eighteen

Helen looked up from a microscope and said, "Lila... I think I found it!"

"What?" Lila's eyes rounded. "Are you serious?"

"Yes," Helen said, grinning ear-to-ear. "The cells stayed attached this time. I think we finally did it. We found the answer to the Breedline aging process. All we need to do now is test it."

"That's wonderful, Helen!"

"Lila, do you know what this means for our species?"

Before she could reply, Helen's cell phone went off. When she retrieved it from the pocket of her white coat, she recognized the number. "Hold that thought, Lila. I've got to take this. It's a call from the hospital."

When Lila nodded, Helen answered the call. "This is Dr. Carrington."

"We've got a trauma case, Dr. Carrington," a nurse's voice said on the other end. "Male in his thirties with a gunshot wound to the chest. Dr. Allman has him stabilized, but he insisted you come in, or do you want me to call Dr. Eaves?"

"No, I'll be there. Tell Dr. Allman I'm on my way."

"Yes, Dr. Carrington."

When the call ended, she refocused her eyes on Lila. "I've got to head to the hospital. You okay to stay here?"

"Sure." Lila nodded. "I'll be fine."

When Helen left the room, she hurried down the hall and into the foyer. Before reached the door that exited the Covenant, she stopped at a mirror above a small entryway table. Her reflection was crystal-clear in the glass, from her white physician's coat to her Mahogany hair, to the signs of middle age starting to appear on her face. If her breakthrough was a success, she wouldn't have to worry about wrinkles or gray hairs anymore.

While Lila waited for Helen to return, she reached inside her purse and retrieved her cell phone. Searching through her contacts, she came upon Casey's number. Before she hit the call button, she took a deep breath.

A few seconds later, he answered, "Hello, Lila."

The sound of his sultry voice spread warmth throughout her body. "Hi, Casey," she bashfully replied. "I hope I'm not calling at a bad time."

"No, no," he instantly said. "I'm glad you called."

"You are?"

"Sure, why wouldn't I be?"

In the awkward silence, she said, "Do you have free time to... maybe... hang out for a while?"

"I'd love to. Where do you want to meet?"

"I'm still in the Covenant's examination room," she said. "Helen got a call from the hospital and had to leave, so..."

Casey chuckled. "And you're stuck here, right?"

She nodded against the phone. "Yeah, I guess. I rode with her, so that leaves me kind of on foot."

"Well, I can't say I hate the predicament you're in. I think it's perfect timing."

"You do?"

"Yeah, it gives me the perfect opportunity to see you." He smiled into the phone. "Sooner is better than later."

Lila blushed at the purr in his voice. "I-I agree."

"How about you meet me in the foyer in say..." He paused to check his watch. "Ten minutes?"

"I'll see you in ten," she said with a smile in her voice.

* * *

The Bates Hospital was state of the art, thanks to the previously added emergency unit. The hospital included twenty-four-hour emergency care, women and infant services, cardiovascular care, behavioral health, orthopedics, and cancer diagnosis along with treatment.

When Helen arrived in the emergency unit, she reviewed the chart of the male patient with the gunshot wound. Five minutes later, the double doors swung open, and a nurse rushed in. "Dr. Carrington, we need you in surgery. The gunshot victim went into cardiac arrest. We got a rhythm back, but his blood pressure is sixty over forty and falling."

Helen nodded. "Let's get a blood type run, and I want his chest X-rays right away. Get an ultrasound of his—"

A scream ripped through the OR and cut her off. Helen instantly rushed toward the sound, with the nurse following behind. As they entered the patient's room, a nurse who'd been assisting him looked as though she'd just seen a ghost, and Dr. Allman was lying on the floor unconscious. For a split second, Helen and the nurse froze. The patient lying on the operating table was *glowing*.

Helen snapped into action and called out commands. Everyone refocused, and the nurse who looked shell-shocked said, "Dr. Allman just touched the patient and... collapsed."

Helen knelt by the physician lying on the floor and checked for a pulse. "He's breathing," she said. "I need him off the floor and out of here."

After the nurse went to get help, within seconds more nurses came into the room with a gurney. While Dr. Allman was rushed out, Helen looked over the patient's X-rays. She was astonished at what she found. The patient's tissue had already healed and there appeared to be no major internal organs damaged. *This can't be right,* she thought.

Helen approached the bed where the patient was hooked up to the anesthesia machines. His chest was prepped for surgery with the regions around it draped in surgical cloth. The Betadine solution made him look like he had an orange tan underneath all the glimmering light that surrounded his entire body. As she looked closer, she couldn't believe what her eyes were telling her. The recent wound to his chest looked to be perfectly fine, like he'd never been injured.

One of the medics who had assisted with Dr. Allman stuck his head in the room. "Dr. Carrington..."

Helen flinched and looked to the door. "How's Dr. Allman doing?"

"He's coming around," the medic said. "He hit his head pretty hard, but other than that, he's fine. It seems that he just passed out."

"Well, I don't blame him," Helen said. "It's not every day your patient starts glowing. But according to the X-rays, there's no internal damage. He appears to be stable, other than..." Helen shrugged as she looked at the patient seemingly lost for words. "...his unexplainable glowing skin."

Lila made it to the foyer and waited for Casey. The moment she saw him at the top of the staircase, she felt her cheeks flush. He was gorgeous. Gorgeous in a way that made her nervous. By the way he dressed, Casey looked like a male model who just stepped off the runway. He looked glamorous, seductive, and out of her league. She blushed even more when he noticed her and waved. Lila smiled and waved back like a giddy teenager. She'd never felt this way with any guy she'd met.

When he made it down the steps and approached her, he said, "Hi, Lila."

She almost melted at the flirtatious tone in his voice. And his scent. God... he smelled wonderful. Off the charts wonderful.

She finally got her mouth to work and said, "Hi, Casey."

"Would you care for something to eat?"

Lila didn't even register his question. She couldn't stop looking into his eyes. The spectacular color was mesmerizing. *Were they real?* she thought. She'd never seen anyone with lavender eyes before.

When she didn't answer, he said, "Lila..."

She flinched. "Oh, sorry. What did you say?"

He smiled. "Are you hungry?"

"Uh, sure..." She blushed even more. "I could eat."

"We have leftovers from last night. How does roast beef sandwiches sound?"

"Delicious."

Casey reached for her hand, and as he led her to the kitchen, he started to think of Lila's family. She'd been born into a prestigious bloodline. He, on the other hand, was not born a full-blooded Breedline. Before his eighteenth birthday, his parents gave him some disturbing news. Not only had he been adopted, he carried the genetics of a Breedline and a Theriomorph. Instead of shifting into a Breedline wolf, he could shape-shift into an enormous black panther. He also had other odd gifts he considered a curse. He had visions of the future and the power of mind manipulation, which the

Breedline species considered a threat to their species. That was the reason for his and his parents' secrecy. He used dopamine to help suppress that side of him he despised.

Although, lately, he'd been having visions of Tessa. And they weren't good visions. The situation put him in a predicament. Casey had to decide if he was going to act on his premonitions, which would give away his secret identity, or just let destiny take hold. No matter what choice he made, it wouldn't change the future.

Nonetheless, he had no business dating Lila. If her family found out, especially her father, they would reject him as an outcast not worthy of their daughter.

He'd never revealed his secret to anyone else in the Covenant. Now that his mother had passed away, his father and his uncle, Tim Ross, were the only family he had left. Although his uncle didn't know the secret his parents had kept, he treated him like family.

As they neared the kitchen, Casey went ahead and held the door open for Lila. Trying his best to be a true gentleman, he pulled out a chair for her. "What would you like on your sandwich, my dear?"

She grinned. "Oh, I'm not picky. I'll have whatever you're having."

He clapped his hands together. "Two roast beef sandwiches with lettuce, tomatoes, and mayo coming up."

Lila sat quietly, nervously fiddling with a napkin while Casey dug around in the refrigerator. She felt a hunger of desire that she'd never experienced before. Deep down she knew what they'd shared earlier. It was the Breedline bonding.

After Casey had prepared their sandwiches, he glanced back at the table. When he looked at Lila, she seemed lost in thought as she twisted a napkin between her fingers.

Finally, when he came over with their plates, she turned in his direction, and all she could do was stare at him with a girlish smile.

"You know," he said as he set the plates on the table and sat down across from her, "I like the way you look at me."

She briefly put her hands over her face. "I'm sorry. Is it that noticeable?"

"Please, don't apologize." He winked. "I'm definitely not complaining."

Her cheeks flushed pink and he adored her bashfulness.

"Shall we?" Casey said, picking up his sandwich.

Lila nodded. "It looks delicious."

After she took her first bite, he waited for her to swallow, realizing she was raised with manners.

"How is it?"

She wiped her mouth with a napkin. "It tastes fantastic. Thank you, Casey."

He grinned at her response, but beneath the surface of him, she sensed he was stressed. His anxiety came out in the tense set of his jaw. It seemed as if he was making an effort to be normal for her benefit. Although she appreciated his politeness, she wondered what was bothering him. She wanted to know everything about him but didn't want to put too much pressure on him. It was too early to start demanding information, even though they'd bonded. Should she ask him about his family? Although they'd just met today, she felt like she already knew all she needed to know, but realistically speaking, she was dying to find out everything.

As she toyed with her napkin, her mind was miles away, and though she wasn't much of a talker, she found herself speaking because she simply couldn't keep it in any longer. Her eyes narrowed, and she glanced up at him in question. "Earlier... we bonded, didn't we?"

His lavender eyes focused on her inquisitive stare. "Yes, Lila." He reached for her hand. "Are you disappointed?"

"No, are you?"

When he shook his head and lightly squeezed her hand, she smiled.

"So..." She cocked her head to the side. "...what do we do now?"

"We could... *kiss*."

Her mouth instantly dropped. His offer made her heart race and her cheeks warm. Given the way those captivating eyes of his were looking at her, she was willing to let him do anything right at this moment. "Okay," she murmured.

When Casey leaned closer and cupped her face, she shivered in anticipation. She sighed against his lips as he softly kissed her. The contact was brief, but still, it took her breath away.

"You're so beautiful, Lila," he whispered with his lips close to hers.

Lila simply stared into his spectacular eyes. At that moment, she knew she was falling in love, and there was nothing she could do to stop it. The Breedline bond was real.

"That was... wonderful."

"Yes, it was," he said.

She felt limp as a noddle but managed to croak out, "Casey..."

"Yes?"

"I-I want to know everything about you."

"You do?"

She nodded. "Tell me about your family. Do they live close by?"

Instantly, his expression tensed. "My mother... died recently," he reluctantly said. "But my father lives close by."

Her brows furrowed. "I'm sorry, Casey. I didn't—"

"It's okay, Lila. You didn't know."

She looked at him with sympathy. "So, does your Breedline twin live in the Covenant?"

He did his best to mask a smile. It was evident to Lila he didn't feel comfortable talking about his family, and she knew better than to press him further.

"I'm sorry, Casey. I don't mean—"

"It's fine," he said. "I was adopted. So, I don't know anything about my twin or my birth parents. But my adoptive parents raised me as though I was their own. My uncle on my mother's side of the family is Tim Ross. He's been a great role model all my life."

"I'm glad you have them in your life. My father has tremendous respect for your uncle."

"Yeah..." Casey laughed a little. "I'm hoping that will help me get in your father's good graces."

"I'm sure my parents will adore you," she said. "I would love for them to meet you. Maybe we could arrange that this weekend."

Casey found himself speechless. Hell, he couldn't say no. Although he dreaded facing her father, worried he'd find out his secret, he simply didn't have the heart to turn down her invitation. He hated lying to her, and he knew he was wrong for her, but she was everything he wanted.

He faked a smile. "I would love to meet your family."

Chapter Nineteen

About an hour later, John Doe—the patient with a gunshot wound, and a body that sparkled like a disco ball—finally stopped glowing. Although Helen was ready to get back to the Covenant to continue what she recently discovered, she wasn't leaving the hospital until she learned more about the mysterious patient. If her intuition was correct, this could be a link to her research. If indeed he was the missing patient she had been looking for, this could be important to her research and the Breedline species. Years ago, she'd found a file in the hospital that was put away marked as confidential. It was a study case by a German physician named Dr. Hans Autenburg. In the reported research, it revealed a patient that had supernatural rapid tissue regeneration he called SPECIMEN ONE—the same ability she found in Jace's and Jem's blood not long ago. Using their blood samples, she all but exhausted herself trying to come up with a cure for the Breedline's aging process. Now, just hours ago, she was finally successful. All she had to do was test it.

Most of the nurses on staff were Breedline and kept the patient's medical information confidential. Helen didn't want it leaking out to the public, especially to humans. If they got hold of what had just happened earlier, it would eventually spread all over the news media and create hysteria.

Before Helen went to check on John Doe, she walked over to the front desk where a pretty blonde nurse sat.

"Hello, Dr. Carrington," the nurse said. "Are you here to check on the patient in room eleven?"

Helen nodded with an exhausted sigh. "Has he woken up yet?"

"No," the nurse replied. "I just checked on him ten minutes ago. All his vital signs are stable, but he's still unconscious. Nurse Jacky is with him now."

As Helen started forward, she stopped and said, "By the way... did we find a next of kin?"

"I searched through his belongings, but unfortunately I came up empty. There was no wallet, no phone... nothing."

Helen shook her head. "I'm not surprised. He was probably mugged right after the attack."

"Yeah, you're probably right, Doctor."

"What about the police?" Helen said. "Have they asked any questions about our patient?"

"After he was admitted, two detectives came in asking about him." The nurse handed Helen a business card. "They left this in case the patient becomes conscious. I guess they want to question him."

Helen glanced at the name on the card that read, *Detective Manuel Sanchez*. She put it in her pocket and said, "Thank you, Kathryn. I'll take care of it."

Nurse Kathryn nodded as Helen waved and headed down the corridor. Room eleven was all the way back, on the left. When she got there, Nurse Jacky looked up from checking the patient's IV and said, "Hello, Dr. Carrington."

Helen reached for the medical record and said, "Hi, Jacky." She looked down at the chart. "How's our patient?"

"He's still stable, which is amazing."

As Helen flipped through the recent stats, she said, "He's a bit of a mystery, all right."

Before Helen looked away from the medical file, she noticed the patient's blood pressure recording. It was back to normal along with everything else.

Nurse Jacky paused at the door. "Let me know if you need anything."

Helen looked up and smiled. "Thanks, Jacky."

As the nurse exited the room, Helen pulled the privacy curtain into place and went over to the patient's bedside. Reaching into her pocket, she pulled out an ophthalmoscope. As she leaned over him, Helen used her fingers to open one of his lids. As she shined the lighted medical device into his retina, she discovered her intuition was right. John Doe had to be one of Dr. Hans Autenburg's patients. The German physician's study also reported abnormal lights that reflected in his patient's irises, exactly as the person lying in this bed.

Helen put her hand on his shoulder and said, "I've got a lot of questions for you when you wake up."

"Helen..."

She flinched and looked over her shoulder. "Jesus, Carl..." She heaved a deep breath. "You startled me."

"Sorry, Helen."

Carl moved to the opposite side of the patient and said, "I just came in to check on him. I still can't believe his wounds healed as fast as they did." He crossed his arms and looked down at the patient. "Our Breedline cells heal faster than any human, but not like this guy. I would give anything to study him, or at least participate in it."

Helen focused on the patient's breathing and listened to the faint beeping of the monitoring equipment. It seemed to swell in the silence between them until her awareness kicked in. She glanced up at Carl and said, "I think we should."

He looked at her in question. "What do you mean, Helen?"

On pure gut instinct, she felt like she could trust Carl. Hell, she'd known him practically her whole life. Helen had been best friends with his wife Shea since college, and co-workers for over ten years in this hospital. So, she went for it and told Carl everything, beginning with the files she found on Dr. Hans Autenburg's patient, her years of tireless research, and wrapping it up with her recent discovery.

"All I need to do is test the cure," Helen finally said.

She waited for Carl to process everything, and hopefully his response would be positive.

A moment later, after he practically had to pick his jaw off the floor, he said, "This is a miracle, Helen. I would be honored to help you in any way I can."

Helen let out a sigh of relief. On some level, she had known this conversation was coming, and she couldn't think of anyone else she could trust more than Carl. He'd been the hospital's Chief of Surgery for the last five years and damn good at his job. It was also to her advantage that he was a full-blooded Breedline as well.

"Thank you, Carl. I knew I could count on you."

* * *

Eve held Sebastian's hand as they traveled through the portal to a charming English manor south of London. The estate belonged to his twin brother. Thomas had inherited his Aunt Carolyn's wealth after she had passed away. Eve glanced around the spacious reception hall, astonished by the beautifully carved staircase.

Sebastian impatiently checked his watch as they stood in the foyer.

"Greetings," came a familiar voice.

As they turned to look, Sebastian rolled his eyes when he saw it was Samuel Mercier. It was a miracle the guy was still alive. Sebastian assumed the bastard would eventually be caught and prosecuted by the Breedline Covenant. After Jace's Beast sent the Chiang-shih demon back to hell, the rest of his cronies—the ones who were still alive—came out of hiding and begged for Sebastian's help, although he flat out turned them down.

Sebastian glared at Samuel. "What the hell are you doing here?"

"Mr. Carlyle asked me, along with some others, to join him."

"Well, don't just stand there like an idiot," Sebastian grumbled. "Where is he?"

Samuel motioned toward the dining area. "Please... right this way."

Sebastian and Eve followed him into a minimalist dining room that occupied a former ballroom. As Sebastian watched Samuel's movements, he had an inkling that the guy was a little light in the loafers. No real man moved like he did. Samuel walked with a feminine stride.

Samuel placed one hand on his hip and said, "Would you care for some tea or perhaps a cup of coffee?"

Sebastian snarled. "Yeah... whatever."

"We'll have some tea," Eve said. "Thank you, Samuel."

"Yes, Miss Eve." He slightly bowed. "Coming right up."

A few minutes later, Samuel returned with two china cups on saucers. Sebastian leaned back in his chair and watched as he poured their hot beverage nice and slow. Sugar was next, and the spoon he used to stir made a soft clinking sound, instantly irritating Sebastian. Samuel would have cheerfully wiped their asses if asked, he thought. At least the tea was decent, although he'd never mention that to Samuel. The idiot would probably tear up with joy.

"Where is my brother, dammit?" Sebastian barked. "I hate waiting."

Before Samuel got a word out, several footsteps drew near.

"Welcome, Brother," Thomas said as he entered the room with two men Sebastian recognized. One of them was frail and pale skinned. The other guy was tall with a muscular build and a tattoo of a dragon on his arm.

"Well, well, well..." Sebastian crossed his arms, practically glaring holes through the tatted guy. "I'm not surprised you managed to rustle up the rest of my father's dumbass council."

Thomas cleared his throat. "I take it you've met Fredrick Mercier and Corbin Azzo?"

"Yeah..." Sebastian curled his upper lip. "How could I forget."

Thomas turned to Eve and lowered his head. "You're looking rather well today, Eve. I'm glad you agreed to come."

Eve nodded in silence.

Sebastian impatiently tapped the bottom of his gold ring on the table. "I'm surprised you invited my father's council members to join you," he said with a hint of brooding sarcasm in his tone. "They've proven on countless occasions to be useless and incompetent."

Corbin scowled at Sebastian. "We were always loyal to your father."

Sebastian smirked at Corbin. For a second, he was tempted to pull the pistol he had tucked inside his jacket and aim for Corbin's family jewels.

"Yes, you might be stupid," Sebastian said, "but at least you're honest. You were loyal to your master. But now, my father is gone. So, where does your loyalty reside now?"

"His loyalty is with us," Thomas spoke out. "All of my men's allegiance is with *Lilith* and us, Brother."

Sebastian rose from his chair and moved next to Corbin, getting face-to-face with the guy. "I'm glad to hear you're still obedient," he gritted out. "Although instead of referring to me as your master, you can call me *God*."

Thomas cut into the conversation before it got heated. "Please, gentlemen. I need to speak with Eve and my brother in private."

While the two men and Samuel left the room, Thomas let out a long sigh. He knew bringing in Sebastian's father's old council members would be like poking at a hornet's nest.

"Tell me, Brother," Sebastian said. "Where's this Lilith you've been talking about? I'm starting to think she doesn't exist."

A second later, a ghostly form entered the room. "I am *Lilith*."

As Sebastian caught sight of the ghostly apparition, his jaw nearly hit the floor. Although she was clearly inhuman, she looked oddly familiar and beautiful. Going by her youthful face, she looked to be only eighteen or nineteen, but her voice clearly sounded more mature, like she'd been alive a lot longer than her age revealed.

"Lilith..." Thomas chimed in. "I'd like to introduce you to my twin brother, Sebastian Crow, and his lovely mate, Eve."

She held out a glowing hand to Sebastian. "It's a pleasure." The *S's* in her words strung out until they sounded like the warning of a rattler's tail.

As he took hold of her hand, he was surprised to find it a solid form.

"If you don't mind me asking..." Sebastian released her hand and stared into her diamond-shaped eyes. "...what... are you?"

"What do you mean?"

"It's obvious you're not human," Sebastian said. "So, what species are you?"

Lilith shook her head. "I do not know what I am. My body was experimented on years ago." She placed her hand in front of her face. "And this is what has become of me."

"You mean..." Eve spoke out, "you were human at one time?"

Lilith lowered her hand and focused on Eve with a smile. "Yes, although I do not remember much of my human life. Some of my memories are gone."

"That's terrible," Eve said. "I'm so sorry."

“Thank you, Eve.”

Sebastian tilted his head a little. “What is it you want from us?”

“The Breedline queen,” she simply said.

Just then, it dawned on Sebastian why Lilith looked so familiar. He stepped closer to Lilith and searched her face like he was looking at her underneath a microscope. “Are you somehow kin to Tessa?”

Lilith nodded. “She is my daughter.”

Chapter Twenty

Jem spooned Mia with his arm wrapped around her waist. As he leaned in to kiss the back of her neck, he was interrupted by the sounds of a baby crying coming from the monitor by the bed. It started out little and quickly escalated into full-blown wailing. The stiffness of Jem's arousal pressing into Mia's hips instantly deflated.

Mia rolled over and faced him. "I'm sorry, honey."

He took her face in his palms. "It's okay, sweetheart. You need help?"

There was absolutely no expression of disapproval in his eyes, or in the tone of his voice. He'd never been resentful of Eve's twins since they took them in. If anything, he'd been helpful.

"No, you stay in bed." Mia eased out of bed and slipped on a robe. Before she left the room, she said, "I'll be back shortly."

"Okay, babe." He winked at her from the bed. "Let me know if you need my help."

Mia went into the room next to theirs and moved toward the crib. When she looked down, Arius was lying quietly next to his upset brother. Both boys had grown miraculously since their birth. Since they were half-succubus, their growth rate was much faster than a full-blooded Breedline. She quickly shifted her focus on Tidus. His face was red from crying and his eyes were soaked with tears.

She reached inside the crib and scooped him into her arms. "Oh, sweetheart." She cuddled him close. "It's okay now. Auntie Mia's here."

She checked his diaper and found that it was dry. Although it wasn't time for his feeding, she wondered why he was so upset. As she eased into a rocking chair, his cries lightened and turned into little hiccups. The rhythm of the rocking seemed to soothe him until finally he closed his eyes.

When Mia let her head fall back against the headrest, she heard soft coos coming from the crib. Carefully, she rose to her feet with Tidus in her arms and carried him back to the crib. After she laid him down, she reached for Arius.

"Hey there, little cutie," she whispered. "What are you doing awake?"

He smiled up at her and cooed.

It was at that moment Mia understood the joys of motherhood. It was as if she'd already bonded with her sister's precious babies.

Moments later, she put Arius back in the crib next to his brother. Before she left the room, she took one last look and gasped in disbelief when she saw Arius's eyes.

"Mia..." Jem whispered as he moved inside the room. "What's wrong?"

She turned toward him and said, "Arius's eyes..."

"What about his eyes?"

"You were right about what you saw after he was born," she said in a hushed voice. "I saw it too. His eyes turned black."

Jem wrapped his arm around her and held her tight. "It's going to be okay, honey. We'll love him no matter what. It's not his fault."

"Oh, Jem..." She pulled from their embrace and looked up into his eyes. "I love you so much."

"I love you too, Mia."

Jem moved next to the crib and looked down. His eyes softened when he saw both boys fast asleep. "Just look at those faces," he said. "How could anything but goodness come from such cuteness."

Mia moved next to him and smiled. "I have a good feeling they're both going to grow up just fine."

"So do I, honey," Jem murmured as he kissed Mia's forehead.

* * *

As Tessa sank deeper into the tub, the water level rose and covered everything but her head and her rounded belly.

The warm water soothed her changing body, now at the beginning of her seventh month. She closed her eyes and smiled, remembering what her father had told her. He'd never given up on her or her birth mother. And all this time, she thought her parents had abandoned her. Now, she knew it wasn't true. Not by her father anyway.

When Tessa reached up to smooth her long hair back, the water felt soothing against her scalp. At this point, she could barely keep her eyes open. She just relaxed in peaceful bliss.

A half hour later, she grasped the side of the tub and pushed to her feet. Carefully, she stepped out and reached for a towel.

"You're beautiful."

Tessa's wet heel squeaked as she turned to look. Jace was standing in the doorway, staring at her without a stitch of clothes on. There was a magnetic moment as their eyes met.

"Tessa, I've never wanted you more than I do right now."

When she let the towel drop to the floor, she felt a sizzle in the air between them and knew it wasn't one-sided.

He held out his hand and winked. "Come here, baby."

A slight smile curved her lips as she came forward.

Jace took hold of her hand and tugged her into his arms. Tessa moaned against his heated embrace and he swallowed the sound with a passionate kiss. It wasn't long before he swept her off her feet and carried her to the bedroom. As though she was a delicate piece of glass, he eased her onto the bed and settled beside her. In spite of Jace's fears that he'd hurt her if he put weight on her belly, Tessa took hold of the reins and reached out to him.

"I promise, I'm not going to break," she whispered. "Please..."

He held back for a moment, but then relaxed, realizing what she needed from him, and finally eased his body onto hers.

Jace leaned forward and placed his lips to hers. As his tongue invaded her mouth and skillfully stroked hers, she writhed against the warmth of his flesh. Goose bumps prickled over her skin as his hand trailed down to her thigh and slowly inched lower. His caressing and sensual touch felt heavenly. In a matter of seconds, she felt a heat bloom within her that nearly took her over the edge. She arched her back and moaned as he rolled his hips against hers, stroking with the promise of pleasure.

As they made love, gasping and panting, Tessa dug her hands into the strands of his long, blond hair, riding out her glorious release.

"Tessa..." he gasped.

She smoothed her hand down the side of his face and watched his handsome features as he strained with pleasure.

Jace finally nuzzled her throat and whispered, "I love you."

"I love you too."

Moments later, he rose from her body and rested alongside her. He gazed into her eyes and said, "Tessa, you're everything to me. Please, don't ever leave me."

She leaned in and pressed her lips to his. "I'm forever yours."

His eyes softened. Then he slid out of bed and moved to the closet.

"Where are you going?" she said, watching his hips flex with each step.

He glanced back at her and winked. "It's a surprise."

"Oh... I like surprises."

A few minutes later, he came back with an acoustic guitar. By the design on the front, it looked vintage.

"Where did you get that?"

"When I first started to show some real skills, my Uncle Jacks surprised me with this bad boy."

"It's beautiful. Will you play something for me?"

"Of course," he said, grinning ear-to-ear. "That's part of my surprise."

When he sat on the edge of the bed, Tessa said, "Are you going to sing us a lullaby?"

He laughed a little and placed his hand on her rounded belly. "Something like that."

Tessa nearly melted the moment his fingers magically strummed across the strings. His soulful voice brought tears to her eyes.

After he finished the heartfelt ballad, she said, "That was beautiful, honey. How did you know that was my favorite song?"

"I have my ways." He smiled. "You're welcome, baby."

They talked for hours about their future. It was mostly about baby things. Then the conversation shifted to their wedding. They'd made plans to tie the knot shortly after the twins were born. Finally, they drifted off in each other's arms. Although Tessa slept peacefully, dreaming of their family, Jace slipped into a different kind of dream. It was more like a nightmare.

In his dream, he was on his knees, leaning over Tessa's body as she struggled to breathe. Her face was pale and her eyelids heavy.

"Please, Jace..." She let out a gasp. "Save our sons."

When her eyelids closed, tears fell from his eyes. "Please, Tessa. Don't leave me."

"Jace..."

Tessa's voice seemed miles away as Jace struggled to open his eyes. He felt trapped in a nightmare, reliving Tessa's death over and over. Her words stuck in his head, repeating until he wanted to scream out.

"Jace..." Tessa raised her voice. "Wake up, Jace."

Finally, he released a moan and croaked out, "Tessa..."

"Jace, you're just having a bad dream."

When he managed to get his eyes to open, the first thing he saw was Tessa.

"I'm sorry I woke you."

"It's okay, honey." She pushed a strand of his sweat-soaked hair away from his face. "You sounded like you were having a nightmare. Are you okay?"

He slowly nodded. "I'm fine, honey. It was just a stupid dream."

"You want to talk about it?"

"Nah," he said, waving it off like it was nothing. "Let's just go back to sleep."

"Okay," Tessa said, resting her head on his chest.

The second he wrapped his arm around her, she flinched and looked up at him. "Did you feel that?"

"Are you kidding me?" He placed his hand over her belly. "How could I not? I think my boys are trying out some wrestling moves in there."

"Yeah." Tessa laughed. "It feels like it."

"Just think, babe." He gathered her close. "Only a few more months and we'll have ourselves a little family."

"I can't wait," she said. "We better enjoy our peaceful nights of sleep now. That will most likely change later."

"Yep." He kissed the top of her head. "Our lives are definitely going to change, but I can't wait."

Tessa smiled. "You make me so happy, Jace."

"You too, sweetheart. I would be lost without you."

As silence drifted between them, Jace closed his eyes with good thoughts on his mind. But underneath it all, his nightmare bothered him. He wondered, was it just a bad dream? He prayed to God it was.

Chapter Twenty-One

Before Helen started the ignition, she sat inside her car in the hospital's parking lot with her thoughts in a state of turmoil. What should she do with John Doe? It wasn't safe for him to be in the hospital, especially if he started to glow again. When she finally came back to focus, she realized she needed to notify the Breedline Covenant. Without further delay, she reached inside her purse and dug around for her cell phone. As she searched through her contacts, she found Tim Ross's number and took a deep breath before she made the call.

When Tim answered, Helen told him everything, starting with her recent breakthrough with the Breedline aging cure. Then she explained to him about the years of research she'd been doing on Dr. Hans Autenburg's missing patient called SPECIMEN ONE, and finally getting to the mysterious John Doe.

At first, there was a long silence on the other end of the phone. After Tim processed everything Helen had told him, he finally said, "We need to get him out of the hospital before the news travels about his incident. If in fact this is the same missing patient from years ago, he'll be safer if he's in the Covenant."

Before Helen could respond, she was alarmed when a van tore through the parking lot. As it skidded to a stop, Helen watched as several people piled out with cameras. That's when she realized it was the news media. She had a crushing prescience that something had leaked out about the patient.

"Dammit."

"Is something wrong, Helen?"

"We're too late," she said. "The news media just arrived."

As Helen watched the camera crew gather in the parking lot, she saw Carl heading to her car. He had a look on his face that read trouble. When he came up to the window, Helen said, "Hang on for a minute, Tim."

She rolled her window down. "What's going on, Carl?"

"Somebody leaked information to the news media about John Doe." Carl kept his voice low. "Apparently they think we're keeping an alien in the hospital."

"Shit... what are we going to do?"

"I've got him moved to a different location in the lower wing. But it won't take long for them to discover he's missing. We need to get him out of here."

"I think I know someone that can help us," Helen said, placing the phone back to her ear. "Tim, I need your help."

It wasn't long after Helen ended the call that Tim and Drakon arrived. As they parked their SUV next to Helen's car, there were police cruisers and a crowd of people nearby. As a reporter stood to address a camera, men in uniform blocked the front entrance to the hospital.

Drakon walked up to a guy who stood among the crowd and said, "What's going on?"

When the guy turned toward Drakon, he instantly took a few steps back. It was obvious he was intimidated by Drakon's presence. Although he didn't take it personally. By now, Drakon was used to the reaction.

Finally, the guy managed to get his mouth to work. "They're saying the hospital is keeping an alien inside."

"Hmmm..." Drakon cocked a brow. "Is that right?"

The guy nodded. "Yeah, and I heard they're bringing in some kind of special forces."

"Sounds pretty serious," Drakon replied before he stepped away.

After Drakon relayed the news back to Tim, he said, "We need to get John Doe out of the hospital ASAP."

Drakon crossed his arms. "So, what's our plan?"

"There's no way we can get him out without being seen. We'll need Jem to use a portal to get him out."

Drakon nodded. "I'll call him."

"Thanks, Drakon. I'll let Helen know what's going on."

As Tim moved across the parking lot toward Helen's car, his thoughts drifted to this mysterious patient. What was his story, and where did he come from? While his mind continued to ponder, he wanted answers. Moving a stranger under the same roof as his family made him feel uneasy. Ensuring the Covenant's safety was on the top of his list of priorities. No matter what, he'd take desperate measures to protect his family.

Before Tim explained the situation to Helen, she introduced him to Carl. After he told them how they were going to get John Doe out of the hospital, Helen felt relieved.

"Although I don't like bringing a stranger into the Covenant," Tim said, "I'm going to trust you on this, Helen. Considering the situation, he'll need to be guarded twenty-four seven."

Helen nodded in agreement. "Thank you, Tim."

* * *

Later that night, after meeting Lilith, Thomas escorted Sebastian and Eve to their bedroom. "If there's anything you need," Thomas said, "please don't hesitate to ask. My home is your home."

Sebastian nodded and Eve said, "Thank you, Thomas."

When they went inside, Sebastian noticed Eve looked out of sorts. And that bothered him.

"Eve, is something wrong?"

She recoiled in silence, staring at him—and as much as it pained her, leaving Sebastian was the right thing on so many levels. She knew he was keeping something from her. She could sense it deep down in her gut. To make matters worse, she desperately missed her boys and her sister.

He took hold of her hand and gently tugged her close. "Please, Eve. Talk to me."

In the silence that followed, her heart was breaking. "I want to know the truth, Sebastian. What are you not telling me?"

"I'm trying to keep you from being punished by the Covenant," he said. "I just want a chance for us to be a family."

"What does all that have to do with your brother and Lilith? And what does Thomas want with Arius?"

"Thomas has promised us a safe home to raise our sons," Sebastian began to explain. "In exchange, he wants my help."

"Help to do what?"

"Lilith wants me to bring Tessa here. While I'm in the Covenant, I'll get our sons."

"Why doesn't Lilith just go to Tessa?" Eve's voice was demanding. "Why do you have to take her against her will? I'm sure Tessa would be thrilled to meet her mother no matter what's happened to her."

"You don't understand, Eve. It's not that easy."

"Nothing is ever easy when it comes to you," Eve groaned. "You're not planning on hurting Tessa, are you? She's pregnant, and if she's hurt, I swear—"

"She's not going to be harmed," Sebastian cut her off, using his ability to smooth-talk her.

"You're not going to kill anyone in the Covenant..." Her eyes narrowed. "...are you, Sebastian?"

"No, Eve. I'm not going to kill anyone."

"I swear, if I find out you're being untruthful, I will take my sons and leave you. Do you understand?"

Sebastian stared back at Eve, bewildered. If he'd thought she was seductive before, now she was in goddess territory. Physical beauty was one thing, but having a spine was another. And she had a point, but he wouldn't give up on destroying the Breedline. He would promise only to give her the family she always dreamed of having. He would tell her what she wanted to hear—the half-truth.

"Yes, Eve," he said, promising her a fabricated lie.

His response surprised Eve. "What about Arius's gift? Promise me you're not going to use our son against the Breedline?"

"I promise to make you happy."

She frowned. "You still haven't answered my question."

Sebastian shook his head, knowing she deserved so much better than he could offer her. "I promise, Eve."

* * *

John Doe came awake in an out-of-body, becoming fully conscious, though he felt trapped in some sort of foggy haze. Without the ability to move his arms and legs, and with his lids so heavy they felt glued together, it appeared that his hearing was the only thing functioning. He heard a conversation going on above him. There were two voices. A woman's and a man's, neither of which he recognized.

As the woman kept talking, her voice became familiar. Her tone was like a male's. She sounded direct and authoritative. *But who was she?*

"Thank God we got him out," he heard the woman say. "If it weren't for Jem being able to use a portal, we would have never got him past all those people."

Suddenly, her identity hit him like a slap in the face. It was the physician at the hospital. A human hospital he'd fallen into after... *Shit,* he couldn't remember.

Anxiety shot through his nerves, getting him precisely nowhere. Although he could hear them, still he was immobile. It was clear they'd sedated him. *Oh, God,* he fearfully thought. *Are they going to experiment on me?* He had to find a way out of here... wherever *here* was. He couldn't take the chance if they discovered what he could do.

Moments later, he finally managed to open his eyes. The first thing he saw was a tall woman wearing a white lab coat that had a name tag that read: HELEN CARRINGTON, MD.

"That was a close call, Helen," the man above him said. "What are we going to tell him when he wakes up?"

Helen looked down at the patient. "Well..." she said as she peered down, realizing John Doe had finally opened his eyes. "Looks like someone's awake."

He averted his eyes from Helen and looked to the male wearing a physician's coat that had CARL EAVES, MD. CHIEF OF SURGERY written at the right of the lapel.

Helen noticed the frightened look on his face and said, "Everything is going to be okay. You're in a safe place, and we're here to help you."

Her reassuring words seemed to ease his worried expression.

"If you can hear me," Helen said, "nod your head."

He blinked a couple of times and then nodded.

"That's good." Helen smiled. "It looks like we're starting off in the right direction."

A knock startled John Doe. His head swiveled to the side as the door cracked open. A man with short-trimmed hair popped his head inside and said, "Helen, could I speak with you a moment?"

Helen put a reassuring hand on the patient's arm. "It's all right. Tim is a friend of mine."

The patient looked anxiously between Helen and the man standing in the doorway. Then, to Helen's surprise, his eyes began to glow.

Tim stepped inside the room and froze in the position he stood. Then he swayed on his feet. Before he pitched forward, he braced his hand against the wall and caught himself.

"What the hell..." Tim gasped.

Helen rushed over. "Tim... are you all right?"

He croaked out, "I-I just saw my life flash before my own eyes."

Helen looked to John Doe and said, "Did you do this?"

When he looked up at her, his neural pathways were like strands of old Christmas lights, flickering and shorting out. That's when he realized what had happened. He'd shifted through the poor guy's memories. His eyes softened and his facial expression looked as though he was sorry for what he'd done.

"Helen..." Tim broke the awkward silence. "Can I please speak with you in private?"

She nodded and looked to Carl. "I'll be right back."

When they stepped out of the examination room, John Doe saw a light spilling in from what looked to be a hallway and a huge man with a black Mohawk. His stern face suggested he might like torturing people, and the glare in his eyes made him wonder if he was his next victim. Hoping to avoid his notice, he closed his eyes and tried not to breathe loudly.

Drakon noticed the serious expression on Tim face and said, "Is everything okay?"

"I want everyone in the library for a meeting in an hour," Tim demanded.

When Drakon nodded, Tim looked at Helen and said, "We need to decide what the hell to do with your patient. Somehow, he got inside my head and shifted through my memories. I feel uneasy about this, wondering what other abilities he has. This puts the Covenant in jeopardy. I fear he could be a danger."

"I completely understand," Helen said. "But please, let me get my patient well enough to speak. I promise I'll find out everything we need to know. If I see that he's going to be a potential threat, I can sedate him until we decide what to do."

Tim heaved a deep breath. "If I agree to this, I want everyone in the Covenant to be isolated from him. Is that doable?"

Helen nodded. "Yes, of course."

"Why do I have a feeling," Tim grumbled, "that this is going to come back and bite me in the ass?"

Chapter Twenty-Two

Jem walked out of the meeting with Mia, his mind a complete whirlwind. He couldn't believe what Helen had just told them. Not only had she found the cure to the Breedline aging process, but she also had an unknown patient downstairs with the same genetics of cell regeneration as him and his twin brother Jace.

As Tim explained to everyone in the meeting about John Doe's ability to get into your head—which he'd personally experienced firsthand—he made it clear that no one was allowed to visit Helen's patient until they knew he wasn't a threat.

Jem walked alongside of Mia until they made it to their bedroom. Before he opened the door, she said, "I need to go check on the twins." She raised up on her tiptoes and kissed him. "I'll be right back, honey."

"Why don't you let me go? I think you're due for a break."

"Are you sure?"

He smiled. "Yes, I'm sure, honey."

"Thank you, sweetheart."

Moments later, Jem came up to the twins' nursery. He put his ear to the door before he went inside. So far, no one was crying. He let out a sigh of relief and quietly opened the door. Instantly, he took in the mixture of scents. The nursery smelled of Mia's perfume and baby powder. He slowly made his way to the crib, and when he looked over the lip, Tidus was curled up in a ball sucking his thumb. And he was twice the size. *What the—?*

Finally, he shifted back to focus and noticed Arius was gone. *For Pete's sake,* he feverishly thought. *He's just a baby. Where could he have gone?* He quickly whirled around and searched the room. He looked under the crib, in the closet, and behind a dresser, but unfortunately, Arius was nowhere in sight. That's when his mind took him to a place he didn't want to think of. *Shit!* Had Sebastian taken him?

Without further delay, he scooped Tidus up and dashed through the open doorway and down the hall. When he rushed into the bedroom, he looked at Mia wide-eyed and said, "Arius is gone."

Mia froze. "Oh God—"

Tim and Helen stayed behind after the meeting to answer questions. Tessa was anxious to know when she could take Helen's cure. Already ten years older than Jace, and due to his cell regeneration, she wanted to stop her natural aging process as soon as possible.

"I haven't had time to test it yet," Helen explained to Tessa. "I'll need to make sure it's safe before I give it to anyone."

Jace crossed his arms. "So, who's going to be your guinea pig?"

Helen shrugged. "That's a good question. I guess after all my years of research, I planned to test it on myself."

"Test it on me," a deep male voice said.

When everyone turned to look, they saw Alexander in the doorway with his hands clasped behind his back. "I want to volunteer myself."

Helen looked at him with a disapproving expression. The last thing she wanted was to take a risk on someone else.

Alexander returned Helen's gaze evenly, almost challengingly. "Please, Helen. Let me do this for the Covenant."

Helen turned toward Tim as if she was asking for his guidance.

"If Alexander wants to be the first to take the cure," Tim said, "we should honor his decision. And I commend you for volunteering yourself."

Helen nodded. "Yes, thank you, Alexander."

"I'm honored," Alexander said with a smile. "It's the least I can do for what everyone has done for me. So, when do we start?"

"Can you meet me first thing tomorrow morning, around eight?"

"You can count on me to be there, Helen."

After their discussion, Tim started for the door. The vibration of his cell phone caught his attention. As he retrieved it from the back pocket of his pants, he saw that it was Angel calling. He swiped to answer, "Hello, sweetheart."

"Hi, honey. How'd the meeting go?"

"I'll tell you all about it when I see you. Are you upstairs?"

"I'm downstairs in the kitchen making Natalie's lunch," she replied. "Would you mind popping in her room to check on her?"

"Sure, honey."

He ended the call and headed upstairs. Before he reached to open the door to his daughter's room, he heard her giggling inside. Surprisingly, he could have sworn he heard laughter coming from another child. "What—?"

He quickly opened the door and couldn't believe what he saw. Sitting on the floor next to Natalie was a little boy. He was almost as big as her. The two toddlers were laughing and playing as though they were long-lost pals.

When the little boy looked up at Tim, he smiled. By the color of the child's eyes, and his dark curly hair and pale complexion, he looked to be one of Eve's twin boys, except he had made one helluva growth spurt.

He sat down on the floor facing them and said, "Arius... is that you?"

The little boy's eyes beamed like he acknowledged Tim's question. He scooped the boy in his arms the second he crawled over.

"Look how big you've grown," Tim said.

In response, Arius chortled with glee.

"Arius..." Tim said with a curious look on his face, "...how in the world did you get in here?"

Natalie instantly pointed to the ceiling.

Tim glanced up and then looked back at his daughter, confused. "Sweetheart... are you trying to tell me he came from the ceiling?"

She bobbed her head up and down.

At that moment, something dawned on him. *Could it be that Arius has the ability to create a portal?*

Tim extended his hand to Natalie and said, "Come to Daddy, sweetheart. Let's take Arius to his Auntie Mia and Uncle Jem. I have a feeling they're missing him."

The minute Tim came to Jem and Mia's bedroom, the door was wide open. He could hear Jem and Mia inside, their voices sounding panicky.

Mia clamped her hand over her mouth when she saw Tim standing in the doorway. He had Arius positioned on one hip and Natalie on the other.

"For Pete's sake," Jem said, releasing a sigh. "We've been worried sick. We thought Sebastian somehow got into the Covenant and took him. Where did you find him?"

"He was in Natalie's room," Tim replied. "And I barely recognized him. He looks like he's had a major growth spurt."

"Yeah..." Jem rolled his eyes. "Tell me about it. This little guy..." He gestured toward Tidus, who was snuggled in his arms. "...about gave me a stroke when I saw him. Not only did he turn from an infant to a toddler in a matter of minutes, his brother there has become a little magician. I can't figure out how in the world he got out of the crib all on his own and then ended up in Natalie's room."

Mia came forward and held out her arms to Arius. "How did you get in Natalie's room, honey?"

When Mia took hold of Arius, Tim said, "I think I have an idea how he did it."

"Oh no," Jem groaned. "Please don't say what I think you're about to say."

Mia shrugged. "What are you two talking about?"

Tim focused on Natalie and said, "Sweetheart, tell Uncle Jem and Auntie Mia where Arius came from."

She pointed to the ceiling and giggled.

"You're not saying..." Mia swallowed hard. "...he used a portal, are you?"

"What other explanation do you have?"

"I guess you could be right," Mia said to Tim. "He could have inherited that from Sebastian." She turned to Jem. "And Sebastian is your half brother. You and Sebastian both were born with the same ability. Maybe Arius was born with it too."

"Well, there's one way to find out," Tim said. "We can have Drakon check the security cameras in the twins' nursery and Natalie's room."

Jem cocked a brow. "Ahh... good idea."

* * *

Later that evening, after Helen had satisfied everyone's questions and agreed to let Alexander be the first to test the cure, she went downstairs to check on John Doe. Tim had explained earlier that he would have him moved to the guesthouse where Eve had been staying, along with guards posted outside his door 24/7.

As Helen opened the door and looked in, Carl was sitting by the patient.

"Is everything okay?"

Carl turned to her, and the patient shifted his eyes in the same direction.

"Yes, come on in." Carl's voice sounded eager. "Guess who's talking?"

The patient placed his palms on the exam table and pushed himself up. "Hello." His voice was raspy and sounded a bit weak. "My name is Steven." He held his hand out to Helen. "Steven Pasquale."

Helen's adrenaline suddenly kicked in. She couldn't believe it. John Doe was talking and had a name. She stepped inside and took hold of his hand. "Hello, Steven. It's nice to officially meet you."

Steven nodded and lowered his hand. "Are you... going to experiment on me?"

"Of course not," Helen said. "Your safety is our first priority. But we do have some questions we'd like to ask you, and I'm sure you have some of your own."

For a split second, Steven believed her, which was nuts. He didn't know where he was, and who they were, but for some strange reason, he felt safe here.

With a slight nod, he suddenly felt drained and eased back onto the exam table. He rubbed his eyes. "I feel exhausted."

"That's understandable," Helen said. "Get some rest, Steven. When you wake up, we'll move you to a more comfortable room. And don't worry... nothing bad is going to happen to you here. Consider us the good guys."

* * *

Later that night, as the grandfather clock in the Covenant tolled ten times, the chimes rang out as if they were inside Casey's head. It was yet another familiar sound he heard on a regular basis, but now, as he sat alone in his bed, he couldn't shut his eyes without thinking of his secret. It was almost too much to bear.

He turned to look when his phone on the nightstand vibrated. He grabbed it and instantly recognized the number. He swiped to answer and said, "Hello, Lila."

"Hi, Casey. I hope I'm not calling too late."

"No, no," he quickly replied. "I'm still awake."

"Oh, good. I just wanted to tell you that I'm looking forward to seeing you tomorrow. My family is anxious to meet you."

"Uh... great."

There was an awkward silence.

"Casey... I'm not pushing you to meet my family, am I?"

"No, Lila." He yawned and tried his best to keep it quiet. "You're not. I'm looking forward to meeting them."

She smiled against her phone. "You're already in bed, aren't you?"

"Yeah. How did you know?"

"Your voice. You sound tired."

"Sorry. I haven't been sleeping good lately. And before you ask the question that's on your mind, you might not want to know."

"Huh... I don't want to know what?"

He lightly chuckled. "If I'm wearing anything."

"Oh..." She instantly imagined him naked. "Okay, I won't ask."

"Are you blushing, Lila?"

She laughed, and he loved everything about the sound.

"How did you know?"

"Just a guess."

She laughed again.

"Lila..." He stopped himself when his Theriomorph urges tried to gain control. He closed his eyes and forced the voices out of his head. He didn't want to manipulate Lila. He wanted her to make her *own* decisions without putting suggestions inside her head.

"Casey, is something wrong?"

"No." His eyes popped open. "I was just thinking. So, what time should I come over?"

"Oh, yeah. I almost forgot to tell you. Dinner starts at six o'clock, but you can come over a half hour early."

"I'll see you then," he said. "And Lila..."

"Yes..."

"I'm glad you called."

"Me too."

When Casey ended the call, he closed his eyes with Lila on his mind and didn't sleep at all.

Chapter Twenty-Three

The following morning, Celina paced back and forth, testing her legs out. She went from the Covenant's dining room through the foyer and back again.

As she stopped in front of the grand piano, she thought about Jem and Mia's wedding she'd missed. When she watched it on the video Kyle had made, it was evident Jem and Mia loved each other unconditionally. Her favorite part of the ceremony was when Mia stood at the top of the staircase in her gorgeous gown with Alexander ready to escort her. The song Drakon sang while he played the piano gave her goose bumps. She'd loved to have been there to witness it personally.

Although she never dreamed of a chance to have a future filled with true love, things had unexpectedly changed. Considering what all she'd been through and overcome, there was no reason to have doubts anymore. She'd found Kyle, knowing he was her bonded mate, and that was a future she would cherish.

As she looked out a window at the blue sky, thoughts of her parents came to mind. It would have been wonderful to share her love with those who had brought her into this world. But they were dead—their death brought forth by her evil twin sister, Taliah.

"Breakfast is ready, babe."

Kyle's voice brought her back to focus. She turned and smiled at him.

He tugged her close. "Whatcha thinking about?"

"Oh... I was just thinking about my parents."

He wrapped his arms around her. He didn't know what to say. The reality of her mother and father's death brought back his own sad memories of his family. "Well, babe," he finally said, "you'll always have me."

She gazed into his caring eyes. "And that's enough for me."

"Good." He grinned ear-to-ear. "Because you're stuck with me."

"Hmmm..." She cocked a brow. "I guess I can live with that."

He laughed. "Come on, babe. Let's go eat before breakfast gets cold."

* * *

When Steven Pasquale—formerly known as John Doe—came to again, it was out of a terrifying dream, one in which he remembered back to the horrific experiments he'd endured most of his life. He wasn't sure what was real and what wasn't because his memory had so many holes in it. The blurry images lingered in his head. It was something he'd tried to bury deep in his mind years ago.

As he sat up and looked around, he realized he was in a different room. He hadn't been afraid in a long time, but now he wasn't sure what was to become of him. Were the strangers in this place trustworthy, or were they just like the others from his past?

The smell of food brought him back to focus. As he looked at the nightstand, he noticed a tray on top. He reached over and lifted the lid, and instantly his stomach growled. Then he saw a note by the tray of food and a cell phone.

Steven rose from the bed and glanced at the clock on the wall facing him. It was eight o'clock in the morning. *What? I haven't slept in this late in what seemed to be forever.* He'd spent a big part of his life on the run, moving place to place, worried his former captors would find him.

Maybe this is nothing but a dream, he thought. *Maybe I just fell asleep on a bus.* Surely, when it stopped, he'd open his eyes and laugh about it while he got a cup of coffee at some dive café. He waited, hoping a bump in the road would wake him. Instead, the clock kept ticking through the minutes, and the food continued to draw his attention.

He came back to reality and reached for the note. As soon as he opened it, he was eager to find out who it was from and what it said.

Steven,

When you wake up, please remember you are safe here. We have moved you to a guesthouse that is attached to the main living quarters. We hope you find it more

After he laid the note down, he was tempted to scarf down the breakfast, change clothes, and make a run for it. But why bother? There were probably guards outside the door and most likely hidden security cameras everywhere.

While he ate, he noticed a barrier on the outside of the windows, the panel so thick there wasn't even a tiny bit of light. They were obviously put there to keep anyone from getting in or getting out.

As he sucked down the last drop of his coffee, he went into the bathroom that joined next to the bedroom. When he saw the shower, he stripped out of his hospital scrubs and turned the faucet to warm. As steam built, he stepped inside and stood under the soothing spray.

When he felt completely clean and refreshed, he stepped out and dried off. Next on his list were clothes. He went to the closet and picked random items and quickly got dressed, mentally preparing himself to call Dr. Carrington. Before he made the call, he slipped a straight-edged razor in his pants pocket that he'd found in the bathroom. It was the only thing he could find for protection in case things here started to take a turn for the worse.

With nervous fingers, Steven searched through the phone and found Helen's number. His hand trembled as he waited for her to answer. After a few rings, she answered. He felt relieved after their conversation. Again, her kind voice and reassuring words made him feel safe. Before the physician ended the call, she told him she would be there shortly.

Moments later, Helen arrived at the Covenant's guest-house where she met two guards outside the door. Bruce Carmichael stepped forward and said, "Good morning, Doctor."

"Good morning, Bruce. I'm here to see my patient."

"Aye," he said, cocking a brow. When he unlocked the door, he opened it for her.

"Thank you, Bruce."

"Aye, ma'am."

When Helen moved inside, she waited for Steven to come downstairs.

Steven kept his hand close to his front pocket and his eyes sharp. As he neared the foyer, he noticed Helen by the door.

When he nodded in her direction, she said, "How are you feeling this morning?"

"I'm still a little weak, but much better than before. Thanks for breakfast... and the clothes."

"You're welcome, Steven." She held up her medical bag. "Would it be possible to check your vitals this morning?"

"Yeah." His voice was hoarse. Wearing a baseball cap, not much of his face showed, but his expression appeared exhausted. As Helen ran a clinical eye over him, she noticed his skin was pale, and his hands shook.

"Please." She motioned to the bar in the kitchen. "Have a seat and make yourself comfortable."

With his hand close to the pocket that had the razor inside, Steven measured the distance between them and decided to remain calm and hang tight. He'd defend himself if needed, although he had a sense the physician wasn't going to do him harm. His best bet was to wait and stick around. If he did manage to get free, where would he go? He was tired of being on the run, moving from place to place. It was exhausting. Maybe after it was said and done, they could be trusted.

"Thanks," he said, reaching for a barstool.

Helen followed behind Steven and waited for him to sit down.

"What do you plan to do with me?" Steven said, looking up at Helen.

Helen's eyes softened. "We want to help you, Steven. I also want you to know I'm aware of Dr. Hans Autenburg and what he's done to you. I found his files a few years ago. I know you have the ability of cellular regeneration."

That name came back to him, haunting him from the past. For some ridiculous reason, he wanted to confide in Helen. "Yes, it's true," he wearily said. "He kept me confined since I was a baby. I never knew my real family. And there were others. Some of his captives were like me, and others were different. We were all held prisoner and tortured."

She was surprised Steven disclosed part of his past, which made two of them.

"Thank you for confiding in me, Steven. I want you to know I will keep your personal information confidential. Everyone in this place is nothing like the people from your past. We want to help you and keep you safe. And I'm sure you have questions, and I promise you will have answers. Later, I would like for you to speak with Tim Ross. He's the man you met yesterday in the examination room."

"Are you talking about the man I made upset? I swear, I didn't mean to get into his head. That was an accident. I was frightened."

"Don't worry, Steven." Helen smiled. "Tim is a great guy. You'll like him once you get to know him, and I'm positive he'll befriend you. He just wants to make sure everyone here is safe."

"Thank you, Dr. Carrington."

"You're welcome, Steven. And please, call me Helen."

Steven nodded. "Okay... Helen."

"Can I ask you some questions about the other day, when you read Tim's memories?"

When he nodded, Helen said, "Have you always had the ability to do that?"

"I was born with the gift. I can see your memories or show you mine."

Helen tilted her head. "Would you show me?"

"Are you sure?"

"I'm a scientist," Helen pointed out, "but nothing like Dr. Hans Autenburg. I love to do research and discover ways to make life better for people, but not if it means harming anyone in the process. I'm all about helping others. That's the reason I became a physician."

"I don't know why... but I do trust you, Helen. I can sense you're a good person."

Then Steven's eyes began to glow, and at that very moment, something between them happened. It was like an exchange of memories of some kind. Helen could see visions of his past. All the painful experiments he'd endured by Dr. Hans Autenburg and his colleagues flashed inside her mind. It was almost too unbearable for her to witness, and she'd seen her share of pain. When tears began to trickle down her cheeks, Steven broke the connection.

"Dear God," Helen gasped. "What they did to you... I'm so sorry, Steven."

He looked at her with regret. "I'm sorry you had to see that. But now you know why I have trust issues."

"I don't blame you. No one should be treated the way you were. Do you have other gifts?"

Steven nodded. "I have the ability to heal."

Her brows went up. "That's remarkable. When did you discover you could do that?"

"My first memory is at a very young age. Dr. Autenburg brought in one of his guards with a broken arm. I remember closing my eyes and wishing with all my heart that I could make his arm better."

"Were you able to heal him?"

"Yes. The break in his arm completely healed. But the next thing I knew, I felt this awful pain. I could literally feel my bones breaking. It took hours before I healed. As I got older, the faster my own healing progressed."

"That's amazing, Steven."

"Sometimes I feel like I was born with a curse."

Helen shook her head. "I can understand why. But I believe God gave you this gift for reasons. It's just a shame that others have taken advantage of you. I promise, that won't happen here."

Steven smiled a little. "Thank you, Helen."

"Is Steven Pasquale your real name?"

"It's the only name I've ever known. But I don't have a birth certificate to prove it."

"What happened to Dr. Autenburg's patient? The one he called specimen one?"

Steven sighed. "His name was Jonah Winthrop. Dr. Autenburg found him and his wife Mary in Budapest. They took them against their will. Jonah was like me and his wife was a Lupa."

Helen looked at Steven confused. "A Lupa? Is that like a she-wolf?"

"Yes. Mary's ancestors descended from the old legend of the lycanthrope, except it couldn't be passed on to others like a virus. It's only passed on to their female offspring. Her species is considered very dangerous. That was one of the reasons why Jonah and Mary lived in Budapest, Hungary. They kept themselves deep in the rainforest, far away from humans. When Dr. Autenburg kidnapped them, Mary was pregnant."

"What happened to the baby?"

"Her name is Abigail, but I call her Abbey."

"Were you close to Abbey?"

When Helen saw the sad look in his eyes, she said, "If I'm pressing you too much, please tell me. I don't mean to—"

"No, no," Steven said. "You're fine, Helen. It's just... Abbey was my life. We grew up together. Dr. Hans Autenburg wanted to mix our species, so he kept us together since we were five years old. As we grew up, we fell in love."

"Oh, Steven..." Helen sighed. "Is Abbey still alive?"

He shrugged. "I don't know. We got separated when Dr. Autenburg's research compound was destroyed. But I can sense her energy. I've been searching for her for years."

"How did the research compound get destroyed?"

"It somehow came under attack," Steven said. "When the facility began to crumble, I got to Abbey so we could escape. But she didn't want to leave her father behind, so when she went after him, we were separated and Dr. Autenburg and his men got to them."

"Do you know who attacked the compound?"

"It's hard to explain, but I think it was one of his experiments. I saw her. She said her name was Lilith."

"Lilith?"

Steven nodded. "She was like an angel of some kind, and very powerful. She seemed kind and wanted to destroy Dr. Autenburg and free all the people he kept prisoner. She's the one that told me where Abbey and her father were taken. That's why I'm here. Lilith told me Abbey was brought to Berkeley, California. I will never stop searching for her."

"Maybe we can help you, Steven."

His eyes rounded. "You would do that?"

"I'll talk it over with Tim, but I'm sure he'll agree to do whatever he can to help."

"I'm glad you found me, Helen."

"So am I, Steven." Helen paused for a second. "There are people here... my friends... that have similar cell regeneration as you. I would like you to meet them."

"I would like that, Helen."

She hadn't realized the time until she glanced at the clock in the kitchen. "Darn... I've got to get going. I have an appointment in ten minutes. But I promise I'll be back as soon as I can. We'll talk to Tim about Abbey. You're going to like everyone here, Steven."

"Thank you for everything," he said. "It's been a long time since I felt I could trust someone."

"You're welcome. If you need anything, you have my number. If you can't get a hold of me, and it's urgent, there's a guard outside your door. He's a great guy. His name is Bruce Carmichael."

Steven nodded and Helen waved goodbye.

Chapter Twenty-Four

Angel opened her eyes when Tim shifted onto his side and away from her. A second later, he flipped back over on his stomach. Then he rolled back over, facing the ceiling.

"Have you slept any at all?" she whispered.

"I'm sorry, honey. I didn't mean to wake you."

"You didn't. I was already awake."

He turned toward her. "Can't sleep either?"

"I'm worried about Arius."

"I know, honey." He reached for her hand. "So am I."

"I can't believe what we saw on the security camera in Natalie's room," Angel said. "Never in my wildest dreams would I ever believe a baby could have that kind of power. I mean... Arius can already create a portal. How in the world are we going to keep him from taking off somewhere? He could get hurt, or what if he can't get back and we can't find him."

"I don't know, honey." Tim lightly squeezed her hand. "Somehow we're going to have to figure something out."

"Have you talked to Helen's patient after yesterday's incident?"

"No, not yet," he said. "I figured it would be best if Steven settles in his new surroundings before we overwhelm him. Helen is supposed to check on him this morning."

"You're worried about him, aren't you?"

Tim nodded. "We don't know anything about him. I just want to keep my family and everyone in this Covenant safe. On top of that, we've got to deal with Sebastian."

"Do you think he'll come back for Arius and Tidus?"

"Oh, I don't put anything past Sebastian. If he had the balls to come for Eve, he'll be back for his sons."

"I think the boys are better off with Mia and Jem," she said. "It's great of them to take them in like they did."

"They're good people. I can already tell they're getting attached to the twins. They'll make wonderful parents someday."

"But..." She furrowed her brows. "...aren't they going to keep Arius and Tidus?"

"I don't know, Angel. If Sebastian can't get his hands on the twins, I think Eve will turn herself over to the Covenant. She's not going to live without those boys. If that happens, she'll be tried for her crimes against the Breedline. She won't be punished for life. The council may not give her much time. It could be a few years, or she could get probation since she helped Sarah escape the Chiang-shih demon. Whatever the case, she'll eventually want her sons back."

Angel sighed. "I'm already getting used to them living here, and Natalie seems to adore them, especially Arius. You see how good they play together."

"If Eve does turn herself in, maybe she'll want to stay close to her sister."

"Are you saying you would allow Eve to stay here?"

"I wouldn't have a problem with her living here with the boys, but the decision isn't all up to me. Tessa would have the final say. But considering how much everyone, including her, seems to care for Arius and Tidus, I'm sure she'll agree to let Eve stay here with the boys. And that's if she would even want to live here."

"Eve doesn't have anywhere else to go," Angel said. "She'll need some help."

"Yeah, I can't imagine how she'll manage on her own with two babies."

Angel scooted higher on her pillow. "So, changing the subject, I'm dying to know more about Helen's new discovery."

"Apparently, ever since she discovered Jace and Jem's ability to regenerate their cells, she's been working on a cure to the Breedline aging process. Just the other day, she made a breakthrough. Although it has to be tested first."

"Is Helen going to test it on herself?"

"She was, but Alexander volunteered himself."

Angel's brows lifted. "How romantic."

Tim chuckled. "Why do you say that?"

"Isn't it obvious? Alexander wants to impress Helen."

"Maybe... or he just wants to help out the Covenant."

"If the cure is safe, I want to take it," she said. "How would you feel about it?"

"Well, I guess that means I will have to take it too. I can't have you looking young while I turn into an old codger." He laughed a little. "You might want to trade me in for a younger man."

She laughed. "I love you, sweetheart."

He lifted higher on his pillow and kissed her. "I love you more, honey. Come on, let's get up and make breakfast. Even though it's the weekend, I've got a big day ahead. After I eat, I'm going to visit Helen's patient."

"I'll start breakfast if you check in on Natalie."

"Sounds like a deal," he said. "I'll meet you downstairs shortly."

Before Tim went into Natalie's room, he walked down the hall to the twins' nursery. When he looked in, they were both gone. Just to ease his conscience, Tim knocked on Jem and Mia's bedroom door. Since no one answered, he figured they were already downstairs with the twins.

As he moved down the hall to Natalie's room, he peeped around the door jamb and saw her sitting up in bed petting the cat. For some reason the black, furry feline mostly stayed with Natalie, following her everywhere she went.

"Want some pancakes, sweetheart?"

Natalie snapped her head in his direction and then pointed at Buddy. "Kiddy-tat."

"Does kitty-cat want pancakes too?"

She quickly bobbed her head up and down.

When he moved inside, he scooped her into his arms. "Let's go fix the kitty some pancakes."

As he started to leave, she stiffened in his arms and squealed, "Kiddy!"

"Sweetheart, I'm not carrying the kitty," he said, recalling the last time he'd picked up the cat. It had sunk its claws into his shirt and hung off like a tie. He was not going to repeat that again.

"Don't worry. Kitty will follow us."

Suddenly, the cat meowed and darted for the open door.

Natalie giggled and kicked her feet.

Moments later, as Tim pushed through the door, he was shocked to see the number of occupants already inside the kitchen. Angel and Tessa were behind the stove cooking. Mia was getting something out of the refrigerator. Jem was putting Tidus in a highchair, and Jace was standing beside him holding on to Arius. Drakon and Cassie were placing the dishes and silverware on the table, and Kyle and Celina were making coffee. The sweet smell of pancakes entered his nostrils. "Everything smells delicious," Tim said as he placed Natalie in the highchair next to Tidus.

"I hope you're hungry," Mia said. "We're making blueberry pancakes and sausage."

Tim rubbed his stomach. "I could eat a—"

"Dang!" Jace yelped. "That hurt!"

When everyone turned to look, Arius had just opened his mouth to release the skin on Jace's arm, leaving imprints of little teeth.

Natalie started to giggle.

"Hey, little girl..." Jace drew his brows tight. "...that's not funny."

Mia quickly came to Jace's rescue and took Arius. "I'm sorry, Jace. He's been teething."

"Yeah..." He rubbed his arm. "I can see that."

Kyle burst into laughter and Jem followed in.

"Go on ahead," Jace said. "Laugh it up now. Just wait until my boys are born. I'll teach them to bite you two assholes."

Tessa glared at Jace. "Honey, don't curse in front of the babies."

"Asss-holll..." Natalie mimicked Jace with a giggle.

Tim grumbled, "Good going, Jace."

Jace covered his mouth. "Oops... Sorry."

Angel clapped her hands, drawing everyone's attention. "All right everyone. Breakfast is ready. Let's eat!"

* * *

As Helen walked back to the Covenant's examination room, she glanced down at her watch. It was almost time for Alexander to show.

When she heard someone clearing their throat, she flinched and whirled around.

"I'm sorry, Helen," Alexander said. "I didn't mean to startle you."

"Oh, you're fine." She motioned him inside. "Please, come on in and have a seat."

As he moved inside and sat down, there was an awkward moment of silence. It was as though words hovered in the air between them, things about their relationship they wanted to talk about but didn't. Alexander wanted Helen to look at him more than just a patient. He wanted those eyes of hers going over his skin, not in a clinical way but romantically.

Before she slipped on a pair of rubber gloves, she said, "Have you had breakfast, Alexander?"

"Uh... actually no. I wasn't sure if I should eat before this."

"Neither have I, and you should eat before we get started. I'm sure there's something in the kitchen we could fix."

"Good idea," he said. He stood and held out his hand. "Shall we?"

Alexander watched as she reached out to take his hand. It happened so fast. He grasped her hand and tugged her forward. The element of surprise shocked her into complete surrender. With quick hands, he stripped her white coat off, handling her as gently as he could while her body eagerly obeyed.

Unexpectedly, he took her wrists in one hand and lifted her arms over her head, trapping her against the wall with his body. She gazed into his blue eyes and moaned her approval. Her scent carried the sultry sweetness of a Breedline female who wanted to be touched. Being in this position of passion not long ago, he'd stopped before things went any further, but now, as they got to know one another, he couldn't wait any longer. Alexander wanted her, and going by the lust in her eyes, he knew it wasn't one-sided only.

He stretched his free hand toward the door and pushed it shut. It clicked when he turned the lock.

He finally released her hands and reached to unbutton his shirt. When he shrugged it off his shoulders and bared his chest, Helen noticed a scar that appeared to have been there a long time. The residual marks seemed reduced to a slight discoloration. She ran her hand over it and said, "What happened?"

"I'll tell you later," he replied as he gently undid her hair clip, watching the long waves fall around her shoulders. "Right now, my focus is all about you."

Helen let out a breathless sigh and Alexander swallowed it up with his mouth. "I want you, Helen," he murmured against her lips. "I can't wait a minute longer."

She eagerly nodded, and with shaky hands she unbuckled his belt. He watched as she worked at his zipper. In a matter of minutes, he was standing before her completely naked. All six feet and six inches of nothing but solid muscle. As she took this spectacular specimen of a man in, she was amazed by his muscular physique. And the lower half of him was as impressive as the top.

Alexander looked at her with pleading eyes. "May I undress you?"

His question nearly took her over the edge. "Please..."

Alexander smiled a little as he proceeded to unbutton her blouse while she slipped out of her heels. It wasn't long before he had her undressed, her pink lace bra gone, and her matching panties tossed aside. His body was blazing for her, stimulated by what seemed like forever to be right where he was. To finally be with his beloved.

"You're beautiful, Helen."

She had to catch her breath. There was nothing more attractive to her than when a man was into intelligent women.

He reached out and said, "I want to touch you."

When she nodded a reply, he smoothed his hand down her shoulders. Goose bumps trailed over her skin as he went lower and moved his hand under the swell of her breast.

Moments later, Alexander scooped her off the floor and into his arms. When he placed her on top of the examination table, he looked at her curiously. "Are you sure this is what you want?"

"Yes." Her voice trembled. "I want this. I want you, Alexander."

There was a beat of silence as he gazed into her eyes. "I just want you to know, Helen... I'm in love with you."

Her heart quickened. "I love you too, Alexander."

Embraced in his loving arms, his mouth came down over hers, kissing her with a passion she had never felt before.

The way he touched her, kissed her, made love to her, was like something she'd only read in romance novels. She'd never dreamed men like Alexander really existed until now.

After their passionate lovemaking, Alexander knew it wouldn't be long before her Breedline wolf took over.

"I promise, Helen. I'm not going to leave your side."

The second she nodded an understanding, she felt the prickling of tiny new hairs as they began to surface. Helen closed her eyes and let the transformation take hold. Her features seemed to have a will of their own, stretching and lengthening at an alarming rate.

Alexander placed his hand on her back and stroked over the coarse layer of brown fur that quickly replaced every inch of her skin.

"Open your eyes, Helen." Alexander's tone was reassuring. "You're magnificent, sweetheart."

The moment Helen lifted her lids, she felt her throat open with a howl, but she did not give in to it. Instead, she nuzzled closer to Alexander and let out a light whimper.

"Don't worry, honey." He smoothed his hand through her soft-coated fur. "You're just fine. Whenever you're ready to shift back, just think of your human form."

Moments later, when Helen had willed her human transformation to return, she stared up at Alexander and simply sighed. Words bubbled up inside her. Finally she said, "That was... incredible."

Alexander reached for her hand and laced his fingers through hers. "*You're* incredible, Helen."

She leaned forward and kissed him warmly, pressing her mouth softly to his. As she pulled her lips from his, she said, "I'm famished. What do you say we get dressed and go scrounge up something to eat?"

He lightly squeezed her hand. "That sounds like a wonderful idea."

Chapter Twenty-Five

When Helen and Alexander pushed their way into the kitchen, they hadn't expected to find anyone inside. To their surprise, they came upon a crowd. It was as though everyone in the Covenant was seated around the table. As Helen met Tim's stare, he appeared to be looking at her in a suspicious way.

Helen did a quick check of her clothes, paranoid something was inside out. *Crap!* Realizing her pant leg was rolled up, she shook her leg until it fell back into place.

"Good morning," she finally said.

An awkward silence stretched through the room. As everyone's eyes seemed to zone in on Alexander, Helen turned to look. Her lips instantly formed a smile when she got a closer glimpse of his tousled hair. It never dawned on her to do a double check before they left the examination room.

"Please, have a seat," Angel said, breaking the silence. "We made enough to feed an army."

"You two look famished," Jace said with a clear smirk in his voice. "Have you guys been working out or something?"

"Jace..." Tessa said in a hushed voice and discretely elbowed him in the ribs.

He flinched. "Ouch."

"Ignore the caveman sitting beside me." Tessa motioned Helen and Alexander over. "Please, come join us."

Alexander smiled and came forward. Before Helen sat down, he pulled a chair out for her.

"Thank you, Alexander," Helen said as she settled in.

As soon as Alexander took a seat, Angel handed them a plate and some silverware. Tim passed down the plate of pancakes, and Drakon gave them the dish of sausages.

"Everything smells delicious," Alexander said as he held the plate of pancakes out for Helen. She took one while he forked three.

Angel smiled at Alexander, and Mia said, "Thanks. It's nice to enjoy a big breakfast with everyone."

As they ate, Tessa occasionally looked up from her food and glanced at Helen and Alexander. Finally, she pushed her plate aside. "I don't mean to pry into your business, but..." She paused and focused on Alexander. "Did you take the cure?"

Alexander lowered his fork. "Actually, Helen suggested that I have something to eat first."

When Tessa saw Helen blushing, she instantly knew why. Going by Alexander's messy hair and by the way he looked at Helen and the way she looked at him, it was obvious they'd made love this morning.

Tessa grinned and finally said, "Oh, that makes sense."

Alexander's brows lifted. "Don't worry, Tessa. I'm going to take it right after breakfast."

Tim's chair squeaked as he scooted closer to the table. "Helen, how's your patient doing this morning?"

"He's a little weak but seems to be healing just fine."

"Would it be okay if I stop by to see him today?"

"Yes, of course. Steven was asking to see you earlier."

While Tim engaged in conversation with Helen, Alexander noticed how beautiful she looked when her face grew serious. She flinched as he reached under the table and grasped her hand.

For a moment, she stayed focused on Tim, and then she turned in Alexander's direction and smiled. He lightly squeezed her hand and shot her a flirtatious grin.

As Tim changed the subject and engaged in conversation with Tessa, Alexander leaned in and whispered something in Helen's ear. Whatever he'd said must have been private by the way Helen reacted. Her skin bloomed and her smile widened. Then she nodded and rose from her chair. "Thanks for breakfast, everyone."

Alexander scooted his chair back and stood. "Everything was delicious. Thank you."

Tessa put her hand out when Alexander reached for his plate. "Oh, we'll take care of the dishes." She turned to Jace. "Won't we, honey?"

Jace frowned. "What—"

"I'll pitch in," Celina said.

When Alexander and Helen said their goodbyes and left the kitchen, everyone sat in stunned silence.

Kyle broke through the stillness and blurted, "They hooked up, didn't they?"

Cassie sighed. "I think it's cute. They make a great couple."

"Really, Cassie?" Jace rolled his eyes. "Gross... I don't want to think of my father hooking up."

"It's not gross," Tessa said. "It's great to see them in love."

"We need to invite Helen out for drinks," Mia chimed in. "I want details."

"That's a good idea," Angel spoke out.

Drakon lightly chuckled. "If you're having a girls' night out, we need to invite Alexander out with the guys."

"Yeah, that's an excellent idea," Jem said as he looked to his brother. "Jace, you can plan it."

Jace shrugged. "Why me?"

"Please, honey," Tessa said. "Alexander would like that."

"I'll help too," Tim said. "It would be nice to go out and relax for a change."

Tessa glared at Jace. "And no strip bars."

"Honey..." Jace cocked a brow. "Come on. You know we'd never do that."

Tessa shot him a look. "Uh-huh, sure."

* * *

Later that afternoon, as it drew close to four o'clock, Casey stepped out of the shower and toweled off. Before he got dressed to go to Lila's for dinner, he'd need at least half an hour to rest after he took his dopamine. He sat on the edge of his bed and wrapped a tourniquet around the middle of his biceps. After he'd filled the syringe, it took him a while to find a vein that was viable. Finally, he pressed on the plunger and watched as the drug's clear solution entered his vein.

As he freed the tourniquet, he stared at his arm and thought of Lila. Halfway through the injection, his cell phone went off. A quick glance at the screen showed his father's number. The moment he withdrew the needle and reached for the phone it went straight to voicemail.

He eased back onto the bed and closed his eyes, waiting for the drug to kick in.

After enough time had passed, he could feel the effects. The voices in his head were silenced for now and his body felt numb. If Lila's family got wind of the secret he kept, they would immediately notify the Covenant. The predicament he was forced to live with was something he didn't want. As he rose on shaky feet, he slowly made his way over to the closet.

He rummaged through his clothes until he picked out the perfect outfit. As soon as he finished getting dressed, he checked his voicemail. As he listened to his father's message, his voice sounded troubled.

When he returned his call, his father answered on the first ring. "Please, son, don't go to the Demonts this evening."

"But... why?"

"Casey, you know why."

"Please, father. I've bonded with Lila."

"This will not end well, son. Please take my advice."

There was a long pause and finally Casey said, "Dad, are you still there?"

When there was no answer, Casey knew his father had ended the call.

In the back of his mind, he knew the reason why his father didn't want him to meet Lila's parents, but he didn't care. He was going. No matter how hard he tried, he couldn't stay away from her.

* * *

As the day ticked away, Lila couldn't wait to see Casey. She watched for him to arrive from her bedroom window. She was anxious to introduce him to her family.

"Miss Lila..."

When Lila turned around, a butler stood in the open doorway.

"Dinner will be served in twenty minutes."

"Thank you, Mr. Sims. I'll be down in a minute."

He dipped his head. "Yes, ma'am."

While she watched for Casey's car to pull in the drive, her mind drifted. She thought of the dream she'd had of Casey last night. It was more like a nightmare than anything. In the dream, Casey was in the middle of a forest. Although the darkness and all the fog surrounding him dimmed her visibility, she could still see that he was naked. He was reaching for her and calling out her name. Then the dream shifted into some bizarre realm where nothing seemed to be real anymore. Casey transformed into a giant black panther. She couldn't understand why she would dream such a thing.

Suddenly, the doorbell brought her mind back to focus. Then she saw Casey's silver Maserati parked in the drive.

After a quick mirror check, she rushed downstairs as Mr. Sims was welcoming Casey inside. He was handsome in his designer clothes, looking like he'd just stepped off the runway. His long brown hair was neatly groomed and pulled back with a leather strap.

Lila met him in the foyer and reached for his hand. "I'm glad to see you," she said with a smile. "Thanks for coming."

"Thanks for having me."

Lila gently tugged at his hand. "Come... I'm dying to introduce you to my parents."

Before she led Casey into the dining room, he took a deep breath and straightened his shoulders. When they stepped inside, the smell of food instantly engulfed their senses.

Lila cleared her throat. "Mom... Dad... I'd like to introduce you to Casey Barton."

Her mother came forward and extended her hand. "It's a pleasure to meet you, Casey."

Casey slightly lowered his head and took her hand. "Thank you for having me, Mrs. Demont. Everything smells delicious."

"Thank you, dear." She smiled. "We're glad you could join us, and please... call me Carol."

Lila's father came forward and looked Casey up and down as though he was sizing him up. Finally, he extended his hand. "It's nice to meet you, Casey."

Casey nodded and took his hand in a firm handshake. "Thank you, sir."

When the butler finished setting up the table, Victor smoothed his hand over his goatee then motioned for everyone to sit down. "Please, let's eat."

As Casey slowly polished off everything on his plate, he had a sinking feeling in his gut. He wondered to himself if her parents approved of him so far.

An hour later, as the butler cleared the table and took their plates to the kitchen, Casey's nerves were on pins and needles.

"Would anyone care for dessert?" Carol said. "I made a homemade peach cobbler."

"No thank you," Casey said, patting his stomach. "Everything was delicious, but I'm full."

Victor cleared his throat. "I'll have a small piece, honey."

Carol reached out and placed her hand on Lila's. "Would you like some cobbler, dear?"

"No thanks, Mom. I couldn't eat another bite."

As the butler served Victor and Carol, he poured Lila and Casey a fresh cup of coffee.

When Victor finished his dessert, he wiped his mouth and said, "Casey, I met your father this afternoon." He looked at Casey with a narrow stare. "We had an interesting conversation over lunch."

Chapter Twenty-Six

Sebastian relaxed in a wingback chair covered in plush, dark velvet in the formal dining room of his brother's estate. Surrounded by stylish, wealthy furnishings, he admired the tasteful artwork that hung above the fireplace mantel. Swaths of beautiful damask drapery that was fringed with gold satin ran from the floor to the ceiling. In their lush splendor, they reminded him of his father's magnificent castle in Paris.

After the Zadkiel—the archangel of forgiveness—freed his father of the Chiang-shih demon's possession, and the Breedline took over the castle, Sebastian missed the elegance of that life. Now living in his brother's mansion, he enjoyed the lavish lifestyle again. He reached out and stroked one of the drapes. It felt thick and substantial, with nothing cheap about it. It made him desire a home of his own and for his family. Soon he would have his sons, and that was all the motivation he needed.

Sebastian looked up when he heard someone talking. As the voice grew near, he snarled his upper lip, realizing who it was. Samuel Mercier entered the dining room with a cell phone to his ear. When he ended the call, he glanced up and saw Sebastian. "Oh... I'm sorry. I didn't realize anyone was in here."

Sebastian shifted in his chair. "I need you to do something for me."

"Of course." Samuel bowed his head. "I'm at your service."

"I need you to find out how many Breedline reside in the California Covenant."

"That's going to be a problem." Panic resonated from Samuel's voice. "I cannot go back there. The Breedline have a warrant out for my arrest. If they catch me, they'll lock me up for treason."

"Just figure something out," Sebastian grumbled. "Work around it."

Samuel remained silent, looking between Sebastian and the doorway in desperation, like a dog that needed to pee. It was evident he equally feared Sebastian as much as he hated him.

Finally, he nodded. "Yes, sir."

Sebastian despised weakness, and Samuel reeked of it. "Well, don't just stand there." He pointed to the door. "Get on it!"

Samuel almost tripped over his own feet as he scurried out of the room.

Sebastian rose to his feet and moved toward the French doors. As he looked over the groomed landscape, his brother's voice came from behind. "Lilith wants to speak with you."

Sebastian wheeled around. "Right now?"

Thomas nodded. "It's important."

"Do you know what it's about?"

"It's about your sons." Thomas motioned him over. "She's in the study. I'll escort you there."

As they headed to the study together, Sebastian wondered what his sons had to do with Lilith. He looked at Thomas as they came to a set of double doors and thought, *Did he reveal to her Arius's powers?*

Thomas tapped on the door before he opened it. Sebastian walked in first and looked at all the rows of shelved books and antique clocks from grandfathers to brass windups. He found the ticking sounds distracting and irritating.

"Please, sit," Lilith said as she motioned toward the chairs across from hers. "Make yourself comfortable."

As Sebastian slowly came forward, he couldn't take his eyes off Lilith's hypnotizing gaze. Her eyes sparkled like diamonds against her brilliant features. The way her skin glowed, it was like looking at an angel without wings. His eyes continued to scan over her ghostly form as he sat down next to Thomas.

Lilith focused on Sebastian. "I have some information regarding your sons." Then she tossed a velvet bag to him.

Sebastian opened it and retrieved the gold pendant inside. "What's this?"

"It's a relic medallion."

He tilted his head. "What's it for?"

"A powerful Wicca has placed a binding spell to protect the Breedline Covenant," Lilith explained. "It keeps anyone from using a portal to get in or out. This pendant will give you access inside. The Covenant also has Guardians who reside there. It will keep them from detecting you."

After Sebastian placed the pendant around his neck, he looked toward Thomas, noticing he had one around his. "I take it you're going to help."

Thomas nodded. "I'll get Tessa while you get your sons."

"You do realize Tessa is pregnant," Sebastian said. "She's not going to go willingly."

"She is not to be harmed," Lilith demanded. "Thomas will give her a sedative that will not harm her or my grand-children."

"What about everyone in the Covenant?" Sebastian said. "How in the hell are we supposed to get close to Tessa without running into someone?"

"We'll go in while they sleep," Thomas said. "The medallion will keep us from being seen. It's like..." He paused as though he was trying to think of the right word. "...having our own visibility shield."

Lilith narrowed her stare. "I've got one more task for you to complete. My son is also residing in the Breedline Covenant. He is in the guest quarters. Bring him back with Tessa."

Sebastian held up a halting hand. "Now wait one damn minute. This is getting risky. How in the hell do you expect me to retrieve my sons while Thomas sedates Tessa... and now you want us to sneak inside the guesthouse and get someone else?" He shook his head. "No can do."

Thomas quickly stood and placed his palm on Sebastian's shoulder. "Don't worry, brother. It won't be a problem. I've got a plan."

* * *

After breakfast, Helen gave Alexander the injection for the cure. She'd kept her fingers crossed and hoped it was a success. Meanwhile, Alexander led Helen upstairs to his room.

When he opened the door for her, his Breedline instincts kicked in. He tugged her close and said, "I want to kiss you."

She gazed up into his gorgeous blues. "So do I."

In all his forty-some years, Alexander had never expected to feel this way with anyone. When it came to Helen, he was like a weak-kneed virgin all over again. It seemed all he could do was stare at her beautiful face.

"So, are you going to kiss me or not?"

Smiling like a bashful teenager, he cupped her chin and whispered, "Sorry, I was just admiring your beauty. I can't seem to get enough of you."

Helen's knees nearly buckled. She felt weak in his presence.

Overcome by desire, he gathered her close and pressed his lips to hers.

After another round of passionate lovemaking, Alexander held Helen in his arms. As he cuddled her, he'd never felt more satisfied. His life's purpose never seemed so clear as it did at this very moment. Now, his priority was to keep her happy and safe. She made him feel whole again.

When Helen let out a contented sigh, he snuggled her closer and stroked her arm. Out of nowhere, he found himself thinking, for no good reason, about a lifetime commitment with her. As far as he was concerned, Helen was already his life mate. She had given him her trust, and he had turned over his heart in return.

Alexander cleared his throat. "Helen... have you ever thought about getting married?"

Her eyes softened. "Yes, but I never thought marriage was for someone like me."

He frowned. "Why would you think that?"

"I've always dedicated my life to medicine, and I'm not exactly the type that stands out among other women, so..."

Alexander reached out and tenderly lifted her chin. In the silence that followed, she could only guess what was going through his mind. The idea that he pitied her made her want to do something to prove she was okay with the person she was.

Abruptly, he lowered his hand and rose out of bed.

"Where are you going?"

He held up a halting hand. "Hold on, sweetheart. I'll be right back."

Moments later, he returned with a mirror in his hand. He held it in front of her. "Helen, look at yourself. Don't you see what I see?"

She stared at her image and shook her head.

"Not only are you intelligent... you're beautiful, sweetheart."

She smiled, and her cheeks turned pink. "Do you really think that?"

"Are you kidding me?" He lowered the mirror. "Sweetheart, you're perfect in my eyes."

She looked up at him and never felt more desirable in her life. She loved that he adored her for what she was. She swallowed the knot that had formed in the back of her throat and said, "Alexander, will you make love to me again?"

He grinned. "Honey, you never have to ask that question twice."

Later that evening, when Helen finally emerged from Alexander's bedroom, she went downstairs to escort Tim to the guesthouse. She needed to check on Steven, and Tim had questions concerning the safety of the Covenant.

When Bruce escorted them inside, Steven had just come downstairs.

"I hope you're feeling like company," Helen said. "I have someone here to see you."

As Tim came forward with his hand extended, he said, "Look... I know we got off on the wrong foot, but I want you to know you're welcome to stay here as long as you need."

Steven reached out and shook his hand. "Thank you, Tim. I was hoping we could start over. And I promise, this time, I won't get into your head."

Tim nodded. "That sounds like a good idea."

Helen moved forward and ran a clinical eye over him. "Your coloring seems better. How are you feeling, Steven?"

He smiled at her. "Much better. Thank you, Helen."

Tim cleared his throat. "Steven, do you mind if I ask you some questions?"

"Yes, of course."

"Do you remember anything about your incident and who shot you?"

"I do recall partial glimpses of faces and a run-down hotel. One of them was Dr. Markus Ludwig. He sent his men to take me prisoner. I'd die before I went back to that place. So, I had no choice but to defend myself. In the process, I killed the physician and most of his men. The last thing I remember is someone attacking me and then a gun going off. After that, I remember waking up on Helen's examination table."

"I don't blame you," Tim said. "You did what you had to do."

"Thanks for understanding. I'm sorry I didn't tell you before. I wasn't sure how you'd react."

Helen cut into the conversation and said, "Steven, I hope I wasn't overstepping my boundaries, but I told Tim about what you showed me. I thought it was for the best in order to help you find Abbey."

"It's okay, Helen. I understand, and I'm grateful for everything you've done for me."

"Going by what Helen's told me," Tim said, "it sounds like you've been through hell. And I want to do everything I can to help, but we need more information to do that."

Steven shrugged. "What do you suggest?"

"Show me your past. Like you did with Helen."

"Are you... sure?"

Tim nodded. "This time, you have my permission."

Chapter Twenty-Seven

In stunned disbelief, Casey stared across the table at Lila's father. He was taken back by what he had just said. His mouth parted, but he was lost for words. *Surely, my father wouldn't have revealed to Mr. Demont about my secret,* Casey feverishly thought.

There was something about the look in Victor Demont's eyes that struck a chord within him. Without warning, Casey's Theriomorph side plastered through the dopamine and shot through his body in an instant. Then Victor's mind opened up and Casey got a glimpse inside his head. He felt a sea of raw emotions radiating from Victor's subconscious. The biggest one was guilt.

All at once, the emotional grids of every single person sitting at the table popped into Casey's head. Mrs. Demont was thinking of horses. Evidently, she'd made plans to visit the country next week to go horseback riding. Lila, on the other hand, was thinking of something entirely different. She was thinking of a strange dream she'd had about him. In the dream, she saw him shifting into a giant panther. *Shit!*

Suddenly, everything surrounding Casey shifted. He drowned out all the voices and focused on Victor's thoughts. Although Casey was relieved when he realized Victor had no idea of his secret, he was distraught by what he'd discovered. Victor was thinking of a woman, and it wasn't his wife. Casey's eyes rounded when he saw images of his mother inside Victor's head. *Why was Victor thinking of my mother?* It seemed as if he was grieving over her death like someone does when they're in love.

Shortly after, the voices started to fade. Juicing up his Theriomorph side was an engine that, once it got going, was hard to stop.

"Your father speaks highly of you," Victor finally said, bringing Casey back to focus. "He seems quite proud of you, Casey."

"My father is too kind, but I have to say... it's nice to hear those words." Casey smiled a little. "Although I give my parents all the credit. My father has been a great role model, and my mother…" He paused and swallowed. "My mother was a wonderful person. No one could ever compare."

Lila put a comforting hand on Casey's arm, and Mrs. Demont said, "Everyone adored your mother, Casey. She was so kind. She will be dearly missed."

Casey nodded. "Thank you, Carol."

Victor cleared his throat and rose from the table. "If everyone would please excuse me, I think I'd like to retire for the evening."

"But, dear…" Mrs. Demont looked at her watch. "It's not even eight o'clock."

"Yes, I know it's early, but I seem to have developed a headache." He averted his eyes from his wife and looked at Casey. "You don't mind, do you, Casey?"

He shook his head. "Of course not, sir. Thanks for inviting me into your home. It was nice to meet you."

"You're welcome." Victor moved next to Casey and extended his hand. "It was a pleasure."

As Casey shook his hand, Victor leaned in close and said in a low voice, "Meet me for lunch tomorrow at Vito's. I need to speak to you about something private."

Casey nodded in silence.

Before Victor excused himself, he turned to Lila and kissed her cheek. "Don't stay up too late, sweetheart."

"I won't. Good night, Daddy."

After Victor left the dining room, Lila said, "Mother, would you please excuse us? I'd like to show Casey the patio before he leaves."

"Of course, darling. Would you like me to have Mr. Sims bring you some sweet tea?"

"Thank you, mother. That would be nice."

"Thank you for dinner, Carol," Casey said. "Everything was delicious."

"We're delighted to have you, honey. You must visit us again."

As Lila escorted Casey to the patio, he wondered what her father wanted to talk about. And did it have something to do with his mother?

For a moment, Steven simply stared off into the distance. He knew there was no getting out of Tim's request. He was going to have to show him the nightmares of his past. It was something he hated to dredge up, much less share with someone else.

In an instant, Steven connected with Tim's conscious mind. The images he shared almost brought Tim to his knees. It was horrifying to see what Steven had endured. All the torture... all the pain... and all the suffering. Finally, when Steven severed their connection, Tim shook his head. "My God..." He gasped. "I'm so sorry, Steven."

"Believe me," Steven sighed. "I wish you didn't have to see that."

"How long have you had this ability?"

"I was born with it."

"So, you think the people who attacked you will send others?"

Steven nodded. "They'll never stop searching for me."

"You're welcome to stay here," Tim said. "I think it's the safest place for you. I'll do some digging on the physician you mentioned. Is there another person linked to this Dr. Ludwig?"

"He had two colleagues: Dr. Hans Autenburg and Dr. Hubert Crane."

Tim narrowed his eyes. "I'd bet everything those bastards are backed up by an underground organization."

"You think someone is funding their research?" Helen queried.

"There's no doubt," Tim replied. "And I bet it has something to do with the government."

"So..." Steven looked between Tim and Helen. "What do we do?"

Tim placed his hand on Steven's shoulder. "You must be on overload by now. As soon as I find something useful, I'll let you know. But for now, get some rest."

"Thank you, Tim."

Tim lowered his hand. "You're welcome. If there's anything you need, don't hesitate to ask."

"He's right, Steven," Helen said. "You have our numbers listed in the phone I gave you."

When Tim and Helen left, Steven thought about what was waiting for him on the outside. No matter where he hid, they always found him. Even though he didn't want to go into the past, Steven couldn't stop himself. He went back to what had been done to him, recalling all the painful experiments he went through. If he were faced with that life again, he would do the same thing he'd done before—*kill.*

* * *

As soon as Jace drifted off to sleep, darkness engulfed him and took him to a place of hell.

"No," Jace cried out, pain tearing through his heart. He fell for what seemed like an eternity until he finally dropped to his knees. The horror of his nightmare unfolded as it always did, and yet it was as fresh as the first time it had come to him. As he reached for Tessa's lifeless body, he saw blood on his hands. Her blood...

"Tessa!"

Jace's outburst instantly woke Tessa. After she quickly switched on the lamp, she shook his shoulder. "Jace... wake up, honey. You're having a bad dream."

When he opened his eyes, he tugged off the blankets to look at his hands. "There was so much blood," he gasped with his hands close to his face.

Tessa reached out to him. "It was just a dream, Jace. There's no blood."

He shifted his eyes from his hands and looked at her face. "I'm so sorry." He let out a deep breath. "I didn't mean to wake you."

"Honey, don't apologize." Tessa smoothed her hand over his shoulder. "You okay?"

He wound his arms around her and held her close. "I love you, Tessa."

"Ah, honey... I love you too."

Finally, she pulled from his embrace and reached for the blankets he'd kicked off. She slipped underneath them and re-covered him. "That must have been some nightmare. You sounded terrified, honey. That's the second one you've had. Do you want to talk about it?"

"Let's just go back to sleep."

Tessa turned off the light and snuggled next to him. "Good night, honey."

"Good night, Tessa."

As much as Jace tried, he couldn't shut his eyes. He battled with idea of telling Tessa about his recurring dreams. He turned his head and gazed at her beautiful profile. He loved the changes in her body and the extra glow she'd gained from the pregnancy. Tessa took his breath away. That's when he decided not to tell her. He didn't want her stressed, especially in her condition. He moved his hand to her rounded belly and softly caressed the taut skin. Instantly, images of his unborn sons came to mind. He wondered how it would be to finally hold them in his arms. The thought made him smile.

"That feels good, honey."

"I'm sorry, Tessa. Did I wake you again?"

She turned toward him. "No. I couldn't sleep either. I was thinking."

"Thinking of what?"

"What it will be like to hold them for the first time."

Jace lifted his head a little and reached for her hand. "I was just thinking the same."

Tessa smiled. "Really?"

"Yeah." He laughed a little.

Then, after few moments of silence, he said, "Tessa... can I ask you something."

"Of course, honey."

"Do you think I'll be a good father?"

"You're going to be an excellent father. Why would you ask that question?"

"I don't know." He thought for a minute. "I guess I'm just worried."

"Jace, stop worrying. You're going to be just fine. I promise."

He lightly squeezed her hand. "Have I told you lately how much I love you?"

"All the time. And I never grow tired of hearing it."

"Good, because I'm going to tell you at least a hundred times a day. Tessa, I don't know what I'd do without you. You're everything to me."

"You make me the happiest woman in the world, honey," she murmured. "I love you to the moon and back."

"Everything is going to be okay, isn't it?"

"Yes, Jace. I don't want you to worry. I'm fine, and the babies are fine."

When Tessa pulled her hand from his, she reached to the necklace around her neck. After she unfastened it, she sat up and said, "I want you to have this."

Jace reached for the lamp on his side and switched it on. As he turned to look at Tessa, he saw the necklace in her hand.

"But, sweetheart, your father gave it to you." He shook his head. "I can't except that."

"Please, Jace." Her eyes softened. "It would mean a lot to me if you wore it. Look at it this way. Something dear to me will always be close to your heart."

He sighed. "Oh, Tessa..."

"Please, Jace. Take it. For good luck."

He finally took the necklace and fastened it around his neck. After he positioned the gold cross in the center of his chest, he smoothed his fingers over the top. Then he looked at Tessa with tears in his eyes. "You'll always be close to my heart. Thank you, babe."

She smiled. "You're welcome."

He kissed her and turned off the light. "Let's get some sleep."

Ten minutes later, Tessa was out like a light, cuddled next to him. As Jace listened to the soft sounds of her breathing, his mind took him to the beginnings of their relationship. It had been a rough period for them both. The memories bore down on him like a tangible weight. During the time Tessa was abducted by Sebastian, it nearly killed him not knowing if she was were dead or alive. But then, she came back to him safe and sound. She'd shown so much courage after what she'd gone through. Tessa was strong. Stronger than anyone he'd ever met. Now, he wanted to be strong for her. Maybe he should confess the dreams he was having to someone other than Tessa. That's when Helen came to mind. She had counseled many of the Breedline, and she was someone he trusted. *Yeah,* he thought. His mind was made up. First thing tomorrow, he'd give her a call.

The next morning, Jace's eyes popped open when he heard a faint cry. It was coming from the hallway. He nudged Tessa. "Honey, did you hear that?"

Tessa opened her eyes, and before she could reply, a loud cry came from the hallway, followed by the murmur of voices.

"That sounds like Angel," she said.

As Jace shot out of bed, he slipped and nearly face-planted on the floor. He caught his bearings and grabbed his pants. While he pulled them up, Tessa slipped into a robe.

As soon as Jace zipped his pants, he shot out the door, with Tessa following close behind. They were surprised to see the crowd of people standing outside Natalie's bedroom. Tim held Angel in his arms while she sobbed in his embrace.

Jace came forward. "What's going on?"

"It's Natalie and Arius," Tim said. "They're missing."

"Oh no," Tessa gasped. "Surely, they couldn't have gotten far."

Angel looked at Tessa in desperation. "We've looked everywhere, Tessa."

"Jem's outside right now searching the grounds," Mia said as she held Tidus in her arms. "We think Arius used a portal and took Natalie."

Jace placed his hand on Angel's shoulder. "Don't worry, Angel. I'm sure they're somewhere outside. I'll go help Jem look for them."

Angel nodded. "Thank you, Jace."

Before Jace made it downstairs, he heard Jem's voice coming from there.

Chapter Twenty-Eight

When everyone went to look over the stair railing, they saw Jem by the door holding on to Natalie's little hand and Arius snugly nestled against his hip. Both toddlers were covered from head to toe in mud.

Angel covered her mouth and mumbled into her hand, "Oh, thank God."

Tim put his arm around Angel. "They're safe and sound, honey."

Mia sighed a relief as tears trickled down her cheeks. "Oh, Arius..."

Jace looked at Angel and smiled. "See... I told you they had to be somewhere outside."

Tessa came up to Mia and held her hands out to Tidus. "Here, let me take him while you go get Arius."

Mia wiped her eyes and placed Tidus in Tessa's arms. "Thank you, Tessa."

While everyone headed downstairs, Angel was the first one to rush over to Jem.

Natalie's eyes were huge in her small face as she recognized her mother's worried expression. Her thumb immediately went to her mouth.

Angel reached for Natalie and enfolded her in her arms. "Oh, sweetheart. How in the world did you get so dirty?"

Jem chuckled. "I found them playing in a mud puddle."

"Yucky..." Natalie crinkled her nose and held out her muddy hands.

Tim came up next to Angel and kissed Natalie's forehead. "Young lady, you had us worried to death."

Mia took Arius in her arms and said, "Just look at you. You're filthy."

Unaware of the trouble he'd caused, Arius simply giggled.

Jem shook his head. "What are we going to do with you, little man?"

Arius nestled his head in the crevice of Mia's neck and murmured, "Ma-ma."

"Oh, sweetheart..." Mia kissed the top of Arius's head. "You make it impossible for anyone to be upset with you."

"I think we need to come up with a plan," Tim said. "Now that Arius can take another person with him through a portal, we need to figure out how we can keep this from happening again. Next time, he might go further from the Covenant."

Jace crossed his arms. "Good luck with all that."

Suddenly, their attention was drawn toward the stairs as Drakon and Cassie moved in their direction. Cassie's hair was still wet as though she'd recently showered.

"Did we miss something?" Drakon said, noticing everyone gathered around Natalie and Arius, who were covered in mud.

"Yeah..." Jace laughed a little. "Jem found those two varmints outside playing in the mud."

Cassie's eyes rounded. "How did they manage to get outside?"

"Arius used a portal and took Natalie with him," Jem replied.

Drakon's eyes rounded. "Are you serious?"

Jace pointed at the two mischievous toddlers. "Well, just look at them. All that mud should answer your question."

Drakon shook his head and Tim said, "We've got to come up with a solution. Drakon, do you have any suggestions?"

Drakon rubbed a hand over his short-trimmed Mohawk. "Man, I don't know. I'll have to think on this one."

Angel cut into the conversation and said, "I think it's time for someone to take a bath."

Mia nodded in agreement, eyeballing Arius. "Yes, I think that's a good idea."

* * *

Later that afternoon, Jace headed toward the examination room. When he approached the facility, the door was open. Helen was sitting in front of Alexander, getting a blood sample, when she noticed Jace looking in.

He stepped back a few steps. "Oh, I'm sorry. I can come back if you're busy."

"I've just got to get one more sample," Helen said. "What can I help you with, Jace?"

"I just wanted to talk to you about something." He held up a hand. "But I can wait in the hall."

"You can wait inside," Alexander said. "I don't mind."

"Are you sure?"

"Please..." Alexander motioned him in. "Come on in. Have a seat, Jace."

When Jace stepped inside, he found a chair next to the door. There was an awkward silence after he sat down.

"So, how's Tessa?" Helen said, breaking the tension in the room.

"Oh, she's fine," Jace replied. "I'm trying to make sure she gets plenty of rest."

"That's good. She needs to take it easy for the next few months."

"Tessa's going to be a wonderful mother," Alexander said. "And you're going to be a great father, Jace."

Jace smiled. "Thanks."

"Okay," Helen said, patting Alexander's hand. "I'm all done. I won't need another blood sample until the end of the month."

Alexander gave her a grateful look as he rolled his sleeve back down. When he rose to his feet, he moved toward the door. Before he left the room, he winked at Helen and waved at Jace. "I'll see you later, Jace."

Jace waved back. "Later."

When the door clicked shut, Helen rolled her chair toward Jace and sat down, facing him. "So, what brings you here?"

He brushed a hand through his long hair and sighed. "I've been having these strange dreams."

Helen cocked her head. "What kind of dreams?"

"They're about Tessa. In the dreams... she's dying."

Helen paused, with her eyebrows clenched, collecting her thoughts not only from a medical standpoint but a personal one too.

"How long have you been having these dreams?"

"They started when I found out Tessa was pregnant. They stopped for a short period, and now they're back."

"Have you told her?"

Jace shook his head. "I'm afraid it will upset her. I don't want—"

"You've got to be honest with her, Jace," Helen said. "Keeping secrets from your mate isn't a good idea."

He shrugged. "But what if..."

As Jace's voice trailed off, Helen placed her hand over his. "She'll be just fine. Tessa is strong-willed. Tell her."

Jace reached up and smoothed his fingers over the cross necklace. "Yeah, you're right. She is strong." He smiled. "I'll tell her."

Helen lightly squeezed his hand. "I think this is just nerves talking. You're about to be a father. It's natural to be worried. If you need help with anything, my door is always open."

"Thanks, Helen."

Before Jace got up to leave, he said, "Can I ask you something?"

Helen nodded. "You can ask me anything."

"How are you and Alexander getting along?"

Helen's eyes brightened. "Everything is great. He's a good man, Jace. And I don't mean to pry into your business, or tell you what to do, but you should try to spend more time with him. He's your biological father. Once you get to know him, you'll see."

"Yeah, maybe I'll do that."

"I know Alexander would be thrilled to get to know you."

He narrowed his eyes. "You really think so?"

"Yes, I know he will. Just give him a chance."

He inhaled sharply and Helen could see the wheels turning furiously in his mind. His indecision was written all over his face, but she also saw the moment acceptance registered.

"Thanks for all your help, Helen."

"Anytime, Jace."

Chapter Twenty-Nine

The following afternoon, Casey descended the curving staircase, preparing to meet Lila's father for lunch. With each step, all he could think of was his mother's death. His memories brought back the day of her funeral.

When he'd entered the funeral home, the scent of her favorite flowers and vanilla candles lingered deep in his nostrils. He wondered how long it would be before he got that smell out of his sinuses every time he inhaled. Feeling sick to his stomach, and not wanting to deal with her death, he was desperate to leave. But instead, he faced his fears. Moments later, he composed himself enough to pay his mother the respect she deserved. As he neared her closed coffin, his nerves were pins and needles. It brought back the horrible memory of how she died. She'd been murdered at the hands of the Chiang-shih demon's death army. Then his thoughts went to a better place. To the place where they used to live. Colorado was beautiful, and he remembered how much his mother loved the snow. Whenever it fell at night, she would turn off all the lights and stare out the window for hours. God... he missed those childhood memories. After her funeral, the days had seemed to pass by in a blur.

Although Casey was curious to find out what Victor wanted to talk about, he was more interested in why he was thinking of his mother during dinner the other night. He also wondered why Victor had met with his father for lunch. He'd never heard his father speak of the Demonts before. Sure, they knew one another because of the Covenant, but they never socialized. Casey frowned as he glanced at his watch. In less than an hour, he'd be sitting across a table from Lila's father. This time, he skipped his dopamine injection. Casey wanted to be able to get inside Victor's head and read his thoughts. It was the only way to find out why his mother was so important to Victor.

A half hour later, Casey entered the restaurant to meet with Victor. As the waitress escorted him to the table, he was shocked to find it empty. When he looked toward the restroom, he saw Victor talking on his phone. Casey exhaled a deep breath and sat down and ordered a glass of wine.

Ten minutes later, Victor strode toward the table in an expensive pin-striped suit and a blue silk tie. "I'm sorry I kept you waiting," Victor muttered in an apologetic tone. "I had an important phone call I had to take."

"Don't worry about it." Casey waved it off like it was nothing. "It's fine."

Victor took a seat and shot Casey a fake grin. "Thank you for being so understanding."

Casey reached for his glass of Chardonnay. "So, what did you want to talk to me about?"

Victor leaned back in his chair and crossed his legs. "Can I ask you something personal?"

Casey instantly brought forth his Theriomorph side and burrowed into Victor's thoughts. What he saw was like looking at a projection screen as Victor's mind displayed his memories. Victor was sobbing as he knelt in front of his mother's coffin. The words Victor babbled didn't make any sense. He called his mother... his *beloved*.

"Casey..." Victor raised his voice. "Did you hear me?"

His voice snapped Casey back to reality. "I'm sorry... what did you say?"

"I would like to ask you a personal question." Victor's voice sounded arrogant. "That is, if you don't mind."

"Uh... sure," Casey muttered.

"Have you bonded with my daughter?"

"Yes, I have."

"I don't think it would be a good idea for you to court her."

Casey furrowed his brows. "Why? Am I not good enough?"

"No, no," Victor said. "That's not the issue. It's just I—"

Casey cut him off and said, "How well did you know my mother?"

Victor's eyes rounded. "What... why would you ask me that?"

"I saw you at the funeral. You were on your knees sobbing. Why did you call my mother your beloved?"

Victor's mouth dropped. "Dear God... I thought I was alone."

* * *

Jace averted his eyes from the computer screen and looked at the clock on the wall. It was time to call it quits. Later tonight he had plans with Tessa to meet her father for dinner. He'd also taken Helen's advice and invited Alexander. After he logged off his computer, he left his office and took the elevator to Jem's department. As he stepped out, he rounded the corner and tapped on Jem's office door.

"It's open."

Jace opened the door and poked his head in. "Hey, I'm heading out."

"Try to behave yourself tonight."

Jace smirked. "Whatever..."

"Hey, wait."

When Jace popped his head back in, Jem said, "Have a good time. I'm glad you're giving Alexander a chance."

Jace grinned. "What can I say?" He shrugged. "I'm a nice guy."

Jem rolled his eyes. "Later."

Jace waved. "Later, bro."

As Jace and Tessa arrived at her favorite restaurant, the waiter escorted them to the outside patio. The moment they saw Kenneth and Alexander sitting in the far corner, Tessa waved at them. Kenneth waved back and motioned them over.

Kenneth rose and kissed Tessa on the cheek as soon as they made it to the table. Then he shook Jace's hand and said, "Thanks for inviting me to dinner."

Alexander extended his hand to Tessa. "You look beautiful. Motherhood definitely agrees with you."

She took his hand. "Thank you, Alexander."

He turned to Jace and offered him his hand. "Thank you for inviting me, Jace."

"Oh, yeah..." Jace grasped hold of Alexander's hand. "You're welcome."

"I hear this is your favorite place to eat, Tessa," Kenneth said.

"Yes, it is. I love their cheese fondue appetizer, and the brick oven pizzas are out of this world."

"Well then..." Kenneth smiled. "I'll take your word and order both."

During dinner, Jace leaned close to Tessa and whispered, "There's something I want to talk to you about when we get home."

"Okay, honey." She looked at him concerned. "Is everything okay?"

He wrapped his arm around her. "Everything is fine, sweetheart."

After dinner, everyone said their goodbyes and left the restaurant. On the way home, Jace dreaded telling Tessa about his dreams, but he knew he had to tell her. He didn't like keeping secrets.

When Jace pulled into Covenant and cut the engine, Tessa said, "What did you want to talk about, honey?"

* * *

Sebastian parked his Mercedes under one of Berkeley's bridges. The black sedan was hidden by the shadows thrown by the massive concrete supports. The digital clock on the dash told him that showtime was near.

After he'd used a portal to get him and his brother here, they'd managed to retrieve his Mercedes from the parking garage at the club. As they waited, Sebastian thought about the meeting with Lilith. In retrospect, he didn't like the demands she'd given him. Getting his sons and Tessa out of the Covenant was going to be a task. Getting out with Lilith's son was another. This kind of shit could get them killed. Timing was going to be everything.

He was still figuring out this new life of his. After everything he'd been through, his main priority was to keep Eve and his sons safe and away from the Breedline Covenant. He'd do whatever it took to keep his family together.

As Sebastian refocused on the task ahead, he turned to Thomas and said, "Where's our backup?"

"Don't worry. They'll be here."

As if on cue, two cars pulled up between the concrete pylons. The Denali SUV was Corbin and Fredrick, and the silver Chrysler was Samuel's car.

Corbin and Fredrick were the first to get out, and when Samuel followed, it was like watching the three stooges live.

As they approached the Mercedes, they were all dressed in black. All Sebastian could think of was if they screwed up, he would cut their throats without so much as a second thought.

Samuel nervously placed a big leather bag on top of the trunk of the Chrysler. Sebastian watched in the rearview mirror as he zipped it open. It appeared to be full of weapons.

Abruptly, a loud pop went off.

Inside the sedan, Sebastian and Thomas quickly ducked down, and Corbin and Fredrick hit the ground.

Samuel jumped back with his mouth wide. And then he looked in their direction and waved his hands in the air. "I'm sorry! One of the guns accidently went off!"

Before he could get another word out, Sebastian flew out of the vehicle and bitch-slapped his lid shut. Then he put a knife to Samuel's throat. "If you pull another stupid-ass stunt like that, I'll personally remove your testicles. Do you hear me?"

Samuel's eyes bulged. "Y-yes, sir."

As Sebastian lowered the blade, he grabbed the bag and got back into the car. He looked at Thomas with a snarl and grumbled, "Samuel is still the same fuckup as always."

Thomas sighed. "Yes, but he's loyal."

"Let's just do this," Sebastian groaned.

Corbin and Fredrick came up to the passenger's window as Thomas explained the plan. After they understood what their responsibilities were, they got back into their SUV and drove off.

Samuel rushed over to Thomas in a sloppy jog like someone who had never moved fast in his life. When he poked his fat face in the window, Thomas pulled out his gun and leveled it at Samuel.

Sweat beaded his forehead. "Please, Mr. Carlyle. Give me another chance. I promise I won't disappoint you again."

Thomas finally lowered the weapon. "This is your last warning. One more screwup, and I'll kill you myself. Do we have an understanding?"

"Yes, Mr. Carlyle." He quickly nodded. "I understand."

As he walked back to his car, Sebastian hit the lights to the Mercedes. Samuel spun around and held up a hand to shield his eyes. Sebastian was tempted to mow him down, but for the moment, he'd let the bastard prove his worth.

When Sebastian accelerated up a ramp and got onto the highway, Thomas's phone went off.

It sparked Sebastian's curiosity when Thomas took the call but didn't say much. It appeared to be a private conversation, which seemed odd. A few minutes later, he ended the call and Sebastian said, "Who the hell was that?"

Thomas waved it off and said, "Nothing important. It was my attorney. He's finalizing my aunt's estate. Apparently, I have some legal documents I need to sign."

Sebastian kept his eyes on the road and didn't buy his brother's bullshit. He didn't trust the bastard as far as he could throw him. The first day he laid eyes on Thomas, he knew he was shady as hell. Sebastian could spot a liar a mile away. It took one to know one. Whatever he was up to, it had to be something cunning and underhanded.

Chapter Thirty

If Victor Demont sounded nervous, it was because he was. He was bloody well terrified. And he didn't scare easily. But if his affair with Casey's mother got out, it would ruin him.

Casey leaned forward and said, "Were you having an affair with my mother?"

Victor appeared lost for words. With a trembling hand, he reached for his cocktail and downed it in one gulp. After he used a napkin to wipe his mouth, he cleared his throat and said, "I promised your mother I would keep our secret, especially from you."

"Does my father know?"

"Not until after..." Victor swallowed hard. "...your mother's funeral."

"How did he find out?"

"Your father found our text messages in your mother's phone. When he asked me the other day during lunch, I thought he deserved to know the truth. Your father has graciously forgiven me and your mother."

"Why didn't my father tell me?"

"He didn't want..." his voice cracked, "...you to have any ill will toward your mother."

Casey's eyes watered. "Is this the reason why my father tried to talk me out of dating Lila?"

Victor nodded in silence.

Casey rose from his chair and squared his shoulders. "For your information, I would never have anything but respect for my mother. What she did in her personal life was none of my business. She's the one that has to face God with the truth." He took a deep breath and continued, "As far as Lila and I are concerned, I'm going to continue our relationship with or without your approval. So, if you'll excuse me, I'm done with this conversation."

When Casey walked away, Victor had to practically reach up and physically close his mouth. Although no one had the balls to cross Victor Demont, Casey just made him eat his own shit. Nevertheless, Victor had to hand it to the kid... he had balls of steel. He'd been the first person to stand up to him, and that deserved respect. That's when Victor decided to let him date his daughter. Besides, it was the least he could do after what he'd done to Casey and his father.

As soon as Casey got back to the Covenant, he headed straight for the bar. After he'd downed his second glass of bourbon, his mood shifted, and his thoughts went to Lila. By the third drink, he decided to give her a call.

When he finally made it up to his bedroom, he flopped down on the bed and propped himself against a mountain of pillows. He felt a little tipsy as he searched through his contacts, but eventually he found Lila's number and made the call.

"Hello…"

"Hi, Lila. Is this a bad time?"

"Are you kidding me?" She laughed a little. "It's never a bad time. I'm always glad to hear your voice."

He sighed into the phone. "Good, because I miss you."

"You do?"

"Heck yeah. I wish you were here."

"Me too."

His brows lifted. "Really?"

"Yes… I do."

* * *

As Tessa waited for Jace's response, he had that deer-in-the-headlights look. Finally, after he built up the courage, he said, "You know those bad dreams I've been having?"

"Yeah…" She nodded. "What about them?"

"They're about you."

Tessa reached for his hand. "Are they the same ones you had before? About my death?"

When he nodded, she squeezed his hand. "Jace, they're just dreams. Stop worrying. Nothing is going to happen to me. I promise."

"But how can you be sure. What if my dreams are visions?"

"You're not having visions. I think you're just nervous about becoming a father, and that's normal. I'm worried too."

"You are?"

"Yes. All new parents worry. I worry about not knowing what to do once our sons are here. I've haven't had much experience other than helping out with the little ones in the Covenant. But I do have confidence, knowing we have a lot of family and friends that will help me along the way. Plus, I have you."

Jace huffed. "I'm not sure how much help I'll be. I have no idea how to take care of a baby, much less two at a time."

She smiled. "Of course, you do. I've seen you with Natalie and Eve's twins. You're great with them. You display patience, especially when Arius bit you the other day. Sure, we need to work on your language, but other than that, all the kiddos in the Covenant seem to be drawn to you. You'll probably be a better parent than me. I have no doubt you'll be an excellent father."

Jace beamed. "God, I love you, Tessa." He tugged her close. "Come here, little mama."

Tessa reached across the console and wrapped her arms around his neck. "I love you too, honey."

When he finally broke their embrace, he placed his hand on the side of her face. "The way I feel about you scares the hell out of me. I can't lose you, Tessa."

She slightly turned and kissed his hand. "I'm not going anywhere. You're stuck with me forever."

His eyes softened. "I won't have it no other way. Although I do have one favor to ask."

Tessa shook her head. "Uh-huh... don't tell me." She chuckled. "You want to put a monitoring device around my ankle?"

"No, but that does sound like a good idea."

She rolled her eyes. "Jace..."

"Okay, okay. No ankle device. But I have something even better," he said, reaching toward the glove compartment. When he opened it and brought his hand out, Tessa noticed he held a gun holster with what looked to be a small caliber inside.

She raised a brow. "Is that what I think it is?"

"Look, it's small enough to fit into your purse, honey. It would ease my mind if you would carry this with you at all times." When Tessa opened her mouth to protest, he cut her off and said, "I already know you can handle a gun, so don't try and talk your way out of it."

"Okay, Jace. Only if it eases your mind."

He leaned in and pressed his lips to hers. "Thank you, babe. I feel better already."

Before they got out of the vehicle, Tessa said, "You know, I don't scare easily. You realize that, don't you?"

"Oh, believe me, I know." He cocked a brow. "I *totally* know."

As Jace and Tessa made their way to the front entrance to the Covenant, little did they know, they were being watched. While Sebastian and Thomas waited for the right time to slip inside, their backup hung back at the edge of the property, readying themselves if things didn't go as planned.

Fresh from a shower, Jace slipped under the covers next to Tessa. She looked incredibly small with her legs drawn up to her body. Her arms were wrapped around her belly as though she was cradling the two little lives inside.

When he reached out and pulled her close, her eyes fluttered open. "Sorry, honey." She yawned. "I didn't mean to fall asleep."

Jace smiled and kissed her forehead. "You should get some sleep, sweetheart."

"I'm not that tired," she whispered, rubbing her leg against his.

"Hmmm..." He looked at her playfully. "What did you have in mind?"

"I need some special attention."

"Do you now." He batted his brows. "What kind of *special* attention are we talking?"

"Stop playing around." She reached for his hand and tugged at him. "You know what I'm talking about."

He laughed. "Oh, no. You'll have to tell me exactly what you want."

"Come on, Jace."

"Tell me, Tessa."

“I want…”

“Go on,” he urged. “I’m listening.”

“I want…” Tessa framed his face with her hands. “I want *you* to make love to me.”

“Okay, now we’re talking.” He made a growling noise in the back of his throat. “I’m pretty confident I can make that happen.”

She moaned as he nestled close to her neck and kissed just below her ear. He inhaled her scent as he moved his lips down to the curve of her neck and to her shoulder.

Goose bumps trailed over her skin at the feel of his soft and sensual kisses.

When he smoothed his hand between her thighs, in a matter of seconds she felt a heat bloom within her.

“You’re so beautiful, Tessa. I’m so in awe of you, sweetheart.”

Her heart tugged at the sincerity in his voice.

“Please…” Her breathy tone was ripe with surrender. “I need you.”

He positioned himself above her and captured her mouth. She arched her back as he deepened the kiss. In one breath, he moved inside of her. The rhythm of his movements took her to a place of exquisite pleasure. Tessa’s hands dug into the strands of his long hair while her flushed body writhed underneath the warmth of his skin.

The soft moans she made and the way she looked at him, brought him to his own blissful release. He let out a breathy sigh and whispered, “I love you.”

“I love you too,” she said, snuggling deeper in his warm embrace.

Moments later, after Jace shifted on his side with Tessa in his arms, it wasn’t long before he drifted into a peaceful slumber. This time, his dreams were filled with good things.

Unable to fall asleep, Tessa stared at the ceiling, replaying Jace’s previous confession in her head. Something was wrong, but she didn’t want to seem bothered by his recurring dream, worried she’d stress him further. Tessa couldn’t wrap her mind around why he was having the dreams again. Maybe she was right and it was just his nerves. Surely they weren't visions, or were they?

She closed her eyes and concentrated on sleep, but it was hard when her mind wouldn't rest. She took several deep breaths. Eventually, her mind eased and she finally relaxed. When her stomach grumbled, her lids popped open again. As she slipped out from underneath the blanket, she sat upright and quietly moved to her feet. Trying not to wake Jace, she tiptoed to the bathroom and grabbed a robe. Focused on food, she crept out of the room and headed toward the kitchen.

* * *

Sebastian heaved a deep breath, impatient with all the waiting. His backup kept silent, readying themselves for his and Thomas's command.

Finally, Sebastian's patience wore thin, until he took the bull by the horns and created a portal. He turned toward Thomas and said, "No more waiting. Let's get this done."

When Thomas nodded, Sebastian cleared his mind and concentrated on their destination. Everything around him became dim as he focused solely on the pathway to his sons. As he stepped through the bright illumination, Thomas followed close behind.

Chapter Thirty-One

With her mind on Sebastian, Eve stared out the window and looked up at the star-filled sky. She was worried what he'd do once he got into the Breedline Covenant. Sebastian was the kind of man who was determined to protect what was his at all costs. She wanted her sons back, but not if it meant taking innocent lives.

The day they'd met, she had been drawn to him by an inexplicable force. But their relationship had been forged in the fires of hell. Both their childhoods were nothing but memories of pain and disappointment. They had endured more than most people would ever experience in a lifetime. They'd been treated as less than human, like caged animals, and yet here they were, clinging to one another, each the salvation of the other.

Yes, she loved him for all he'd done for her. She didn't refute it. But now that she was a mother, she'd changed. Sebastian remained ruthless and cruel, greed overriding everything else. Eve wanted to right her wrongs, walk a different path in life, one that didn't include hurting others. She longed to have a life filled with love and children and family.

It sounded so simple, Eve thought. And yet their path remained complicated, heading down a road of disaster. How could she ever hope to achieve such a thing when she felt doomed from her past.

While Eve desperately wanted her children back, she didn't want them to live a life of darkness and destruction. She needed her sister's help now. She had no choice but to ask it of her. Although the idea of betraying Sebastian seemed wrong, she had to do what was right.

A year ago, she would have never imagined she'd feel this way. She never felt programmed like other women. Living a tortured childhood damaged and ruined her thinking process. She'd spent her adulthood punishing others for her suffering.

Eve closed her eyes and brought forth her succubus side. She could sense Sebastian's whereabouts. Her eyes flew open and her lips parted in a gasp. It was at that moment she realized he was inside the Breedline Covenant.

* * *

It wasn't long before Tessa made her way to the kitchen. The aroma of chicken soup coming from inside smelled like heaven. The second she pushed through the door, she saw Casey in front of the stove.

He turned and immediately smiled at her. "Hey, Tessa," he said, tapping a wooden spoon on a pot with steam rising above it. "I made chicken noodle soup. There's plenty if you'd like some."

"Oh yes..." Tessa put her hands on her rounded belly and moved to the table. "That sounds delicious."

Casey sat down next to her and placed a steaming bowl of soup in front of her with a spoon inside. "Couldn't sleep either, eh?"

Tessa picked up the spoon and glanced down at her tummy. "Nope. This pregnancy has really revved up my appetite."

Casey chuckled. "Well, you are having twins after all."

"Yeah," she said, laughing a little. As she took a sip, she let out a sound of approval. "The soup is perfect, Casey. The twins say thank you."

He laughed again. "Tell them they're welcome."

Before Casey dipped his spoon into his bowl, he said, "I'm sorry, Tessa. Would you care for something to drink?"

She smiled. "No thank you, Casey. The soup will be just fine."

Moments later, as Tessa leaned back in her chair and let out a contented sigh, Casey said, "Would you like seconds? Remember, you're eating for two."

Tessa rubbed her belly. "No thanks, I'm stuffed." Then she noticed it was already past midnight. "Besides, it's getting late. I better get back to bed before Jace notices I'm missing."

"Yeah, I think I'll head that way myself."

Before Tessa rose from her chair, she noticed the look in Casey's eyes. It was as though he had something heavy weighing on his mind. Although he was sitting at the table, and carrying on a conversation, he looked miles away. She wondered if he was thinking of his mother since it hadn't been long since she'd passed. Tessa debated whether to press the issue. She was curious about him but didn't want to make him uncomfortable either. Casey was reserved and mostly kept to himself. There was a lot she didn't know about his personal life, other than his modeling career and his impressive skills as a keyboardist in Jace's band.

"How's your father doing, Casey?"

He looked at Tessa as if he was lost for words. Finally, he said, "He's doing okay." The corners of his mouth lifted slightly. "Thanks for asking."

Tessa smiled and scooted her chair back. "Thanks for the soup."

When Casey started to get up to collect their bowls, Tessa said, "Don't worry about the dishes. I'll get those."

"Are you sure? I don't mind."

"It's the least I can do since you made the soup."

Tessa washed the dishes, and before she stepped out of the kitchen, she said, "Try to get some sleep, Casey."

He nodded. "Good night, Tessa."

As soon as Tessa left, Casey's expression tensed. The moment Tessa mentioned his father, he felt uneasy. He wasn't entirely certain how he was going to handle the awkward situation about his mother's infidelity with Victor Demont the next time he was around his father. Then his thoughts quickly drifted to Lila. During dinner with her parents, he'd used his Theriomorph side and briefly got into her mind, more to reassure himself she didn't suspect his secret. He caught a vague image of a dream she'd had. It was of him shapeshifting into a black panther. *Could it be*, he wondered, *that she already knows?*

It went against his nature to lie to the people he respected and loved. He hated lying. It wasn't like he wanted to be different. He'd give anything not to live the rest of his life taking drugs to control his Theriomorph side. As much as he feared revealing his secret, he couldn't live the rest of his life pretending to be normal. How could he expect everyone in his life to accept what he was when he couldn't accept himself?

* * *

As Tessa moved toward her bedroom, she noticed a bright light coming from underneath the door to Arius and Tidus's nursery. Then she was caught by surprise when someone grabbed her from behind and clamped a hand over her mouth. She struggled and tried to scream, but it did no good. The person who had her from behind only tightened their hold.

"Sebastian... don't hurt her," Thomas said in a hushed voice. "Lilith's orders were that under no circumstances were we to harm her."

Oh God... Tessa thought before she felt a sharp stick in her arm.

"Remember me?" Sebastian whispered in her ear. The familiar, seething voice immediately sent cold chills all through her body. Seconds later, Tessa's vision blurred, and her eyes felt heavy.

As she went limp in Sebastian's arms, he lifted her off her feet and carried her toward Thomas.

"Take her." Sebastian kept his voice low. "I'm going to get my sons."

Although Tessa was too drugged to make out her surroundings, her hearing seemed to be working. It was at that moment she realized Sebastian was here for Arius and Tidus.

It wasn't long before she heard him say, "We're running out of time. We'll have to come back for Lilith's son."

Tessa's eyes rolled back into her head, and still she fought to remain conscious.

"*Jace...*" she linked her mind with his, "*...help me.*"

Her telepathic voice was weak, a mere whisper. She pleaded for Jace to hear her. But all that awaited her was suffocating darkness that closed in from every direction.

Jace suddenly came awake at the sound of a faint whisper. It was Tessa's voice and she sounded distraught. He aimlessly searched for her in the darkness but found her side of the bed empty. A panic flew over him as he reached for the light and scrambled out of bed.

Chapter Thirty-Two

As Casey finally made his way up the staircase, and before he turned the corner that led to his room, he saw Sebastian standing outside the nursery with Arius and Tidus. Next to him was a man who looked to be Sebastian's twin. He had Tessa in his arms, and she appeared to be unconscious.

Casey shouted and rushed forward, but it was too late. They were gone within seconds, vanishing through a portal, taking Tessa and the twins with them.

Jace rushed to the bathroom and called out to Tessa in desperation. When there was no answer, he hurriedly slipped on a pair of jeans. He rushed to the door, and before he opened it, the sounds of pounding came from the outside. When he sprung the door wide open, he came face-to-face with Casey. The look on his face said without words that something bad had happened.

"Where's Tessa?"

Casey shook his head. "Sebastian took her and the twins."

"No..." Jace gasped and clutched at his chest. Fury momentarily clouded his vision, and images of the past flashed before him. He recalled the memory of Tessa the last time Sebastian had taken her and what he'd done to her. Every marking instinct in his body fired off at once, and there was no holding back the Beast within him.

Casey took a few steps back. "Jace... listen to me. You've got to calm down before—"

A deep roar instantly cut Casey off, and the blast of light emanating from Jace temporarily blinded him. He quickly looked away and covered his ears.

As the noise echoed throughout the Covenant, it sent everyone on alert. Tim and Drakon were the first ones to come out of their rooms. When they rushed down the hall and came up to Jace and Tessa's room, they stopped in their tracks. The bright light that engulfed Jace's entire body made it difficult to see.

Tim called out, but Jace's thundering roars drowned the sound.

Drakon looked at Tim and raised his voice, "Something bad has happened. Jace is about to shift into his Beast."

Fear knotted Tim's gut. *Shit!*

Before Tim could get a word out, someone nudged his shoulder. When he turned to look, Jem stood behind him. "The twins are gone," he said as loud as he could. "Somehow Sebastian got into the Covenant. I think he took Tessa too."

Tim briefly closed his eyes and heaved a deep breath. "Jem, you've got to calm your brother before it's too late."

Meanwhile, Casey managed his way past Jace's room and shot toward the others. He looked at Jem fearfully and said, "I saw Sebastian and someone who looked identical to him. Before I could stop them, they disappeared through a portal with Tessa and the twins."

"Dammit," Jem said.

Drakon shook his head. "How in the hell did Sebastian get into the Covenant? I thought Celina made sure that couldn't happen?"

"She did," Tim replied. "But another Wicca could break her spell. Sebastian must have outside help."

"It's the only explanation," Jem said. "There's no way anyone could have got past the Guardians without being seen. This must be one helluva powerful Wicca."

Drakon shrugged. "So, what's the plan?"

"Let me try to talk to Jace," Jem said. "Hopefully I can persuade him to calm down."

Casey clapped a hand over Jem's shoulder. "Good luck, buddy."

While the others gathered back, Jem slowly moved down the hall and tried to connect with Jace telepathically. *"Listen to me, Jace. We'll get Tessa back, but you've got to calm down so we can find her."*

Jace glanced back and forth between Jem and the others as indecision rolled through him. The last thing he wanted to do was hurt the ones he loved, but he was hanging by a thread and the Beast was clawing at his insides.

As Jem went to reach out, a voice stopped his hand in midair. "Please, Jace... this is not helping Tessa."

When Jem turned to look, his sister came up from behind.

"Cassie, wait," Jem said, reaching out to stop her.

"Please, Jem." Cassie looked at him with pleading eyes. "Let me try."

"All right…" Jem sighed. "But be careful, sis."

She averted her eyes from Jem and focused them on Jace. "Look at me, brother. Everything is going to be okay." She slowly reached out to him. "Let me help you."

The moment her hand made contact, it seemed as though time had stopped. Cassie felt a shift in the air, and then everything inside the Covenant changed. It was as if a gust of wind had magically appeared out of nowhere.

Jace opened his mouth and a raw scream erupted into the air.

Cassie covered her ears and closed her eyes, cutting off the sound of her brother's agonizing screams.

The burst of energy that followed was so intense it shattered all the stained glass windows above the staircase. Shards splintered and scattered while everyone ducked for cover. The floor underneath shook with such force it felt like the walls were going to collapse.

The air whipped around Jace like a whirlwind, lifting him off the floor. A bright light blasted from his body followed by a screeching howl. When the light disappeared, it took Jace with it, leaving everyone behind in stunned silence.

"Jace…" Jem called out as he pushed his way into the room.

Cassie followed in behind him and said, "Jace…" Her eyes searched the room and then looked at Jem for an answer. "Where did he go?"

Jem shook his head. "I don't know."

"But how could he just up and disappear like that?"

Jem wrapped his arm around her and tugged her close. "It's going to be okay. We'll find him. And I promise, we'll get Tessa and the twins back too."

As everyone came out of their rooms and crowded around, Tim finally spoke out, "Right now we need to stay calm. Not only did Sebastian mysteriously find his way inside the Covenant, it's apparent he has a twin brother. By the way he was able to use a portal to get inside, we'll assume he has a powerful Wicca helping him. There's no other way he could have broken through Celina's spell. I don't have an explanation for what just happened to Jace, but I do know one thing. We are going to do everything we can to find Tessa and the twins." He focused on Drakon. "First, we need to view the video surveillance to get a closer look at what happened. Then we'll figure out our next move."

After everyone took a few minutes to collect themselves, Tim followed Drakon to the security room to view the cameras. Drakon rewound the footage to start just after a bright light emerged from outside Tidus and Arius's nursery.

As Jem came in, Drakon held up a hand in absent greeting before turning his attention back to the screen. Tim stood beside Drakon and stared at the monitor. When Sebastian and Thomas came into view, Drakon frowned and then hit the keyboard to pause the video.

"Son of a—" Jem said through gritted teeth. "Am I seeing what I think that is?"

Tim looked at Drakon and said, "Can you zoom in on their faces?"

Drakon nodded and typed a rapid succession of commands. As the screen zoomed in and the image sharpened, he said, "Casey was right. It looks like Sebastian has a twin."

When Alexander and Kyle walked into the surveillance room, Kyle said, "Well, what did you find out?"

Drakon pointed to the image on the monitor. "Take a look for yourself."

Kyle's mouth dropped. "What the hell? I can't believe there's two of them."

Jem glanced at Alexander and said, "Did you know anything about this?"

Alexander shook his head. "No... I had no idea."

Tim looked at Jem and said, "You'll need to notify your parents and tell them about Jace. I'll contact Kenneth. He needs to know about Tessa."

Chapter Thirty-Three

Tessa slowly cracked her lids. When she didn't see any-one, she opened them wider and quickly scanned her surroundings. Her heart started to pound as the memories of the kidnapping took hold.

"Oh, God... no."

The horror of it all was overwhelming. The face of her captor swept through her brain: his deathly pale skin, his inky black hair, his yellow catlike eyes and the hateful way he glared at her. Then she recalled what Sebastian had said. He sounded evil... sinister. She struggled to cut out the voice in her head, but no matter how hard she tried, it wouldn't go away. She clamped her hands over her ears, desperately trying to drown it out. "Please, God," she pleaded. "Help me."

After several deep breaths, she lowered her hands and finally calmed down. Slowly, she pulled herself up and shifted her legs off the bed. Her head began to spin the instant she got to her feet. Before she toppled over, she sank back down and took a few more deep breaths. Whatever Sebastian had given her, hopefully it wouldn't harm the twins.

When she smoothed her hand over her stomach and felt a little movement, it quickly eased her mind. Then she cleared her thoughts and tried to telepathically connect with Jace.

"Jace... can you hear me?"

Suddenly, pain splintered inside her head. It felt as though her skull was going to split in half. She let out a strangled cry and covered her face. Something was wrong. Instinctively, she knew something had happened to Jace.

Moments later, when the pain finally subsided, she felt a hand on her shoulder. Tessa reacted on instinct and lashed out with the heel of her hand.

The impact sent Thomas stumbling back with his hand covering his nose. When he regained his composure, he grabbed a fistful of her hair. The last thing Tessa remembered was his fist and then everything went dark.

* * *

Jem opened the door to his and Mia's bedroom and saw her sitting on the edge of the bed with her head down. When she looked up, her eyes were filled with tears.

He moved closer and pulled her into an embrace. Mia's incomprehensible words mixed with sobs until they finally coalesced into some meaning. "What are we going to do? How are we going to get them back? Oh, God... Tessa's pregnant. She's due in a few months. And what happened to Jace?"

"Shhh..." Jem soothed. "I promise, Mia. I'll do everything I can to bring them back."

With so many emotions bombarding her, she rested her head on his shoulder and clung to his every word.

Jem slipped his fingers under her chin and gently nudged it up. "Trust me, honey. I'm not going to rest until I find them."

"I know you will." She blinked tears. "I love you, Jem."

"I love you too," he said, wiping at her tears. "I won't let you down, Mia."

* * *

After days of total darkness, Jace couldn't understand why the sun was suddenly shining on him, unless he'd died and was crossing over to the other side.

He squinted his eyes and shielded his face, trying to focus on the bright image that was moving in his direction. As Jace maneuvered himself upright, he realized he was in too much pain to be dead. *Nope*, he painfully thought. *I'm definitely still alive.*

"Here... drink this," an angelic voice said.

As Jace parted his lips, the taste of cool water soothed his dry throat. When he got to the last drop, he was desperate for more.

"Hold on," the voice whispered. "I've got another bottle."

Jace savored every sip like it was his last. Then, to his surprise, the damp air around him shifted. As he surveyed his surroundings, he realized he was sitting in the middle of a grassy field.

He rubbed his weary eyes, and when he looked up, he saw someone standing above him. It appeared to be a giant man-angel. He stood to the height of at least ten feet with long dark hair and green, catlike eyes.

"Who... are you?"

When the angel smiled, his pointed teeth shone like ivory pins. "I am the archangel of healing." His voice was deep but gentle. "My name is Raphael."

"I don't understand." Jace tilted his head. "Why are you here?"

The angel unsheathed his enormous black wings. "Come with me, Jace." He extended his hand. "Your family needs you."

"Wait..." Jace hesitated before he took the angel's hand. "Please, tell me. Is Tessa alive?"

The angel dipped his head, and the instant he grasped Jace's hand, everything faded into darkness.

* * *

As Jem headed to the library to meet with the others, it felt like the days had passed by in slow motion. The Covenant seemed empty after Tessa and the twins were taken. Then there was the mysterious incident with Jace. Not only was everyone devastated by what had happened, Natalie was heartbroken over the cat's disappearance. For some strange reason, when Jace vanished, Buddy went missing.

Time was now of the essence. After Jace went missing, their sibling telepathic connection had severed. It left him feeling helpless. He had no idea where to search for Jace.

When Jem finally made his way into the meeting, he sat down next to Drakon. Everyone around the table looked as defeated as he felt.

Sweat beaded on Jem's forehead as they waited for John and Sarah to arrive. It was hard to tell his adoptive parents what had happened, but they deserved the truth.

As the door opened and John and Sarah walked in, pain sliced through Jem's heart. They looked completely devastated.

Jem stood and motioned them over. After he pulled a chair out for Sarah, she nodded in appreciation and took a seat. When John sat down beside her, Jem slid into the chair next to his mother and placed his hand over hers and said, "I know you're worried, Mom, but I promise... everything will be all right. This family has faced difficult times, and we always come out on top."

Sarah's lips quivered as tears slid down her cheeks. John reached into his pocket for a handkerchief and wiped them away. "Jem's right, sweetheart. We'll get through this."

Alexander leaned across the table and took hold of Sarah's other hand. "Jace and Tessa are both strong," he said. "I have faith that they can survive just about anything."

The others nodded, and it was all Sarah could do not to break down completely. Her family was everything to her, and now it extended to the fullest with everyone at this table she'd come to adore. She finally composed herself enough to say, "You're all so kind." Her voice trembled. "Thank you."

John looked at Jem. "Where's your sister?"

"She called an hour ago. She had an emergency at the hospital. I told her I would fill her in when she gets back."

"Okay," John replied, his heart breaking with every breath.

Finally, Tim stood and addressed the table. "I know this is difficult, but there's no doubt in my mind that we will prevail. It's just going to take some time, but we will eventually locate Tessa and Jace. We've all got to stay positive."

"Has anyone contacted Tessa's father?" Alexander said.

Tim nodded. "I promised Kenneth I would keep him updated."

"What about the Guardians?" Kyle spoke out. "Maybe there's something they can do to help."

Tim rubbed his jaw and sat back down. He felt like he'd aged in the last few days, he really did, but he was also wired and twitchy. He leaned back in his chair, his weight making it creak in protest. Everyone in the room looked at him, anxiously waiting for his response.

Before he could get a word out, the doors to the library burst open. Mia rushed inside and said, "Chester found Jace!"

Sarah covered her mouth and muttered into her hand, "Oh... thank God."

Jem shot to his feet so fast his chair tipped over. "Where is he?"

"They're outside," Mia said, motioning everyone to follow her.

When everyone rose from their chairs, Mia led them to the front entrance and to the outside gate.

Jem put his arm up to shield his eyes from the bright sunrise. At first, all he could see was the silhouette of a tall man moving in their direction, and it looked as though he had someone draped over his shoulder. As he got closer, Jem recognized that was Chester and his brother.

Jem's face lit up as he turned to Mia and said, "How did you know Chester found him?"

"Amelia came to me this morning. She said Chester found him lying on the ground beside the front gates."

Before Chester made it over, Jem took off and ran as fast as his legs would carry him. He froze in his tracks when he came up to Chester and got a glimpse of Jace. He looked like he'd been to hell and back. His jeans were torn and filthy, and his long hair was a tangled mess.

As everyone crowded around Chester in a tight circle, Sarah said, "Oh, dear God. Let's get him inside."

Soon after, Chester eased Jace from his shoulder and onto a nearby couch. Sarah smoothed his long hair back and said, "Jace... it's your mother." She placed her hand on the side of his face. "Can you hear me, sweetheart?"

He slowly lifted his lids and gasped, "Ma... is that you?"

"Yes, honey." Tears spilled down her cheeks. "I'm so grateful you're back."

Jace rubbed his eyes. "Where's Tessa? Did you find her?"

"Honey, we're doing all we can to find her," Sarah said. "Now that you're back, maybe she'll connect with you... I mean telepathically."

When Jace nodded, she looked over his body for injuries. "Are you in any pain?"

"My eyes are a little blurry, and my body is weak," he groaned. "But I'll live. Where's Dad?"

"Right here, Son," John said. "You sure are a sight for sore eyes."

Jace's brow creased. "Is Jem here?"

"I'm right here, Brother," Jem said as he knelt beside Jace and grasped his hand. "We've all been worried sick over you. Where the hell have you been?"

Jace shook his head. "I have..." He let out a deep breath. "...no freakin' idea where I was. I just remember waking up, surrounded by darkness, thinking I'd died. Then I saw a bright light, and someone gave me water. I was so thirsty." He swallowed hard. "The next thing, I was outside sitting in the middle of a field."

Sarah smoothed her hand over his brow. "But how did you get back, sweetheart?"

"You wouldn't believe me if I told you."

"After everything I've come to learn about you, your brother, your sister, and everyone in this Covenant," Sarah said, "nothing would surprise me."

Jace frowned. "Is Kyle and Casey here?"

"We're right here, buddy," Casey said as moved beside Jem with Kyle standing next to him.

"If I tell you how I got back, I better not hear shit from you two."

"I swear, man," Kyle chimed in. "We're not gonna give you any crap."

"Okay," Jace finally said. "It was an angel."

There was a moment of silence and finally Alexander came forward. "I want to know what this angel looks like, because if I ever see him, I want to personally thank him for bringing you back to us."

Jace looked through all the people surrounding him, and when he spotted Alexander, he smiled. "Thanks, Alexander."

"Well..." Kyle shrugged. "Aren't you going to tell us? What did *this angel* look like?"

Jace rolled his eyes. "Do you really want to know?"

"Heck, yeah."

"He wasn't exactly what you'd expect an angel to look like. He had to have stood at least ten foot tall, and he had huge black wings. He said he was the archangel of healing. He called himself Raphael. He had fangs like a vampire."

"Jeez…" Kyle muttered. "Sounds like you've been trippin' on acid, buddy."

Jace grumbled, "Dammit, Kyle."

Kyle held up his hands in protest. "Sorry… just saying."

"We're just glad you're back in one piece," Tim cut in as he came up next to Kyle. "Although I think while you were gone, I got a few more gray hairs."

"Sorry…" Jace's voice trailed off when his cat jumped on the couch next to him. "Hey, Buddy." He smoothed his hand over the feline's back. "Did you miss me too?"

"Believe it or not," Tim said. "That cat has been missing the whole time you were gone. Natalie had me looking for him every day. She'll be thrilled when she finds out he's back."

Jace rubbed the cat's head. "You were out searching for me, weren't you, Buddy?"

The cat purred and rubbed against Jace.

Moments later, when Jace tried to sit up, he felt light-headed and quickly lowered back down.

Sarah placed her hand on his shoulder. "You stay put, honey. Going by the dark circles under your eyes and your pale complexion, it obvious you're dehydrated."

"I'd like to get a shower," Jace said. "I feel like I've been drug through a mudhole."

Kyle laughed. "And you smell like it too."

Jace huffed out a frustrated sigh.

"Let us help you," Jem said. "The last thing we need is for you to take a fall and crack your head."

"Yeah," Kyle said with a light chuckle. "It's sounds like you've been knocked in the head a few times—"

"Kyle…" Tim cut him off. "Why don't you head down to the examination room and bring back a wheelchair." Then he looked at Sarah and said, "I've contacted Helen. She's on her way here. I think it's best Jace gets a full examination as soon as possible, wouldn't you agree?"

Sarah nodded. "Absolutely."

Jace muttered something under his breath and then said, "All right, all right. Get the damn wheelchair, already."

Tim padded Jace's shoulder. "Hang tight. You'll be back on your feet before you know it."

Chapter Thirty-Four

When Tessa finally came to, her head pounded. It felt like someone had hit her with a baseball bat. She was so overwhelmed with nausea that even breathing was difficult. As soon as she tried to sit up, the room started to spin. All this was because of Sebastian Crow. She was angry and tired of dealing with him. And now... there were two of him.

Then her thoughts went straight to Jace. She wanted to try and reach out to him, but she was afraid. The agony was already so overwhelming she didn't want to take the risk. But still, she had to try. What other options did she have? If she couldn't get through to Jace, there was no way anyone would find her.

For several moments, after Tessa was finally able to sit up, she rubbed her temples and focused on clearing her mind. Maybe it was the drugs keeping her from connecting with Jace.

She took a deep, soothing breath and then whispered his name in her mind. The pain returned and intensified. She lowered her face into her hands and breathed through the pressure inside her head.

When the door abruptly opened, she flinched and looked up. Panic shrieked through her as Sebastian's doppelganger stepped inside. Tessa scrambled back against the headboard of the bed and clutched her hand over her belly in an automatic protective measure. Fear trickled up her spine, wondering where Sebastian was.

"Hello, Mrs. Fairchild," he said. "It seems that we got off to bad start." He smiled in amusement. "Wouldn't you say?"

She gritted her teeth and forced back the obnoxious reply that hovered on her lips.

He sat down on the end of the bed and faced her. "Let's get one thing straight. If you try anything stupid, I will bring in my guards. Trust me, it won't be pleasant. If you cooperate, no harm will be brought to you. Do we have an understanding?"

Tessa nodded. "Who are you?"

"I'm sure you see the undeniable resemblance and realize Sebastian and I are related. We were separated at birth and had no knowledge of each other's whereabouts. Sebastian was told I died at birth, but of course, as you can plainly see, that is not the case." He dipped his head a little. "My name Thomas Carlyle. I was raised by my aunt in England. Unfortunately, she passed recently. Her estate now belongs to me." His smile broadened. "Welcome to my abode."

She looked at him, confused. "Are you telling me I'm in England?"

When he nodded, she said, "But... I don't understand. Now that Sebastian has his sons back, what does he want with me?"

"It's not Sebastian who wants you, nor me."

She pursed her lips and stared at him unflinchingly. "Then who?"

"Your questions will be answered in due time, my dear. For now, please get some rest. You'll need it." His smile faded as he glanced at her rounded belly. "Especially in your vulnerable condition."

* * *

Eve flinched at the sound of a knock but relaxed when Sebastian called out to her. When she opened the door, she instantly covered her mouth.

"Oh..." she muttered into her hand. "My babies."

Sebastian smiled. "I kept my promise."

Arius reached out to her and mumbled, "Mama..."

Eve's eyes filled with tears as she took hold of Arius and snuggled him into her arms.

"My precious boy," she whispered close to his ear. "Look how big you've grown."

Tidus crinkled his little nose and let out a light whimper.

When Eve directed her attention toward him, his eyes were pleading, and his arms strained for her to hold him.

Eve smiled. "Come to Mama, sweetheart."

As Sebastian made the trade-off, Eve cuddled Tidus in her arms. "I've missed you both so much."

When a light knock came from the open doorway, Eve looked up and Sebastian turned around.

"Sorry to interrupt your little family reunion," Thomas said, focusing on Sebastian. "But I need to speak with you in private."

Sebastian glared at him. "Can't this wait?"

"This won't take long."

Sebastian sighed and handed Arius to Eve. "I'll be right back, darling." He kissed her forehead and smiled at the boys before he stepped out of the room.

* * *

Jem leaned back in a chair next to Jace as he watched him rest. He hadn't moved in hours. After Helen gave him a thorough examination and hooked him up to an IV, he was out like a light. It seemed that everyone in the Covenant, except for Jem, had settled into their rooms as exhaustion finally set in. After several attempts, he was unable to shut his eyes. Jem felt restless, his mind on Tessa and the twins. It was obvious why Sebastian came for Arius and Tidus, but he couldn't grasp why he took Tessa. The thought took him to a place he didn't want to think about.

As time passed, and if they hadn't found Tessa, Jem wasn't sure how Jace would react. Things could take a turn for the worse. Although Tessa wasn't here in physical form, she would always be a part of Jace, no matter what happened. There was no looking at Jace without seeing Tessa. The two had been inseparable in life, and that would continue even after death. That was just how it was with bonded mates.

Abruptly, Jace's lids popped open. There was an ache inside him, under his ribs, which had nothing to do with an injury. He reached up and clutched his chest. It felt like his heart was breaking into a million pieces. He had never been one to believe in the prophetic meaning of dreams, and yet it was a possibility his had come true.

Jace sensed someone sitting next to him and lifted his head. He rubbed his eyes and focused his blurry vision. "Jem... is that you?"

* * *

While everyone in the Covenant retired for the night, Casey headed to PulseZero.

It wasn't long before he arrived at the club located in one of the biggest drug districts. As he sat in his car staring into the rearview mirror, he looked at his features. It was as if a stranger was looking back at him. He could sense the Theriomorph urges overriding his thinking. The visions of Tessa's death and all the voices in his head nearly took him over the edge. He inhaled a deep breath and eased back against the headrest.

When the voices wouldn't stop, Casey covered his ears and pressed until his arms shook. He was desperate to drown them out. His chemical fix was only a few feet away and time was of the essence. He had only an hour to score before closing time. Fortunately, there was no line outside, so getting in would be quick and easy. After he locked up his car, he went inside and maneuvered through the crowd. PulseZero was known for addicts and drug dealers, which was the only reason he'd chosen this place. Before he met with the owner, he decided to take the edge off with a few shots of vodka. He took a seat at the bar and watched as the lights flickered over the dance floor.

"Rough night?"

Casey swiveled on the barstool and came face-to-face with a female bartender. Instinctively, his Theriomorph side took over. As he burrowed into her head and read her thoughts, he felt a rush like he was free-falling off a building in a downward spiral. Her thoughts were of him... in a bed of tangled sheets.

"Hey, sweetheart, you okay?"

He snapped back to focus. "Uh... sorry. What did you say?"

"You look miles away, honey. How 'bout a drink?"

Casey nodded. "Sure. I'll take a shot of Patrón."

She winked. "Coming right up, cutie."

A few minutes later, when she came back with his drink, Casey downed it in two swallows.

"Are you ready for a second round?"

Before Casey could reply, the sounds of someone carrying on caught his attention. As he turned to look, a booming voice said, "I want my drink now!"

Two barstools down sat a guy with massive biceps and a good dozen prison tats. He was arguing with a waitress, clearly drunk off his ass. He watched as the loudmouth grabbed the waitress's arm and sent the tray of drinks in her hand crashing to the floor.

Instantly, Casey rose to his feet and glared at the bigmouth that had put his paws on the poor waitress.

"Hey, asshole..." Casey raised his voice. "I think you've had enough for the night."

The guy lumbered out of his seat to the height of six-five or more. He narrowed his stare at Casey. "Are you talkin' to me, pretty boy?"

Casey balled up his hands but kept them at his sides. "I think it's time for you to leave."

"Is that right?" The guy smirked. "And what if I don't?"

"I'll drag your sorry ass out of here myself."

The guy was so shell-shocked, his pie-hole popped open. When he managed to get his mouth to move, he said, "Is that so?" He moved closer and looked Casey up and down. "How 'bout instead, I break that pretty face of yours."

Casey snarled his upper lip. "Bring it, asshole."

The second the guy threw a punch Casey grabbed his wrist in midair and cranked his beefy arm to the middle of his back. When he shoved the loudmouth off balance, he fell to the floor, knocking the breath out of him.

Casey's motto was, in order to keep the peace, sometimes you had no choice but to get your hands dirty.

Then he bent down and grabbed the guy's collar. Everyone surrounding them was surprised when Casey dragged the burly guy, who sputtered like a whiny schoolgirl, toward the bar's exit.

The waitress hurried ahead and held the door wide-open. Before Casey tossed him out on his ass, he got down in the guy's face and said, "I don't want to see your ugly mug here again. You hear me?"

Casey clamped a hand on his ear and twisted when he didn't respond quickly enough.

"I'm sorry... what did you say?" Casey twisted harder. "I didn't hear you."

"Okay, okay." The guy groaned in agony. "I get it."

When Casey finally released the guy's appendage, he got to his feet and stumbled through the exit.

As Casey turned to head back to the bar, he looked at the waitress as she closed the door. She pointed at him. "Your eyes." Her voice trembled. "They're glowing."

He used his Theriomorph skills and wiped her memory and then disappeared to the back with a single-minded focus—get the drugs and get the hell out.

* * *

Jem quickly got to his feet. "I'm right here, Jace."

"How long have I been out?"

"A couple of hours."

"Damn," Jace groaned. "My head... it feels like it's going to split in half."

"You want me to get Helen?"

"Nah. I just need a few minutes to get my bearings."

Jem nodded. "Jace, can I ask you something?"

"As long as it doesn't make my head worse."

"What happened to you? I mean... how in the hell did you just up and vanish like you did?"

"Hell if I know." Jace shrugged. "All I remember is feeling intense pain after I heard Tessa's voice in my head."

"You heard her?"

"She called out to me in my sleep. When I woke up, she was gone. That's when Casey came to my door and told me what had happened. After that, everything else seems like a blur, except for the angel thing."

"We're going to get her back, Jace. I swear. I'll die trying if that's what it takes."

"I know, Brother." Jace sighed. "I know you would."

Then he looked at Jem with weary eyes. "If for some reason we don't get her back, I'm not sure if I will be able to move on." He swallowed hard. "You know that, right?"

Jem leaned over and hugged Jace. "I'll be strong enough for the both of us."

"You always are," Jace said. "Just like when we were kids."

When Jem pulled from their embrace, he said, "How's that head of yours?"

"A little better, but I've got to pee like a racehorse."

Jem extended his hand. "Let me help you."

As Jem helped him sit up, Jace said, "Thanks. I can take it from here."

"You sure?"

Jace slid his legs off the examination table. "Yeah, I got this."

He shuffled to the bathroom like an old man, but he managed it on his own. A few minutes later, Jem heard the toilet flush.

A half hour later, the door to the bathroom opened and Jace stepped out. He was wearing a robe, and his hair was wet from a shower.

"I'm going to get Helen," Jem said. "She wanted me to let her know when you came around."

Jace nodded. "Okay."

Before Jem stepped out, he looked over his shoulder and said, "Hey, Jace..."

"Yeah?"

"I love you, Brother."

Jace smiled a little. "Love you too, bro."

Chapter Thirty-Five

When Sebastian stepped out into the hallway, Thomas said, "We need to go back to the Breedline Covenant. We still need to get Lilith's son."

Sebastian narrowed his eyes. "You don't get shit from me until you tell me what the hell is going on." He pointed his finger in Thomas's face. "I know you're hiding something, and I want to know what it is."

Something dark flickered in Thomas's eyes. "You have no idea what I'm dealing with, Brother. There are people after Lilith, and they don't give a damn who lives or dies as long as they get their hands on her."

"What people?" Sebastian shook his head. "What the hell are you talking about?"

Thomas gritted his teeth and glared at Sebastian in silent menace.

"We're wasting time, Thomas." Sebastian eased back against the wall and crossed his arms. "Spill it, or I'm not lifting a finger to help you."

Thomas moved closer until he was face-to-face with Sebastian. "The people I'm referring to are dangerous. You don't understand..." He stepped back and heaved a deep breath. "They're threatening me. If I don't give them what they want, they'll—"

"Kill you?" Sebastian said as Thomas's voice trailed off. When Thomas nodded, Sebastian said, "So, are you going to hand her over to them?"

"I don't know what to do. I'm trying to come up with a plan."

"You better come up with something soon," Sebastian said. "My family is here. If anything happens to them, I'll kill you myself."

"Give me a few days. I'm sure I'll figure something out."

"While you're figuring things out," Sebastian continued, sounding irritated, "explain something to me, because it doesn't make any damn sense. If Tessa and Steven are siblings, how is it she can shift into her Breedline wolf? Am I missing something? I thought they had to be identical twins to do that."

Thomas shrugged. "It has something to do with the tests they did on Lilith when she was pregnant. Lilith told me one of Tessa's unborn twins will inherit Jace's genetics."

Sebastian cocked a brow. "You mean, his Beast?"

"Yes, and that's not all. Steven has the genetics of a Breedline and an Adalwolf. He has the power to heal any injury or illness."

"You're full of shit."

Thomas's eyes grew shadowed. "I'm not full of shit. What reason would I have to make something up like this?"

Sebastian shook his head. "Christ. This is some messed up shit. At least give me a damn smoke. I'm going to need something to calm my nerves after all this."

Thomas reached inside his blazer and pulled out a cigar. When he handed it to Sebastian, he dug out a lighter and tossed it to him.

Sebastian placed the end of the cigar into his mouth and then raised his hand to light it. A moment later, he inhaled deeply and then exhaled a long plume of smoke. Finally, he said, "So, does Tessa know anything about this?"

"No. She doesn't even know Steven is her brother."

"Really..." There was an intense interest in Sebastian's usual inscrutable gaze. "Why weren't you straight with me in the first place? You knew about all this the whole time, but you never thought about mentioning it?" He stared at Thomas like he'd just committed a crime. "That's bullshit, and you know it."

"We don't have time to argue about this right now," Thomas said. "I promise to keep you in the loop from here on, but you have to help me go after Steven and bring him back."

Sebastian stared at him with such cold severity the look would freeze Jack Frost. After he took another drag from his cigar, he exhaled in Thomas's face. "Before I do anything, I want to speak with Lilith. And I promise, if you keep anything from me again, I won't hesitate to cut your throat."

* * *

As soon as Jem stepped out of the examination room, he noticed Chester in the hallway, pacing the floor. Before he managed to get a word out, his twin brother's cry of agony alerted his attention. Jem whirled around and rushed back into the room with Chester following close behind. He found Jace huddled on the floor, covering his head as though he was in extreme pain.

Jem dropped to his knees. "Jace, what's wrong?"

Jace gritted his teeth, feeling like his head was going to explode. He could hear Tessa's voice. It was laced with insufferable agony. For some unexplainable reason, their pain was somehow linked.

Chester knelt on the other side of Jace and looked up at Jem. "I think he's somehow physically linked to Tessa."

"He's right..." Jace gasped. "Something's wrong with her."

Then images of Tessa flashed before his eyes. She was lying in a fetal position, gasping in pain.

"I have to..." Jace groaned. "...help her." He tried to push himself up, but the lingering waves of pain—her pain—crippled him.

"Please, Jace," Jem pleaded, "what can I do to help?"

After a few minutes, the agonizing pain in Jace's head eased and the link with Tessa finally faded. He cracked his lids and said, "Please, help me up."

While Jem took hold of Jace's hand, Chester grasped his other hand, and between the two of them, they got him to his feet.

For a moment, Jace leaned into his brother for support as he helped him to the examination table. When he plopped down, he took a deep breath. "I heard Tessa's voice. I felt what she was feeling." His voice trembled. "There was so much pain."

Jem slid his hand over Jace's shoulder and squeezed lightly. "Did she tell you anything... anything to give us a clue to where she might be?"

"No." Jace shook his head. "She was begging me to help her."

"Listen to me, Jace," Jem said. "Tessa is strong. She'll make it through this."

Jace nodded and averted his eyes from Jem and looked at Chester with pleading eyes. "Chester, can you help me find her?"

Chester's eyes softened. "I'm sorry, Jace. Someone with a great deal of power is blocking my ability to connect with her. But I will not give up trying."

* * *

As Casey headed for the back of the club to see the owner, the voices in his head taunted his sanity, trying to overtake his thoughts. With all the strength he had left, he forced it out of his mind and focused on the task ahead. Finally, when he came to the end of a narrow hallway, he spotted a huge bouncer standing outside the owner's door.

"I'm here to see Hugo."

The guy nodded at Casey and reached for his phone. After he made a call, he opened the door and said, "He'll see you now."

The second Casey stepped inside, he looked to the goateed guy behind a desk with a shot glass in his hand. He appeared more businesslike in his pristine, black, tailored suit than a drug dealer who owned a ratty-ass nightclub.

Casey glanced toward the door as it closed. When he shifted his eyes back to Hugo, he said, "I need twice as much as last time."

"I'm sorry..." Hugo put his glass down on his desk and leaned in closer. "I didn't quite hear you. Do you mind repeating that?"

Casey raised his voice, "I want a double order."

Hugo cocked a brow. "You sure about that?"

Casey heaved a deep breath. "Yes, please."

After a few moments of silence, Hugo leaned back in his chair with his eyes on Casey. "Okay. I believe I can make that happen. You got the cash?"

Casey nodded as he reached for his wallet. After he pulled out several bills, he dropped them on the desk. "Is four hundred enough?"

Hugo smiled as he retrieved his phone from the inside pocket of his expensive suit. It wasn't long after he ended the call that the door opened. The bouncer brought in a small bag and placed it on top of the desk. "Will there be anything else, boss?"

"I believe that will do."

The bouncer nodded, and when he stepped out, Hugo eyed Casey with a serious stare. "Remember, my stuff is high quality. I'd advise you to use it sparingly. That shit can kill you."

"Yeah, I know what I'm doing."

As Casey left with the drugs and headed back to his car, his inner voice kept repeating the words over and over in his head. *"Junkie... you're nothing but a damn junkie."*

It wasn't long before he made it back to the Covenant and rushed upstairs to his room. As he sat on the edge of his bed, he opened the small bag and fixed his eyes on the contents inside. His mind seemed to wander the longer he continued to stare at the liquid drug, realizing how desperate he was. A knock at the door startled him.

"Who's there?" he said, shoving the bag underneath a pillow.

"It's Kyle."

Casey heaved a deep breath as he moved to his feet and opened the door.

"Sorry, I know it's late," Kyle said. "I came by earlier, but you were out. I saw you pull into the drive a few minutes ago. Is everything okay?"

"Yeah, I'm good." Casey quickly changed the subject. "Have you heard how Jace is doing?"

Kyle nodded. "I talked to Helen earlier. She said he's physically fine, but emotionally... he's a wreck. I know firsthand what he's going through. When Celina's sister kidnapped her, I thought I was going to go out of my mind not knowing if she was hurt, or even alive."

In the silence that followed, Casey thought of Lila. She was so beautiful and sophisticated. For the first time in his life, he felt like a nerdy teenager, all clumsy and awkward every time he was in her presence. He couldn't imagine what he would do if something happened to her.

Casey shook his head. "I just couldn't imagine."

"It sucks, man," Kyle groaned. "Well, I'm ready to call it a night. Later, buddy."

Casey nodded. "Yeah, later."

After Casey went back to the bed, he sat down and reached for the bag. As he held it in his hand, he said a silent prayer, wishing he could be something other than what he was.

* * *

Steven rested against a stack of pillows he'd used to prop his head up and stared into the darkness with his thoughts in turmoil. When Helen had stopped in to check on him earlier, she relayed the news about Tessa and Eve's twins. His nerves were shot. He could understand why Sebastian trespassed to get into the Covenant for his sons, but why did he take Tessa? When he'd asked Helen questions, she was reluctant to give him all the details. Then he wondered if this had something to do with the people who were after him.

He glanced at the clock next to the bed and realized it was already two o'clock in the morning. He felt exhausted, but every time he shut his eyes, they popped back open. He felt restless and unsure. Nearly an hour later, his lids finally gave in and sleep took hold.

An overwhelming feeling of sadness brought him back to wakefulness. He could hear a woman crying as if she was in pain. The sounds were crisp and clear as if someone was in the room with him. He instantly sat up and reached for the lamp next to the bed. As the room lit up, he said, "Is anyone there?"

"*Please...*" He heard the voice again. "*Can you hear me? I need help.*"

Steven caught his breath. "Wh-where are you?"

Then a suffocating wave of agony swept through him. He gritted his teeth and gasped in pain. He closed his eyes as the woman's pain mingled with his. Using all the strength he had, he merged more fully with her mind. When they linked, Steven took on the blunt force of her pain.

218

The woman whispered into his head, *"I don't understand. How did you... do that?"*

Tears ran freely down his cheeks as the full extent of her suffering blew over him like a blazing inferno. It took everything he had to maintain the link between them. He could feel it fading. It took him a moment to collect his thoughts after the pain cleared in his head.

"I have the power to heal," he finally said.

"Who are... you?" Her voice drifted into his mind.

"My name is Steven," he said. *"Steven Pasquale. Who are you?"*

"Tessa..." Her voice was a mere whisper, fading into the distance. *"Steven... this is Tessa Fairchild."*

Steven felt their connection slip from his mind.

"Tessa are you there?" he called out in desperation.

Tessa focused on her ability to telepathically communicate with Steven, but when she realized it was gone, she started to weep. Despair and darkness consumed her like a never-ending cloak. Although everything seemed grim, she wouldn't give up. She was determined to find a way out of here and back in Jace's arms.

Steven listened and waited for a moment, but when Tessa didn't respond, he got out of bed and moved to the bathroom. He stared at his reflection in the mirror and shook his head. How was it possible that he could telepathically communicate with the Breedline queen? It was impossible. Maybe he was losing his mind. But he swore he'd heard her voice. Could it be, after so many years of being held captive and tortured with lab tests, it had finally eaten away the last bit of his sanity? The memories of what Dr. Hans Autenburg and his colleagues had done to him made him angry. To them, he was only a nameless, faceless research project. Regardless of the powers he inherited at birth, he was treated as less than human.

Although he had no idea how to explain what he'd just experienced, still, it was imperative that he contact Helen. If indeed the voice in his head was real, there could be a chance he could help the Covenant locate Tessa.

Chapter Thirty-Six

After Helen finished her shift at the hospital, she had one more patient to see before she turned in for the night. As she entered the Covenant, she headed straight for the examination room to check on Jace. He was clearly not too happy about being poked and prodded. After she gave him a thumbs-up to rest in his bedroom, she said, "You need to take it easy for a few days. Please, don't do anything strenuous for at least a week."

"Okay, Doc," Jace said as he slid off the examination table. Jem stood close by, waiting to help him to his bedroom.

Jace waved him away. "Thanks, but I've got this, Brother."

"Come on, Jace. You heard Helen."

Jace rolled his eyes. "Okay, fine."

A few minutes later, as Jem opened the door to Jace's bedroom, he said, "Do you think you could do me a favor?"

Jace shrugged. "What is it?"

"Promise me—"

Jem's voice trailed off when his phone buzzed in his back pocket. "Hang on. I got a call. Let me see who it is."

When he retrieved his phone, he looked at the caller ID, but didn't recognize the number. He tucked it back in his pocket and let it go to voicemail.

"As I was saying... promise me you'll come talk to me if something happens. I don't care where I'm at or what time it is, just talk to me. Don't let things bottle up until it's too late. You know I'm always here for you, right?"

"Yeah, I know." Jace extended his hand. "Thanks, bro."

"Come on, Brother." Jem took hold of his hand and tugged him forward. "Let's hug it out."

When Jace pulled back, Jem said, "You look like hell. Go get some rest."

Jem stood back and watched as Jace went into his room. At that moment, he thought back on their childhood. The death of their mother nearly destroyed Jace, but when he met Tessa, it was like she resurrected his soul. If something happened to her, Jem wasn't sure if he possessed the power to rescue his brother. He'd never felt so helpless in his life.

Before Jace headed for bed, he went into the bathroom and flipped on the light. Instantly, he noticed the gold chain on the sink. It was the necklace Kenneth had passed down to Tessa. It was supposed to be for good luck. He picked it up and smoothed his thumb over the cross. "Please, Tessa," he whispered. "Come back to me."

As much as Jace wanted to rest, he couldn't get his lids to close. Every neuron in his brain was restless and on edge. Although he wanted more than anything to use his Breedline telepathic ability he shared with Tessa, he didn't want to take the risk. Every time she tried to communicate with him it caused her pain. Forcing himself from thinking of her was going to be near impossible.

It was torture not knowing if she was all right. He wanted the reassurance she wasn't suffering. He'd already gotten luckier than any one man could ever hope for by having her restored to him after Sebastian had kidnapped her. And now that bastard had taken her again. Was he doomed to lose her to fate after all?

Jace blew out an agonizing breath. It was evident that Tessa and his unborn sons were in danger, and it infuriated him that there was nothing he could do. His thoughts were consumed of revenge, hate, and hopelessness, but mostly revenge.

Before his anger and frustration got out of control, he tried to focus on something else. His thoughts took him back to his childhood. As he recalled the good memories, he imagined himself at the age of five sitting at the kitchen table with his twin brother and his little sister. He could almost smell the chocolate-chip pancakes his adoptive mother always made on Saturdays. He would never forget her smile and the glow in her eyes as she served them breakfast. That's when the image of his adoptive father came to mind. He admired and respected John for giving them a good life. Jace smiled as he remembered their cat Jiggles and their dog Pongo. Those were happy times he'd never forget.

As he started to drift off, a feeling of shame slid through his chest. He felt guilty for failing to keep Tessa safe. At that moment, he made a solemn promise to himself and to God. He would search the ends of the earth for her. Giving up was not an option. He wouldn't stop until he took his last breath.

* * *

Casey woke to the sound of his ringtone, and when he shot out of bed, his center of gravity shifted. As he pitched forward, he threw out his arms to keep from face-planting onto the floor. When he landed on all fours, he groaned and cursed but managed to get back to his feet.

For a split second, the room started to spin, causing his body to sway. He briefly closed his eyes and took a deep breath. Finally, he regained his bearings and reached for his phone on top of the dresser.

When he saw it was Lila calling, he plopped back down on the bed and took a deep breath. "Hello, Lila."

"Hi, Casey." Her voice was soft, and soothing, instantly causing his heart to race. "Would you like to meet for breakfast?"

"I would love to," he replied, his voice masking how nervous he felt. "Do you have a place in mind?"

After they agreed to meet at a quiet café downtown, they talked for nearly an hour. When Casey ended the call, he thought about the secret he kept and all the lies and upkeep it required. He hated deceiving everyone he cared about, but what other choice did he have? And now that he'd bonded with Lila, he couldn't bring himself to tell her the truth. The last thing he wanted was to hurt her or anyone else. He couldn't bear the thought of losing Lila and living a life as an outcast. He'd rather be dead.

When he got back to his feet and took a few steps, he realized gravity wasn't his best friend. The dopamine he'd taken last night calmed the voices in his head, but it came with side effects, so the trip to the bathroom took a lot of effort. The minute he stepped through the door, he stripped off his boxers and flipped on the shower. As he waited for the water to heat up, he looked at himself in the mirror and thought about the previous night. It had been a close call. He'd let himself go without the drug he needed for too long. Something he'd make damn sure never happened again.

As he stepped under the shower, an image of Lila came to him. She was like an angel sent from the heavens to save him. She was worth fighting for regardless of the odds weighing against them.

A half hour later, as he headed downstairs, he met Kyle on the way down.

Kyle smiled and said, "I was just coming up to see if you were coming down for breakfast. Celina made blueberry waffles."

"Thanks, buddy, but I'm on my way out to meet Lila for breakfast."

"Oh..." Kyle cocked a brow. "Sounds like you two are moving things along. How's that going?"

Casey's lips instantly curved up. "Okay, I guess."

"You got that look, bro."

"What look?"

"You know." Kyle chuckled. "The same look a dude gets when his head's stuck in the clouds over a female."

"Yeah..." Casey smirked. "I remember, smart-ass."

Kyle nudged Casey's arm. "I want details on this one."

Casey rolled his eyes and laughed a little. "I'll catch up with you later."

As Casey arrived at the place where Lila wanted to meet for breakfast, he reached over to the passenger's seat for the single lavender rose he'd picked up for her. It was the size of a grapefruit. This type of rose had a meaning. It meant love at first sight. Casey hoped Lila would be pleased he'd done so.

The instant he stepped inside the café, he spotted her in a booth in the back. The sight of her took his breath away. She had her long blonde hair arranged in a ponytail and her sun-kissed skin reminded him of the beach. He could so picture her lying on the sand, wearing a little bikini.

At first, she didn't notice him. She had her head down, focusing on the menu. When he approached the table, she looked up and smiled.

Casey dipped his head and extended the rose that was in his hand. "I picked this up on the way. I hope you like roses."

Her smile broadened. "It's beautiful. Thank you, Casey."

As she reached forward, he tried to warn her about the thorns, but it was too late. She yelped and quickly drew her hand back. When a drop of blood formed on the tip of her finger, Casey leaned down and placed his lips over the tiny prick. In the back of his mind, he realized what he'd just done. He released her finger and looked at her with an apology written all over his face. "I, ah—"

"It's okay," she said, warding off the awkward moment. "I think it's sweet of you."

He breathed a sigh of relief. "Sometimes I don't think before I act."

"Well, neither do I," Lila said, gesturing to the empty chair across from her. "Please, join me."

"Thanks." He sat down and faced her. "So, what are you hungry for?"

"I'm leaning toward the special of the day."

"That sounds delicious. I think I'll have the same."

After the waitress took their order and left, Lila and Casey easily fell into a conversation. While they talked about her research with Helen, to his modeling profession and the band he played in, Casey tuned out the background noise and simply absorbed her every word.

When the waitress brought their food and sauntered off, Lila said, "Everything smells wonderful."

"Yes, it does," Casey said. "But not as wonderful as you."

Lila blushed. "Oh, thank you."

Soon after they finished eating, he inched his hand close to hers and said, "May I?"

When she nodded, he intertwined his fingers with hers. "Lila, I have something I'd like to ask you."

The sound of his seductive voice made her mind wander. She imagined his body as a cage locked around her, warming her from the inside.

"Sure, what is it?"

"May I have your permission to date you?" He cleared his throat. "Exclusively, that is."

Lila's eyes brightened. "Yes, I would like that."

Chapter Thirty-Seven

When Jem woke the following morning, he reached for his phone, remembering the caller from last night. Since he didn't recognize the number, he'd let it go to voicemail. He scrolled through his missed calls and noticed there was a voice message from the same number. After he punched in his password, he listened carefully and recognized the caller's voice. *Shit!* The message was from Helen's patient. As he continued to listen, his eyes grew wide and his mouth nearly dropped to the floor.

Mia crowded in close, straining to hear the message. She only got bits and pieces, but what she heard chilled her to the bone.

Apparently, Steven tried to get hold of Helen and Tim, but when he couldn't reach them, he called the last person Helen listed in the contacts she'd given him. His voice sounded distraught as he explained his telepathic connection he'd had with Tessa.

Jem stared at Mia in stunned disbelief.

Mia finally broke the silence and said, "What are you going to do?"

"I've got to let Tim know." He scrambled out of bed and grabbed a pair of jeans. "If this is true, it could be our only shot at finding Tessa."

Mia hurriedly got out of bed and slipped on a robe and followed Jem as he headed for Tim and Angel's room.

Angel opened the door and instantly realized something was wrong by the look on their faces. "Oh, no," she said. "What's wrong?"

"It's about Tessa," Jem said. "Is Tim here?"

"Of course." Angel motioned them inside. "Please, come in."

As Jem and Mia came into the room, Natalie was giggling while Tim bounced her on his knee. The moment he saw the look on their faces, he handed Natalie to Angel.

"Something tells me you two are not here just for a visit."

Jem held up his cell phone. "I got a message from Steven. It has something to do with Tessa."

"What is it?"

"It's hard to explain," Jem said. "You need to listen for yourself."

After he played Steven's message, Tim said, "Does Jace know?"

Jem shook his head. "I came here as soon I heard Steven's message."

While Tim contemplated what to do, he went to the window that overlooked the guesthouse where Steve was staying. His mind was full of questions. How was it possible that Tessa could telepathically communicate with Steven? Unless, for some strange reason, Steven had some other special power he did not mention. According to the Breedline, the only two people they could link their mind with was their identical twin or their bonded mate. Although there had been a few cases, like Jace and Alexander's, that a parent could telepathically communicate with their child. It was obvious Steven and Tessa weren't identical twins, and their close age ruled out the other possibility, and they damn sure weren't bonded mates, so how could this happen?

Tim turned to Jem and Mia. "Go ahead and tell Jace while I call Helen. As soon as she gets here, we'll talk to Steven. If he can indeed communicate with Tessa, maybe he'll be able to locate where Sebastian has taken her."

Jem's brows went up. "You know Jace is not going to wait for Helen."

"Yeah..." Tim sighed. "You're probably right. I'll head that way and meet you there as soon as I contact Helen."

After a couple of knocks, Jace opened the door. He looked between Jem and Mia. "Hey, you two, what's up?"

"Something has happened. It's about Tessa."

"No..." Jace instantly braced himself against the door frame. "Please don't tell me she's—"

"No, no." Jem held up a halting hand. "It's not that. As far as I know, she's okay."

Jace clutched his chest and exhaled a deep breath. "You 'bout give me a damn heart attack."

Jem lightly patted his brother's shoulder. "I'm sorry, Jace. What I said didn't come out right. This could be good news.

Maybe something that can help us find Tessa." He put his phone on speaker and proceeded to replay Steven's message. "You need to hear this."

As Jace listened, Mia wanted to reach out and comfort him when she saw his reaction. Instead, she wrapped her arms around herself and held back tears. Jace wasn't the type to accept pity. Besides, you had to admire him for surviving a lifetime of suffering.

When the message ended, Jace's brow creased. "I don't understand. How can Steven and Tessa telepathically communicate with each other?"

"That part I don't know, but maybe Steven has the answer."

Jace started forward. "I want to talk to him."

Jem threw out a hand. "Hold on, Jace. We're supposed to wait for Helen before we do anything."

"I don't have time to wait around. Tessa's life could be at risk."

"Look, Jace. I get it. I know you want answers, but please, let's wait for Helen."

"Sorry, Brother." Jace pushed past him. "I'm not wasting any more time."

"Dammit, Jace." Jem groaned and then turned to Mia. "Honey, please stay here while I go after him. I don't want him going by himself."

Mia rose on her tiptoes and kissed him. "Please, be careful."

* * *

Tessa held her hand over her belly, desperate to feel movement while she kept quiet lying in an unfamiliar bed. Then, to her relief, one of the twins shifted. A single tear slid down her temple and disappeared into her hair. It worried her that all the drugs she'd endured would affect her babies.

In her mind, an endless loop played, and she saw the familiar evil glare in the eyes of her captor. He was Sebastian's twin brother. Tessa shut her eyes and wiped the image of his face from her thoughts. She was more afraid than ever, terrified someone was going to take her babies away. *But why did they take her? And what did they want?*

Fear gripped Tessa by the throat just thinking about it. Putting her fears aside, she scanned the bedroom and searched for anything that would give her clues to where she was. But what was she looking for? There wasn't much in the tiny room. As she focused on the small, open closet across the room, she could see clothes inside. Next to the closet, there was a bathroom. On the far side of the room, tucked in a corner, was a shelf loaded with books.

She let out a deep breath and slowly sat upright. With all the strength she had, she stood and moved toward the bookshelf. Located on the second shelf, she spotted what looked to be a journal and reached for it. For some strange reason, her pulse quickened when she read the name on the outside. The journal belonged to Lisa Wellington. The date listed below the name was the exact year she was born. *How strange,* she thought.

Although Tessa felt as though she was invading someone's privacy, she was curious to find out who this person was and what was written inside. As she moved back to the bed and sat down, anticipation weighed heavily on her mind.

Her fingers gripped the edges as she opened it, almost like she was afraid of what she'd find. As she read along, her eyes widened, and she exhaled. *How could this be?* she feverishly thought. *Could this journal truly belong to my... mother? And how in the world did it get here?*

Tears burned the edges of her eyes as she continued to read her mother's documented life, discovering she had a fraternal twin brother named Steven. She wiped her eyes and wondered if the Steven she'd connected with earlier, the same person Helen had brought into the Covenant, was indeed her real brother?

Her hand trembled as she turned page after page, finding out everything she'd thought she'd ever known about herself— her life—was all a lie. She swallowed back tears and continued to read her mother's beautiful handwriting.

Her mother had been seventeen and pregnant with her and Steven the day she'd been taken against her will. A top-secret group of scientists who were funded by government military officials were responsible for her mother's kidnapping. They kept her, along with others who were gifted with special abilities, prisoners for years. Further into the memoir, her mother outlined the horrific experiments she'd suffered by a physician named Dr. Hans Autenburg. Born with the Breedline genetics and the power to heal, she'd been forced to take on other people's injuries, both physically and mentally. After Tessa and Steven were born, her mother grew increasingly concerned about their future, worried Dr. Autenburg would torture them with the same endless experiments.

As Tessa turned to the next page, a letter slipped out and fell into her lap. When she picked up the envelope, she noticed the letter was addressed to her. Her face instantly softened, and tears gathered in her eyes. Carefully, she removed the letter and started to read her mother's words.

My dearest Tessa,

Please forgive me for making the hardest choice of my life. I had to find a way to keep you out of harm's way. I will never give up on you or your brother. Know that no matter what, I always wanted you. I will forever keep you both in my heart. I love you my darlings.

Your mother,

Lisa Wellington

Tessa's lips quivered. She sucked in a deep breath and wiped the tears from her face. Without breaking down completely, she was determined to finish reading her mother's journal. After all these years, not knowing if her parents wanted her, she finally had the answer. Not only did they love her, she'd found her fraternal twin brother. Knowing the truth gave her strength.

Chapter Thirty-Eight

As soon as Tim notified Helen about Steven, he headed to the guesthouse, realizing Jace was not the person to reason with when it came to Tessa. He was like a bull in a china shop. When he finally got to the guarded entrance, Jace was arguing with Jem, getting face-to-face.

"I'm tired of waiting around," Jace grumbled with his hands fisted at his sides. "What if it was Mia? You'd want answers. And you'd want them now."

Jem stared at his brother, knowing he was right. If it had been Mia, he'd already broken down the door by now. He gripped the back of his neck in frustration and looked at Bruce Carmichael, who stood guard outside the guesthouse.

"Come on, Brother," Jace continued to argue. "We have no idea what's happening to Tessa. Please..."

Uncertainty rolled through Jem. He couldn't stand to watch his brother suffer. And going by what Jace had experienced earlier, it was obvious Tessa was in trouble. Considering her condition, it didn't look good. Although allowing Jace to confront Steven in his current frame of mind wasn't the best idea. Things could end up getting dicey.

He put his hand on Jace's shoulder. "I don't want you losing your cool. Before we go inside, I want you to take a breather and settle down. The last thing we need is the Beast to rear its ugly head, if you get my meaning."

Before Jace could reply, Tim stepped forward and said, "Bruce, unlock the door."

"Aye, sir."

There was a moment of silence as everyone stood back while Bruce inserted the key. When he opened the door, Jace sucked in a deep breath and followed everyone after they stepped inside.

* * *

As Sebastian anxiously waited for Lilith to arrive, he paced back and forth inside the study. He wanted more information before he'd agree to go back into the Breedline Covenant to get her son.

Meanwhile, after Eve put her twins down for a nap, she went downstairs toward the kitchen. Before she rounded the corner, she heard voices coming from the study. She paused and listened. She realized it was Sebastian and Thomas in some sort of heated discussion. She became curious when she heard Sebastian mention Tessa's name. Quietly, she moved alongside the wall next to the open doorway and eavesdropped on their conversation.

"I've already brought Lilith Tessa," Sebastian said, "and before I go back to get her son, I want to know what her plans are?"

Eve's mouth dropped open. *No,* she thought. *It can't be true.* Did they truly have Tessa somewhere held hostage? And what were they going to do to her? A knot welled in her throat as she slowly backed away and headed back upstairs.

"I don't know," Thomas replied. "Maybe she just wants to see her children after all these years."

"Whatever," Sebastian grumbled. "I think there's something she's not telling us."

Thomas shrugged. "What other reason would it be?"

"I hope I'm not interrupting."

When Sebastian and Thomas looked at the open doorway, Lilith stepped inside.

"Such silence," Lilith said, focusing on Sebastian. "That seems unusual for you."

Sebastian cocked a brow. "I choose my words carefully."

"You want to know why I had you bring my daughter here," she said. "Instead of telling you... let me show you." She extended a glowing hand and placed it on Sebastian's shoulder.

The second her hand made contact, images flashed through his head. His knees nearly buckled. The pain and suffering she'd endured was almost too much for him to bear.

When she finally removed her hand, he fell to his knees, and as he tipped forward, he caught himself before he face-planted on the floor. He looked up and said, "How... did you do that?"

"I have powers you could never comprehend," Lilith said and then looked away from Sebastian and focused on Thomas. "Bring Tessa to me."

Thomas bowed his head. "Yes, Lilith."

* * *

After Bruce led Tim, Jace, and Jem inside the guesthouse, everyone seemed tense and ill at ease. While they waited in the small foyer, Bruce went upstairs to retrieve Steven.

Jem put his hand on Jace's shoulder when he noticed him nervously fidgeting. He shifted from one foot to the other until, finally, Jace stopped and crossed his arms.

Their attention was drawn to the top of the stairs as Bruce came down with Steven. When Jace started forward, Tim flung his hand out to stop him. "Let me talk to him first."

Jace nodded and took a few steps back.

"Hello, Steven," Tim said. "We'd like to ask you some questions about Tessa."

Steven came forward. "I take it you got my message."

"We did," Tim replied. "I notified Helen. She's on her way. Do you have any idea how you were able to telepathically connect with Tessa?"

"I'm not completely sure." Steven shrugged. "I was hoping you would have some answers."

Jace shot past Tim and got into Steven's face. "We're wasting time, Steven. Tell us what you know. Did you find out anything? Tell me... where is she?"

Tim stepped between them. "You need to calm down, Jace. Give him a chance to tell us what happened."

"Okay, okay..." Jace backed off. "I'm sorry. I just want to find her."

Tim expressed a look of sympathy and averted his eyes from Jace and looked at Steven. "Did Tessa tell you where Sebastian has her?"

Steven's eyes grew weary. "I'm sorry. I lost the connection before I could find out." His tone was disheartening. "Although I was able to take away whatever pain she was experiencing."

Jace shook his head. "How were you able to do that?"

"I've always had the ability to heal others. But this was the first time I was able to do it without physical contact."

"Did she say anything about her condition?" Jace asked. "I mean, she's pregnant with our twins, and she's due in a few months."

"We were linked only for a few minutes. After I took away her pain, we exchanged names, and then her voice faded."

"I'm sorry..." Jace sighed. "I'm having a hard time wrapping my mind around this. It doesn't make any damn sense. How are you able to telepathically communicate with her?"

"I don't know," Steven said. "I've never experienced anything like this. I don't even have the ability to connect with my Abbey that way."

Jace narrowed his eyes. "Who's Abbey?"

"She's my beloved. Both of us grew up in a research facility. When it was destroyed, we were separated." Steven lowered his head. "I've been searching for her for years."

"Is Abbey a Breedline?"

Steven lifted his chin and looked at Jace. "No, she's a Lupa. She inherited her genetics from her mother. Dr. Hans Autenburg wanted to use our DNA to create a new species. I know firsthand how it feels to lose the person you love, and I will do whatever it takes to help you find Tessa."

"Why would you care?" Jace snorted. "You don't even know her."

"Because..." Steven swallowed hard. "...there's a possibility that Tessa is my fraternal twin sister."

"What?" Jace blasted. "You've done lost your damn mind."

Tim held up a halting hand. "Wait a minute. How could that be? There's never been a Breedline born with a fraternal twin that could shift. Only identical twins have that ability."

Steven cocked a brow. "Are you sure? Just because you've never heard of it doesn't mean it can't happen. Remember, I've spent most of my life in a research facility. I've been through all kinds of tests and experiments. It's possible Tessa may have suffered through some of Dr. Autenburg's lab tests as a child. They could have affected us somehow. Maybe that's the reason why we have the power to shift."

Jace rolled his eyes. "Don't you think she'd remember something like that?"

"Maybe not," Steven said. "If she was taken from the facility at a young age, she wouldn't remember."

"But her mother's older sister and her husband raised her," Jace said. "They told Tessa her mother ran off after she was born. Why would they lie to her?"

"They could have lied to keep her safe."

"Safe from what?"

"The same people who kept me locked up for most of my life," Steven said. "You have no idea what kind of monsters I'm talking about. They don't look at me or you as human beings. Our kind are disregarded. To them, we are nothing but animals."

"He could be right," Jem spoke out. "You have to consider the possibility. Besides, what other explanation do we have?"

"It's a bizarre theory," Tim said. "But I have to admit, it's the only thing that makes sense at the moment."

"Steven..." Jem hesitated for a second. "...do you think you could communicate with Tessa again?"

"I could try." Steven looked at Jace. "It's worth a shot, don't you think?"

"I don't know," Jace said. "What if this causes her more pain? I'm worried about the twins."

Helen stepped inside the foyer and said, "Let him try, Jace."

When everyone looked at Helen, she moved close to Jace. "It's the only way we'll find her. Tessa would want us to do everything we could. Right now, it's our only option."

"Helen's right, Jace," Steven said. "If Tessa experiences any discomfort, I promise I will do everything I can to take it away."

Jace heaved out a deep breath. "Okay, do it."

Steven nodded. "Do you have a photo of her?"

"Yeah," Jace said as he reached for his phone and brought up a photo of Tessa. "This is a recent photo. I took it the day before..." His voice trailed off as he looked at her picture, remembering the conversation they'd had before he'd snapped that photo. They were talking about the twins' nursery and what colors they were going to paint the room.

Jace looked up when Steven reached out and placed his hand on his arm. "It's going to be okay. We'll get her back."

Jace's lips turned up into a half smile. "I hope so. And hey... I'm sorry about your Abbey. Maybe we can help you find her too."

"Thank you, Jace."

When Jace handed Steven his phone, he sat down and said, "I'll need complete silence. It will help me clear my mind in order to connect with Tessa."

Moments later, as Steven relaxed, he used his mind to call out to her. *"Tessa... can you hear me?"*

* * *

Tessa chewed at her bottom lip while she read her mother's journal, wondering how it got here. Did Sebastian or his twin brother have anything to do with it? And were they keeping her mother captive somewhere in this place?

She rubbed at the tension building in the back of her neck. *If only I knew where this place was,* she thought. *Then maybe, if I could connect with Steven again, he could get a message to Jace.* Tessa put the thought aside and continued to read on. According to her mother's recorded events, a guard at the research facility where she was held captive befriended her. His name was David. After a time, he'd promised to help her escape. The plan was to get out with both twins, but unfortunately, Dr. Hans Autenburg's men got to Steven before David managed to get to him. Although David promised Lisa he would help her get Steven back after they took Tessa to a safe place. Her older sister Wanda and her husband John were the only two people she could trust...

Tessa averted her eyes from the page when a faint voice whispered inside her head. She closed her eyes and said, *"Steven... is that you?"*

"Yes, it's me." His voice brought tears to her eyes. *"I'm here with Jace and the others. We're here to help you, Tessa. Do you know where Sebastian is keeping you?"*

A sudden wave of agony hit her like a ton of bricks. Tessa pressed her hands to her head and gasped in pain.

"Stay with me, Tessa." Steven's voice felt soothing to her ears, already easing some of the pain. *"I'm going to help you through this."*

Steven used all the energy he had and concentrated solely on lifting her pain. As he willed it into himself, a warm sensation flooded Tessa's body with instant relief.

As Steven's agony finally subsided, he focused his thoughts back to her. *"Tessa, are you still there?"* When she didn't immediately reply, he got worried. *"Please... talk to me, Tessa."*

"I'm here, Steven," Tessa said. *"Whatever you did... thank you."*

"You're welcome. Can you tell us where you are?"

"I'm somewhere in England. It's an estate that used to belong to Sebastian's twin brother's aunt. His name is Thomas Carlyle. That's all I know."

"Okay... that's something," Steven said with a heavy sigh.

"And there's something else," Tessa said. *"It's a journal I found in my room they're keeping me in. I'm not sure how it got here, but it belongs to a Lisa Wellington. Do you recognize that name?"*

"No, why?"

"It's my mother... our mother, Steven. According to the journal, you're my fraternal twin brother."

Steven was quiet for a moment.

"Steven, are you still there?"

"Yes." His voice was shaky. *"I'm here, Tessa. I had a feeling we were siblings. It's the only explanation for our ability to telepathically communicate. I promise I'm going to do everything I can to find you."*

"Thank you, Steven. Please, tell Jace—"

Tessa words abruptly broke off and Steven could sense her fear. *"Tessa... are you okay?"*

When she didn't reply, he knew he'd lost the connection.

"Damn it," Steven cursed out loud.

"What happened?" Jace demanded. "Is Tessa all right?"

"I lost her," Steven gasped, lowering his head. "But she's okay."

Jace dropped to one knee and got face-to-face with Steven. "Tell me, dammit. Did you find out where she's at?"

Steven lifted his chin and nodded. "Tessa is in England. She wasn't sure exactly where, but the estate used to belong to Thomas Carlyle's aunt."

Jace breathed out a sigh of relief. "Good work, buddy." He patted Steven's shoulder. "Did she say anything else? Are the twins okay?"

"Tessa and the twins are fine, but..."

Jace's expression turned grim. "What is it, Steven?"

"Tessa found a journal in the room where Sebastian is keeping her. She said it belongs to our mother."

Jace stood straight and stared down at Steven. His mouth opened, but he found himself lost for words. Finally, he managed to say, "Freakin' unbelievable. I honestly don't know what to think."

Tim came forward with Helen and said, "Well, that explains a lot. I would have never thought it could be possible, but I guess you were right, Steven."

Helen knelt next to where Steven was sitting. "Did Tessa happen to mention how she came across your mother's journal?"

"Tessa said she had no idea how it got there. But... I wonder if Sebastian has my mother held hostage."

"It sounds rather peculiar," Helen said. "How would Sebastian or his brother get possession of your mother's journal?"

"And what purpose would it serve them?" Tim chimed in. "Did Tessa mention your mother's name?"

Steven's eyes softened, realizing he'd never known who his real parents were. He cleared his throat and said, "Lisa Wellington."

"Did Tessa get the chance to tell you if there was anything else in your mother's journal that would link her to

Sebastian?" Tim asked. "Something that could help us locate her whereabouts in England?"

"No," Steven said. "For some reason, we were cut off. I think someone came into her room. I could sense her fear."

"Dammit," Jace said. "I swear, if anyone lays a hand on her..."

Jem reached out to Jace. "You've got to stay positive. Besides, Tessa is fierce. She can take care of herself."

Jace grumbled. "I know, but still..."

"I'll do what I can to find out who this Thomas Carlyle is," Tim cut in before Jace got overheated. "I'll also do some digging into this Dr. Hans Autenburg and his facility. It could lead us to some of his other colleagues." He looked at Steven. "I'll almost bet Sebastian and his brother are working with these people to get to you and Tessa." When Steven nodded, Tim turned toward Jem and said, "Would you check to see if Mia might help us out? Maybe she might recall Eve mentioning some of Sebastian's family."

"That's a good idea," Jem said. "I'll ask her if she knows anything."

Tim nodded. "Every bit of information we can gather will be helpful."

Jace looked at Tim and said, "Now that we know Steven and Tessa are siblings, I think we should tell him about Kenneth."

Steven shot to his feet. "Who's Kenneth?"

"Your biological father," Tim said.

Steven plopped back down. "My father..." He looked up at Tim bewildered. "Do you know where he is?"

"Steven, your father is an orthopedic surgeon at the San Francisco General Hospital," Tim replied. "He's a good man. He's been searching for your mother for years."

Jace clapped a hand over Steven's shoulder. "Tim's right. Kenneth is a great guy. He'll be ecstatic when he finds out you're here."

"I can arrange for you to meet him," Helen said. "Kenneth is going to be so thrilled. He told me how much he loves your mother. Before she disappeared, he proposed to her. He was devastated when she took off without a trace. He said it was like she vanished from the face of the earth, but he has never given up hope."

"After all these years," Steven exhaled a deep breath, "I never knew my real identity. So, do you know my true name?"

Helen smiled. "Steven Craven."

Steven closed his eyes briefly. To finally have an identity, not to mention a family, was something he'd never dreamed would come true.

Jem patted Steven's shoulder. "Welcome to our family, Steven."

He looked up at Jem and smiled. "I can't tell you how much this means to me. And I swear on my life... I will do everything in my power to get my sister back. I'll die trying if that's what it takes."

"You and me both," Jace said.

Chapter Thirty-Nine

Before Eve went inside the nursery to check on the twins, she placed her hands over her face. *Oh God,* she thought. *What is Lilith planning to do with Tessa? Maybe Thomas was right. Maybe she just wants to reunite with her children after all these years.* Although she sensed something wasn't right. Deep down, she knew someone was keeping secrets. Could it be that Lilith and Thomas were lying to Sebastian? Then it dawned on her. Were they planning on using Sebastian just to get to Arius for his powers? And were they planning on using Tessa against the Breedline Covenant? *No,* Eve thought as she lowered her hands and fisted them at her sides. It couldn't be. Lilith seemed to be genuine when it came to Tessa's safety. Maybe this was all about Thomas. Was he hiding something from Lilith and Sebastian? Eve knew one thing for sure. She didn't trust anyone, including Sebastian. One way or the other, she was going to find a way out of here and warn the Covenant.

As Eve reached for the door, her first thought was to take Arius and Tidus and run. She'd go back to the Covenant and beg for their help. But how would she get away?

She took a deep breath and gathered her thoughts before she went inside the nursery. Finally, she opened the door and moved next to the crib. Eve smiled when she caught sight of the twins snuggled together. They looked content, especially Tidus. He had his thumb tucked between his parted lips. At that moment, she vowed to do whatever it took to keep them safe even if it meant giving up her freedom. The idea of being separated from them brought tears to her eyes. Eve prayed the Covenant would show some sort of leniency for her past crimes if she found a way out of here. But how would she accomplish such a task? Somehow, she had to come up with a plan. While she formulated her getaway, she had to pretend to Sebastian—who she had foolishly believed—that her heart wasn't breaking into a million pieces.

"Eve... is something wrong?"

Eve flinched at the sound of Sebastian's voice. It took every bit of strength she possessed to compose herself enough to turn around. As she looked in his direction, she wondered if he had been lying to her all along. The naive part of her wanted to believe it had all been a misunderstanding and he'd explain everything to her. *Don't be stupid,* she thought.

"No," she said. "I'm just tired, that's all."

Sebastian slightly tilted his head to one side and narrowed his eyes. He stared at her in a way that made her think he knew she was lying. Then a smile emerged from his tight lips. "Let's take advantage of the moment." He extended his hand. "Come join me in our bedroom."

"I'm sorry, but I don't feel well," she said, avoiding his hand. "Maybe I just need to rest. I've been up most of the night with the twins."

She had to make up an excuse. The last thing she wanted was intimacy. Anyway, it wasn't a complete lie. Her stomach was upset, but not from lack of sleep.

"Is there anything I can do?"

"No, I'm sure I'll be fine after a few hours of sleep."

Sebastian moved close and took hold of her hand. "Come..." He gently tugged her forward. "I'll rest with you."

Eve nodded in silence and went with Sebastian as he led her to their bedroom.

* * *

Tessa quickly tucked the journal beneath a pillow and scrambled to the far side of the bed as the door to her room swung open. Within seconds, Thomas stepped into the room with a burly man following him.

"Up and at 'em." Thomas snapped his fingers. "Let's go, Miss Fairchild."

Tessa shivered at the calculated way he looked at her. "Where are you taking me?"

"I don't have time for questions." He raised his voice. "Let's go."

"I'm not going anywhere until you tell me where you're taking me."

Thomas looked at the man standing beside him, who was the size of a mountain, and said, "Garrett, please help Miss Fairchild to her feet."

As Garrett came forward and grabbed Tessa by the arm, she struggled against his hold. Then, to her surprise, Thomas flashed a gun in her face. "Don't make this more difficult than it has to be."

"Please…" Tessa looked down the end of a barrel, fearing what fate lay ahead. "Just tell me and I'll go peacefully."

"Garrett…"

When the back of Garrett's hand smacked across Tessa's face, her head forcefully snapped to the side. She put her hand over her cheek and looked at Thomas with fire in her eyes. "You're just as evil as your brother," she said, gritting her teeth.

"You're rather brave considering your condition," Thomas said, lowering his gaze toward her rounded belly. "Be careful, my dear." He looked back up at her face. "I promise, bravery can lead you down a road you'll soon regret."

"You and your rotten brother are not going to get away with this," Tessa said, her voice seething. "That's something I can guarantee."

Thomas cocked a brow. "You don't learn, but you will…" He paused and nodded at Garrett. "…the hard way."

Tessa suddenly felt the sharp sting of a needle as it plunged into her arm. Then, to her despair, she fell limp as everything began to fade and blur. Her knees wobbled, and before she lost her footing, Garrett lifted her off the floor.

"Take her to Lilith," Thomas demanded.

His words seemed jumbled as Tessa slipped into a state of unconsciousness.

* * *

When Eve finally drifted off, her dreams tormented her with immeasurable flashes from the past and the present. They swirled together in one never-ending stream of terror.

Her stepfather had her in his grip again, but instead of Sebastian saving her, the demon had been standing there, his dark gaze piercing right through her.

The demon's voice whispered in Eve's mind, "You will always belong to me, Eve. And this time... you'll learn to obey."

The nightmare slowly began to shift. It drifted into something much more terrifying, something Eve never dreamt before, but far beyond her reality.

She found herself in the middle of a dark, wooded field. As the sound of footsteps approached, she whirled around in a circle but saw nothing but trees and darkness. Her shoulders sagged in relief, and as she inhaled a deep breath, the pungent smell of blood was sharp in the air. It hung in the back of her throat like the taste of rusted metal. She swallowed and stared off into the night, realizing it wasn't the demon from her haunted past; it was something else.

Suddenly, the sound of a growl made her flinch. She froze where she stood, her pulse racing and her nerves on edge. Eve clenched her hands until her knuckles went white and listened for the slightest noise. Whatever you do, *she thought,* don't turn around. *But the longer she waited, the more her curiosity grew. The not knowing was unbearable. As she whirled around to face whatever it was, she instantly wished she hadn't.*

Eve's movement alerted the thing. It lowered its big head and drew back a snarl. It was a wolf, yet not a wolf... some unknown and ungodly hideous mutation of a Breedline. Its long sleek body was low to the ground, and blood covered its thick, black fur. While Eve watched in horror, it began moving in a tense circle, pacing back and forth. And then, without warning, it stopped and raised its head toward the sky.

The howl it gave was unearthly. It let out a shrieking bellow of unbearable agony like an animal... and a human. Their eyes met and held as the creature lowered its head and turned to confront her.

"No," Eve pleaded. "Please, no..."

Eve instantly awoke, startled. Sweat beaded on her forehead and chills prickled her skin. She sat up in bed and trembled in fear.

She glanced over to find Sebastian lying beside her, sleeping peacefully. Careful not to wake him, she quietly breathed a sigh of relief and eased out of bed. She went into the bathroom and dabbed her face with a cool washcloth.

Before she slipped out of the bedroom, she grabbed her robe and headed for the nursery. After a quick peek inside, and relieved to find the twins fast asleep, she took the stairs to search for Tessa. She had to be somewhere in this estate.

Suddenly, Eve heard two male voices moving in her direction. She quickly ducked around the corner and flattened against the wall. As they grew near, she recognized Thomas's voice, but not the other.

When their footsteps seemed to change course, Eve peered around the corner. What she saw nearly made her cry out in fear. She covered her mouth to silence her gasp.

Eve watched in horror as Thomas opened the door to the study while a man twice his size carried Tessa, who was limp in his arms.

As Eve started forward, she was caught off guard by Sebastian's leery voice.

"What are you doing?"

She turned to face him with a startled look on her face.

"It's almost time for the boys to wake up." She swallowed back fear. "I was going to the kitchen to get their formula ready."

"Do you need any help?"

"I'll be fine." She faked a smile. "The boys are no trouble."

"I'm going out," Sebastian said, "but I won't be long."

"All right," she said, afraid to ask where he was going. "I'll be upstairs with the twins."

He kissed her forehead. "I love you, Eve."

"I love you too."

Moments later, as soon as Sebastian closed the door behind him, Eve hurried over to the study. When she noticed the door was partly open, she positioned her back against the wall and eavesdropped on the conversation coming from inside.

Chapter Forty

As Eve listened to the exchange between Thomas and Lilith, she wanted to burst into the room and demand answers. But she was afraid. If anything were to happen to her, there would be no one to protect her sons.

"My beautiful daughter," Lilith whispered as she reached out to touch Tessa's face. She halted her movement when she noticed a pink mark that looked to be a large handprint.

"What is this?" Lilith said as she looked up at Thomas.

Thomas took a few steps back. "I-it was an accident. She was proving difficult."

"You were supposed to keep her safe, not harm her," she bit out. "And why is she drugged?"

"I had to no choice but to sedate her. She refused to leave her room."

"If any harm is brought upon her again..." Lilith gritted her teeth. "Do you understand?"

"Yes, Lilith."

She peeled her eyes off Thomas before she lashed out, realizing he was the only one she could trust to retrieve her son from the Breedline Covenant. When she refocused her attention back to Tessa, she used her mind to try and connect with her. Unfortunately, the pathway was difficult due to all the drugs she'd been given. With gentle hands, she lifted Tessa into her arms as easily as plucking a flower from the ground.

"Open your eyes, Tessa," she whispered softly.

As Tessa's lids began to open, she didn't acknowledge Lilith. She merely stared blankly at the ceiling.

Lilith turned to look at Garrett like the boneless swivel of an owl's head. "You..." She narrowed her eyes. "What did you do to my daughter?"

"I-I..." Garrett swallowed on impulse. "I just gave her a small dose. Only enough to calm her down."

"You will suffer for this."

Garrett shook his head and took careful steps back. "Please... I beg you."

Seconds later, he froze, his face seemingly stoic. Then his eyes fixated on the door. As he started forward, Thomas noticed the hypnotic look in Garrett's eyes. It was as if he was in some sort of trance, like someone had taken over his mind.

When Garrett pushed through the door, Eve nearly jumped out of her skin. She expected to be caught, but instead, Garrett kept his eyes forward and moved past her without a word. He suddenly stopped in his tracks and reached inside his jacket. Eve placed her hand over her mouth when he put a gun to his head and pulled the trigger.

The blast echoed like a firecracker, and when Garrett fell to the floor, Eve scurried away.

Lilith looked at Thomas and said, "Leave us."

The moment he left, she lowered Tessa and placed her palm over her rounded belly. As she kept it there, she smiled when she felt movement inside. Then a brilliant light suddenly emitted from her body, surrounding Tessa with the warmth of healing.

Tessa blinked, until finally her eyes came back to focus.

"You're going to be just fine," Lilith said.

Tessa couldn't believe what her eyes were telling her. It was as if she was looking into the past at her younger self, except the person looking down at her had eyes like diamonds. They shimmered so brightly it was almost painful to gaze upon them. And her skin was... ghostlike.

Lilith sensed Tessa's fear. "Don't worry. I'm not going harm you."

Tessa's mouth dropped open. It took her a moment to find her voice. "Who are you?"

"My name is Lilith. And I'm your mother."

"Your real name is Lisa..." Tessa sat upright and tilted her head a little. "Lisa Wellington." When Lilith nodded, Tessa said, "How is this possible? You look so... young."

"If you'll allow me, I can show you."

Tessa flinched as Lilith brought her hand forward.

"Trust me, Tessa."

When Tessa nodded, Lilith placed her hand on the side of her face. With a sigh, she leaned into the warmth of Lilith's palm. As their minds connected, images were shown to Tessa like photos of a picture book, flipping pages through Lilith's past. Her eyes softened at the memory of her mother telling her how much she loved her. But sadly, Dr. Hubert Crane and his evil colleagues captured her mother and tortured her with painful tests for many years. After they altered her DNA, Lisa had been reborn as Lilith.

Tessa exhaled a deep breath when Lilith removed her hand. She looked at her mother with tears in her eyes. "It's true. Everything in your journal is true." She shook her head. "But I don't understand. What does Sebastian and his brother have to do with all this? Why did you have them take me from my family?"

"I'm sorry, Tessa. There was no other way. I had to keep you safe."

"Sebastian is a monster," Tessa said. "How is that keeping me safe? You could have just come to me alone."

"There are people..." Lilith briefly paused, trying to find the right words to explain. "The people that did this to me are after you and your brother."

"My Covenant is my safe place," Tessa said. "My fiancé has probably been worrying himself sick over all this. I have to let him know I'm okay."

"Your Covenant cannot keep you safe. I'm the only one that has enough power to keep you and your unborn children out of harm's way. You must understand."

"Then why not work together?" Tessa looked at Lilith in frustration. "Whoever these people are, the Covenant can help you destroy them."

"I'm sorry, Tessa. But after everything I've been through, it's hard to trust anyone. I was afraid your Covenant would turn against me. When I met Thomas, he swore he would help me. I had no one else I could go to."

"You trust me, don't you?"

"You are my daughter," Lilith said. "How could I not trust you?"

"If you trust me, you can trust my Covenant," Tessa said. "I promise, they will help put an end to the people that have done this to you." Then her thoughts went to Steven. "I almost forgot," she went on to say. "I was able to telepathically connect with my brother a few times. He's staying at the Covenant."

"I know, and we will go to him," Lilith said. "I will have Thomas make the arrangements."

"Kenneth," Tessa said, "he must be worried sick. You do remember my father, don't you?"

Lilith's eyes widened and suddenly filled with tears. As the droplets slid down her cheeks, she reached up and wiped her finger across her translucent skin. Looking down at the wetness on her fingertip, she had a crushing sensation enter her body. Throughout her memories, she didn't recall ever expressing this emotion. After all the torture she'd been through, it had gotten to the point that she believed she'd been born without tear ducts. But feelings of sorrow crept into her empty chest, and squeezed her dead heart, replacing it with a beating rhythm. For the first time in years, she could feel the thump of her heart beating with a fast tempo.

As she placed her hand over her chest, her gaze met Tessa's. "It's been so long... and with all the horrible lab tests... my memories of him over the years seemed to fade. But now, I remember." More tears fell from her eyes. "I can see his handsome face and hear his tender voice." She wiped her eyes and looked at Tessa, confused. "But how did he find you?"

"Although, at the time, it seemed purely coincidental," Tessa said, "but now I believe it was fate that brought us together. We ran into each other at the hospital. He was the surgeon that helped a friend of mine. He told me later after a DNA test proved I was his daughter, the moment he saw me, he instantly knew. He said I looked so much like you. He has never stopped loving you and vowed to never give up hope in finding you."

In the silence that followed, Lilith felt as though her beating heart was about to break. Her lips trembled. "I'm so sorry, Tessa."

Thomas exhaled a deep breath as he came upon Garrett's body. He was lying in the floor in a pool of his own blood, staring out of glassy dead eyes.

"Dammit," he said as he reached inside his jacket for his phone. After he searched through his contacts, he initiated a call. "It's Thomas Carlyle." He kept his voice low. "I need more time. A few days tops. I swear... I'll get you Lilith's son."

"I've waited long enough!" an angry German voice shouted on the other end. "We go now! Rendezvous with my men at the Covenant in an hour."

"Please, Dr. Crane. Just give me one more day."

"You've had more than enough time. If you and your brother are not there within the hour, you'll both be lying on a cold slab. I'll have my men come for Lilith's daughter. Be ready."

Thomas's face turned pale. "You'll still keep your side of the bargain, right? You promised to leave Lilith alone if I brought you her children."

As he waited for an answer, he became worried until, finally, he realized Dr. Crane had ended the call. He tucked his phone back into the pocket of his jacket and prayed the deal he'd made with the physician would still go as planned. He would do anything to keep Lilith safe, even if he had to betray her trust.

"What the hell happened to Garrett?"

Thomas turned to face Sebastian. "It was Lilith. She got into his head."

"What?" Sebastian's eyes rounded. "Are you saying she did this?"

Thomas nodded. "Garrett hurt Tessa."

"Is she okay?"

"I don't know."

Chapter Forty-One

In a wave of panic, Eve hurried upstairs to the nursery. As she neared the door, she could hear one of the twins crying. She released a deep breath, and when she opened the door, she could see the top of Tidus's head peering over the crib. His face was red and scrunched up with unhappiness. The sound of the gun going off, she thought, most likely woke him.

"It's okay, sweetheart," she whispered. "Mommy is here."

Tidus reached out his tiny hands, whining for Eve to pick him up. The moment she lifted him into her arms, he quieted and nestled his head in the crevice of her neck.

When Eve heard laughter, she peered down at Arius. He was sitting up in the crib, playing patty-cake with his hands. The image made her smile. Regardless of what his father and Thomas had said about Arius's powers he'd inherited from the Chiang-shih demon, he was such a happy little boy. Never once had he cried.

She reached down and smoothed her free hand over his dark, curly hair. "You're such a good little boy. I love you so much, sweetheart."

Arius looked up at her and grinned. Then, to her surprise, a bright light engulfed his entire body.

Eve instantly put a hand up to shield her eyes. Before she got the chance to grab Arius, the light dissipated, taking him with it.

"Arius..." Eve frantically called out.

The hair on the back of Sebastian's neck rose when he heard a scream coming from upstairs. It sounded like Eve. "The twins," he gasped. "Something is wrong."

In a split second, Sebastian took off upstairs with Thomas on his heals. When they stepped inside the nursery, Eve's face was wet with tears.

"Eve..." Sebastian reached for Tidus. "What happened?"

"It's Arius." Her voice cracked, emotion knotting her throat. "He's gone."

"What do you mean he's *gone?*"

Eve dropped to her knees and sobbed. "He just disappeared."

Sebastian knelt beside her with Tidus in his arms. "It's going to be okay. Try to calm down and tell me exactly what happened."

"There was a bright light, and when it vanished..." She swallowed back tears. "...it took Arius with it."

"I think I know what happened."

Eve wiped her eyes and looked at Sebastian, confused. "What are you talking about?"

"Arius must have the ability to use a portal."

"But he's just a baby. Where would he go?"

"There's a possibility..." Sebastian gritted his teeth. "...he could have gone back to the Covenant."

Eve shook her head. "But why?"

"That's where your sister is, and the only place he could remember to go."

Eve instantly broke down into more tears.

Sebastian reached out to her. "I'll get him back."

The sound of someone clearing their throat caught their attention. As Thomas, Sebastian, and Eve looked at the open doorway, Lilith and Tessa stepped inside.

"We heard screams," Lilith said. "Is everything all right?"

"It's Arius," Sebastian said, his eyes going from Lilith to Tessa and back again. "He disappeared, and we think he has the ability to use a portal."

Tessa's eyes flashed wide, remembering the few times she'd witnessed Arius vanishing from his room. "It's true," she spoke out. "When he was living in the Covenant, he used a portal a couple of times, but he didn't go far. We saw him on the security cameras. The first time, we found him in Natalie's room. Another time, we found him outside, and he took Natalie with him."

Eve covered her mouth, shocked by what Tessa had just revealed. Slowly, she lowered her hand and stood. "Do you think Arius went back to the Covenant?"

"More than likely," Tessa replied. "I'm sure he misses your sister and Natalie."

Sebastian rose to his feet and kept his eyes on Tessa, staring at her like he wanted to strangle her. "Why didn't you say something about this sooner?"

"How could I?" Tessa pursed her lips. "I've been locked up for days and drugged half the time."

Lilith reached out and took hold of Tessa's hand. "My daughter is not a prisoner here. She's to be treated as our guest." She looked at Sebastian and narrowed her eyes. Then she shifted her focus on Thomas. "Does everyone here understand, or do I need to explain it like I did with Garrett?"

Eve cringed as the image of Garrett pointing a gun at his head came to mind.

Sebastian snarled his upper lip and finally nodded an understanding.

Tessa glared at Sebastian with hatred. It took everything in her power not to allow him to see the paralyzing fear from the past. She wouldn't give him the satisfaction. There was no way she would go back to being that scared, helpless woman she'd been when he had kidnapped her. Now, she was the Breedline queen... and this time *she* was in control.

"You have our word," Thomas finally said, bowing his head. "Please forgive me, Miss Fairchild. From here on, you can trust that I will treat you with the upmost respect."

"I don't just give my trust to anyone," Tessa said. "You must earn it. And so far, Mr. Carlyle, you're a long way from it."

Tessa's smug words burned Sebastian to the bone. He balled his hands up and looked at her with daggers in his eyes.

"If you want Arius back," Tessa said, "I can help you."

"Why would you help us?" Sebastian said. "And how can we trust it's not just a trick?"

"What other choice do you have?"

Sebastian smirked. "So what's your plan then?"

"You can make a trade," Tessa said. "Me for Arius. And one more thing. My mother goes with me."

Thomas's left eye nervously twitched. Although the thought of betraying Lilith created a painful ache in his chest, he had no other choice. If he didn't hand over Tessa and Steven to Dr. Crane within the next hour, he was a dead man, which now involved his brother.

Lilith looked at Thomas. "You will make the arrangements. Contact the Covenant first thing in the morning. Tessa will give you the number to their head council."

He nodded. "Of course, Lilith."

* * *

As Angel stood outside the door to her and Tim's bedroom, she watched him stride in her direction. He had a contented look on his face. He'd just tucked their daughter in for the night.

He approached Angel with his hand extended, inviting her to take hold. When she clasped her hand on to his, he tugged her close.

He arched a brow. "Ready for bed, sweetheart?"

"But I'm not tired."

"I didn't say anything about being tired," he said playfully. "But I'm ready to go to bed. Sleep, however, is not on my mind."

"Umm..." she murmured. "I like the sound of that."

He led her inside, and when he closed the door, he reached up to her face. She shivered as he trailed a finger over her cheek.

"I love you, Angel."

"And I love you."

While he started to unfasten his jeans, he gave her a look of desire. "I want you in our bed, naked with me." Then he leaned in and whispered close to her ear, "I want your legs wrapped around me... with me inside you."

His words made her weak in the knees. The demanding tone of his voice created a needy sensation between her thighs. She couldn't wait to feel his touch. She wanted his feather-light caresses on every inch of her body.

"Undress for me," he whispered.

Angel sucked in a breath and licked her lips nervously. She kept her eyes focused on his while she lifted her blouse over her head. By the time she got down to her bra and panties, she hadn't even managed to remove them before he was standing in front of her completely naked, his eyes impatiently waiting for her.

"Would you like to help me undress?"

He cocked a brow. "I guess I can make the sacrifice."

She smiled as he started to unfasten her bra. His fingers worked quickly, pulling it forward, slowly guiding the straps down her arms. Then he knelt on one knee and slid down her lace panties, letting the tiny scrap fall to the floor.

As he rose back to his feet, his eyes followed the path of her smooth skin. He made a sound in the back of his throat that resembled a low growl. "You're beautiful."

The moment he eased down on the bed, she lightly pushed at his shoulders. They tumbled down together and landed with a soft bounce. When she positioned her body over his, they molded together perfectly as though they were destined for one another.

With the tip of her tongue, she licked over his bottom lip and then slid it inside his mouth. Instantly, heat raced through his body like a blazing inferno.

He shifted on top of her and said, "I need you."

Anticipating his touch, she looked up into his half-lidded eyes and whispered, "I'm all yours."

When his fingertips trailed over her skin, drifting and circling closer to her inner thighs, she let out a soft moan. His touch was sensual and gentle.

She twisted against him, arching into his hand as his fingers grew more insistent. He knew how to touch her and just the right amount of pressure, caressing the exact spot that created wave after wave of intense pleasure.

Moments later, she went limp in his arms, content in the aftermath of his magic touch. Slowly she came back to awareness when he rained a trail of soft kisses over the curve of her shoulder and to the crevice of her neck.

"That felt wonderful," she whispered.

"I'm glad you approve. I love..." his voice trailed off as he turned toward the baby monitor on top of the nightstand.

"What's wrong, honey?"

"I heard voices," he said. "They're coming from Natalie's room."

Angel lifted her head and listened. Her eyes rounded when she heard laughter coming from the monitor.

"Someone is in the room with Natalie," she said. "Hurry, let's get dressed."

Tim quickly got to his feet and grabbed his jeans. While he shrugged them over his hips, Angel hurriedly reached for a robe and slipped it on. Seconds later, they were out the door. As they stood outside Natalie's bedroom, they could hear chatter coming from inside.

As Tim flung the door open, Buddy the cat leaped off the bed and darted between his feet.

Angel's eyes widened. "Oh my gosh... it's Arius."

"Baa-bee," Natalie mumbled, pointing her finger at Arius.

Tim turned to Angel and said, "Stay here, honey. I'll go get Jem and Mia."

As soon as he left, Angel stepped inside the room and reached for Arius, who was sucking his thumb. "Come here, sweetheart," she said, lifting him into her arms. "We've missed you and your brother." She kissed his cheek. "Where in the world have you been?"

Arius looked at Angel and grinned with his thumb angled further into his mouth.

Natalie reached for Arius, openly pleading with her mother to put him down.

"Okay, Natalie," Angel said, placing Arius back on the bed.

It was such an endearing sight as Angel sat down next to the two toddlers. As she watched them play, she was struck by the rightness of it all. But she knew this put her family and the Covenant in danger. Somewhere out there, Sebastian would be waiting for the right opportunity to come back for his son.

Chapter Forty-Two

When Sebastian handed Tidus back to Eve and stepped outside the nursery with Thomas, Tessa looked at Lilith and said, "Would it be okay if I visit with Eve and Tidus for a little while?"

"Of course, Tessa. You're a guest here. Feel welcome to do as you please."

Tessa smiled. "Thank you."

As she watched her mother leave, she turned to Eve. "Is Sebastian keeping you here against your will?"

Eve shook her head. "I came here willingly, but now..." She looked at Tessa with weary eyes. "I don't trust Thomas. I think he's hiding something."

"Do you think Sebastian knows?"

"No. I think he's lying to Sebastian and your mother."

Tessa looked at her in question. "Have you mentioned this to Sebastian?"

"That's the thing," Eve said. "I don't know if I can trust him either."

"Why?"

"Sebastian and his brother mentioned Arius's birthmark. It has something to do with the powers he inherited from the Chiang-shih demon. I think they plan to use my son against the Covenant."

Footsteps passed in the hallway and Tessa knew she only had moments before Sebastian came back. "Would you be willing to go back to the Covenant with me?"

When Eve nodded, Tessa sagged in relief. "Okay, good. But whatever you do, please don't tell Sebastian. He'll do anything to keep you and your sons from going back."

"Before the incident with Garrett," Eve reluctantly said, "I was actually going to search this place for you. I knew Thomas and Sebastian had you stashed somewhere. For some reason, your mother trusted Thomas to keep you safe. I don't think she knows what kind of person he truly is. I was going to figure out how I could get you back to the Covenant. I was also planning on turning myself in, hoping Jem and Mia would take care of my boys while I stood trial."

"You're making the right decision, Eve. And I promise, I'll make sure you get a fair trial."

"Thank you, Tessa."

When Tidus started to fuss, Tessa reached out and said, "Do you mind if I hold him?"

"Of course," Eve said, handing him to her.

As Tessa gathered Tidus in her arms, she rocked him gently. She looked up at Eve and said, "I was just curious. Where in England is this place?"

"I believe it's seventeen Curzon Street in London."

Tessa silently nodded, and then suddenly, Steven's voice whispered into her mind.

"Tessa... it's Steven. Can you hear me?"

Her brows creased in pain, and it took every bit of strength she had to keep from reacting in front of Eve.

The moment Steven absorbed most of Tessa's pain, the tension in her head eased and relief was stark in her eyes.

"Yes," Tessa finally said. *"I'm okay, Steven."*

"Have you figured out where Sebastian is keeping you?"

Before she could respond, Tidus—who was unaware of Tessa and Steven's telepathic connection—chortled in glee and grasped a handful of her hair. He pulled a long strand to his mouth.

Tessa pried her hair from his little fingers and handed him back to Eve. "I think he's hungry."

"I'm in London," she quickly told Steven. *"At seventeen Curzon Street."*

"Thank God. As soon as I tell the others, I promise, we'll come for you, Tessa."

"Wait, Steven..." Tessa called out to him in desperation, but the link ended when she saw Sebastian enter the room.

"I'll give you two some privacy," Tessa said as she went for the door.

Sebastian grabbed her arm. "Not so fast."

"Sebastian..." Eve's tone was firm. "Don't hurt her."

He turned toward Eve. "What did you say?"

"You heard what Lilith said. Please, Sebastian, just let her go."

Sebastian cocked a brow. "Is there something going on here that I should be aware of?"

Eve shook her head. "I don't want our son to witness anything that has to do with violence. Is that so much to ask?"

He released Tessa and said, "Before you go, you might want a bit of advice. If you're thinking of connecting with Jace to give him your location so he can rescue you..." His lips formed a smug grin. "...I wouldn't if I were you. But I'm sure you've already tried. The drug Thomas was using to sedate you has a nasty side effect. It will cause you a great deal of pain as well as Jace. It can also be lethal to both of you after so many doses."

Tessa nodded, and before she walked out, she turned to Eve and smiled. As she descended the stairs, someone from behind grabbed her and yanked her back. She opened her mouth to scream but was silenced by a large hand.

"Be easy with her," Thomas said to the huge man who had his hand over Tessa's mouth. "Dr. Crane ordered that she is not to be harmed."

Tessa tried to make a connection with Steven, but her efforts were cut off when she felt a sharp stick in the side of her arm. Then she felt herself being lifted by a strong pair of arms and carried until she felt the warm breeze on her face.

Thomas opened the back door of a dark sedan that was parked in the drive. "Hurry, get her inside."

The man who had Tessa placed her in the back seat and climbed in beside her.

"Take her straight to Dr. Crane," Thomas directed.

When the driver in the front nodded, Thomas looked back at Tessa with guilt written all over his face. "I'm sorry, Miss Fairchild."

He closed the door and watched as the car drove away.

* * *

An overwhelming relief burned brightly in Mia's eyes when she saw Arius sitting on the bed next to Natalie. They were chattering gibberish like two magpies and acting like they were long-lost playmates. It filled her heart with joy. As she turned to look at Jem, he smiled at her and said, "I think someone missed us."

Mia nodded. "If only he'd brought his brother back with him."

When Arius heard Mia's voice, he pointed at her and said, "Ma-ma."

Mia instantly came forward and scooped him into her arms. "I missed you so much, sweetheart."

Arius rested his head on her shoulder, and when he noticed Jem standing in the doorway, he said, "Da-da."

Mia looked to Jem to gauge his reaction. But he didn't seem to mind in the least. Jem's entire face softened, and a gentle smile emerged from his lips. When he moved next to Mia, he extended his arms out to Arius. "Come here, little buddy."

Arius's eyes flickered with glee as he latched on to Jem.

Mia's heart lurched, and a knot formed in her throat. Tears clogged her eyes, and she blinked as the drops fell down her cheeks.

Jem leaned over, and to Mia's surprise, he kissed her softly. Nothing prolonged, just a quick brush. But it was intimate all the same.

"Who wants pancakes?" he said, ruffling Arius's hair.

Natalie clapped her hands. "Yummy..."

Tim leaned close to Angel and said, "Honey, would you and Mia take the kiddos to the kitchen while I gather everyone for a meeting? I've got to put everyone in the Covenant on alert. I'm sure it won't be long before Sebastian comes for Arius."

Angel nodded. "Of course, honey."

"I know it's late," Tim said, his focus solely on Jem. "But we've got to prepare for the worst."

Jem nodded and handed Arius back to Mia. "Take Arius and go with Angel while I help Tim," he said. "I'll send one of the guards to the kitchen to watch over things just as a safety precaution."

As Mia snuggled Arius in her arms, Jem leaned down and kissed the top of his head. "Be good, little man."

Before Tim stepped out of the room, his cell phone went off. He dug it out of his back pocket and noticed it was Steven calling.

When Tim answered, everyone stood back and waited, wondering who was on the other end.

"Okay, Steven," Tim finally said. "I'll gather the others. We'll meet you in the library."

He tucked his phone back in his pocket and said, "That was Steven. He's got Tessa's exact location."

Jem sighed. "Thank God."

"We need to move fast," Tim said. "I'll inform Drakon while you tell Jace. We'll meet up in the library so we can figure out our next move."

As Mia watched Jem turn away and leave with Tim, her gaze shifted across the room to Angel. When she saw Mia's helpless expression, she nodded an understanding. "Don't worry, Mia. Everything will work out. We'll get Tessa and Tidus back."

Mia smiled a little. "Thanks, Angel."

Moments later, as they stepped out of Natalie's room, Mia saw Jem standing outside Jace's bedroom door. As she followed Angel down the stairs, she could hear Jace's voice in the background. It was obvious Jem had delivered the news about Tessa by Jace's joyful outburst.

Chapter Forty-Three

While an anxious group of Breedline gathered inside the library, the mood was grim and tense. Everyone's nerves were on edge. Tim stood at the head of the table next to where Drakon sat as they surveyed the other occupants of the room.

Jace and his twin brother Jem sat close to one another in utter silence, waiting for the rest of the crew to arrive. Under normal circumstances, when Jem had to face unusual situations involving one of their family members, he had the ability to remain calm and focused. But Jace... he was altogether entirely different. He was like a ticking time bomb ready to explode. And now that Tessa had been taken by Sebastian for the second time, his nerves were just about shot. Things could end up getting dicey if Jace's Beast emerged.

Kyle and his best friend Casey sat in the chairs across the table from Jace and Jem, looking nervous as hell. Sitting at the same table with a guy who could shift into a seven-foot werewolf that could rip your head clean off your shoulders wasn't exactly something you looked forward to. If something provoked Jace, things could quickly take a turn for the worse.

Moments later, the other members of the Covenant arrived. Alexander came in with Helen and Steven. They sat down in the empty chairs alongside Casey. Finally, Jem and Jace's sister Cassie and their Uncle Jackson stepped into the room. Celina came in behind them and sat in the vacant chair next to her boyfriend Kyle. When everyone was seated, Tim cleared his throat and said, "We've finally located where Sebastian has Tessa. And that's not the only reason why I've called this meeting. About ten minutes ago, Angel and I found Arius in Natalie's room."

Everyone looked at Tim in complete shock. When Tim began to explain how they were going to rescue Tessa, he was interrupted as Bruce Carmichael barged into the room. By the look on his face, Tim knew something was wrong.

"Someone has breached the Covenant's grounds," he said, trying to catch his breath. "The outside alarm has been tripped."

Tim's gut tightened and Jace shot out of his chair, anger creasing his forehead.

"It's Sebastian..." Jace growled. "I'm going to rip him into pieces."

Tim quickly stepped in Jace's path as he went for the door. "Now is not the time to lose control. We've got to stay focused. I need you to pull it together and keep a level head."

"This is bullshit." Jace puffed out his chest. "I'm tired of waiting around, dammit. It's time to fight for our family and this Covenant."

A course of agreement circled the room.

"He's right, Tim," Jem spoke out. "There is no reasoning when it comes to Sebastian. It's time to put an end to this."

Tim looked at Jem, and then his eyes roamed over the faces of everyone seated at the table. He knew Jem was right. He rubbed a hand over his short-trimmed hair and said, "You're right. I—"

He was cut off as Angel moved past Bruce with Natalie in her arms. Her eyes were filled with fear and her voice was panic-stricken. "It's Mia and Arius... They're gone."

Everyone instantly rushed over while Tim did his best to calm Angel. "What happened, honey?"

"Mia took Arius in the other room to change him." Angel's voice trembled. "I wasn't worried since one of the guards went with her. When I realized how much time had passed, I went to check on them. The guard... his throat had been cut, and Mia and Arius were gone."

"Son of a bitch," Jace gritted out.

Jem lowered his head and buried his face into his hands. He couldn't bear the thought of losing Mia. His hands shook as rage and sorrow battled for equal control of his emotions.

"It's time," Jem finally said as grief knotted his throat. "We have to end this now."

Tim briefly closed his eyes, the nightmare only growing more horrific with every passing second. His family was getting ripped apart in front of his eyes, and he wasn't going to be helpless and watch it all happen. He was forced to do the unthinkable, which meant they would have to take lives. It was a reality of what they had to do to survive. The decisions they were faced with were difficult, but at the end of the day, they lived with the choices to keep their family safe. When it came down to saving this Covenant from monsters like Sebastian Crow, he'd play dirty. He'd fight dirty. And he'd take down anyone by any means necessary.

Tim focused on the guard and said, "Bruce... I need you to stay here with the women and children. I'm guessing it was Sebastian who took Mia and Arius. He must have used a portal to get inside." Then he looked between Alexander and Jackson. "Stay here and help Bruce. Although the Guardians cannot help us fight, they have the power to keep whatever's on our doorstep from entering this Covenant."

Jackson nodded. "I'll do whatever it takes to keep them safe."

When Alexander opened his mouth to protest, Tim held up a halting hand. "Before you say anything, Alexander... let me speak. I know you want to help us fight, but I need you to stay here. Your strength is needed to keep our family out of harm's way."

Alexander reluctantly nodded. "Okay. I promise to protect them with my life."

"Thank you, Alexander."

Drakon came forward. "So what's our next move?"

"Sebastian may not be the only one we're dealing with," Tim pointed out. "I'll need you to bring up the surveillance cameras so we can get a look at what we're up against."

Shortly after, everyone gathered in the security room. Drakon's hands shook as he punched in codes and brought up the surveillance footage of the Covenant's grounds.

"Oh shit," Drakon said as the images on the monitor came into full view. "What the hell is that?"

"Breedline hybrids," Steven spoke out. "They were created by Dr. Hans Autenburg and Dr. Hubert Crane."

"What the hell are they doing here?"

"If I had to bet," Tim chimed in, "they're working with Sebastian and his twin brother."

"Jeez..." Jace groaned. "Can they be killed?"

Steven nodded. "They're as strong as any Breedline, but they're not indestructible."

"What will kill them?"

Steven looked at Jace and simply said, "Me."

* * *

With a firm hold on Arius, Mia stared up at Sebastian and shivered at the calculated way he looked at her. There was no mistaking the expression of triumph in his eyes. He knew he'd won, and he was relishing every moment of her fear and helplessness.

"Well, well, well," Sebastian said in a dragged-out fashion. "I bet you're surprised to see me."

She gritted her teeth. "What did you do with Tessa?"

"Tessa is none of your concern," he said with a clear smirk in his voice.

Mia lowered her head. Grief welled in her heart, spreading until her entire chest ached. When silence fell between them, she looked back up and shot him a look of pure hatred.

"Ready to admit defeat, Mia?" Sebastian said as he circled around her. "Jem cannot help you now."

Her knees wobbled, but by sheer grit alone she managed to remain on her feet. "You can go straight to hell."

His lips curled up like a bow. "As I recall," his voice settled over her like a suffocating fog, "it wasn't long ago that you loathed the Breedline. So, tell me, Mia. What changed that dark heart of yours?"

"If Jem doesn't find you first," she hissed, "I swear, I'll kill you myself."

Sebastian's eyebrows went up. "You're a scrapper, aren't you, Mia?" He laughed. "I like that in a woman."

A spark of rage flashed in her eyes. "What about my sister? Does Eve know you've brought me here?"

"What Eve doesn't know won't hurt her. Besides, she'll be too busy taking care of my sons."

"You're a sick bastard. You don't give a damn about Eve or your sons. It's all about control. You don't care about anything but yourself and what you can take. You're God in your own mind, and you think everyone is a pawn to do what you want, when you want."

"Whatever," he said in a smug tone. "It doesn't change the fact that I'm holding all the cards. You belong to me now. Forget all about Jem. You're mine to do with as I please."

Mia's mouth gaped open. She was so furious that she couldn't even see straight.

Sebastian clapped his hands, and when the door opened, Mia turned to look. When a tall, muscular male covered in tattoos came into the room, she recognized his face. It was Corbin Azzo. He was wanted for his crimes against his own Breedline Covenant.

When Corbin looked between Mia and Sebastian, it was obvious by the way he glared at Sebastian they weren't long-lost pals.

"Corbin," Sebastian snarled his upper lip, "take my son to his mother."

Mia tightened her arms around Arius as Corbin moved toward her.

"Don't make this difficult," Corbin said, holding out his hands. "Give me the baby."

She nodded in defeat and handed Arius over.

As Corbin started for the door, Arius looked back at Mia with his brows scrunched. In that moment, she wanted to slap Sebastian across the face.

"He'll be fine," Sebastian said. "He's just confused, that's all. It's because you look so much like Eve. As he gets older, he'll know the difference."

Before Mia could respond, Sebastian extended his hand and created a portal. In a matter of seconds, he stepped into the light and vanished, leaving Mia in the room all alone. Her mind was a whirlwind. Somehow, she had to figure a way to escape. There was no way she was going to live her life as Sebastian's personal concubine.

Chapter Forty-Four

Tessa's sanity was on edge as she woke up completely immobilized. Her arms were strapped to a thinly padded table and bands were attached to her ankles and around her neck. The worst of it all was having no idea where she'd been taken.

She struggled against the restraints, but it was hopeless; they were too tight. Exhaling a deep breath, she peered out of the corner of her eye and surveyed her surroundings. Tessa gasped when she saw her mother. She was lying motionless inside what looked to be a clear incubator. She could feel tears brimming in her eyes until they spilled over and flooded from the corners.

Oh God, please, she begged silently. *Please help us.*

When two men wearing face masks and white lab coats moved in her field of vision, she cried out, "Please... where am I? What do you want with me?"

They ignored her pleas and acted as though she didn't exist. As they moved about, attaching some sort of electrode pads to her forehead, she felt frightened and unsure of what their intentions were.

"Please... please don't hurt my babies."

Within seconds, she felt an electrical shock all the way down to her toes. As she screamed in agony, there were no reactions, no emotions, on the masked faces looking down at her.

Finally, when the pain eased, she closed her eyes and concentrated on Steven. He was her only hope for a way out of here.

* * *

Jace cocked his head and looked at Steven, confused. "Are you saying you're the only one that can kill those things?"

"Like me, they're impervious to silver. But if you're fast enough, and they don't kill you first, go for the neck. That's their weakness."

"So you're saying if we break their necks, they'll die?"

Steven nodded. "Or, in your case, you could just rip their heads off. That'll do."

"Now you're talking my language." Jace clapped a hand over Steven's shoulder. "I think I'm really starting to like you, Steven."

Drakon pointed at the monitor as two dark sedans pulled up to the outside gate. "Take a look, guys. We've got more company."

The second everyone turned to look, at least a dozen hybrids, if not more, scurried over the gate and across the lawn.

"Shit..." Tim cursed under his breath, feeling the hairs on the back of his neck rise. "Get ready, everyone. We're about to go into battle." He swallowed hard. "We'll have to shift since silver bullets won't kill those things. Steven and Jem... I need you two positioned at the front entrance while the rest of us slip out the back and attack them from behind."

Steven gave a quick nod and then turned to Jem. "It's now or never."

"I'm ready," Jem replied. "Let's do this."

Tim looked at Jace and said, "You ready to wake up the Beast?"

"Hell yeah!"

Before their transformations began, everyone reached back for the wall to steady themselves when a distant explosion shook the Covenant.

"What the hell?" Jace growled.

Tim looked at Steven and Jem. "Okay, guys, on my count, you two go to the front. The rest of us will hit them from behind. One, two... *three!*"

Steven broke off into a run, and Jem followed close behind. In the blink of an eye, Steven started transforming. His skin took on a luminous sheen and his eyes glimmered like diamonds. When his transformation was complete, he took out two shooters outside the entrance while Jem extended his palm and blasted a fireball, downing two more.

Seconds later, a shot came from behind, and Jem went down, clutching his arm. When Jem heard a cracking noise like the sound of bones breaking, he turned to look. That's when he saw Steven releasing a gunman with his neck twisted at an unnatural angle.

Steven rushed to Jem and knelt next to him, eyeballing the blood on his shirt. "You think you're strong enough to stand?"

"Yeah," Jem grunted. "It's just a graze."

Steven extended his hand. "Come on, then."

When Jem took hold of Steven's hand, he hauled him to his feet.

"You ready?"

Jem nodded. "Let's finish this."

As the gunfire escalated, Jace's adrenaline shot through the roof. He quickly looked at the others in alarm. It was then they all realized they had not a second to spare.

Jace was the first to begin shifting. He yanked his shirt over his head and toed off his boots. His body expanded as if something within him was overtaking his natural form. For a moment, he hovered in that in-between state, flickering between human and Beast and said, "Bastards..." His words were deep and distorted. "I'm going to rip them into pieces."

Kyle shot Casey a look. "Let's go kick some ass."

Casey nodded, realizing what had to be done. Exposing his secret was something he had to risk in order to save his friends he considered family.

Jace's body quaked with fury, the creature within itching to be released. It curdled in his veins, calling to the Beast inside him.

At first, it looked as if there was something inside of his body too large for his skin. His face began to bulge and move in odd ways. In a matter of seconds, white, coarse hairs grew out of his pores and covered his skin.

Kyle's eyes widened as he looked up at Jace's Beast. *Shit!*

Tim, Drakon, Casey, and Kyle stepped back as Jace's seven-foot creature let out a thunderous roar. The Beast lowered his big head and snarled before he tore off, leaving the others to complete their transformations.

Relieved to still be in one piece, Kyle heaved out a deep breath. "Okay guys... here goes nothing."

The muscles in his body began tremble as the Breedline rose inside him with raw power. Straining muscles rippled beneath his skin while the tendons in his neck stood out like drawn bowstrings. Thick hairs sprouted from his pores as the change came upon Kyle instantly. Faster than the human eye could perceive, dark fur covered his entire body. The Breedline wolf in him wanted nothing more than to take down his enemies in battle. Throwing his head back, he howled a purely inhuman sound and rushed onward.

Drakon suddenly dropped to all fours when an uncontrollable rush broke out all over his body. Spasms twisted his gut and thick veins bulged from his skin, bringing forth his rogue wolf.

Tim watched the beginnings of Drakon's transformation while he felt the change within his own body begin to take hold.

A low growl caught Casey's attention. He averted his eyes from Drakon and focused on Tim's gigantic wolf as he charged onward with Drakon on his heels.

Casey closed his eyes and did what he had to do. He focused on his Theriomorph side and called to the panther within him. Embracing the animal, he surrendered to the change.

As he bounded forward on padded feet, the shrill roar of his panther echoed throughout the Covenant and beyond.

As the Beast smashed through the back door, wood splintered into pieces, and masses of Dr. Crane's hybrid wolves rushed toward him with their powerful gaping jaws. The weight of their impact knocked him off balance, and as he fell to the ground, they attacked him like any animal of the wild moving in for the kill.

Although the Beast was at a disadvantage, he was not alone. Drakon's enormous rogue-wolf charged forward. Using his dagger-size teeth, he snatched one of the hybrids off the Beast and flung him like a rag doll. Before Tim and Kyle jumped in to help, Drakon grabbed another hybrid and pinned it to the ground. He snapped his jaws and crushed its skull like an eggshell.

As Tim and Kyle surged into action, they got attacked from both sides. There were so many hybrids they couldn't even fathom the amount, only hear the growls of the monsters.

The battle had only begun, Tim realized, and he knew they were all outnumbered. Hot hybrid blood sprayed as the Breedline fought tooth and nail.

A hissing noise came from beyond, catching Tim's attention. In the split-second he turned to look, an enormous black panther leaped in midair. When it landed, a deafening scream came from its jaws. With one quick swipe of its massive paw, a headless body of a hybrid dropped to the ground.

In anger, Jace's Beast had not only the instincts of the savage killer but his Breedline blood and something else left from the man he used to be. He remembered his beloved and his unborn sons. It was his job to protect them. Using his razor-sharp claws, the Beast slashed into the flesh of his enemies. As his claws struck them, slicing through their hide, the hybrids howled in pain—pain that brought the Beast into focus, fueling his rage.

Tim had never heard such anguish from animal or human like the wails coming from the hybrids.

Out of nowhere, the giant panther bounded after a black sedan. First, it leaped onto the roof and then dropped down in front of the windshield as the vehicle swerved. Glass exploded as it came to a screeching halt.

The battle was still raging when Steven and Jem stepped out of the fog and into the heat of the conflict. The air reeked of blood and war. A scene of utter chaos and carnage greeted their eyes. Their attention was drawn to a wrecked vehicle with a man screaming inside while an enormous black panther attacked him through the shattered windshield.

They shifted their focus and looked toward the sound of Jace's Beast. Its white pelt was covered in blood as it fought with a vengeance. Although they had already taken out many hybrids, they were still severely outnumbered. Jem counted at least a dozen or more. Despite the grim situation, he refused to give up. He would die fighting if that's what it took. His family needed every ally they could spare if any of them hoped to survive this bloodbath.

The second Jem blasted a blazing fireball from the palm of his hand, flames torched several of their enemies and filled the air with smoke and death.

In the speed of a blur, Steven tackled a monstrous hybrid the size of two Breedline wolves without it even registering his movement. He had one arm locked around the creature's throat as it thrashed and struggled against his tight grip. With a forceful twist, he snapped its neck, sending the unholy creature to its death.

Chapter Forty-Five

All at once, the remaining hybrids suddenly turned and retreated. Jem looked beyond Steven to where Jace's Beast stood, his body positioned, ready for another attack. The longer they stood around in the silence, the more Jem grew uneasy. His gut was screaming, and the hairs prickled and rose on the back of his neck.

There was something odd and decidedly wrong with this picture. Jem was about to say something to Steven when a shiny metal object catapulted over the gate. The round projectile caught a glint of the moonlight before it plummeted to the ground.

He realized it was a grenade and shouted, "Everyone get down!"

Jem dove behind a concrete statue as it exploded on impact. His ears rang, and the smell of gunpowder filled his nostrils.

In the aftermath of the explosion, he peered over the statue, but the smoke and dust clouded his visibility. He could only hear the groans of pain.

As Jem rushed to his feet to search for the others, Steven staggered from the debris with his hand over his side, gasping in pain.

Jem got to him just as his knees started to buckle and helped him take cover behind the statue.

"Dammit," Steven winced in pain. "I got hit."

When Jem saw a sharp piece of shrapnel embedded in Steven's rib cage, he said, "In order for that wound to heal, we've got to remove it."

"Do it," Steven said.

While Steven gritted his teeth, Jem removed the object, and as he applied pressure to the wound, another blast went off.

As they flattened on the ground, broken chunks of dirt and debris came from all directions.

The instant Jem looked up, he saw a man wearing a mask who was about to launch another grenade. At first, it looked as though the masked man intended to throw it toward the back of the Covenant, but to his surprise, he hurled it in his and Steven's direction.

Although silver wasn't lethal to either of them, being blown up might very well send them to their deaths. As Jem watched the explosive soar high in the air, he quickly acted on instinct and shot a firebomb straight out of the palm of his hand. He let out a sigh of relief as the grenade exploded in midair.

When the smoke and dust cleared, Jem rose to his feet and looked for the others. But to his dismay, he saw Sebastian and what looked to be his doppelganger dragging Jace's body. He started forward, and before he could reach them, they disappeared through a portal, taking his brother with them.

The moment Jem opened his mouth to call out, he was distracted by a black panther as it charged toward him. He ducked just as the majestic animal leaped high in the air. Everything seemed to move in slow motion. The huge cat lunged at the disguised assailant who was attempting another attack. Casey's panther took great pleasure in the man's pleas for mercy as he disarmed him by sinking his sharp teeth into his flesh.

"Please..." the masked man pleaded. "I have information about Tessa."

The panther backed off when Steven yelled, "Wait... don't kill him!"

"He's right," Jem said, keeping his eyes trained on the panther. "Whoever you are... please... we need him alive. He's offering to help us."

Jem noticed the confusion in the panther's eyes. Then, to his surprise, a gentle peace descended over the majestic animal as it began to shrink. Jem was amazed as every pore in its skin absorbed all the hair that had covered its body until the animal was no more and Casey's human form took its place.

"Casey..." Jem's jaw dropped. "But... how?"

Naked and exposed, Casey tucked his knees in and lowered his head. "I'm sorry..." His chin began to slowly lift. "I didn't know how to tell you. Please, forgive me."

When their enemy revealed his identity by removing his mask, it made Jem's veins boil. He looked away from Casey and said, "Samuel Mercier, we've been looking for you. Shame on you for turning against your own kind."

"I-I can make it up to you," Samuel muttered. "Please, I can tell you where Sebastian and Thomas are keeping Tessa."

Jem glared at him. "What about my brother?"

"Some people Thomas has been working with are coming for Jace."

"Where are they taking him?"

"I swear... I don't know the location," Samuel babbled. "But I heard Thomas mention a research facility."

Tim staggered forward with Kyle trudging slowly behind. Neither one had a stitch of clothes on.

"My head..." Kyle gasped with his hand over his forehead. "Why does it feel like I've been hit with a baseball bat?"

"Me too," Tim said hoarsely. "What happened?"

"We got hit with a couple of grenades," Jem said. "Thanks to Samuel Mercier."

When Tim looked at Samuel, his expression shifted from confusion to anger in a split second.

"Before you kick his ass," Jem said, "he gave us some information about some people Thomas has been working with. They have Tessa at a research facility."

"Do we know where?"

"No," Jem said, "but they're coming back for Jace."

"Hopefully, we can get there before it's too late," Tim said. "Let's gather everyone..."

Tim's voice trailed off as Drakon came forward, naked as a jaybird, and said, "I saw Sebastian and someone who looked just like him take Jace through a portal." He looked at Jem sympathetically. "I'm sorry, Jem. I couldn't stop them in time."

"It's not your fault, Drakon," Jem replied and then brought him up to speed on everything Samuel had told them.

Drakon focused on Samuel with a menacing stare. He cracked his knuckles and moved forward. "Are sure you're telling us everything?"

"I swear, that's all I know. Please," Samuel pleaded, "don't hurt me."

Kyle rolled his eyes. "What a pussy." Then he got a glimpse of someone sitting on the ground nearby. As he turned to look, he saw Casey. He was naked and had his knees drawn up to his chest.

"Are you okay, buddy?"

Casey looked up at Kyle. "There's something I need to tell you." He swallowed hard. "Something I've been keeping from all of you."

"Casey," Tim looked at him, concerned, "I've always known. You're my nephew. How could I not know?"

"But why didn't you say anything?"

"Because I wanted you to tell us when you felt ready."

"Wait a minute," Kyle chimed in. "Will someone please clue the rest of us in?"

"I'm a... Theriomorph," Casey reluctantly said.

Kyle's eyes rounded. "Are you freakin' serious?"

"I'm sorry," Casey said. "I should have told you. I can leave the Covenant if it makes you feel uneasy."

"Leave?" Kyle shrugged. "Why the hell would I want you to leave?"

"Because I'm different," Casey said. "I know my kind is considered dangerous."

"I do agree with one thing you said," Kyle grumbled. "You should have told me. For fuck's sake, man. You're my best friend."

"I know," Casey said. "I'm sorry."

"So, you're really a Theriomorph?"

When Casey nodded, Kyle said, "I think that's the coolest thing ever!"

Casey looked surprised. "Really?"

"Hell yeah. That's bragging rights, buddy. To have the ability to turn into a freakin' black panther... Damn, I'm envious, dude."

Casey's expression brightened. "I don't know what to say."

Drakon sighed. "Casey, did you really think we'd turn our backs on you?"

"I don't know. I guess I thought you'd all be disappointed."

"Come on." Tim offered his hand to Casey. "You're a part of this family no matter what."

When Casey got to his feet, Tim went on to say, "Besides, your panther kicked ass. It'll be a great asset to this Covenant."

Jem came forward and said, "We're honored to have you and Steven as part of our team, and our family."

Steven smiled, and Casey said, "Thanks, guys. You don't know what this means to me. I feel so stupid for thinking the worst. Can you ever forgive me?"

"There's nothing to forgive." Tim clapped a hand over Casey's shoulder. "Let's get inside. We need to make sure everyone's okay and get ready to go after Sebastian and his brother. But before we do anything, let's get some damn clothes on."

Chapter Forty-Six

As soon as Sebastian stepped through the portal, he released Jace's arm. When he looked away from his half brother, who was sedated, he glared at Thomas with fury in his eyes. "You son of a bitch!"

He knocked Thomas down with one punch, sending him sprawling across the floor. As Sebastian went down after him, the dining room erupted in chaos.

Corbin Azzo and Fredrick Mercier attempted to pry Sebastian from Thomas, but it took the combined efforts of the two and one other man to finally pull him off.

While Thomas picked himself up, he wiped the blood from his nose and shot Sebastian a look. "What the hell is wrong with you?"

When Sebastian lunged for him again, Corbin placed his massive body between them. "Cool down, Sebastian."

Eve stood in the shadows and watched the events unfold.

Sebastian pointed his finger at Thomas. "Explain to me what the hell just happened back there. What were those *things* attacking the Breedline, and why the hell did we bring Jace back here? I thought we were there to get Steven."

Thomas's hand shook as he dragged it through his hair. "You have to know I didn't intend for this to happen."

"What the fuck are you talking about?"

Before Thomas could explain, Fredrick interrupted, "Where's Samuel?"

"I'm sorry, Fredrick." Thomas looked at him wearily. "Your brother didn't make it back."

Fredrick went white. For a moment Thomas worried he might pass out. His knees started to buckle, and before he pitched forward, Corbin reached out to steady him.

Fredrick sucked in a deep breath. "I-it can't be true. I don't sense his death."

Sebastian smirked. "If that fat ass of a brother of yours isn't dead, he'll spill his guts to the Breedline Covenant."

"We need to prepare for the worst," Thomas said. "If indeed Samuel is still alive, it could be possible they have questioned him already."

Fredrick's eyes darkened. "We need to go back for him now."

Thomas got face-to-face with Fredrick. "Sorry, but there's no way we can go back for your brother. Right now, I've got bigger issues to deal with." He looked away and focused on Corbin. "Take Fredrick and leave. I need to speak with Sebastian alone."

"Come on, Fredrick," Corbin said as he placed a hand on his shoulder. "Let's go."

When Corbin escorted Fredrick out of the room, Sebastian impatiently waited for answers. "So, are you going to tell me what the hell is going on?"

"I'm sorry." Thomas exhaled a heavy sigh. "I screwed up. I had no idea that you would be this involved. Someone is threatening me."

"It's time for you to start talking," Sebastian said. "Tell me what the hell is going on here."

"They said they would kill me if I didn't agree to help them find Lilith and her children."

Sebastian furrowed his brow. "Who are *they*?"

"A team of scientists backed up by top military officials and wealthy prospects," Thomas explained. "They started a project over thirty-six years ago. At first, they were interested in psychic and telepathic power. They wanted a way into the heads of foreign government so they could steal their top-secret weapons. It sounds crazy, yes, but then a whole lot of in-depth research was discovered after they found out about the Breedline species. Then they found Lilith. What they did to her is beyond anything I've ever heard of. Before they made her what she is now, she was a Breedline with the ability to heal. She's not the only one gifted with this power. Her son Steven has the power to heal any wound or illness."

In the brief silence that followed, Sebastian finally said, "Well, go on. I'm sure that's not all of it."

"When they discovered Lilith's special abilities, it marked a complete turn for other possibilities. They studied every case like hers."

"Are you saying there are others like Lilith and Steven?"

"Yes," Thomas said, "but none of them were as powerful. Years went into searching out people with other exceptional gifts. They tested extensively until some of their experiments turned into a monstrosity. An abomination such as the hybrids you witnessed earlier."

A sudden thought occurred to Sebastian. "You're getting paid for this, aren't you?"

"Yes. At first, I did it for the money. But when I met Lilith..." He swallowed the knot that had formed in the back of his throat. "I fell in love with her."

Sebastian rolled his eyes. "So, instead of handing over Lilith, you're giving her children in exchange, am I right?"

Thomas reluctantly nodded. "I've betrayed her."

"What do they want with Jace?"

"Isn't it obvious?" Thomas shrugged. "The government is funding Dr. Crane's research. They want to use his DNA to create an army. That's why they want Tessa's unborn children."

"If Lilith finds out you've double-crossed her, she'll wipe you from the face of the earth."

"I know." Thomas lowered his head. "And I deserve it."

"Wait a minute." Sebastian pursed his lips. "You didn't tell these people about my son Arius, did you?"

Thomas looked up and shook his head. "For what it's worth, I kept him out of this. They have no idea he even exists. If word got out, they would take him too."

Although the tension in Sebastian eased, he sensed his brother's anguish. "They didn't just take Tessa, did they?"

Thomas briefly closed his eyes and swallowed back tears. "Since I failed to deliver Steven, they took Lilith."

"Is that why you wanted to bring Jace back? Are you planning to exchange him for Lilith?"

"I know you must think I'm a monster," Thomas said. "But I cannot bear to live without her."

Sebastian huffed. "I could give a shit what you do as long as you don't involve my family."

"But Jace is our half brother."

"True," Sebastian said. "But he would have me killed if he had the chance. He'd kill you just because you look like me."

"Why would he want to kill you?"

"It's a long story," Sebastian said, "one that would open your eyes to who the real monster is here. Jace has reason to want me dead. Oh well..." He shrugged. "It is what it is. We all have our dark sides. Jace will always be gunning for me, and no matter what I do, it won't change the past."

"Something tells me this has something to do with his mate?"

Sebastian grudgingly nodded. "Yes, it does."

"Well, I can understand his anger then."

"Oh, you have no idea." Sebastian cocked a brow. "Jace won't ever stop until he finally kills me. What can I say... if the circumstances were reversed, I'd want me dead too."

Distracted by moaning sounds, Sebastian glanced down at Jace. "You better do something fast. He's coming around."

Thomas quickly reached inside his jacket and when he brought his hand out, he held a syringe filled with clear liquid. He knelt next to Jace and uncapped the needle. "This will keep him sedated long enough to make the trade," Thomas said as he inserted the tranquilizer into Jace's arm.

It took Eve only a few moments of eavesdropping on Sebastian and Thomas's conversation to come to a decision. She had no other choice but to leave now. One way or another, she'd find a way back to the Breedline Covenant even if she had to hitchhike to get there.

She rushed upstairs to the twins' nursery and grabbed a bag from the closet. After she packed a few things, she searched for a pen and paper. Before she took off with Arius and Tidus, she wanted to leave Sebastian a note. Saying goodbye to him was going to be the hardest thing she'd ever have to do. By the time she finished, her eyes burned with tears. She folded it in half, and after she wrote Sebastian's name on the outside, she placed it on the nightstand.

With the overnight bag strapped over her shoulder, she picked up Tidus and placed him on a daybed next to the crib. Then she scooped up Arius and sat down next to Tidus. She looked at Arius and said, "Take us to Auntie Mia, sweetheart."

Arius's features immediately brightened. In a matter of seconds, a bright light engulfed Arius's body. It spread and lengthened until it surrounded Eve and Tidus. As the light dissipated, it took all three of them with it.

From one heartbeat to the next, they reappeared in what looked to be the same estate, although they were inside someone else's bedroom.

Arius pointed his finger at a woman lying on a bed. "Mama, mama, mama…"

When Eve realized who the woman was, her jaw dropped. "Oh my God… Mia."

After she placed the boys on the floor, she rushed to Mia's side. "Mia…" She lightly shook her. "Please wake up. It's me, Eve."

Dread hit her when Mia didn't respond. It was then she knew her sister had been drugged. It had to be Sebastian who kidnapped Mia and brought her here. But why?

Eve quickly went to pick up her sons. She went to Tidus first and placed him next to Mia. Then she lifted Arius in her arms. As Eve placed him on the bed, she noticed he looked at Mia with tears in his eyes.

"Oh, sweetheart," she softly whispered. "Auntie Mia is just sleeping."

Tidus whimpered and crawled over to Eve, his forehead creasing in concern.

She reached for Tidus and cuddled him close. "It's okay, sweetie."

Suddenly, Mia let out a light moan, and when Eve turned to look, she couldn't believe what she saw. Arius had his hand on Mia's cheek, and he was glowing.

"Arius?" Eve said in stunned disbelief.

At that moment, Mia opened her eyes and smiled up at the little angelic face looking down at her.

"How'd you get here, sweetheart?" Mia said hoarsely.

"Thank God." Eve breathed a sigh of relief. "Are you okay?"

Mia nodded as tears fell from the corners of her eyes. "I am, thanks to this little darling." Then she looked at Eve confused. "I don't understand. How did you find me?"

"It was Arius," Eve said. "I wanted to go back to the Covenant. Something bad has happened and I wanted to warn everyone. I prayed Arius could get us there with a portal. When I told him to take us to you, this is where we ended up. Somehow he knew you were here."

"Sebastian kidnapped me when he came back to the Covenant for Arius."

Eve shook her head. "But why?"

"To punish me and Jem for taking the boys."

"I'm sorry, Mia. And I'm not sure if you know, but Sebastian and his twin brother have Jace. Thomas is planning to hand him over to a group of scientists for research."

"Oh my God..." Mia's eyes rounded. "What about Tessa? Do you know if she's all right?"

"They have her too. That same group of scientists are planning on using her unborn children for research. The government plans to use their DNA to create a new species for an army."

"We've got to find a way back to the Covenant before it's too late."

"What about Arius?" Eve said. "Maybe he can take us there using a portal."

When Arius heard his name, he looked at Eve and smiled.

"I think he understands what we're saying," Mia said.

"There's only one way to find out." Eve reached for his hand and lightly squeezed. "Arius... can you take us to see Natalie?"

His smile broadened and in an instant, his body began to glow.

Eve quickly took hold of Tidus's hand and said, "Hurry, Mia. Grab hold of Arius's other hand."

As Mia laced her fingers around Arius's hand, the light that engulfed him surrounded all three of them. When the illumination completely vanished, it took them with it.

Chapter Forty-Seven

As Sebastian read the note Eve had left in the twins' nursery, his eyes filled with tears. He couldn't believe she had deserted him and taken their sons. That's when he wondered what could have driven her to leave. Was it possible she overheard his and Thomas's conversation? Although the letter stated her reasons. Eve was afraid of his twin brother and fled to the only place she felt safe, pleading for him to stay away. At that moment, he knew she had somehow found a way back to the Breedline Covenant.

Was this a final good-bye? His heart ached just thinking about it. The more he thought about it, his body responded to the memories of their past and how they'd always survived the worst. He brought his hand up and rubbed the center of his chest. Eve's words were heartbreaking.

He dropped the note when the door came open. As he turned to look, Thomas stormed inside and said, "Mia is gone."

Sebastian pursed his lips and gave his twin brother a look that said without words he was furious.

"By the look on your face," Thomas said, "I get the idea you're pissed about something entirely different."

"Eve is gone," Sebastian said through gritted teeth. "And she took my sons."

"What!" Thomas's jaw dropped. "But... I don't understand. Where could she have gone?"

"Where the hell do you think?"

"No..." Thomas shook his head. "Not the Breedline Covenant."

"Where else would she go?"

"There's no possible way Eve or Mia could have got past my men," Thomas said. "And they've searched this entire place."

"She must have got Arius to use a portal," Sebastian said. "That's probably why Mia is missing."

"Do you think it's possible Eve overheard us talking?"

Sebastian sighed. "She left me a note."

"What did it say?"

"She said she's afraid of you."

"Me?" Thomas shrugged. "Why me?"

"Are you seriously asking that question?" Sebastian raised his voice. "Look at what you're doing, and you've involved me in this shit. No wonder she took off. This is all your damn fault."

"I'm sorry. What do you want me to do?"

"You're going to help me get her back."

Thomas shook his head. "We'll have to take care of this later. Right now, we've got bigger problems. I'm sure it won't be long before Samuel gives away our location to the Covenant. We've got to get out of here."

"Where in the hell do you suggest we go?"

"Dr. Crane's men are here," Thomas said. "We're going with them to a secure location."

"What about Lilith?"

"Dr. Crane promised he'd make the trade as soon as we arrive with Jace. When this is over, I swear on my life... we'll go back for your family."

Sebastian smirked. "And you trust those bastards?"

"What choice do I have?"

Sebastian moved closer and snarled his upper lip. "If I agree to this and you double-cross me, I will slit your throat. Do you understand?"

Thomas nodded. "You have my word."

* * *

Jem nearly dropped to his knees when he saw Mia descending the stairs with Arius in her arms. Eve followed close behind, holding on to Tidus.

"Mia..." he called out. "Thank God."

As soon as Mia's feet hit the floor, Jem rushed forward and gathered her and Arius in his arms. "I can't believe it," he whispered close to her ear. "I thought—"

"Shhh..." she said, pulling from his embrace. "We're okay, honey."

Jem looked at her bewildered. "But how did you get here?"

Mia turned toward her sister and smiled. "Eve and Tidus... and this little guy." She kissed Arius on the cheek. "He came to my rescue."

Jem reached out and ruffled Arius's hair. "Good job, little man." Then he looked at Eve and said, "Thank you, Eve."

Her eyes softened. "I'm so sorry all this happened."

"Do you know if Jace is okay?"

"Thomas is going to hand him over to a scientist named Dr. Crane. That's where they have Tessa."

"Do you know where this place is?"

Eve shook her head. "I'm sorry, Jem."

"We were attacked by some type of hybrids not long ago," Jem said. "This could be linked to the scientist you mentioned."

Mia's eyes rounded. "Oh my God. Is everyone okay?"

"Everyone is fine, honey," Jem said. "We managed to capture Samuel Mercier. He told us everything about Thomas and a group of people he's working for. We've got to get that location in order to find Tessa and Jace."

"What are you planning to do?"

Before Jem got the chance to reply, Tim, Drakon, Kyle, and Casey moved in their direction, all relieved to see Mia and the twins.

"Thank goodness you're okay," Tim said, focusing on Mia. "How did you get here?"

"Eve found me, and we got Arius to get us here with a portal."

"You did a good thing, Eve." Tim placed his hand on her arm and lightly squeezed. "Your help speaks volumes."

"I just wish I would have done something sooner. I had no idea what Thomas was up to and neither did Sebastian."

"The important thing is we know where Thomas's estate is located," Tim said. "If we're lucky, we'll get there before Thomas and Sebastian try to make a getaway. I'm sure they're worried Samuel spilled his guts."

Drakon chimed into the conversation and said, "You can't tell me a bunch of science nerds are the masterminds of all this. I'll bet you anything this Dr. Crane is following orders. Someone has to be funding his research."

"I did overhear Thomas mention the government," Eve pointed out. "They want to create an army using Jace's DNA."

"What about Tessa?" Jem asked. "Did they mention her?"

"They want her unborn children's DNA too."

"We've got to get moving," Jem said. "There's no telling what they're doing to her."

Tim nodded. "I agree. You can get us there using a portal. But first, I'd like to see if Steven can connect with Tessa. Maybe she can tell us where this facility is."

Steven stepped into the room. "I'll do it under one condition."

"And what's that?" Tim asked.

"I'm going with you. I want to help put an end to those bastards."

"Oh, don't worry." Tim cocked a brow. "After what we saw you do to those hybrids, you're definitely going."

Jem clapped a hand over Steven's shoulder. "I'm not trying to rush you, but do your best to make this fast. Time is of the essence."

Seconds later, Steven took a seat at the far end of the room so he could clear his mind. He closed his eyes and let everything else drift away. *"Tessa... can you hear me?"*

Suddenly, he sensed her. It felt like a burst of warmth, but with it, came a flood of terror, and an agonizing pain.

Steven squeezed his lids and gritted his teeth. The images that flashed through his mind infuriated him. Tessa was bound to an examination table with steel bands clamped around her neck, wrists, and ankles. He could see electrode pads attached to her forehead with wires connected to some type of machine. Although he wanted to destroy everyone that caused her pain, instead he concentrated on sending her waves of comfort.

As soon as he washed away her pain, she relaxed and said, *"Steven... please. You've got to help me."*

"You have to hold on, Tessa. We're coming for you, but I need you to focus. Do you have any idea where they've taken you?"

"I'm in some type of lab, but that's all I know. The people here..." She swallowed back tears. *"They're starting to*

experiment on me with electricity. I'm afraid they're going to hurt my babies. And Steven... they have our mother too."

"Gather all your strength. I promise, we'll find you."

When their connection ended, Steven opened his eyes and rose to his feet. He looked to the others and said, "Tessa is in a lab, but she doesn't know where. We don't have much time. She's in a lot of pain. Those bastards are treating her like a lab rat. They also have our mother."

"Let's go now," Tim said.

"How do we know we're not walking into a trap?" Casey spoke out. "I'm sure Thomas realizes Samuel will sing like a canary. They'll be expecting us. Don't you think we should locate Thomas's address and check the layout of this place before we go rushing in?"

"Let's put nerd boy on it," Kyle popped off. "That's Drakon's expertise, right?"

"Watch it, Kyle." Casey smirked. "He'll kick your ass. Drakon has moves that I don't even think there are names for."

Drakon rolled his eyes, and Tim said, "We don't have time. We've got to move in now."

Chapter Forty-Eight

When Jem created a portal, Drakon was the first one to step through. Instead of waiting on the others, he quickly moved toward Thomas's estate. His mind was focused on one important task that would hopefully, if he didn't get caught, lead them to the research facility.

Following Drakon was Steven, and then Kyle and Casey. As Tim crossed through the opening, Jem shot in behind him and closed the portal.

"Where's Drakon going?" Jem said, crouching behind a tree while the others took cover among the manicured shrubbery and colorful foliage.

"Don't worry," Tim said. "He's got a plan."

They kept their distance and watched, waiting for Drakon to return. When two men stepped from the front entrance, Jem cursed under his breath. By the tailored suit and smug look on his pale face, he immediately recognized Sebastian. The other guy was obviously his twin brother. They looked almost identical. As soon as they climbed into the back of a black sedan, it quickly drove off.

"Shit..." Kyle said. "Are we just going to sit on our asses and let them get away."

"Be patient." Tim held up a halting hand. "Let's wait for Drakon."

A glimmer of a smile curved Drakon's lips as he suddenly appeared. "We're set," he said, waving a small device at his comrades. "I attached a tracking device to their vehicle. It'll take us straight to that research facility, assuming that's where they're going."

"Wait a minute," Casey spoke out. "How are we supposed to follow them without a vehicle?"

"I spotted a Hummer H2 parked on the west side of the estate with our name on it," Drakon said. "It'll be a tight fit, but it's big enough for the six of us."

"I hope you have the keys."

"I don't need keys."

"What are you planning on doing?" Casey smirked. "Hotwiring it?"

Drakon nodded. "Yep."

Kyle held out his fist. "Drakon... you're the man."

Drakon bumped knuckles with Kyle and said, "Time is ticking. Let's get moving, ladies."

* * *

When the driver pulled up to the research facility's security gate, Thomas and Sebastian watched as a bearded man got out of a parked SUV. He motioned to another guard to open the gate as he came forward. He was dressed head to toe in full combat attire with a black beret atop his head and a rifle strapped over his shoulder. His expression appeared focused and disciplined. As he moved closer to the car, Sebastian noticed the guy had a silver whip attached to his waist.

He walked up to the driver's window and looked toward the back seat. "My name is Heinrich," he said in a thick German accent. "Dr. Crane is expecting you." He motioned Thomas and Sebastian to get out. "I will escort you from here."

As he led them through the gate, Thomas got into Heinrich's vehicle first, and Sebastian slid in the back seat next to him. He leaned forward and said, "So, Heinrich... what kind of place is this? I hear your boss does some freaky experimentations here."

Thomas turned toward Sebastian and slowly shook his head. The look on his face warned Sebastian to tread carefully.

Heinrich glared into the rearview mirror at Sebastian. He ignored his arrogant bluster and continued to drive onward. A few minutes later, he stopped in front of a building that looked more like a military base than a research facility. There were armed guards stationed all over the place.

"We're here," Heinrich said as he stepped out from behind the wheel and waited for Thomas and Sebastian to get out. Before they went inside, two armed guards checked them for weapons. As they entered, a man in a white lab coat greeted them. He was tall like Heinrich, but thin and pale-looking. "Welcome, gentlemen." He dipped his head a little. "My name is Elias. I'm Dr. Crane's assistant. Unfortunately, he is currently preoccupied, but he should be available to see you in an hour or so. Until then, I will take you to your quarters." He motioned them forward. "Please, follow me."

On the south side of the research facility, Dr. Crane's guards had Jace's wrists and ankles shackled to chains that were embedded deep in the floor. He was so incapacitated from all the sedatives and the restraints made of silver he could barely hold his head up.

Suddenly, blurred images flashed before him. Jace remembered the battle with the hybrids and then, out of nowhere, he'd been rendered unconscious by a huge blast. The moment he regained consciousness and opened his eyes, he immediately recognized the person peering down at him. No matter how hard he tried to forget, seeing his half brother brought back all the dark memories of the past. He'd never forgive him for what he'd done to Tessa. Before he got the chance to rip that smug look off his face, someone from behind had drugged him. Although he had no recollection at all of who it was, the memory of Sebastian's face was still fresh in his mind.

His head was spinning. He tried to gather himself, tried to think, to shake off the effects of the drugs and call upon his Beast.

I need to focus, he feverishly thought. *I've got to save Tessa.*

Shaking, he prayed for a miracle. "Please, God," he choked the words out. "Please help..." His voice trailed off when he heard the door burst open.

Jace looked forward and watched through blurred vision as several people in white lab coats entered the poorly lit room. He nervously glanced side to side as they formed a circle around him. Desperate to be free, he tugged at the chains that were bound to his wrists, but it was hopeless. He was too weak.

"Dammit," he gasped.

When a pale, thin man wearing round spectacles stepped forward and faced him, Jace stared at him in silent menace. The pale-faced man looked evil and unrelenting in his Neo-Nazi uniform, oddly resembling Adolf Hitler.

"Bring forth your Beast," he ordered in a callous, German accent.

Jace shook his head. "I can't..."

"You will do as I say!"

"Go to hell," Jace said, snarling his upper lip.

"Bring in Heinrich!"

Seconds later, a bearded man came into the room with what looked to be a silver whip in his grasp. He wore army fatigues and a black beret. As he moved behind Jace, Hitler's doppelganger backed away.

Jace braced himself and gritted his teeth, preparing to feel the burn of the whip. It whirled high in the air, end over end, and struck his back like a blazing torch. He instantly dropped to his knees and howled in pain.

The bearded man seemed to have no end as he continued his vicious savagery. He slashed his flesh again and again, until finally, Jace went limp against his restraints.

"Enough!" the Hitler look-alike shouted. "Leave us!"

After everyone filed out of the room, Hitler's doppelganger came forward and leaned over Jace's bloodied body. "Do you know who I am?"

With all the strength Jace could muster, his lifted his chin to meet his captor's eyes and said, "Go fuck yourself."

"You're very stubborn, Mr. Chamberlain. You remind me of Steven."

Jace narrowed his eyes. "You're that bastard Dr. Crane, aren't you?"

"My name is Dr. Hubert Crane, and you are my prisoner."

"Why? What did I do to you?"

"It's not what you did *to* me. It's what you're going to *do* for me."

Jace lowered his head and spat blood on the physician's boots. "I'm not going to do shit for you."

"Oh..." Dr. Crane lifted a brow. "I think I can persuade you. If you do not produce your Beast within the hour, your precious mate will pay the price for your defiance."

Jace tried to lunge at him, but the chains held him back. "Don't you touch her," he growled.

As the physician walked away, Jace yelled, "I swear... I'll kill you!"

Before he left the room, he glanced over his shoulder at Jace. "You have one hour."

When the door slammed shut, something deep within Jace overrode the drugs and the silver. An unbridled fury took control and reawakened the Beast.

At first, nothing happened. Then Jace's breathing suddenly became deeper and more guttural. It was at that moment he gasped in relief, realizing the impending changes were rising fast. Already, straining muscles rippled beneath his skin, while coarse white hairs sprouted from every pore and began to cover the bloody welts on his back. The shape of his face twisted and stretched until his human features were no more. Jace felt himself expanding as if his skin could no longer contain its natural state. His inner Beast throbbed with power and a lust for blood—the blood of the physician who had threatened to hurt Tessa.

With a thunderous roar, he tugged at the silver shackles, snapping them apart as though they were twigs.

The noise coming from inside instantly alerted Dr. Crane's men who stood guard outside.

"Sound the alarm!" Heinrich ordered as he flung open the door.

When the Beast turned to look, he saw the bearded man reach for his whip. Fueled with anger, Jace's Beast charged at the speed of lightning with broken chains dangling from his wrists. He sent them slicing through the air, giving Heinrich a taste of his own medicine. The force of the impact knocked him off balance and shattered his torso. As he toppled over in agony, the Beast threw his head back and howled in triumph.

* * *

When Drakon parked the Hummer not far from the research facility, everyone piled out to form a plan.

"Our only option is to blast our way in," Tim said as he looked at Drakon and the others. "Once we're inside, we're going to split up into teams." He focused on Jem. "I want you and Steven to go in first. There will be casualties, and some human. It's a risk we'll have to take. Speak now if that's going to be a problem." When everyone remained silent, Tim looked at Kyle and Casey. "Drakon and I will follow in behind. I want you two to locate where they have Tessa. Once you find her, contact me." He handed Kyle a two-way radio. "I've got your radio linked to mine."

"What about my mother?" Steven spoke out. "We can't just leave her behind."

"Don't worry, Steven," Tim said. "We'll do everything we can to find your mother and get her to safety."

When Steven nodded, Tim went on to say, "Any questions?"

In the silence that followed, Drakon clapped a hand over Tim's shoulder and said, "Let's get this done."

Chapter Forty-Nine

While the others hung back and waited, Jem and Steven charged forward. As they neared the security gate that led into the research facility, Jem wasted no time and launched a fireball straight out of the palm of his hand. The two guards posted outside took notice of what was coming and made a run for it. When it made contact, it exploded and ripped the steel barricade blocking the entrance.

On cue, Tim, Drakon, Kyle, and Casey came rushing forward. It wasn't long before they were met by Dr. Crane's men. The second they opened fire, Jem took them by surprise with another blast. It exploded when it hit the ground. After a few minutes, the smoke and dust finally cleared. It looked like a bomb had gone off. The front entrance to the facility had been destroyed, and at least a dozen guards were scattered among the debris.

As they hurried past all the wreckage, Drakon stopped long enough to snatch a security access card from one of the guards. He caught up with Kyle and said, "This should give you clearance to all the doors."

Kyle smiled as he took the key card. "Like I said... you're the man, Drakon."

Drakon smirked. "Let's just pray it works."

When everyone gathered outside the entrance that had a hole in it big enough to drive a semi through, Tim said, "This is where we split up." He focused on Kyle and Casey. "I'm counting on you guys to locate Tessa and her mother. Use your radio to stay in contact."

Kyle nodded and rushed inside with Casey right on his heels.

On the other end of the facility, an alarm echoed, bringing forth armed guards. As they charged into the room where Jace was held prisoner, they opened fire when they saw he had shifted into his Beast. As the hail of bullets slammed into his chest, his body thrashed wildly, and blood streamed from his white pelt. He crouched into a fighting stance and howled as the silver-tipped slugs burned his hide.

"Hold your fire!" Dr. Crane ordered as he rushed inside with a tranquilizer gun. "I want him alive!"

The gunfire finally came to a halt, and before Dr. Crane managed to sedate the Beast, its supernatural speed outweighed his human pace. As the Beast shot forward and pummeled into the physician, the bone-jarring force knocked the tranquilizer gun from his grasp. Momentum hammered him into one of his men and sent them tumbling across the floor.

Dr. Crane gritted his teeth and grunted but managed to pull himself up. The second it took him to grab the tranquilizer gun, wolfish fingers closed around his throat and hoisted him off the floor. He instantly dropped the gun and gasped for breath. He clawed at the Beast's tight grip and kicked his feet.

When bullets nailed the Beast from behind, he quickly released the physician and spun around to face the shooter.

Then the sound of a doleful clicking noise took the gunman by surprise. He realized he was out of bullets and wearily stepped back.

Hungry for the taste of blood, the Beast locked on to the man's jugular and peeled back his lips. As he prepared to attack, an explosion of glass and gunfire momentarily distracted him. Then an impact rocked the facility so hard it felt as though it had been hit by a meteorite. A portion of the ceiling came crashing down, nearly hitting the Beast. Fluorescent tubes shattered in an explosion of sparks, barely giving them enough light to see by.

"Release the hybrids!" Dr. Crane called out as he pushed his way through all the fragments of rubble and broken glass.

As much as the Beast longed to sink his teeth into the human's flesh and rip out the physician's throat, something more important drove him forward. He dropped on all fours and bolted out of the room and made his way through a long corridor that led to the heart of the facility.

Meanwhile, Kyle and Casey moved slowly down a hallway, checking every room. As they came to an open doorway, they went inside, but unfortunately, there were no signs of Tessa or her mother.

"Tim... do you read me?"

Tim heard Kyle's voice over the radio as bullets zinged by him and the others. When they took cover, Tim reached for his two-way radio and said, "Kyle, did you find Tessa?"

"So far, nothing. What about the rest of you?"

"We're making our way to the other wing as fast as we can. Keep looking, Kyle. Tessa has to be somewhere—"

Tim's voice cut off as bullets kicked up plaster close to where he and the others had taken cover.

"Tim, are you guys okay?"

After a few moments, Tim said, "Don't worry about us. We're okay. Just ran into a few hiccups. Keep searching for Tessa and her mother."

"Roger that," Kyle said. "We won't stop looking until we find them."

As soon as Tim put away the radio, something immense and heavy thundered close by. It sounded like a stampede of onrushing bulls.

Tim rolled his eyes. "What the hell now?"

Drakon peered around the corner to get a closer look, and as soon as he saw what was heading in their direction, he motioned toward the others and shouted, "Run!"

In a matter of seconds, the floor beneath their feet began to tremble as they took off in the opposite direction.

Steven's eyes bulged as he glanced over his shoulder and saw about a dozen hybrids charging after them.

When Jem spotted a door a few feet ahead, he directed the others toward it, praying the damn thing was unlocked. He let out a sigh of relief as he pushed through it and held it open for the others. As soon as everyone made it inside, Jem slammed it shut.

They listened at the chorus of howls as the hybrids tore past the door, seemingly focused on something else.

"Shit," Drakon said, breathing hard. "That was close."

"They weren't after us," Jem said.

"Then... what the hell are they after?"

Before Jem could respond, a thunderous roar echoed in the distance.

Drakon exchanged glances with Jem and the others. "Is that who I think it is?"

"Yep." Jem heaved out a deep breath. "That is definitely Jace's Beast."

"He's going to need backup," Tim said. "There's no way he can take on all those hybrids alone. We're going to have to shift."

Kyle put his radio away and looked at Casey with a grim expression on his face. "We've got to find them."

"We will," Casey said, praying he was right. "Let's move on. They've got to be in this building somewhere."

Kyle put on a brave face, but underneath, he was afraid. He feared what they'd find when they came across Tessa and her mother.

As they continued to search through the maze of small rooms, which looked to be more like torture chambers rather than examination rooms, Casey abruptly stopped in his tracks.

Kyle noticed him staring at a door across the hall. "What is it?"

"This is it, Kyle." Casey pointed at the door. "This is the room where they have Tessa."

Kyle quickly moved past him and swiped the security card. When the lock clicked, he opened the door and froze as he stepped inside. "Oh, God," he gasped.

As Casey came up behind him, he feared the worst. When he saw Tessa, he nearly fell to his knees. Beside Tessa was a woman that looked a lot like her, but younger. She was lying in a clear cylindrical tube and she was glowing.

Kyle rushed over and placed his hand on Tessa's shoulder. "Tessa..." He gently shook her. "Tessa, can you hear me?"

He waited for her to open her eyes, to make a sound... anything to let him know she was all right. When she didn't respond, he leaned over to see if he could hear her breathing.

Casey moved next to Kyle and choked out, "Is she..."

Kyle straightened and let out a deep breath. "I can hear her breathing, but it's shallow." He grabbed the radio. "Tim, we found Tessa. I repeat, we found Tessa. Over."

There was static, and then Tim said, "Thank God. Is she all right?"

"She's unconscious, and her breathing is shallow. They've got her hooked up to some type of electrical machine."

"What about her mother? Did you find her?"

"We found someone who looks like Tessa, but I'm not sure if she's her mother. This girl looks like her teenage sister. And she's glowing."

"Listen to me, Kyle. I want you and Casey to get them out of the building as fast as you can. We've got the front cleared, but I'm not sure for how long. Radio me as soon as you make it out."

"Roger that. We're on it."

When Kyle tucked his radio away, he looked at Casey. "We've got to get them out of here."

Casey nodded. "While you get Tessa out of those restraints, I'll see if I can free..." He paused and looked at the young girl in the cylinder. "...her mother?"

"Whoever she is," Kyle said, "I'm sure she's been a prisoner here. God knows what they've done to them."

"Come on," Casey said, "let's get them out of here."

As Kyle started working on Tessa's restraints, Casey rushed over to a computer that was attached to the plastic capsule and began tapping furiously on the keyboard, praying he could get the thing to open.

"Casey, what's the holdup?"

When Casey looked up from the computer, Tessa's limp body looked tiny in Kyle's arms. "I'm hurrying as fast as I can," he said. "I can't get this damn contraption to—"

Casey blew out a deep breath when the lid to the tube suddenly cracked open. The second he started to speed up the process by forcing it to open wider, he felt something cold press against his throat.

"Stop right there," a male voice said from behind. "One move and I'll cut your throat."

Casey recognized Sebastian's voice and froze in the position he stood. By the look on Kyle's face, he knew shit was about to go down.

Then, out of nowhere, Thomas came forward with a pistol in his hand. "Don't try anything stupid." He aimed it at Kyle's head. "The bullets in this gun are tipped with silver."

Casey gritted his teeth, yearning for his Theriomorph side to break free.

Chapter Fifty

The Beast's roar mixed with the howling hybrids alerted Jem as he looked at the others and said, "I've got to help Jace before those hybrids tear him apart."

"Take this with you," Tim said, handing him the two-way radio. "You'll need this to keep in contact with Kyle and Casey. As soon as we shift, we'll meet you in battle."

Jem nodded and clipped the radio to his belt. Before he took off, his eyes searched over the occupants of the small room, who he considered his family, and said, "I'll see you all soon."

As Jem rushed into the heat of the battle, his throat tightened, and dread hit him like a ton of bricks. Although the hybrids outnumbered the Beast, attacking him from all sides, he fought back with pure savagery.

Ready to help his brother even up the odds, Jem palmed up a fireball in the shape of a sphere. Careful not to hit the Beast, he aimed it toward several hybrids and sent it rolling. The force of the impact instantly ignited three. As they went up in flames, Jem prepared for round two. In one continuous motion, he discharged another firebomb and took out three more hybrids.

Rage burned through Tim's veins as he exploded into action and barreled his way through the hybrids surrounding the Beast. Drakon and Steven followed close behind.

With an appetite for vengeance, they leaped and bounded through the hybrid hordes, leaving several dead in their wake.

Jem merely stared aghast as he witnessed an unforgettable scene of carnage right before his own eyes.

Steven lunged out and grabbed one of the hybrids by the torso and flipped it to the ground. Before the monstrous creature could get up, he stomped on its head and crushed its skull. Steven was a force not to be reckoned with. Which, considering he was on their side, was a good thing.

* * *

Sebastian glared at Kyle and said, "Put Tessa down, or your buddy will pay the price."

"All right, all right," Kyle said as he gently placed Tessa back on the examination table. "But for the love of God... she's pregnant and her breathing is shallow. Let me get her some help."

Sebastian shrugged. "Why should I care?"

"You selfish bastard." Kyle raised his voice. "At least let her brother try to heal her. Is that so much to ask, or is your heart that dark?"

Thomas looked at Kyle and said, "Steven is here?"

"Yes," Kyle instantly replied. "Please... let me use my two-way radio to contact him."

Thomas eyed Kyle as though he was weighing his words. "Go ahead, but if anyone comes with him, we'll kill both of you."

"Tim..." Kyle said into the two-way radio, "...do you copy?"

When there was no immediate response, he called for Tim again, but still he got nothing.

"Shit... something must be wrong."

"Looks like your friends might have finally met their end," Sebastian said. "I mean, how could they possibly take on all those hybrids?"

"Go to hell," Kyle gritted out.

"Maybe I should get it over with and cut his throat now," Sebastian said as he pressed the blade deeper into Casey's throat.

Kyle looked past Casey with a look of horror, and said, "What the—"

As Thomas turned to look, he lowered the gun and took a few steps back.

When Sebastian glanced over his shoulder, his jaw dropped. He instantly removed the blade from Casey's throat and muttered, "How the hell..."

To their surprise, Lilith had somehow awakened. She was surrounded by a blaze of fire as though she had fallen into the heart of the sun. Her eyes were like torches and her body hovered in midair. The second she saw Tessa, the air around her warped, as if her anger were the source of her power.

"Who did this?" her voice traveled in an echo.

Thomas melted to his knees. "I'm sorry, Lilith. Please, forgive me."

"You…" She looked at him confused. "You did this to my daughter?"

"It wasn't me." Thomas quickly shook his head. "I swear. It was Dr. Crane. I tried to stop him, but—"

"Liar," Sebastian interjected.

Thomas looked at Sebastian with his mouth agape.

Sebastian gave Thomas a hateful glare and said, "He's been working with Dr. Crane and all his cronies this whole time."

"Is this true, Thomas?" The confusion in her expression softened like her heart was breaking into million pieces. "Did you betray me?"

Thomas pleaded with his hands together as if he was praying for his life. "I had no choice. Dr. Crane was threatening me. If I didn't hand over Steven and Tessa, he was going to kill me and take you instead."

"For God's sake, Thomas." Sebastian rolled his eyes. "Be a man. Stop groveling like a dog."

Lilith looked back at Sebastian. "How are you tied into all this?"

"I'm not," Sebastian said. "I had no idea what the bastard was up to until recently. All I wanted was my family back. And now, because of him, everything is fucked up."

Lilith released a sigh. Then her eyes darted away from Sebastian. She looked between Kyle and Casey. "Who are you and how are you two involved?"

"My name is Kyle, and this is my best friend Casey. We're here to get you and your daughter to safety." He glanced down at Tessa. "Please, something is wrong. She needs help."

Lilith peered down at Tessa and whispered, "I've been so foolish." As she went to see to her, an explosion took her by surprise.

As the walls started to crumble, Kyle and Casey simultaneously acted on instinct and lunged for Tessa. They used their bodies to shield her from all the falling debris.

When gunfire ripped through the room, Casey yelled for everyone to take cover. While Sebastian dropped to the floor, Thomas leaped in front of Lilith.

When all the dust and smoke finally cleared, Sebastian saw Thomas lying motionless on the floor with blood covering his chest.

Chapter Fifty-One

A fervent howl suddenly rang out across the many dead and wounded hybrids, proving that there was no chance against the Beast and his deadly companions.

To the astonishment of both Jem and Steven, the remaining hybrids tucked tail and retreated. Drakon's rogue wolf, along with Tim's Breedline wolf, sprinted after the pack, making sure they didn't change their minds.

In a matter of seconds, the Beast's thick white pelt began to shrink and disappear as if his skin was miraculously willing it back inside his body. Jem watched the creature's fast transformation right before his eyes. It wasn't long before his brother's naked and bloodied body took his human form again. As Jace started to pitch forward, Jem quickly reached out and caught him before he fell.

"Thanks, Brother."

"No problem," Jem replied. "But I have to say..." He chuckled a little. "You look like shit."

"Jeez, thanks," Jace said, rolling his eyes. "And by the way, you're welcome."

Jem shrugged. "For what?"

"For saving your ass."

"Uh, I think you got that mixed up," Jem said. "I'm the one that saved your ass."

"Whatever..." Jace grumbled. "But you did find Tessa, right?"

Before Jem could get a word out, a loud blast shook the facility.

"Shit." Jace flinched. "What the hell was that?"

Steven came forward and said, "It came from the other side of the building."

"Dammit." Jem heaved out a deep breath. "That's where Kyle and Casey are." He looked at his brother with dread stamped all over his face. "Jace, they found Tessa and her mother."

Despite his injuries, Jace managed to stand on his own. "Oh God, please tell me. Are they—"

"Yes, Jace. Tessa and her mother are alive, but they've been sedated."

"We've got to go—"

Jace was cut off by the sound of gunfire. When bullets whizzed past them, hitting the back wall, Steven shouted, "Get down!"

As they ducked for cover, Jem scrambled over to one of Dr. Crane's men who'd been caught in the crossfire. Quickly, he peeled the guy's trousers off and shot back to where Jace and Steven had taken cover.

"Here," he said, tossing them to Jace.

Jace frowned at the pants that looked to be too small. "What the hell?"

"Sorry..." Jem held up his hands. "Would you rather go naked? It's the best I could do."

Jace groaned, although he managed to pull the skintight pants over his legs and hips.

Jem handed him the two-way radio. "This is linked to Kyle's radio. You take care of finding Tessa while Steven and I take care of things here."

Jace stared at the radio in his hand as though he was weighing the decision to leave his brother and Steven to fight alone.

"Don't worry, Jace," Steven said as he began to transform back into his Adalwolf. "We've got this." Then he focused on Jem with a sinister look on his face. "Come on. Let's get this over with."

The second Jace agreed, Drakon and Tim showed up in the nick of time and charged forward.

Jem looked at Steven and said, "Well, I guess that's our cue."

As Jem took off to help the others, he glanced back at Jace. "Good luck, Brother. I'll see you later."

* * *

Sebastian stood back as Lilith knelt next to Thomas. She placed her hand on the side of his face. "Thomas, can you hear me?"

His eyelids flickered and his breathing was labored. Lilith briefly turned toward Sebastian with a grim expression. As she looked back at Thomas, she said, "Please... open your eyes."

Thomas could hear the pain in her voice and wanted to reach out to comfort her, but as he tried to lift his arm, for some strange reason it would not move.

I'm dying, he feverishly thought. And if he was going to die, he wanted nothing more than to see Lilith's face one last time. He wanted to tell her he was sorry and that he loved her.

Thomas struggled, forcing his eyes open. As he focused on her face, he realized the fire that had surrounded her before had vanished. And her eyes were no longer shaped like flames. Instead, they were a bright emerald green. They stared at one another in silence until finally he said, "Lilith—"

"It's all right," she said. "Try to save your strength."

He shook his head. "I need to tell you..." His voice was hoarse. "I'm sorry. Please, forgive me." Then a look of sadness passed over him. "I... I love you."

A faint smile curved her lips. "I know, Thomas. I forgive you."

In that moment, he smiled and looked past her as though his eyes were fixed on something far away.

"Thomas..."

When he did not respond, she sensed he was gone and reached up to close his lids.

"Why didn't you heal him?"

Lilith looked up at Sebastian and simply said, "It was his time."

Sebastian placed his hand on her shoulder. "For what it's worth, I'm sorry."

Lilith nodded, and at that moment she knew what had to be done. She had to finally put an end to all this madness. And the only way was to turn this place to ash and Dr. Hubert Crane along with it. She looked at Kyle and Casey. "Please, get my daughter to safety."

Casey nodded and Kyle said, "I promise, come hell or high water, we're getting her out of here."

Lilith shifted her eyes back to Sebastian. "We have to end this, and I'm going to need your help."

Sebastian extended his hand, and as she took hold, a bright light surrounded them. When it completely vanished, they disappeared as though the light had swallowed them whole.

"Shit," Kyle muttered under his breath. "Once again, as always... Sebastian somehow always manages to escape."

"It sounded like Tessa's mother needed his help."

"You think she's going after this Dr. Crane guy?"

Casey nodded. "I hope so. And let's pray she ends that SOB."

"Whatever the case," Kyle said, "we've got something more important to deal with, like getting Tessa the hell out of here."

As soon as Kyle went to get Tessa, he heard footsteps outside the room. He reached for his gun and signaled to Casey.

Casey nodded and positioned himself beside the door while Kyle stood on the opposite side.

When two armed men charged into the room, Casey stayed back and guarded the door. Kyle came up behind them and said, "Drop your weapons!"

Both men whirled around, and as they attempted to lunge at Kyle, Casey darted forward with his weapon poised and ready to fire. "Don't even think about it," he said with a low growl rumbling deep in his chest.

The guy wearing dark-rimmed glasses shrunk back and looked at Casey wide-eyed. "What the hell are you?"

Casey snarled his upper lip. "Your worst nightmare."

"Start talking," Kyle demanded. "Where's Dr. Crane?"

The other guy spit on Kyle. "We're not telling you a damn thing."

Before the guy could register his movement, Kyle doubled up his fist and pummeled him square in the face. The impact knocked him back and sent him skidding across the floor.

Kyle quickly moved forward and grabbed the guy by the scruff of his shirt and dug the pistol into the side of his head. "I said... where's Dr. Crane?"

When he didn't reply, Kyle pointed his gun at fly of the guy's pants. "Don't make me shoot off part of your anatomy. You might want to keep those."

"Okay, okay," the guy sputtered. "Dr. Crane went after the man-beast. Him and the others are heading toward the north side of the facility."

Kyle stood straight and waved the pistol. "Hands behind your back." He glared at the other guy and said, "You too, asshole."

* * *

With retribution blazing through his veins, Steven rushed at Dr. Crane's men and engaged in brutal combat. He fought his way through the chaotic free-for-all to get to the physician who had taken his sister and mother.

In the midst of it all, Jem's powers by far were the most lethal. With one flick of his wrist came a blazing inferno of destruction. It had the capability of incinerating through flesh and bone.

While they fought side by side along with Tim and Drakon, Dr. Crane was amazed by Jem's extraordinary powers. His beady eyes bulged behind his silver-rimmed spectacles, realizing for the first time, he might lose this battle. Then he was caught off guard when a bright light appeared out of nowhere. He briefly lifted his hand to shield his eyes. When it faded, two figures stood in its place. The minute they came forward, disbelief passed over the physician's face. He looked decidedly less sure of himself when he recognized Lilith. She looked angry as she moved closer, glaring at him with fire in her eyes.

307

Chapter Fifty-Two

"Kyle... this is Jace. Do you read me?"

"Copy that."

As Kyle's voice came over the radio, Jace sighed in relief. "Where are you?"

"We're near the south side of the facility. We ran into two of Dr. Crane's men. We've got them contained. You need to watch your back. His men are gunning for you."

"Thanks for the heads up, but please... tell me you have Tessa?"

"That's affirmative," Kyle replied, swallowing back his nerves.

"Is she all right?"

"Jace..." Kyle briefly hesitated, "...we need Steven. Something's wrong with Tessa. She's unconscious and her breathing is shallow."

Jace sucked in a breath. *Oh God, no...* "Get her out of the building," Jace said. "I'll go after Steven and meet you outside the front."

"Roger that. And don't worry, Jace. We'll take good care of your girl."

The second Jace took off, he instantly stopped in midstride when he felt a sharp object slam into the back of his leg. It burned like fire. As he peered down, he saw a dart embedded in his left calf. *Shit!* That's when he realized Kyle was right. Dr. Crane's men were after him and armed with tranquilizer guns. With no time to spare, he gritted his teeth and removed the dart.

As soon as Jace started forward, he was hit again. He immediately reached for the back of his neck. It felt like his entire body was on fire. The second he ripped the dart free, his vision clouded, and his body weakened. When he could no longer stand, he tipped forward and dropped to his hands and knees.

No, he feverishly thought. *I've got to get to Steven.*

Jace refused to give up, and as he struggled to stand, he felt the Beast within him yearning to break free. Not yet ready to surrender his human form, he closed his eyes and fought against the impending changes.

I've got to remain human. Just long enough to find Steven.

Finally, Jace managed to get his bearings and ducked behind a desk. He used what energy he had left and telepathically called out to his twin brother.

"Jem, can you hear me?"

Instantly, Jem linked with Jace's mind.

"Jace... where are you?"

He scanned his surroundings and said, *"I think I'm close to the entrance. I had to take cover behind what looks to be the front desk. I've been hit with tranquilizers."* He squeezed his eyes tight, resisting the change. *"Tessa needs help."* He took a deep breath. *"I need to get to... Steven. He can heal her. I can't hold back much longer. One more hit... and I won't be able to control the Beast."*

"Hold on, Jace. I'm coming for you."

As Jem created a portal and went after Jace, Dr. Crane faced Lilith with a calculated stare. "I'm warning you, Lilith," he said, reaching inside the pocket of his white coat. "Don't take another step."

"You're nothing but a monster." Lilith continued to move forward. "It's time for you to be punished for all the innocent lives you've taken."

"I gave you this power." A vengeful grin stretched across the physician's face when he brought his hand out. "And I can easily take it away."

As he aimed a gun at Lilith, the orbs of her eyes glowed with a harsh acidic light.

Everything after that seemed to happen in slow motion. The second Dr. Crane squeezed the trigger, Sebastian shouted a warning. But it was too late. The bullet slammed into Lilith's chest, but not before she used her powers and set the physician on fire.

Steven merely stood back and watched as Dr. Crane's body engulfed in flames. At that moment, he felt redeemed. It was like a weight had been lifted. As he looked away, he got an overwhelming ache in the center of his chest. The young woman who had finally put an end to all this madness was lying on the floor, clutching her chest. He remembered her from years ago. She'd been the one who destroyed the research facility where he and Abbey had spent most of their lives in captivity. Going by the uncanny resemblance between the young woman and Tessa, he wondered if somehow they were kin. Finally, he snapped back to reality and focused on the man kneeling beside her. He instantly recognized him. It was the same bastard that kidnapped his sister. With fury blazing in his eyes, he glared at Sebastian. As he started forward, a bright light stopped him in his tracks. He held up his hand to shield his eyes. As soon as the illumination faded, Jem and Jace suddenly appeared.

Sebastian concentrated on Lilith. "Come with me," he said, offering her his hand. "I can get us out of here."

"It's too late," she said in a weak voice. "Please... just go."

"Please, Lilith," Sebastian persisted.

"I want to see my son," she gasped. "One last time."

"Are you sure this is what you want?"

She slowly nodded with tears in her eyes.

As Sebastian rose to his feet to search for Steven, Jace charged forward with lightning speed. The flicker of a shadow offered Sebastian only an instant's warning before he even knew what hit him.

Jace grabbed him by the throat and pinned him down. "What did you do to Tessa?"

"It wasn't me," Sebastian said, struggling against the tight grip on his throat. "Dr. Crane." He choked. "It was... Dr. Crane."

"You're the bastard who took her." Jace squeezed harder. "It's time for you to pay for what you've done."

In that moment, it felt like time stood still as Sebastian struggled for air. Blurry images of Eve and his sons filled his mind. As he thought of them, he pondered the extent of God's forgiveness. If he could forgive humans for their vanity, their cruelty, and their lust, why couldn't he forgive him? All he'd ever wanted was to be loved. Instead, his life had been filled with lies and cruelty.

God... he feverishly thought, *why have you forsaken me?*

Suddenly, a miracle happened. A light fell from overhead, sheltering Sebastian, warming him, saturating him with something unexplainable, something he'd never felt before. His tortured soul, darkened by his childhood past, had been released from years of suffering.

Sebastian stared in sorrow at his half brother, praying he would show leniency, if only the smallest, despite everything he had done to him.

"Please..." he croaked out, "forgive me."

Shocked by Sebastian's words, Jace looked at him, confused. "What did you just say?"

"I'm..." Sebastian strained to get the words out, "...sorry."

When Jace let go, Sebastian opened his mouth with a string of raspy breaths.

"Why should I believe you?"

"I know what it's like to hate," Sebastian said in a gravelly voice, "to want revenge. But now, all I want is to live to protect my sons."

"Protect them from what?"

"My sins."

Although Jace could not deny that Sebastian had done so many rotten things to the ones he loved, it was not his place to be judge or jury. It was God's decision to decide his fate. Besides, time was ticking, and he needed Steven's help.

As Jace turned away from Sebastian to look for Steven, he saw him kneeling next to the young woman who looked to be Tessa's younger sister. It was hard to comprehend that she was Tessa's biological mother. In all his years, he had experienced many unexplainable things, but this was definitely at the top of his list.

Steven placed his hand over Lilith's and said, "I remember you. Your name is Lilith. You destroyed Dr. Autenburg's research facility and freed all those people."

She gathered all the strength she had left and looked up at him. "Yes..." Her voice was weary. "If only I'd known you were my son." Emotion knotted her throat. "I'm so sorry, Steven."

"But..." His eyes rounded in disbelief. "...how can this be? You're so young."

"I was kidnapped at a young age due to my ability to heal. At the time, I was pregnant. A few weeks after I gave birth, Dr. Crane wanted to experiment on you and Tessa. I wanted a better life for you and your sister, so I tried to escape." She briefly paused, breathing through the pain. "But Crane's men took you before I could get to you. I managed to get Tessa to a safe place and when I came back for you..." She swallowed back tears. "...I was captured. For years, they experimented with my genetics until they were able to stop my aging process. Not only did Dr. Crane systematically use you as a threat, they erased most of my memories and transformed me into this." She slowly lifted her glowing hand. "When I began to regain some of my memories, I wanted to reunite with you and Tessa."

"Then why did you have Tessa kidnapped?"

"I was afraid she wouldn't understand." Her voice trembled. "I just wanted to keep you and your sister safe from Dr. Crane. But I know now I should have asked the Breedline Covenant for help. Please... forgive me, Steven."

"It's okay," Steven said, lightly squeezing her hand. "You didn't know. It's not your fault."

She struggled through the pain that wrapped around her body like a burning vine and smiled. "You look so much like your father."

Then Lilith felt the stroke of his hand against her cheek. So caring and soothing. She closed her eyes and leaned into the warmth of Steven's palm.

"You're going to be just fine," he whispered, directing his hand over the wound to her chest. "I can heal you."

A moment later, as Lilith felt the effects of Steven's healing energy, her lids snapped open. It was as though her body had been reborn. When she brought her hand close to her face, it was no longer translucent and glowing. It appeared human again. She sucked in a fortifying breath and focused all her attention back on Steven. By the tense expression on his face, she realized he was taking the brunt of her pain. "Steven... please. I can't bear to see you in pain."

"I'll be fine," he said in a raspy voice. "It's only temporary for me."

After a few minutes had passed, Steven moved to his feet and offered his hand to Lilith.

When he helped her to her feet, she scanned her body in utter disbelief. It was as though she'd been magically transformed back to the body she had long ago. Then she looked up at Steven and said, "How is this possible?"

Steven instantly turned when he felt a hand press down on his shoulder.

"Please, Steven," Jace said. "Something's wrong with Tessa. Kyle and Casey are heading to the front of facility with her. Will you help her?"

Chapter Fifty-Three

Before Steven could get a word out, one of Dr. Crane's men aimed his weapon at Lilith. Before he pulled the trigger, Sebastian did the unbelievable. He dove between her and Steven, using his body as a shield. He was hit in the throat, and the bullet sliced alongside his carotid artery.

As Sebastian fell to the floor, Jem shot a blazing fireball out of the palm of his hand and took out the gunman. Then he looked at what was left of Dr. Crane's men and said, "Unless you want to become ashes, I suggest you drop your weapons and keep your hands where I can see them."

As soon as they surrendered, Lilith knelt next to Sebastian and said, "Why did you risk your life for us?"

He looked up at her with teary eyes. "Because..." he said in a strained voice, "...you both deserve to live a normal life."

As she placed her hand over his wound, blood seeped through her fingers in a steady flow. "Hang on, Sebastian," she said. "I'm going to try and heal you."

"No!" Steven yelled as he scrambled to his knees. "Please... don't do this. Your body isn't what it was. You won't survive a fatal wound."

Lilith looked into Steven's pleading eyes. "I'm sorry, but I have to help him. It's not his time."

"This will kill you," Steven urged. "He's not worth dying for. Please..." He placed his hand on her shoulder. "I won't be able to heal you from this."

Jace stood back, feeling helpless as precious time continued to get away. Then, to his surprise, a crackling noise came from his radio.

"Jace, do you read me?"

He grabbed the radio and said, "I'm here, Kyle. Where are you?"

"We're outside the facility with Tessa."

"How is she?"

"You need to hurry, Jace." Kyle's voice sounded grim. "It doesn't look good."

Steven helplessly watched as his mother ignored his pleas and took on Sebastian's wound. In a matter of seconds, Lilith released Sebastian and put her hand over her throat.

"Mother…" Steven reached for Lilith as she started to tilt back. He caught her before she collapsed and eased her down on the floor.

"No, no, no…" he painfully cried out, cradling Lilith's limp body in his arms. "Stay with me."

Lilith shook her head and grasped his arm. "Steven…" Tears spilled from her eyes. "I don't have… much… time."

"You can't leave me." Steven pulled her closer. "I've just found you."

Through all the pain, she forced a smile. "I love you." She closed her eyes, and before she took one last gasping breath, she said, "Tell Tessa… I love her."

"Please…" he sobbed, caressing her lifeless face. "Don't go."

Desperate for help, Jace turned toward Jem and said, "Please, Brother. Will you help Tessa?"

"But, Jace, I've never used my powers to heal. What if I can't control it? It could hurt the twins or… kill Tessa."

"They could die regardless," Jace said. "Please… I'm begging you."

Jem nodded. "I'll try."

Jace pressed the talk button on the two-way radio and said, "Kyle, stay put. We're heading your way."

"Copy that," Kyle replied.

Before Jem created a portal, he quickly explained the situation to Tim and Drakon, leaving them to take care of the rest of Dr. Crane's men and Sebastian.

The moment they stepped through the portal and Jace saw Tessa in Kyle's arms, he instantly rushed over.

"Oh my God…" Jace said, reaching for Tessa. "Is she still breathing?"

Kyle placed Tessa in his arms and said, "Yes, but it's weak. Where's Steven?"

Jem shot Kyle a despairing look. "He's not coming."

Kyle's eyes rounded. "What the fuck, man?"

"I don't have time to explain," Jem said. "I'm here to take Steven's place..." He briefly paused and released a sigh. "...to try and heal Tessa."

"But what if—"

Jem cut Kyle off with a halting hand. The last thing they needed was to upset Jace any more than he already was. Besides, Jace knew his healing powers could end in disaster.

Jace pressed his lips to Tessa's forehead and concentrated on linking his mind with hers. *"Please, Tessa...fight your way back to me."*

Jace flinched when he felt a hand on his shoulder.

"Brother," Jem said, "I need you to put her down."

Jace eased Tessa onto the ground like she was a piece of glass in danger of shattering. When he looked down at his hands, they were covered in blood. Instantly, he looked for an injury. His heart nearly stopped when he noticed blood between her inner thighs. "Oh, God..." In that moment, he realized all those nightmares of her death had become real. He looked up at Jem and stared at him for a few seconds, but it seemed to last forever as time slowly ticked by.

"Please..." Jace finally said, "tell me you can save her."

"I think it's best if we get her back to the Covenant," Jem said. "I'm afraid if I try to heal her, it might further complicate her pregnancy. Please, Jace, let Helen examine her first."

Jace nodded and carefully gathered Tessa back into his arms.

Jem looked at Kyle and Casey and said, "Guys... go back inside the facility. The others are going to need your help."

"Don't worry," Kyle said. "We'll take care of things here. You just take care of our girl."

Casey, who had been totally silent since Jem and Jace got here, looked at Jace with sympathy written all over his face. He felt guilty and irresponsible for not telling him about the visions he'd had of Tessa's death. Would it have made any difference? After all, no matter how hard you tried, you couldn't cheat death. Fate was inevitable. With all the courage he could muster, he parted his lips and said, "Tessa is going to be all right, Jace. She's too stubborn not to."

After Jace, Jem, and Tessa disappeared through the portal, Kyle and Casey hurried back inside the research facility to search for Tim, Drakon, and Steven. It wasn't hard to find them. The trail of dead hybrids and the bodies of Dr. Crane's men led them straight there. As they got closer, they could hear someone sobbing. They looked to where it was coming from and saw Steven. He was kneeling next to the young woman who they'd discovered with Tessa earlier. It couldn't have been thirty minutes since they last saw her vanish through a portal with Sebastian. Now she was lying motionless on the floor, and going by all the blood on her throat, things didn't look good.

Shit... Kyle thought. *Poor Steven.*

On the opposite side of Steven was Sebastian, and he too was covered in blood. He was on his knees, silently watching as Steven fell apart. Oddly, it looked as though Sebastian was fighting back tears.

Kyle averted his eyes from the heartbreaking display and looked at the others with a bewildered expression on his face. He could tell Tim and Drakon had shifted at some point by the pants they were wearing. They looked to be the same camouflage trousers as Dr. Crane's men, and neither one had shoes or shirts.

"What the hell happened?" Kyle finally said.

"One of Dr. Crane's men fired his weapon," Tim said. "Sebastian..." He paused and shook his head. "...believe it or not, he jumped in the line of fire."

Casey shrugged. "So, if Sebastian took a bullet, why isn't he dead?"

"Steven's mother healed Sebastian," Drakon chimed in. "I'm not sure why, but when she took on his injury, she didn't survive."

"Damn..." Kyle huffed. "Who the hell would risk their life for that piece of shit?"

"I hear ya," Drakon said. "I was just wondering that myself."

"Shit..." Tim rolled his eyes. "I was so wrapped up with all this, I almost forgot to ask. What's the situation with Tessa?"

"It's not good," Kyle regretfully said. "It looked as though she was hemorrhaging. Jem thought it was best if they take her back to the Covenant so Helen could examine her before he tried to do anything."

"My God..." Tim sighed in frustration. "Well, he did the right thing. She'll be in good hands. All we can do now is pray."

"So," Casey briefly hesitated, "what are we going to do about Steven?"

"I'll take care of it," Tim said. "While I go talk to him..." He paused and looked between the two of them. "...I want you guys to stay here with Drakon and make sure the rest of Dr. Crane's men are contained."

"What about Sebastian?" Kyle said. "How are we going to stop him from using a portal to escape?"

"That's a good question," Tim replied. "Maybe he'll do the right thing and surrender to the Covenant."

Kyle smirked. "Yeah, good luck with all that."

"You never know," Tim said as he turned to look in Steven's direction. "Stranger things have happened."

Moments later, as Tim went over and knelt next to Steven, he said, "I'm so sorry—" Tim suddenly went silent, his jaw nearly hitting the floor when a ghostly form appeared from out of nowhere.

Behind him, Sebastian looked shellshocked as he stared up at what looked to be Lilith, except she was no longer corporeal—a beautiful ghostlike figure of some sort. Even Dr. Crane's men looked pale and shaken.

Tim tapped Steven on the shoulder. "Steven... are you seeing what I'm seeing?"

He didn't hear a word Tim said because he couldn't believe his eyes. It was his mother... sort of. It was her face and her body, only she was... an angel.

"Mother?"

Steven slowly got to his feet, and after a brief hesitation, he reached out to her and put his hand to her glowing face.

"Is this really you?" he said.

Lilith nodded and leaned into his hand. She could tell he'd been crying by the tears on his face and the redness in his eyes.

"I'm finally at peace," she said, her lips forming a smile.

"I thought..." Steven's voice trembled, "...I'd never see you again."

"I'll always be with you and Tessa," she said. "Right here." She placed her hand to his chest. "Close to your heart."

Steven gulped in steadying breaths, but God, he wanted to break down and cry like a baby. He opened his mouth to speak, but instead he wrapped his arms around her.

Lilith closed her eyes and gently enfolded him in her embrace. "I love you, Son," she whispered close to his ear. Then, in the blink of an eye, she was gone.

"Steven?"

He turned to see Tim. Standing next him was Sebastian. The others stood back with grim expressions stamped all over their faces.

"We need to get back to the Covenant," Tim said.

Pain flashed in Steven's eyes. "Something's wrong with Tessa, isn't there?"

"Come on." Tim gestured at Steven. "We don't have much time."

* * *

Through Jace's eyes, everything seemed to move at the speed of a snail: Helen and Cassie rushing over the instant they arrived at the Covenant. Their mouths were moving, but he couldn't hear what they were saying. Jem looking at him, trying to tell him something, but whatever it was, it didn't register in his brain. It was as if the volume in his ears had been turned all the way down. He felt frozen in the place he stood, completely incoherent, holding Tessa in his arms. Then suddenly, Helen's voice rang loud and clear. It was like someone had cranked up the volume, snapping him back to focus.

"Jace..." Helen put her hand on his shoulder. "Did you hear what I said?"

He flinched. "What...?"

She raised her voice, "Put her down, so I can get her to the examination room."

Instantly, Jace obeyed Helen's orders and carefully placed Tessa on top of a gurney.

Moments later, as they wheeled Tessa inside, other members of the Covenant gathered outside the hallway, and they all had looks of concern written on their faces. When the door to the examination room closed, Angel, Jackson, and Celina leaned against the wall next to the door, while Mia and Eve stood against the opposite wall, facing them. Alexander stood a few feet away, his head hung low. He looked worried as like the others.

Celina turned to Angel and said, "Have you heard yet from Tim or any of the others?"

"Don't worry, Celina," Angel said. "Tim called me a few minutes ago. Everyone is fine."

Celina nodded and released a sigh of relief. "We should contact Tessa's father. I'm sure Kenneth would want to be here."

"Oh dear," Angel groaned. "Where's my head at? I completely forgot. I'll get a hold of him."

"What about John and Sarah?" Mia mentioned.

"Of course," Angel replied. "Thanks, Mia. I'll make sure I call them as well."

"You get a hold of Kenneth," Jackson chimed in. "I'll take care of John and Sarah."

"Thanks, Jackson," Angel said with a slight smile. "I'd appreciate that."

In the silence that followed, Eve grudgingly spoke out, "Did Tim mention anything about... Sebastian?"

"Yes, Eve," Angel said. "He turned himself in."

Eve looked at Angel, bewildered, and for a moment, she was lost for words. "I-I'm glad," she finally said. "It was the right thing to do."

"There's something else you need to know," Angel continued. "Sebastian risked his life and took a bullet for Tessa's mother."

Eve's eyes rounded. "What...?"

"He's not hurt," Angel went on to explain. "It would have been fatal, but Tessa's mother healed him. When she took on his injury, she wasn't able to heal herself."

"But I don't understand," Eve said. "Why couldn't she heal herself?"

Angel shook her head. "I don't know, Eve. That's all the information I have so far."

Eve glanced at the closed door. "Sebastian..." She swallowed hard. "Did he hurt Tessa?"

"No, Eve," Angel said. "Whatever was done to Tessa, Dr. Crane's men are responsible."

Eve slowly nodded as tears gathered at the corners of her eyes.

Mia laid a hand on Eve's arm and squeezed reassuringly. "All we can do now is pray." She looked at the others. "If I know Tessa like I think I do, she'll fight tooth and nail to pull through this." She looked up at the ceiling and closed her eyes. "Please, God... we need you now more than ever."

Chapter Fifty-Four

Jace watched closely as Helen and Cassie traded clinical terms while examining Tessa. As soon as they went silent, Jace looked between them and said, "Please... tell me she's going to be okay."

"I promise, Jace," Helen said. "We'll do everything we can."

Jace bent down and pressed his lips to Tessa's forehead. "I love you, baby," he whispered close to her ear. "Please come back to me."

"Jace..."

Jace glanced up to see his brother standing next to him, his expression pained.

"Come on, Brother." Jem lightly tugged at Jace's arm. "Let's give them some room."

Jace swallowed and nodded numbly, allowing himself to be pulled away.

It wasn't long after Jem and Jace stepped back that Helen said, "We're going to have to do an emergency C-section."

"But... the twins," Jace said with a panicked look on his face. "They're not due yet."

"I don't have a choice," Helen replied. "The babies are in distress and Tessa has lost a lot of blood."

Jem came forward. "Helen, do you want us to step out?"

"Stay close," she said. "I may need you, Jem."

While Cassie started an IV, and Helen laid out surgical tools, Jace went pale. When he started to sway, Jem grabbed his arm. "Jace, are you going to be okay?"

He took a deep breath. "I'll be fine."

Jem lightly squeezed his arm. "Tessa is a survivor. She'll get through this, Brother."

"She's got to," Jace said, despair seeping into his soul. "I'd be lost without her."

"If Helen can't save her," Jem reluctantly said, "you know I'll do whatever it takes to bring her back."

Jace nodded. "I know you will."

As they watched Helen and Cassie prepare Tessa for delivery, Jace closed his eyes and said a silent prayer. Then, at the sound of a baby's cry, his lids popped open. It nearly brought him to his knees.

"This one has definitely got a set of lungs on him," Helen said, handing the first baby to Cassie. "Now, let's get baby number two."

After Cassie did a quick examination, she swaddled the tiny infant in a blanket. "Even though he's early," Cassie said, handing the baby to Jace, "his vital signs are great."

Jace was silent for a moment, and he looked over at Jem with tears in his eyes. "I'm..." He sucked in a breath. "...a father."

The corner of Jem's mouth lifted. "Congratulations, Brother."

Jace lowered his gaze to the tiny bundle in his arms. "My son..." He bit back tears and looked at Jem again. "I'm naming my first born after you."

Jem's eyes brightened. "I'm honored."

"Cassie," Helen called out, "I've got baby number two."

As Cassie took the baby from Helen, Jace noticed he wasn't crying. He patiently waited while Cassie worked fast with a suction syringe over the baby's mouth and nose. Shortly after came a high-pitched cry, relieving some of the tension in the room.

"He's just fine," Cassie said, wrapping the baby in a blanket.

Jem reached out as Cassie placed the baby in his arms. "Hey there, little man," he said with tears brimming in his eyes. "I'm your Uncle Jem."

"Tessa and I decided to name our second born after Uncle Jacks. Except we're spelling it a little different."

"I think that's a great idea," Jem said, smiling down at the baby. "The name suits him."

Jace opened his mouth to respond but hesitated at the urgency of Helen's voice.

"Quick, Cassie... I need your help. She's hemorrhaging."

Jace stood with his son in his arms while Cassie and Helen worked on Tessa, feeling like the life had gone right out of him. He was sick with worry that this might be his last memory of her. His anxiety only increased when got a glimpse of the amount of blood covering their surgical gloves. It took every bit of strength he had not to rush over, but he stayed back so they could do their jobs.

It felt like an eternity as Cassie and Helen continued to do everything possible to stop the bleeding. Then, out of nowhere, Jem heard a voice whisper softly inside his head.

"Jem... use your powers."

He turned to Jace and said, "Did you say something?"

Jace shrugged. "What?"

"I-I thought I heard..." He broke off, his voice laced with confusion. "...someone say something."

"I didn't say anything."

"You have the power to save Tessa." The voice spoke to him again. *"Hurry, Jem. There's not much time."*

Jem linked his mind with the voice and said, *"Who... are you?"*

"My name is Lilith. I'm Tessa's mother."

"I don't understand. How is this possible?"

"Listen to me, Jem. There's no time to explain. You have a special gift of healing. Please, you must save my daughter."

He lowered his head in frustration. *"But... how?"*

"All you have to do is take hold of her hand." Lilith's voice started to fade. *"Concentrate on thoughts of healing."*

"How can you be sure it won't harm her?"

When there was no response, Jem put everything he had into reaching out to Tessa's mother. *"Lilith... are you still there?"*

Fear and uncertainty paralyzed him. He warred with the consequences if his powers didn't heal Tessa but instead killed her. If it came down to it, he'd give her life at the expense of his own. And then he heard another voice.

"Jem..."

He instantly snapped back to focus and looked up.

"We've done everything we can," Helen said, her expression grim. "The bleeding... it won't stop. Whatever has been done to her, it's interfering with her natural Breedline healing. You're her last hope, Jem. You've got to try to use your powers."

"Do it, Brother," Jace said, releasing a strangled breath. "Please..."

As Jem turned to face his twin, he could see the fear and desperation etched into every groove of his face.

"I promise I'll do everything in my power to save her."

Cassie hurried over and gently took the baby from Jem's arms. As he went over to Tessa's bedside, Jace followed close behind, holding on to his son.

Jem took a shuddering breath as he peered down at Tessa. She was so pale and lifeless. If he hadn't previously known what a strong-willed and determined person she was, he'd have thought she'd already given up the fight. The moment he took hold of her hand, he closed his eyes and blocked out everything around him: the beeping noise coming from the portable heart monitor, the sound of his own heartbeat pounding in his ears, and even Jace, who loomed over Tessa.

As death closed in, Jem knew that it was almost too late for her. With all the strength, and all the perseverance he could muster, he concentrated on a pathway to link with Tessa's mind.

And then a warm presence surrounded her, replacing the darkness with light.

"Tessa..."

She instantly recognized the voice in her head. It was Jem. Tessa was desperate to respond to his soothing voice, but she was so weak. In the silence, she waited, praying to hear his voice again.

"Tessa... if you can hear my voice, give me a sign. Please, Tessa. You've got to help me. I can't do this all alone. Fight with all your strength. Fight for Jace and your newborn sons."

In that moment, she felt warmth radiating from his body to hers. That's when she realized he was fighting for her... healing her. And she was pretty damn positive Jace was right by his side. She drew on every ounce of strength she had left and sent him a message.

When a single tear slipped out of the corner of her eye, Jem said, *"That's it, Tessa. Keep fighting. I know you can do this."*

As more tears fell from her eyes, she linked her mind with Jem and Jace, forming a telepathic pathway between the three of them.

"I'm here." Her voice was faint. *"Please... don't let me go."*

"No one is letting you go, Tessa," Jem said.

"Oh my God..." Jace gasped.

"Jace... is that you?"

"I'm here, baby," he said, pressing a gentle kiss to her forehead. *"And I'm not letting you go. Please... fight your way back. Our sons need you. I need you."*

"It's okay now, Tessa," Jem said as warmth spread to every pore in her body. *"You're going to be just fine. All you have to do is open your eyes."*

Tessa's long eyelashes fluttered, and as her lids slowly opened, she became aware that she wasn't alone. Although her vision was blurred a little, she could still make out the image looking down at her. Jace was leaning over her, his eyes filled with tears. His long, blond hair hung over his shoulders, some of it falling forward into his face. He was smiling so big that his cheeks dimpled. God... she'd never grow tired of looking into his gorgeous face and those baby blues that stared at her with such intensity. Not only was Jace standing above her, but Jem, Cassie, and Helen were hovering close by.

"Welcome back, sweetheart," Jace softly said. "How are you feeling?"

"Tired," she replied, her voice hoarse. "But it feels good to be alive."

She lifted her head and searched for the twins. Her brows furrowed when she didn't see them anywhere.

"My babies... where's my babies?"

"Shhh, it's okay," Jace said, leaning over with the tiny baby in his arms. "They're perfectly fine, honey."

Tessa's eyes brightened with joy and relief when she saw her baby for the first time. The instant she reached up and smoothed her hand over his soft, fine hair, he turned to her and cooed.

"He's beautiful," Tessa said in a tear-laced voice. "Just like his daddy."

Jace lowered the baby into Tessa's arms. "Meet our firstborn."

"Hello, little Jem," Tessa murmured, cradling the baby close. "You're so tiny." Then she looked up at Cassie and said, "Is that little Jax?"

"It sure is," Cassie said, placing the baby next to his twin brother. "They're both the cutest babies I've ever seen."

"But they're premature," Tessa said, her brows clenched with worry. "Don't they need some kind of special care?"

"I don't know how to explain it," Cassie said, "but they're perfectly healthy. I checked them myself. Other than their small size, they're developed to full-term." She patted Tessa's hand. "Maybe it's their strong genetics. Whatever the case, don't worry. They'll be fine."

When some of the anxiety in Tessa's features appeared to ease, Cassie said, "I'll go tell the others that Mommy and babies are doing just fine. I'm sure everyone is worried sick."

Tessa smiled. "Thank you, Cassie."

The minute Cassie headed for the door, Tessa gazed into little Jax's bright blue eyes and said, "Well, aren't you just the spitting image of your father."

"I don't know," Jem chuckled. "I think he takes more after his uncle."

Jace wrapped his arm around Jem and tugged him close. "Ha-ha. Very funny, Brother."

Tessa laughed a little and then focused on Jem. "It was you, wasn't it? You're the one who saved me."

Jem merely smiled. "Well... sort of. I have to admit I had a little help."

"What do you mean?"

"Your mother spoke to me, Tessa. She told me what to do."

"But... I don't understand." Tessa shook her head. "How is that possible?"

Jem kept silent for moment, trying to find the right words, and before he opened his mouth to speak, Tessa said, "She's gone, isn't she?"

Jem regretfully nodded. "I'm sorry, Tessa."

For a moment, what he'd said didn't sink in, but when it did, tears burned her eyelids and ran freely down her face. Her mother's death tore her to shreds. She'd only recently found her, and now… she was gone.

Jace wiped at the tears running down her cheeks. "It's going to be okay, honey. I'm here for you. We're all here for you."

Tessa's lips crooked up a little, her throat aching with emotion as the too-short memories of her mother flooded her mind.

"I hate to interrupt," Helen said, her eyes focusing on Tessa, "but I need to give you a quick examination, just to make sure there's no more bleeding."

When Tessa nodded in agreement, everyone stepped back so Helen could do her thing. It wasn't long before she faced Tessa and said, "I've never seen our kind heal this fast. Your incisions are completely gone. If I hadn't done the C-section myself, I wouldn't believe you had one." She looked over at Jem. "Whatever you did, it worked a miracle."

"Where's everyone else?" Tessa asked. "Does my father know about my mother? And what about Steven? Has anyone told him?"

Jace moved next to her and slid his hand over hers. "We haven't said anything to Kenneth, but Steven…" He hesitated for a second. "…he was there when your mother passed. He tried to save her."

Tessa's brow wrinkled and she stared questioningly up at Jace. "How did my mother…?" She bit her lip, but Jace could still see her mouth trembling.

"Oh, sweetheart." Jace lightly squeezed her hand. "You've been through so much. How 'bout we talk about this later, after things settle down."

"You're right." She nodded. "We can talk about it later."

A knock at the door drew their attention. When everyone turned to look, the door cracked open and Cassie stuck her head in. "I brought someone to see you. I just wanted to make sure you're up for visitors."

"Of course," Tessa said.

When Cassie opened the door further and stepped inside, Kenneth came in behind her. His eyes lit up when he saw that

Tessa was awake. To his further surprise, there were two tiny babies nestled contently beside her.

"Hey, sweetheart," Kenneth said. "Are you sure it's okay?"

"Don't be silly." She smiled and waved him over. "Come meet your grandbabies."

When Tessa held up an arm to hug him, he leaned down and carefully embraced her.

"I love you, Tessa."

"I love you too."

Finally, as Kenneth pulled from their embrace, he said, "I was so worried for you. Everyone has been worried, honey."

"I'm too stubborn to give up that easily. Besides, I have too much here to live for."

"You take after your mother," Kenneth said with a light chuckle. "The stubborn part, that is."

At that moment, Tessa thought about telling him the dreadful news about her mother, but instead, she decided against it. Besides, this was supposed to be a happy occasion and a moment to celebrate new life.

"So..." Kenneth raised a brow. "What does a grandpa have to do around here to get permission to hold his grandsons?"

Tessa laughed. "When it comes to family, permission is always implied."

"On that note," he said, reaching for one of the babies, "I start with this little guy."

"His name is Jem," Jace said to Kenneth.

"I like it. He looks like a Jem." Then he carefully scooped the baby in his arms and softly said, "Hello, little Jem. I'm your grandpa, and I'm going to spoil you and your brother rotten."

A series of chuckles from the others seemed to lighten the tension in the room.

After moments of coddling and admiring his grandson, Kenneth swapped babies with Tessa and said, "And who do I have here?"

"That's Jax," she said. "He was born four minutes after his big brother."

"Whoa..." Kenneth smiled down at the baby. "A whole four minutes. What took you so long, little fella?"

Jax's lips curved up into the biggest smile.

"Well, look at that," Kenneth said. "He's a happy little guy. He smiled at me."

Jace smirked. "Are you positive that was a happy smile or a poopy smile?"

Tessa rolled her eyes. "Jace..."

"Well, whoever is holding the baby when he makes a poopy has to obey the golden rule."

"Oh?" Kenneth looked at Jace in question. "And what's the golden rule?"

"You're the one stuck with changing the poopy diaper."

Kenneth laughed. "I'll have to remember that rule."

"Is it okay if we come in?" a small voice came from the open doorway. "It sounds like we're missing out on all the excitement."

When everyone looked at the door, Angel, Mia, Eve, and Celina were anxiously waiting with anticipation stamped all over their faces. Angel had a hold of Natalie's hand, and Mia had Arius positioned on her hip, and his twin brother Tidus was in Eve's arms. Behind them, Alexander and Jackson gathered.

Tessa motioned everyone inside. "Please, come meet little Jem and his twin brother Jax."

As they all filed inside and gathered around Tessa's bedside, there was a chorus of oohs and ahhs all around. Everyone admired the twins and congratulated the new proud parents. There wasn't a dry eye in the room.

"They're both adorable," Angel spoke out. "I'm so relieved you're all right, Tessa."

Tessa smiled. "Thank you, Angel."

"If you ever need a babysitter," Mia said, "all you have to do is ask. I'd be more than happy to help out."

"So would I," Eve said.

Tessa grinned. "I may take you both up on that offer."

"Count me in too," Celina chimed in.

Jackson came forward. "And me too."

Alexander came up behind Jackson. "Don't forget about me. I have grandpa rights." He looked at Jace, gauging his reaction. "Only if that's okay with you, Jace."

"It's okay by me," Jace replied. "Would you like to hold your grandsons?"

Alexander's eyes glistened. "Yes, I would like that very much."

As Jace handed the baby to Alexander he said, "We named this little guy after Jem."

"Hello, little Jem." Alexander bit back tears. "I'm going to cherish every moment I get to spend with you and your little brother."

Jace clapped a hand over Jackson's back and said, "Uncle Jacks, we named our secondborn after you."

He looked at Jace as though he was lost for words. His eyes suddenly teared up. "I don't know what to say." He wiped at his eyes. "I'm so honored. But why me?"

"Because..." Jace swallowed back tears. "...you were very dear to my mother. Although I was just a kid at the time, I can still remember how important you were to her. You looked after us all. Besides, I think it would make her happy to know I named her grandchild after her only brother."

Jackson instantly enfolded Jace in a huge hug.

Jace returned his hug, holding on tightly. Just holding on.

"That means a great deal to me," Jackson choked out. "Thank you, Jace."

"You're welcome, Uncle Jacks."

As soon as Jackson released Jace, he whirled around as several new voices flowed into the room.

"How'd you guys get back so fast?" Jace asked.

"It's a long story," Tim said, reluctant to explain how they made it back to the Covenant all the way from England. It had been Sebastian. After he'd turned himself in, he used a portal to get them all back here. Tim decided it was best to tell everyone later, especially Jace. "I'll explain later," he went on to say. "Right now, since everyone got their turn, I'm ready to meet those boys of yours."

"Yeah, count me in," Drakon said, grinning ear to ear.

"Don't forget about me and Casey," Kyle said as he stepped in behind Drakon with Casey alongside him. "And how's the little mama doing?"

"I'm just fine, Kyle," Tessa said. "Thanks to you and Casey." She motioned them over. "Come on, guys. Come meet our boys."

Drakon noticed as everyone gathered around Tessa that Steven stayed back.

"Come on," Drakon said, smiling at Steven. "Don't you want to meet your sister and your *father*?"

Steven's jaw nearly hit the floor. "My father... is here?"

"You ready to meet him?"

A timid smile wavered on his lips. "Yes..."

Drakon led him where everyone gathered and cleared his throat. "Everyone, listen up." He raised his voice. "I'd like to introduce a new addition to *our* family."

Steven peeked around him and nervously scanned the occupants of the crowded room.

Drakon stepped back. "This is Steven, Tessa's brother."

Although almost everyone already knew Steven was Tessa's brother, all eyes turned in his direction. Kenneth was the first to react. His eyes rounded, and his expression looked one of utter disbelief. Tessa's face went blank for a second, and then tears rimmed her eyes.

A round of cheers rang out over the room, and Steven didn't know how to react. He stared from face to face, wondering if this was what it felt like to have a real family.

"Welcome, Steven," Jem said. "We're glad to have you as part of our family."

Jace reached out and clapped Steven on the back. "Glad to have you back, buddy."

Steven nervously looked up at Jace. "You're not upset with me, are you?"

"Hey, I get it," Jace said. "I would have done the same if it had been my mother. Besides, it all worked out in the end."

Steven's eyes softened. "For the first time in my life, I finally know what it feels like to have a real family."

"Yep," Jace said. "Like it or not, you got all of us. Warts and all."

Steven chuckled. "I'll take each and every one."

"Come on." Jace nudged him forward. "Let's go meet your sister and your new nephews."

As Jace directed him over to Tessa, Steven looked down at her with an apologetic expression. "I'm sorry, Tessa. I wasn't there when you needed me."

"It's okay, Steven." She placed her hand on his. "I understand what you had to do. We can talk about the rest later. Right now, let's enjoy the moment."

"Steven..."

Steven looked toward the voice and saw a man with salt-and-pepper hair and emerald-green eyes standing next to him.

"My name is Kenneth Craven." He extended his hand. "I'm your father, Steven."

As Tessa watched her father and her brother shake hands, she never felt so happy as she did right now. Then she looked up at Jace and said, "I love you."

He smiled down at her. "I love you more."

Just as Jace leaned down to kiss her, Sarah swept into the room, arms waving. "We got here as soon as we could."

Her husband John came in behind her. "And she nearly killed us on the way here."

"Oh hush," Sarah groaned, rolling her eyes at John. "I got us here in one piece, didn't I? Now... where's my grandbabies?"

Jace came forward with a baby in his arms. "Right here, Ma."

When Sarah got a look at the baby, she instantly covered her mouth. "Oh my..."

John wrapped his arm around her. "Look, sweetheart, it's official. We're finally grandparents."

Sarah lowered her hand and instantly reached for the baby. As Jace placed him in her arms, he said, "That's our firstborn, little Jem."

"My sweet grandbaby." She cuddled him close. Then she looked up, her eyes searching the room. "Where's his little brother?"

When Jem came over with baby Jax, John extended his arms. "Hand that boy over here."

The minute he handed him the baby, Jem was surprised to see big fat tears rolling down his father's cheeks.

Unable to resist, Jem said, "Dad... you're not crying, are you?"

"Oh, be quiet," John said. "I'm allowed to cry over my grandchildren, aren't I?"

Jem and Jace both chuckled.

After John and Sarah took turns holding the twins, they crossed through the crowded room to check on Tessa.

"Thank the Lord you're okay." Sarah reached out to hug Tessa. "I love you, sweetie."

"I love you too, Sarah."

Before Sarah drew away, she kissed Tessa on the cheek. "Congratulations, honey. I'm so proud of you and Jace."

"Don't smother her, Sarah," John abruptly said. "Let her have some breathing room so I can hug her too."

Tessa smiled as John put his arms around her. "I love you, sweetheart. I don't know what we'd do without you."

"I love you too, John."

Although everyone in the Breedline Covenant had experienced more than their share of life's trials and tribulations, one important thing stood true. Life had taught them that nothing worthwhile came easy, but everything was all the more rewarding for the sacrifices made.

To be continued...

"There are many soulmates,
but only one can understand the howling of your heart."
—L. L. Musings

Take a sneak peek into the fourth book of the Novels of the Breedline series, *Sins of Chaos: revised edition*, available now!

Chapter One

Berkeley, California, present day

Even after time had passed, his mother's death still haunted Steven. Giving her life over to save Sebastian's had taken away a part of Steven's soul. Unable to heal her fatal wound, he felt cheated. From the moment he was born, his life had become derailed. The story of his life was *"what might have been."* No relationship with a family, just a life caged in a cell, enduring endless torture, the happy memories expected of a normal childhood switched out at birth for years of lab tests. He'd felt like years of his life had been taken away.

All this time, the woman Steven had crossed paths with years ago—who called herself *Lilith*—was his mother. Indeed, their indifferent paths did not change how he felt. It layered his emotions with a cloak of bittersweet longing to have a family. But sometimes your destiny led you down a winding road of endless pain.

The loss of his mother was a horrible reminder of the disappearance of his beloved Abbey. Steven hadn't seen her in ten years, though he maintained that he could sense she was still alive. Maybe in some future era Abbey would come back to him. He'd rely on hope, no matter how long it took, because love in its many forms always endured.

Steven had ambition for a future after he'd found his twin sister, Tessa, and his father, Kenneth, especially since Sebastian had lost his mind and was institutionalized. Living the remainder of his life in a white, padded cell was enough gratification for all the evil Sebastian had done in this world. Death would be too easy.

After Steven's father revealed he'd inherited the genetics of his Adalwolf from his grandfather, his fraternal twin sister's special gift still remained a mystery. There had been no documented knowledge of any Breedline born without an identical twin that could shift into their wolf, although his sister Tessa possessed the rare ability.

* * *

Now that peace had finally settled into the Breedline Covenant, Jace and Tessa were married barefoot just before sunset as a golden glow from the west settled on the beach and the cliffs behind it. The soothing sounds of the waves rolling onto the beach and fading away created a peaceful ambiance for the occasion.

It was a simple, romantic ceremony. Tessa was breathtaking, her age frozen in time. After Dr. Helen Carrington had approved the cure she'd discovered—which stopped the natural aging process for the Breedline—Tessa was eager to take it. Already ten years older than Jace, and the fact that he would stop aging when he reached thirty, she wanted to stay young and youthful along with her beloved.

Tessa's hair was elegantly pulled up into a bun with a single lavender rose tucked in. The soft, cream, strapless gown she wore accentuated her slim, petite figure and flowed slightly above her knees.

Jace wore beige slacks and a white linen long-sleeve dress shirt rolled up just below his elbows. His blond hair was pulled back, the long strands stirring in the light breeze.

As the happy couple stood facing one another, fingers entwined, their family and close friends assembled in a half circle, anxiously waiting to witness two bonded mates promising each other a lifetime of love and devotion. Jem was standing next to Jace, representing as his best man, and Mia was alongside Tessa as her bridesmaid.

With only the soft sounds of the ocean breeze, Reverend Mike's voice broke the silence. "Family and friends, we are gathered here in this beautiful place, in the presence of God, to celebrate the very special love between Tessa and Jace. They have each prepared their vows to share with one another."

At that moment, after the Reverend said his part, Jace dropped to one knee and looked up into Tessa's emerald-green eyes. "My beloved, you have already given me the three greatest gifts of my life: your love and our two precious sons. Today I pledge to you what has already been yours all this time—my eternal love. As we have always done, I promise to walk hand in hand with you through life's journeys. No matter what lies in our path, it will be our path, together. In the joys and troubles that lie ahead of us, I will be faithful and loving to you. I vow to love and cherish you for all the days of my life."

When Jace got to his feet, he gently slid the beautiful ruby ring that belonged to his great-grandmother onto Tessa's finger. As tears fell from the corners of her eyes, he wiped them away and whispered, "I love you, Tessa."

She smiled as more tears slipped freely down her cheeks. "Jace, I love you. You are my best friend and the love of my life. Today I give myself to you in marriage. I promise to encourage and inspire you, to laugh with you, and to comfort you in times of sorrow and struggle. I promise to cherish you and always to hold you close to my heart. These things I give to you today, and all the days of our life."

After Tessa had placed a white-gold band on Jace's finger, he leaned down and pressed his lips to hers. In their passionate embrace, Reverend Mike spoke out, "I present to you... Mr. and Mrs. Chamberlain."

All at once, the sound of clapping erupted as Jace and Tessa turned to face their guests. Jem smiled, his eyes glistening as he turned to Jace with his hand out. "Congratulations, Brother. It does me good to see you both so happy."

When Jace took his hand, he pulled him into a tight embrace. "Thanks, bro. Thanks for always having my back."

As Jem pulled away, he patted Jace on the shoulder. "I'll always have your back. I love you, Brother."

"I love you too, bro."

Mia was the first to congratulate Tessa with a hug. "You look gorgeous, Tessa. I'm so happy for you and Jace."

"Thank you, Mia."

As Tessa pulled from Mia's embrace, she looked up to see Jem with his arms held out. "How about a hug for your new brother-in-law?" he asked, smiling ear to ear.

"How could I possibly refuse?" Tessa giggled, wrapping her arms around him. "Thank you for everything, Jem."

"You're welcome, Tessa. I'm the one that should be thanking you."

Tessa lifted her chin, looking up at him with a puzzled expression. "For what?"

"For saving my brother. Just when I thought there was no hope for Jace, you came into his life and turned everything around."

She smiled. "Jace saved me too."

"Okay, Brother…" Jace came up behind Jem and placed his hand on Jem's shoulder. "No hogging the bride."

Jem stepped back. "She's all yours."

With his arm around Tessa's waist, Jace led her toward the guests. As her eyes roamed through family and friends, Tessa's attention shifted to her twin boys, who were tucked securely in loving arms. Her father, Kenneth, held little Jem, and Alexander had Jax anchored to his hip. Both boys were identical and were already starting to crawl. They had Jace's blond hair and his gorgeous blue eyes. Everyone she loved was here except for her mother. Deep down in her heart, she knew her mother was here in spirit, a beautiful angel finally set free.

"You look stunning, Tessa," Steven murmured, his eyes glowing in approval. He wrapped his arms around her. "Congratulations, sis. I'm so happy for you."

"Thank you, Steven."

Embraced with hugs by all their family and friends, the wedding party was in full swing. John and Sarah Chamberlain had arranged a large tent beautifully decorated in lavender and ivory with an opening facing the breathtaking view of the ocean. Now that peace had finally settled with the Breedline, John and Sarah moved back home but visited the Covenant frequently to see their grandbabies.

Everyone enjoyed the food, champagne, and dancing. As the end of the night drew near, Jace put his mouth close to Tessa's ear and whispered, "Let's get out of here."

She shivered as his breath tingled her skin. "Where are we going?"

He winked at her. "It's a secret."

"A secret?" She arched a brow. "You mean like a secret honeymoon?"

He shrugged. "Maybe."

"What about the boys?"

"Everything's already been arranged." Jace grasped her hand and pulled her close. "Mom and Dad are taking care of them."

"Don't we need to pack?"

"It's already taken care of," he murmured, pressing a kiss to her forehead. "Mia and Cassie prepared everything you'll need. The car is packed and ready to go."

"Well... it sounds like you've been busy," she said with a coy smile. "How long have you been planning this... *secret?*"

"Um, a few weeks." His lips curled up like a bow. "Ready?"

She smiled. "Yes."

* * *

In a dark padded cell, Sebastian lay with his arms bound inside a straitjacket and his ears tensed for the slightest noise. The buzzing coming from the fluorescent lights outside the door and the rhythm of his beating heart were the only sounds to be heard. Since Sebastian lost his ability to use a portal, this was the first time in his life he felt utterly helpless. When he'd told the Breedline of hearing Thomas's voice—his dead twin brother—they thought him insane, including Eve, and committed him to a Breedline psychiatric institution... *a lunatic asylum.* It was like a punch to the gut. Even though he was guilty of many things, death would be more merciful than eternal insanity.

He hadn't heard Thomas's voice for hours. Forcing himself to think of something else, he wondered how his sons were faring and thought of what Eve had said in the note she left him. Maybe she was right. Perhaps they were better off without him.

Although the sedative he was given made him doze off a couple of times, he concentrated on staying awake. As much as he fought to keep his eyes open, he lost the battle and sleep finally overtook him.

Out of nowhere, he sensed an eerie presence looming over him. He kept his lids closed and pretended to be asleep. He shivered when the temperature in the room dropped. Steam exhaled as he parted his lips.

Something prodded his leg with sharp fingers and whispered, "Wake up, *Sebastian*."

When an unknown presence leaned over Sebastian, a rank breath crept into his nostrils. Then strong hands grabbed a fistful of his hair and wrenched his head back and said, "I know you're awake, you worthless piece of crap."

He recognized his brother's angry voice and opened his eyes. Although it was impossible. Thomas was dead. The monster taunting his sanity was something entirely different. But who was it? And what did it want?

Sebastian felt enraged but remained calm. In his current condition, he was helpless against whatever this *thing* was. If only he could manage to free himself of the restricting constraint.

"Where are you?" he called out as his eyes darted over the poorly lit room. "Show yourself."

He flinched at the sound of a chair scuffling along the floor. When it slid into his field of vision, he came face-to-face with his twin brother. His features appeared haunted and his eyes were black... *soulless*.

Thomas reached inside his jacket and pulled out a dagger. As he reached forward with it, Sebastian clenched his eyes shut and stiffened, preparing to feel the burn of the blade. Oddly, he found exquisite relief instead. His arms were now free.

"Why did you free me?" Sebastian asked. "You're not really Thomas, are you?"

"So many questions," his look-alike said in a smug tone. "The answer to your first question... who am I?" He arrogantly grinned, his fangs shining like ivory pins. "I was once God's favorite angel, and *now...*" he paused, drawing his lips tight. "I am the darkness of night."

"Lucifer," Sebastian muttered, narrowing his stare.

"Yesss..." he answered with the S lingering. "I have been called by that name for centuries now, along with many others. The devil... *Satan.* But if you prefer Lucifer, it's your choice."

"Why?" Sebastian said, swallowing the knot in his throat. "Why are you taking Thomas's form?"

"Why not?" Lucifer asked, leaning closer. "Does this body make you feel guilty?"

Sebastian gripped the bare mattress and pulled himself upright. "Why would I feel guilty? Thomas caused his own death."

Lucifer threw his head back and laughed. The short, sharp bark sent shivers up Sebastian's spine. "You hated your brother. You wanted Thomas to die."

"No!" Sebastian fired back. "That's not true!"

Lucifer crossed his arms. "Isn't it?"

"What the hell do you want with me?" Sebastian urged. "And why can't I use my powers?"

Lucifer rose to his feet, straightened his black, tailored suit, and leaned against the padded wall of Sebastian's cell. "I want something that belongs to you, but I cannot take it freely. You must convince your beloved Eve to give it to me of her free will. Give me what I want, and I will release you from this misery. I will then restore your power to create a portal."

Sebastian went quiet for a minute. He wondered what Lucifer wanted that was so precious. Then he realized it was his son. Lucifer wanted Arius for his powers.

Another surge of rage swept over Sebastian. He stood up on shaking legs, preparing to lunge at Lucifer, but found himself strangely confined in his straitjacket again. "Stay away from my son..." Sebastian snarled his upper lip. "I swear I'll—"

"You'll what?" Lucifer smirked. "Kill me?"

Sebastian looked at Lucifer, his yellow eyes shooting daggers.

"You know..." Lucifer cocked a brow. "...we're not that different."

"I'm nothing like you!"

"Aren't we?" Lucifer said, pursing his mouth in a self-satisfied grin. "I have to say, what you did to Tessa is an all-time low. Raping your half brother's mate is a detestable sin."

"I didn't rape her!"

"Same difference," Lucifer said. "You used your succubus skills and put those images in her head, leading her to believe it." He slowly shook his head. "Only to piss off Jace. By my book, that's shady as hell."

Sebastian glared at Lucifer. "Go to hell!"

"That," Lucifer said in a tone laced with promise, "can be arranged."

Before Sebastian knew what hit him, Lucifer shot over with incredible speed, so fast he was nearly a blur, and gripped him around the throat. "Give me what I want." He bared his sharp pointed teeth. "Or suffer your fate."

Sebastian choked and thrashed against Lucifer's hold.

Eve gasped as she peered through the tiny glass window of Sebastian's cell.

"Guards!" Eve yelled. "Open this door!"

Lucifer curled back his upper lip. "You will suffer my wrath with eternal sleep, reliving the horrors of your childhood past."

Panic seized Sebastian. "No," he gasped. "Please... no."

Sebastian braced himself as Lucifer bit into his throat.

As the door sprang open, Lucifer instantly vanished. Eve caught her breath when she saw Sebastian drop to the floor. Blood trickled down his throat as though he'd been bitten.

Eve hesitated, but only for a moment, and rushed over to Sebastian. When she knelt beside him, she gently placed her hand on the side of his face. "Sebastian, talk to me, please," she helplessly cried out. "Sebastian..." She wiped at the blood on his neck. "Can you hear me?" When there was no response, she glanced up at the guard. "Get this damn thing off him. He needs medical attention, now!"

After the guard had called for backup, he quickly removed Sebastian's straitjacket.

When Bruce Carmichael, Eve's guard who escorted her each time she visited Sebastian at the mental institution, stepped into the room, he froze in his tracks, taken aback by the bizarre spectacle before him.

Eve looked down when she heard a light moan. Sebastian had his eyes slightly cracked. He strained to keep them open.

"Oh, thank God, Sebastian," Eve sobbed.

"Eve..." he said hoarsely. "Please... listen to me."

"You're going to be fine, Sebastian," Eve said in a tear-laced voice. "You just need my blood."

He shook his head as she held her wrist close to his lips. "No, Eve."

"Sebastian, please," Eve persisted. "I can fix this. Take my blood."

"You must save Arius... from Lucifer." He started to weep while struggling to keep his focus. "I love... you." Then he closed his eyes and went limp, falling deeper into a state of unconsciousness. The fault of his son's destiny was his. To keep Arius from the hands of evil, Sebastian was willing to suffer a thousandfold. Now his fate had come, the thing he had dreaded and feared long ago. His punishment was now a reality. Sebastian would be lost in the horrors of his childhood past, reliving each day he'd fought so hard to forget.

"No," Eve cried. "Please, Sebastian. Don't leave me. I believe you. Did you hear me?" She shook his shoulders, desperate for him to open his eyes. "You're not crazy. I saw him. I believe you, Sebastian."

The succubus side in her confirmed what her brain had been denying. Sebastian wasn't crazy. Someone had attacked him. She saw it with her own eyes. Eve had no idea how she was going to do it, but she had to fight to bring Sebastian back and protect her son from... *Lucifer*.

About the Author

Following a career in health and fitness, Shana Congrove has always had a passion for the arts, and her idea of heaven is a whole day of nothing but creating new adventures for her Breedline characters. She's an avid reader of fantasy, romance, and action, and loves to entertain readers with her Breedline series. In 2015, Shana was ranked the fifth novelist in FanStory.com and has continued in the year of 2018 to rank in the top ten. In 2019, she ranked second. She very much enjoys interacting with new readers:

Facebook/A Novel of the Breedline

Reference for terms and cast of characters

BREEDLINE – A species of humans that have the ability to change from human form into wolf form if they are born an identical twin. They are not like the old legend of the Lycanthropy myth. The Breedline species can shift into their wolf at will. The moon has no power over them. They do not pass their ability to other humans. Although they live among humans, their species is secret. In wolf form, they have superstrength, speed, and heightened senses. Compared to humans, Breedlines have tremendous advantages when it comes to health. Their bodies heal fast and are not subject to illness or diseases. The only thing that slows their healing process is silver. It is their kryptonite. Besides old age, a silver bullet to the brain is the only way to kill a Breedline.

All male Breedlines change into their first wolf at the age of eighteen. Female Breedlines do not go through the change until they make love to their Breedline bonded mate.

BREEDLINE TWINS – They have a strong, unbreakable bond from birth. Born with telepathic abilities, they have the power to sense their twin's emotions or injuries. In some cases, the bond between twins is so strong they cannot live without the other.

BREEDLINE BONDING – The male Breedline spends his life searching for his bonded mate. When two Breedline species experience a bond, they instantly feel a simultaneous, desirable attraction. The bond is for life. It is possible for them to have more than one mate in their lifespan.

BELOVED – A word used by a Breedline to express the bond to their mate.

DOUBLE BONDED – In some cases, male Breedline twins bond with the same female.

BREEDLINE COVENANT – The Breedline species must live within the boundaries of their Covenant. There is one in every state. A council governs its laws and oversees the species population.

THE BREEDLINE QUEEN – A Breedline queen is born once every one hundred years. Her massive stature, black fur, and red eyes are the queen's trademarks. Her alpha wolf has twice the strength, speed, and size of any Breedline. She rules over all the Breedline Covenants. She is their absolute law.

TRUE LAW – All Breedline Covenants have a book of laws. If disobeyed, they must face the Breedline council. Punishment for taking another life out of revenge, or evil—other than protecting their life and the life of another—they will instantly shift into a rogue wolf for life and be shunned by the Breedline Covenants.

ROGUE WOLF – A Breedline wolf who has killed with the intent of evil. They can never shift back into their human form.

RED (BLOOD) MOON – During this time, all Breedline species have a strong desire to create offspring. This is a time when Breedline females are more fertile for the conception of twins.

CHIANG-SHIH DEMON (Kiang shi, a.k.a. Ramael Arminius) – An ancient demon that can inhabit the body of a Breedline fetus or during a Breedline's death. It continues to take the soul over the natural lifespan of a child or the deceased Breedline. When the demon possesses a fetus, it breaks the bonding and telepathic abilities with its twin. If the demon possesses a deceased Breedline's body, it must do so before the soul passes on. If the soul is not intact, the body will soon die. The demon's sole purpose is to seek world domination.

THE BEAST – It is the second-born son of the Chiang-Shih demon. When provoked into a rage, he will shift into the Beast instead of the Breedline wolf. The Beast is also known as the Great White due to his white fur and enormous, two-footed stature. One bite from the Beast has enough venom to kill the Chiang-Shih demon, leaving the soul of the person the demon possessed unharmed.

SHADOW WALKER (a.k.a. Shadow Figure, or Black Mass) – When a Breedline species dies and their soul continues to roam the earth as a shadow of themselves—a ghost—because they have unfinished business before their death.

ZADKIEL (Tzadqiel, a.k.a. "Righteousness of God") – The archangel of freedom, benevolence, and mercy, and the patron angel of all who forgives. The Breedline species considers Zadkiel the Angel of Mercy.

SUCCUBUS (a.k.a. Creepers) – A succubus feeds off the blood of a Breedline species. They are skilled with hypnotic abilities and capable of using their beautiful features to influence the thoughts of the Breedline species and humans.

HALF-BREED – A species born with the genes from both a Breedline and a succubus. They can bond with either species. Although they cannot shift into a wolf, they need blood from a Breedline to survive.

WICCA (or Wise One) – According to the Breedline species, a Wicca is the Goddess of magic, witchcraft, the night, the moon, ghosts, and necromancy. They can do white magic (good) or dark (evil).

GUARDIANS (a.k.a. Spirits of the Forest) – They originated during the Middle Ages with the purpose of protecting the Breedline from the destruction of any creation of a dark Wicca. They can stay invisible, with the power to move through any barrier and over any distance instantly.

THERIOMORPH – They are born with the genes of a Breedline, but do not shift into a wolf. They shapeshift into an enormous black panther. They possess powers of mind manipulation and random visions of the future. They must use the drug dopamine to suppress their urges. Their eye color shifts into a bright lavender when their Theriomorph nature takes over. In some cases, the Breedline see them as a threat to their species.

ADALWOLF – A species that has the power to shift from their human form into a beautiful creature, twice the size, resembling half man and half wolf. Born with superstrength, they can move from one place to another with supernatural speed. Their eyes take on the appearance of two shimmering diamonds. With the power to regenerate their own cells, an Adalwolf will stop aging at thirty. The moon has no power over them, and they are immune to silver. They can bond with any species.

LUPA (she-wolf) – The ancestors descended from the old legend of the lycanthrope, but the moon has no power over them. The species only affects female offspring. A Lupa is a dangerous creature which shapeshifts into a therianthropic hybrid wolf-like creature.

Jace Chamberlain (a.k.a. the Beast) – He is a Breedline species who later discovers he was born with a curse of the Beast, inherited by the Chiang-Shih demon. His bonded mate is Tessa Fairchild. He's an IT engineer and the lead singer and plays acoustic guitar in the band Chaos.

Jem Chamberlain (a.k.a. the Chosen Son) – He is a Breedline species and Jace's identical twin brother. He carries the gene of the Chiang-Shih demon, which gives him the power to create a portal and a force of electrical energy used as a weapon—and other powers he discovers later. His bonded mate is Mia Blackwood. He's an IT engineer and the drummer in the band Chaos.

Tessa Fairchild (the Breedline queen) – She was born into the human world and later discovers she's a Breedline. Abandoned by her parents, and raised by her aunt and uncle, Tessa has no knowledge of being born a twin. After she meets Jace, they become bonded mates. During her first change into her Breedline wolf, she shifts into the new Breedline queen. She is an aspiring artist.

Dr. John and Sarah Chamberlain – They are Jace, Jem, and Cassie's adoptive human parents. They are physicians in a children's unit, donating their time to the emergency center.

Chester and Amelia Ewan – They are called Guardians—a species originated during the Middle Ages—with the purpose of protecting the Breedline from the destruction of any creation made by a dark Wiccan.

Katlyn Gray – She is a Breedline and Jace and Jem's biological mother.

Jackson Gray – He is Jace and Jem's biological uncle, Katlyn Gray's older brother. Although he carries the gene of the Breedline, he does not shift into a wolf. He's a medical supply pilot.

Mia Blackwood – She is a half-breed and Jem's bonded mate. Abandoned at birth and raised in human foster care, she later finds her identical twin sister, Eve.

Eve – She is a half-breed, and Sebastian's bonded mate.

Sebastian Crow – He is a half-breed and Eve's bonded mate. He has the power to summon a portal.

Alexander Crest – He is a Breedline species, Jace and Jem's biological father. He is bonded to Dr. Helen Carrington.

Tim Ross – He is a Breedline species and the council head of the California Covenant.

Angel – She is a half-breed and Tim's bonded mate.

Natalie – She is a half-breed and Tim and Angel's daughter.

Kyle Jones – He is a Breedline species that resides in the California Covenant. Celina Baldolf is his bonded mate. He's a mechanic and plays bass in the rock band Chaos.

Casey Barton – He is a Theriomorph and lives in the California Covenant. He is a clothing model and plays backup bass and keyboards in the band Chaos.

Dr. Helen Carrington – She is a Breedline species and a physician at the California Bates Hospital for both Breedlines and humans. She later bonds to Alexander Crest.

Drakon Hexus – He is a Breedline species and bonded to Cassie Chamberlain.

Cassie Chamberlain – Adopted at age two by Jace and Jem's adoptive parents after her mother abandons her. Later, she discovers she is a Breedline species and bonds with the handsome Drakon Hexus. She is a nurse practitioner, specializing in the neonatal intensive care unit.

Celina Baldolf – She is a Breedline species with the power of a Wiccan, but only practices white witchcraft. Her twin sister, Taliah—a dark Wicca—murdered their parents when they were twelve years old. Dr. Helen Carrington is their aunt, and Kyle Jones is Celina's Breedline bonded mate. She is an editor for a local publishing company.

Lila Demont – She is a Breedline, born into a wealthy, prestigious family. She is a lab technician and assists Dr. Helen Carrington with the cure to the Breedline aging process. She later bonds with Casey Barton.

Victor Demont – He is a Breedline and Lila's father. He is a retired council member of the Pennsylvania Breedline Covenant.

Raphael (a.k.a. Buddy the cat) – He is the angel of healing who secretly disguises himself as a black cat who resides in the Breedline Covenant as their pet. He guards the children in the Covenant.

Nathan Gage (a.k.a. Nate) – He is a Breedline and the owner of several upscale nightclubs in the largest metropolitan areas of Northern California.